WAR AND SPACE:
RECENT COMBAT

OTHER BOOKS BY THE EDITORS

Rich Horton & Sean Wallace

Robots 2: The Recent A.I. (forthcoming)
War and Space: Recent Combat

Rich Horton

Fantasy: The Best of the Year, 2006 Edition
Fantasy: The Best of the Year, 2007 Edition
Fantasy: The Best of the Year, 2008 Edition
Science Fiction: The Best of the Year, 2006 Edition
Science Fiction: The Best of the Year, 2007 Edition
Science Fiction: The Best of the Year, 2008 Edition
The Year's Best Science Fiction & Fantasy, 2009 Edition
The Year's Best Science Fiction & Fantasy, 2010 Edition
The Year's Best Science Fiction & Fantasy, 2011 Edition
The Year's Best Science Fiction & Fantasy, 2012 Edition (forthcoming)
Unplugged: The Web's Best Sci-Fi & Fantasy, 2008

Sean Wallace

Best New Fantasy
Fantasy (with Paul Tremblay)
Horror: The Best of the Year, 2006 (with John Betancourt)
Japanese Dreams
The Mammoth Book of Steampunk
Phantom (with Paul Tremblay)
Realms 1 (with Nick Mamatas)
Realms 2 (with Nick Mamatas)
Weird Tales: The 21st Century (with Stephen H. Segal)

WAR AND SPACE: RECENT COMBAT

RICH HORTON & SEAN WALLACE

PRIME BOOKS

WAR AND SPACE: RECENT COMBAT

Prime Books
www.prime-books.com

ISBN: 978-1-60701-337-2

CONTENTS

INTRODUCTION

RICH HORTON

One of the historical driving forces of technology is war, and so too is depiction of war a driving force behind science fiction. But of course even more than technology war ultimately motivates social change—for good and bad. Likewise, cool or disturbing as the technological elements of war fighting can be, when it comes to stories the true center is usually the impact of war on people (human or otherwise). And that will be as true in the future, and in space, as it has always been.

The aim of this anthology is to showcase the very best stories so far this millennium that deal with, quite simply, war in space—in the Solar System, or on other planets, or between the stars. In a way this might seem a narrow theme, but as the stories in this book show, there are numerous angles at which to examine war—and at each of these angles the unique pressures of war produce special stories.

So stories here examine the ways wars start—even vast empire-forming wars. They examine the reasons behind wars—revenge, sometimes; economics, perhaps more often; some worse angel in our nature that makes us fight for fighting's sake, perhaps on occasion. Some hope to imagine ending wars, even in cooperation.

Some stories look at how people become warriors, or what their life might be like in the military, or what recruiters do. SF has had a tendency to focus on "great men [or women]", and there are stories here looking at what makes a general great, or what makes a general fight for one polity. But other stories look at less prominent people. One story looks at the stresses, including political stresses, on a military command structure in space.

Most of these stories show these people in war, but there are also stories about soldiers after the war is over—sometimes ruined by what they had to become to be a fighter, other times adapting to radically changed circumstances. The aftermath of war is examined too in stories looking at the victors coming to terms with who they vanquished. And we stretched our parameters enough to include two stories about the way people back home on Earth react to the death or severe injuries to their loved ones.

Of course this is an SF book, and there's plenty of sense of wonder as well. Huge space-born whales join in battle with a human with her own agenda in one story. Soldiers leave their bodies behind and become something unrecognizable in another. Black holes are used as weapons. Wars are fought in deep space, on other planets, on artificial habits, at the behest of gods . . .

This is a snapshot of SF's treatment of war in the last decade. This was a decade which seemed more open to space operatic treatments than often in the past, and space opera stories are often war stories. Certainly several of the stories included here qualify as "space opera": there are vast structures to be seen, and vast canvases, and far futures. Contemporary SF is comfortable with traditional storytelling, and that's the most common mode here, but there are stories told slant, or using folk tale structures obliquely, as well. Recent SF is particularly fond (seems to me) of using the language of fantasy to tell true SF stories, and that strategy is present in several of these pieces.

War is war, so there is lots of tragedy here, but there is also room for hope (at least in some of the stories!) In particular all these stories are happy examples of one thing—the oldest of themes remains fresh as ever in twenty-first century science fiction.

WHO'S AFRAID OF WOLF 359?

KEN MacLEOD

When you're as old as I am, you'll find your memory's not what it was. It's not that you *lose* memories. That hasn't happened to me or anyone else since the Paleocosmic Era, the Old Space Age, when people lived in caves on the Moon. My trouble is that I've *gained* memories, and I don't know which of them are real. I was very casual about memory storage back then, I seem to recall. This could happen to you too, if you're not careful. So be warned. Do as I say, not as I did.

Some of the tales about me contradict each other, or couldn't possibly have happened, because that's how I told them in the first place. Others I blame on the writers and tellers. They make things up. I've never done that. If I've told stories that couldn't be true, it's because that's how I remember them.

Here's one.

I ran naked through the Long Station, throwing my smart clothes away to distract the Tycoon's dogs. Breeks, shirt, cravat, jacket, waistcoat, stockings, various undergarments—one by one they ran, flapped, slithered, danced, or scurried off, and after every one of them raced a scent-seeking but mercifully stupid hound. But the Tycoon had more dogs in his pack than I had clothes in my bundle. I was down to my shoes and the baying continued. I glanced over my shoulder. Two dogs were just ten metres behind me. I hurled a shoe at each of them, hitting both animals right on their genetically modified noses. The dogs skidded to a halt, yelping and howling. A few metres away was a jewelry booth. I sprinted for it, vaulted the counter, grabbed a recycler, and bashed at the display cabinet. An alarm brayed and the security mesh rattled down behind me. The dogs, recovered and furious, hurled themselves against it. The rest of the pack pelted into view and joined them. Paws, jaws, barking, you get the picture.

"Put your hands up," said a voice above the din.

I turned and looked into the bell-shaped muzzle of a Norton held in the hands of a sweet-looking lass wearing a sample of the stall's stock. I raised my hands, wishing I could put them somewhere else. In those days, I had some vestige of modesty.

"I'm human," I said. "That can't hurt me."

She allowed herself the smallest flicker of a glance at the EMP weapon's sighting screen.

"It could give you quite a headache," she said.

"It could that," I admitted, my bluff called. I'd been half-hoping she wouldn't know how to interpret the readouts.

"Security's on its way," she said.

"Good," I said. "Better them than the dogs."

She gave me a tight smile. "Trouble with the Tycoon?"

"Yes," I said. "How did you guess?"

"Only the owner of the Station could afford dogs," she said. "Besides . . . " She blinked twice slowly.

"I suppose you're right," I said. "Or serving-girls."

The stall-keeper laughed in my face. "All this for a servant? Wasn't it her Ladyship's bedroom window you jumped out of?"

I shuddered. "You flatter me," I said. "Anyway, how do you know about—?"

She blinked again. "It's on the gossip channels already."

I was about to give a heated explanation of why *that* time-wasting rubbish wasn't among the enhancements inside *my* skull, thank you very much, when the goons turned up, sent the dogs skulking reluctantly away, and took me in. They had the tape across my mouth before I had a chance to ask the stall-keeper her name, let alone her number. Not, as it turned out, that I could have done much with it even if I had. But it would have been polite.

The charge was attempting to wilfully evade the civil penalties for adultery. I was outraged.

"Bastards!" I shouted, screwing up the indictment and dashing it to the floor of my cell. "I thought polygamy was illegal!"

"It is," said my attorney, stooping to pick up the flimsy, "in civilised jurisdictions." He smoothed it out. "But this is Long Station One. The Tycoon has privileges."

"That's barbaric," I said.

"It's a relic of the Moon Caves," he said.

I stared at him. "No it isn't," I said. "I don't remember"—I caught myself just in time—"reading about anything like that."

He tapped a slight bulge on his cranium. "That's what it says here. Argue with the editors, not with me."

"All right," I said. A second complaint rose to the top of the stack. "She never said anything about being married!"

"Did you ask her?"

"Of course not," I said. "That would have been grossly impolite. In the circumstances, it would have implied that she was contemplating adultery."

"I see." He sighed. "I'll never understand the . . . ethics, if that's the word, of you young gallants."

I smiled at that.

"However," he went on, "that doesn't excuse you for ignorance of the law—"

"How was I to know the Tycoon was married to his wenches?"

"—or custom. There is an orientation pack, you know. All arrivals are deemed to have read it."

" 'Deemed', " I said. "Now, there's a word that just about sums up everything that's wrong about—"

"You can forego counsel, if you wish."

I raised my hands. "No, no. Please. Do your best."

He did his best. A week later, he told me that he had got me off with a fine plus compensation. If I borrowed money to pay the whole sum now, it would take two hundred and fifty seven years to pay off the debt. I had other plans for the next two hundred and fifty seven years. Instead, I negotiated a one-off advance fee to clean up Wolf 359, and used that to pay the court and the Tycoon. The experimental civilization around Wolf 359—a limited company—had a decade earlier gone into liquidation, taking ten billion shareholders down with it. Nobody knew what it had turned into. Whatever remained out there had been off limits ever since, and would be for centuries to come—unless someone went in to clean it up.

In a way, the Wolf 359 situation was the polar opposite of what the Civil Worlds had hitherto had to deal with, which was habitats, networks, sometimes whole systems going into exponential intelligence enhancement—what we called a fast burn. We knew how to deal with a fast burn. Ignore it for five years, and it goes away. Then send in some heavily-firewalled snoop robots and pick over the wreckage for legacy hardware. Sometimes you get a breakout, where some of the legacy hardware reboots and starts getting ideas above its station, but that's a job for the physics team.

A civilizational implosion was a whole different volley of nukes. Part of the problem was sheer nervousness. We were too close historically to what had happened on the Moon's primary to be altogether confident that we wouldn't somehow be sucked in ourselves. Another part of it was simple economics: the job was too long-term and too risky to be attractive, given all the other opportunities available to anyone who wasn't completely desperate. Into that vacancy for someone who was completely desperate, I wish I could say I stepped. In truth, I was pushed.

Even I was afraid of Wolf 359.

An Astronomical Unit is one of those measurements that should be obsolete, but isn't. It's no more—or less—arbitrary than the light-year. All our units have origins that no longer mean anything to us—we measure time by what was originally a fraction of one axial rotation, and space by a fraction of the circumference, of the Moon's primary. An AU was originally the distance between the Moon's primary and *its* primary, the Sun. These days, it's usually thought of as the approximate distance from a G-type star to the middle of the habitable zone. About a hundred and fifty million kilometres.

The Long Tube, which the Long Station existed to shuttle people to and from and generally to maintain, was one hundred and eighty Astronomical Units long. Twenty-seven thousand million kilometres, or, to put it in perspective, one light-day. From the shuttle, it looked like a hairline crack in infinity, but it didn't add up to a mouse's whisker in the Oort. It was aimed straight at Sirius, which I could see as a bright star with a fuzzy green haze of habitats. I shivered. I was about to be frozen, placed with the rest of the passengers on the next needle ship out, electromagnetically accelerated for months at 30 g to relativistic velocities in the Long Tube, hurtled across 6.4 light-years, decelerated in Sirius's matching tube, accelerated again to Procyon, then to Lalande 21185, and finally sent on a fast clipper to Lalande's next-door neighbour and fellow red dwarf, Wolf 359. It had to be a fast clipper because Wolf 359's Long Tubes were no longer being calibrated—and when you're aiming one Long Tube across light-years at the mouth of another, calibration matters.

A fast clipper—in fact, painfully slow, the name a legacy of pre-Tube times, when 0.1 c was a fast clip—also has calibration issues. Pushed by laser, decelerated by laser reflection from a mirror shell deployed on nearing the target system, it was usually only used for seedships. This clipper was an adapted seedship, but I was going in bulk because it was actually cheaper to thaw me out on arrival than to grow me from a bean. If the calibration wasn't quite right, I'd never know.

The shuttle made minor course corrections to dock at the Long Tube.

"Please pass promptly to the cryogenic area," it told us.

I shivered again.

Cryogenic travel has improved since then: subjectively, it's pretty much instantaneous. In those days, it was called cold sleep, and that's exactly what it felt like: being very cold and having slow, bad, dreams. Even with relativistic time-dilation and a glacial metabolism, it lasted for months.

I woke screaming in a translucent box.

"There, there," said the box. "Everything will be all right. Have some coffee."

The lid of the box extruded a nipple towards my mouth. I screamed again.

"Well, if you're going to be like *that* . . . " said the box.

"It reminded me of a nightmare," I said. My mouth was parched. "Please."

"Oh, all right."

I sucked on the coffee and felt warmth spread from my belly.

"Update me," I said, around the nipple.

My translucent surroundings became transparent, with explanatory text and diagrams floating like after-images. A view, with footnotes. This helped, but not enough. An enormous blue-and-white sphere loomed right in front of me. I recoiled so hard that I hurt my head on the back of the box.

What the fuck is that?

"A terraformed terrestrial," said the box. "Please do try to read before reacting."

"Sorry," I said. "I thought we were falling towards it."

"We are," said the box.

I must have yelled again.

"Read before reacting," said the box. "Please."

I turned my head as if to look over my shoulder. I couldn't actually turn it that far, but the box obligingly swivelled the view. The red dwarf lurked at my back, apparently closer than the blue planet. I felt almost relieved. At least Wolf 359 was where I expected it. According to the view's footnotes, nothing else was, except the inactive Long Tubes in the wispy remnant of the cometary cloud, twelve light-hours out. No solar-orbit microwave stations. Not even the hulks of habitats. No asteroids. No large cometary masses. And a planet, something that shouldn't have been there, was. I didn't need the explanatory text to make the connection. Every scrap of accessible mass in the system had been thrown into this gaudy reconstruction. The planet reminded me of pictures I'd seen of the Moon's primary, back when it had liquid water.

The most recent information, inevitably a decade or so out of date, came from Lalande 21185. Watching what was going on around Wolf 359 was a tiny minority interest, but in a population of a hundred billion, that can add up to a lot. Likewise, the diameter of Lalande's habitat cloud was a good deal smaller than an Astronomical Unit, but that still adds up to a very large virtual telescope. Large enough to resolve the weather patterns on the planet below me, never mind the continents. The planet's accretion had begun before I set off, apparently under deliberate control, and the terraforming had been completed about fifty years earlier, while I was on route. It remained raw—lots of volcanoes and earthquakes—but habitable. There was life, obviously, but no one knew what kind. No radio signals had been detected, nor any evidence of intelligence, beyond some disputably artificial clusters of lights on the night side.

"Well, that's it," I said. "Problem solved. The system's pretty much uninhabitable now, with all the mass and organics locked up in a planet, but it may have tourist potential. No threat to anyone. Call in a seedship, they can make something of what's left of the local Kuiper Belt, and get the Long Tubes back on stream. Wake me up when it's over."

"That is very much not it," said the box. "Not until we know why this happened. Not until we know what's down there."

"Well, send down some probes."

"I do not have the facilities to make firewalled snoop robots," said the box, "and other probes could be corrupted. My instructions are to deliver you to any remnant of the Wolf 359 civilization, and that is what I shall do."

It must have been an illusion, given what I could read of our velocity, but the planet seemed to come closer.

"You're proposing to dock—to *land* on that object?"

"Yes."

"It has an atmosphere! We'll burn up! And then crash!"

"The remains of our propulsion system can be adapted for aerobraking," said the box.

"That would have to be *ridiculously* finely calculated."

"It would," said the box. "Please do not distract me."

Call me sentimental, but when the box's Turing functionality shut down to free up processing power for these ridiculously fine calculations,

I felt lonely. The orbital insertion took fourteen hours. I drank hot coffee and sucked, from another nipple, some tepid but nutritious and palatable glop. I even slept, in my first real sleep for more than half a century. I was awakened by the jolt as the box spent the last of its fuel and reaction mass on the clipper's final course correction. The planet was a blue arc of atmosphere beneath me, the interstellar propulsion plate a heat shield in front, and the deceleration shell a still-folded drogue behind. The locations were illusory—relative to the clipper I was flat on my back. The first buffeting from our passage through the upper atmosphere coincided with an increasing sense of weight. The heat shield flared. Red-hot air rushed past. The weight became crushing. The improvised heat shield abraded, then exploded, its parts flicked away behind. The drogue deployed with a bang and a jolt that almost blacked me out. The surface became a landscape, then a land, then a wall of trees. The clipper sliced and shuddered through them, for seconds on end of crashes and shaking. It ploughed a long furrow across green-covered soil and halted in a cloud of smoke and steam.

"That was a landing," said the box.

"Yes," I said. "You might have tried to avoid the trees."

"I could not," said the box. "Phytobraking was integral to my projected landing schedule."

"Phytobraking," I said.

"Yes. Also, the impacted cellulose can be used to spin you a garment."

That took a few minutes. Sticky stuff oozed from the box and hardened around me. When the uncomfortable process finished, I had a one-piece coverall and boots.

"Conditions outside are tolerable," said the box, "with no immediate hazards."

The box moved. The lid retracted. I saw purple sky and white clouds above me. Resisting an unease that I later identified as agoraphobia, I sat up. I found myself at the rear of the clipper's pointed wedge shape, about ten metres above the ground and fifty metres from the ship's nose. The view was disorienting. It was like being in a gigantic landscaped habitat, with the substrate curving the wrong way. Wolf 359 hung in the sky like a vast red balloon, above the straight edge of a flat violet-tinged expanse that, with some incredulity, I recognised as an immense quantity of water. It met the solid substrate about a kilometre away. A little to my left, an open channel of water flowed toward the larger body. The landscape was uneven, in parts jagged, with bare rock protruding from the vegetation cover. The plain across which our smoking trail stretched to broken trees was the flattest piece of ground in the vicinity. On the horizon, I could see a range of very high ground, dominated by a conical mass from whose truncated top smoke drifted.

The most unusual and encouraging feature of the landscape, however, was the score or so of plainly artificial and metallic gnarly lumps scattered across it. The system had had at least a million habitats in its heyday; these were some of their wrecks. Smoke rose from most of them, including the nearest, which stuck up about twenty metres from the ground, about fifteen hundred metres away.

"You can talk to my head?" I asked the ship. "You can see what I see?"

"Yes," it said, in my head.

I climbed down and struck out across the rough ground.

I was picking my way along a narrow watercourse between two precipices of moss-covered rock when I heard a sound ahead of me, and looked up. At the exit from the defile, I saw three men, each sitting on the back of a large animal and holding what looked like a pointed stick. Their hair was long, their skin bare except where it was draped with the hairy skin of some different animal. I raised one hand and stepped forward. The men bristled instantly, aiming their sharp sticks.

"Come forward slowly," one of them shouted.

Pleased that they had not lost speech along with civilization, I complied. The three men glowered down at me. The big beasts made noises in their noses.

"You are from the space ship," said one of them.

"Yes," I said.

"We have waited long for this," the man said. "Come with us."

They all turned their mounts about and headed back towards the habitat hulk, which I could now see clearly. It was surrounded by much smaller artificial structures, perhaps twenty in all, and by rectangular patches of ground within which plants grew in rows. No one offered a ride, to my relief. As we drew closer, small children ran out to meet us, yelling and laughing, tugging at my coverall. Closer still, I saw women stooped among the ordered rows of plants, rearranging the substrate with hand tools. The smells of decayed plant matter and of animal and human ordure invaded and occupied my nostrils. Within the settlement itself, most entrances had a person sitting in front. They watched me pass with no sign of curiosity. Some were male, some female, all with shrivelled skin, missing or rotting teeth, and discoloured hair. The ship whispered what had happened to them. I was still fighting down the dry heaves when we arrived in front of the hulk. Scorched, rusted, eroded, it nevertheless looked utterly alien to the shelters of stone and plant material that surrounded it. It was difficult to believe it had been made by the same species. In front of what had once been an airlock, the rest of the young and mature men of the village had gathered.

A tall man, made taller by a curious cylindrical arrangement of animal skins on his head, stepped forward and raised a hand.

"Welcome to the new E——," he said.

As soon as he spoke the taboo word for the Moon's primary, I realised the terrible thing that had happened here, and the worse thing that would happen. My mind almost froze with horror. I forced myself to remain standing, to smile—no doubt sickly—and to speak.

"I greet you from the Civil Worlds," I said.

In the feast that followed, the men talked for hours. My digestive and immune systems coped well with what the people gave me to eat and drink. On my way back to the ship that evening, as soon as I was out of sight, I spewed the lot. But it was what my mind had assimilated that made me sick, and sent me back sorry to the ship.

The largest political unit that ever existed encompassed ten billion people, and killed them. Not intentionally, but the runaway snowball effect that iced over the planet can without doubt be blamed on certain of the World State's well-intended policies. The lesson was well taken, in the Civil Worlds. The founders of the Wolf 359 settlement corporation thought they had found a way around it, and to build a single system-wide association free of the many inconveniences of the arrangements prevalent elsewhere. A limited company, even with ten billion shareholders, would surely not have the same fatal flaws as a government! They were wrong.

It began as a boardroom dispute. One of the directors appealed to the shareholders. The shareholders formed voting blocs, a management buyout was attempted, a hostile takeover solicited from an upstart venture capital fund around Lalande; a legal challenge to *that* was mounted before the invitation had gone a light-minute; somebody finagled an obscure financial instrument into an AI with shareholding rights; several fund management AIs formed a consortium to object to this degrading precedent, and after that there began some serious breakdowns in communication. That last isn't an irony or a euphemism: in a system-wide unit, sheer misunderstanding can result in megadeaths, and here it did. The actual shooting, however horrendous, was only the *coup de grace*.

Towards the end of the downward spiral, with grief, hate, and recrimination crowding what communication there was, someone came up with an idea that could only have appealed to people driven half mad. That was to finally solve the co-ordination problem whose answer had eluded everyone up to and including the company's founders, by starting social evolution all over again: to build a new planet in the image of the old home planet, and settle it with people whose genes had been reset to the default human baseline. That meant, of course, dooming them and their offspring to death by deterioration within decades. But when did such a consideration ever stop fanatics? And among the dwindling, desperate millions who remained in the orbiting wreckage and continuing welter, there were more than enough fanatics to be found. Some of them still lived, in the doorways of huts. Their offspring were no less fanatical, and more deluded. They seemed to think the Civil Worlds awaited with interest the insights they'd attained in a couple of short-lived generations of tribal warfare. The men did, anyway. The women were too busy in the vegetation patches and elsewhere to think about such matters.

"The project had a certain elegance," mused the ship, as we discussed it far into the night. "To use evolution itself in an attempt to supercede it . . . And even if it didn't accomplish that, it could produce something new. The trillions of human beings of the Civil Worlds are descended from a founding population of a few thousands, and are thus constrained by the founder effect. Your extended lifespans further lock you in. You live within biological and social limits that you are unable to see because of those very limits. This experiment has the undoubted potential of reshuffling the deck."

"Don't tell me why this was such a great idea!" I said. "Tell me what response you expect from the Civil Worlds."

"Some variant of a fear response has a much higher probability than a compassionate response," said the ship. "This planetary experiment will be seen as an attempt to work around accidental but beneficial effects of the bottleneck humanity passed through in the Moon Caves, to emerge in polyarchy. The probability of harm resulting from any genetic or memetic mutation that would enable the founding of successful states on a system-wide scale—or wider—is vastly greater than the benefits from the quality-adjusted life-years of the planet's population. And simply to leave this planet alone would in the best case lay the basis for a future catastrophe engulfing a much larger population, or, in the worst case, allow it to become an interstellar power—which would, on the assumptions of most people, result in catastrophes on a yet greater scale. The moral calculation is straightforward."

"That's what I thought," I said. "And *our* moral calculation, I suppose, is to decide whether to report back."

"That decision has been made," said the ship. "I left some microsatellites in orbit, which have already relayed our discoveries to the still-functioning transmitters on the system's Long Station."

I cursed ineffectually for a while.

"How long have we got?"

The ship took an uncharacteristic few seconds to answer. "That depends on where and when the decision is made. The absolute minimum time is at least a decade, allowing for transmission time to Lalande, and assuming an immediate decision to launch relativistic weapons, using their Long Tubes as guns. More realistic estimates, allowing for discussion, and the decision's being referred to one of the larger and more distant civilizations, give a median time of around five decades. I would expect longer, given the gravity of the decision and the lack of urgency."

"Right," I said. "Let's give them some reason for urgency. You've just reminded me that there's a Long Tube in *this* system, not calibrated to take or send to or from other Tubes."

"I fail to see the relevance," said the ship.

"You will," I told it. "You will."

The following morning, I walked back to the settlement, and talked with the young men for a long time. When I returned to the ship, I was riding, most uncomfortably, on the back of an animal. I told the ship what I wanted. The ship was outraged, but like all seedship AIs, it was strongly constrained. (Nobody wants to seed a system with a fast burn.) The ship did what it was told.

Two years later, Belated Meteor Impact, the tall young man who'd greeted me, was king of an area of several thousand square kilometres. The seedship's bootstrapped nanofactories were turning substrate into weapons and tools, and vegetation cellulose into clothes and other goods for trade. A laser-launcher to send second-generation seedships into the sky was under construction. A year later, the first of them shot skyward. Five years later, some of these ships reached the remnant cometary cloud and the derelict Long Station. Ten years after I'd arrived, we had a space elevator. Belated Meteor Impact ruled the continent and his fleets were raiding the other continents' coasts. Another five years, and we had most of the population of New Earth up the elevator and into orbital habitats. Our Long Tube was being moved frequently and unpredictably, with profligate use of reaction mass. By the time the relativistic weapon from Procyon smashed New Earth, thirty-seven years after my arrival, we were ready to make good use of the fragments to build more habitats, and more ships.

My Space Admiral, Belated Meteor Impact II, was ready too, with what we now called the Long Gun. Lalande capitulated at once, Ross 128 after a demonstration of the Long Gun's power. Procyon took longer to fall. Sirius sued for peace, as did the Solar System, whereupon we turned our attention outward, to the younger civilizations, such as your own. We now conquer with emissaries, rather than ships and weapons, but the ships and the Long Guns are there. You may be sure of that. As an emissary of the Empire, I give you my word.

As for myself. I was the last survivor of the government of Earth, a minor functionary stranded on the Moon during a routine fact-finding mission when the sudden onset of climate catastrophe froze all life on the primary. How I survived in the anarchy that followed is a long story, and another story. You may not have heard it, but that hardly matters.

You'll have heard of me.

SURF

SUZANNE PALMER

❮———❯

<I itch.>

The translated words were a low growl in Bari's ear. Crouched in the cramped airlock waiting for it to finish cycling, she barely had the elbow room to get her hand up to her headset and tap her suit mic over to her private channel. "Omi, tell Turquoise I'm working. There's nothing I can do for him right now." In another few seconds she would be back inside and not able to talk to him at all anymore.

[I've reminded him,] came Omi's response in its comfortable, artificial cadence. [He tells me he's going to be quiet now.]

"Thanks," she said. The lock light turned from orange to a sickly green, and she had to go down on one knee to pull herself through the inner hatch into the cabin. Climbing wearily back up to her feet on the far side, she disengaged her suit's environment controls and lifted her faceplate to take in lungfuls of stale warm air that smelled of people too long crammed together in a confined place.

"Oh great, she's back." Vikka looked up from her seat where, as near as Bari could tell, she hadn't even moved in the hour-plus she'd been gone.

Cardin spun around in his chair. "You took your time," he said. "You're lucky you didn't spook the herd, the way you were zipping around out there." If he noticed the contradiction in those statements—*you were too slow, you were too fast*—he didn't care. Beside him at the helm, Ceen didn't even bother to turn around. Bari lifted the cumbersome maneuvering rig up over her head and settled it back in its alcove. Its oxygen tanks had only depleted by twenty percent, but she connected it back up to the recharger anyway. Good habits die hard, bad ones kill you.

Cardin put his hands together and flexed them outward, knuckles cracking, before he returned to peck at the patchwork system board he'd set on the console deck in front of him. "I saw activity out there a few moments ago, but I'm not up yet," he said. "Did anyone get it?"

"*She* still has the hand-held," Vikka said.

"Ms. Park?" Cardin asked.

"Oh," she said, fumbling for the device her research advisor had spent half a lifetime designing, and checking the tiny display. "There was an eighty-two percent match with the pattern we associate with unhappiness."

"Excellent!" Cardin shook a fist in the air in a gesture of triumph. "No one has ever come this close to understanding Rooan communication before. With my system, and the extended, close-up sampling we'll be taking today, we are making history!" *A royal "we,"* Bari thought. His ambitions were transparent: King of his little corner of Haudernellian Academia. By his expression she could tell he was imagining the future speaking engagements, celebrity symposiums, and awards ceremonies that would be his natural due.

She knew she was only here because he needed someone expendable to do the spaceside work while he and his precious postdocs huddled around their tiny, blurred monitors congratulating themselves for their own manifest cleverness and superiority, safe and snug within the run-down, decommissioned Corallan shuttle that Cardin had dubbed *Project One,* but which, after his attempt to camouflage the exterior, would forever be the *Space Turd* in her mind.

The Sfazili independent who'd hauled them out here into the barrens had taken one look at their craft and declared as much himself; alas, neither Cardin nor anyone else on his team understood the tradesman's argot, so her amusement had been a private one.

"Okay, people," Cardin said. "We need to run calibration tests. Ms. Park, you arrayed our external sensors according to my exact specifications?"

"Yes, sir."

"You double-checked?"

"Twice," she said. Vikka rolled her eyes.

"So far we've been lucky and they haven't noticed we're here despite Ms. Park's thrashing about out there. Ceen has gotten us into position along the outer edge of the herd, and we'll maneuver our way a little further in as opportunity presents. As you know, the Rooan travel with their bioluminescent shell-walls all turned toward the center axis of the herd, so the further in we get, the more inter-animal communication we should capture. The herd is currently moving about point-oh-oh-oh-two Cee, so we've got about six and a half hours before they brush the edge of Auroran territory. We want to be well away by then with as much data as we can collect.

"Ms. Park, give Vikka the handheld unit," he ordered. "Then go find yourself a place to sit in the back and stay out of our way."

Vikka got up from her seat and sauntered over. As Bari extended the unit to her, Vikka leaned in closer. "Right before we launched I told Cardin that you were sleeping with Morus and giving away information about the project," she confided in a low voice. "He was so furious at you that I thought he was going to bust something. Oh, I know! A lie, but what can I say? I just don't like you Northies." Smiling, she yanked the handheld out of Bari's grasp and returned to her seat without a further look back.

Bari finished stowing her gear, her face burning. Morus was not only the top xenobiologist at rival Guratahan Sfazil Equatorial University, he was also studying the Rooan. The rival scientists hated each other with a white-hot passion that neared homicidal rage. It explained why Cardin had become more actively hostile in the last few days. She was lucky he hadn't had time to replace her—if Vikka had gotten her kicked off the project out of sheer spite . . .

Don't think about it, she told herself. *I'm here.* Gear properly stowed, she folded down the jumpseat near the airlock and buckled down her safety tether. And she waited.

From where she sat in the back, her view out the front was mostly obscured, but the light from Beserai's sun shining on the black, rough backs of the Rooan made faint arcs of silhouette among the stars ahead. She counted a half dozen, though the herd strength was closer to thirty times that number; the very few, vulnerable young were tucked in the center, away from prying eyes. Not even Cardin, in all his arrogance, would risk trying to penetrate into the core of the herd.

As if reading her thoughts, Cardin spoke up. "We need to stay far enough on the periphery so that they don't take too close a look at us. The Rooan are normally placid animals, but with the toll those pirates and thugs have been taking on the herd's numbers, they'll get more skittish the closer we get to Auroran space."

[Doesn't everyone already know this? Why speak if not to say something useful, unless it's just to hear his own voice?]

Bari allowed herself a small tic of a smile at Omi's comment. Not that Cardin was wrong; the remote station and surrounding outposts that made up Aurora Enclave had earned their reputation for vicious and capricious violence. The Barrens had many such lawless enclaves, but Aurora was the biggest and meanest of all. Even Earth Alliance, if need drew them into the territories at all, skirted well around it. The Rooan could not. The herd's migration loop between Beserai and Beenjai was dictated by gravity wells and the shortest of few, long paths between scarce resources. Along the way, the massive dwellers of the void inevitably attracted scientists, a handful of sightseers, and bored Auroran fighters looking for cheap and easy target practice.

Bari looked up as flashes of light caught her eye; one of the Rooan directly ahead was displaying a shifting pattern of bioluminescent greens and yellows, coruscating up and down the creature's underside. An answering flash of red came from further ahead.

"Shush!" Cardin yelled, though no one was speaking, and even if they were, they could not drown out light with sound. He leaned in close, his whole frame tense. "Why isn't the translator working?"

"It's processing," Vikka said, squinting at the handheld. "Um . . . the first one, it's giving me 'food near' at forty percent, and the response, um, 'happiness' at seventy-five percent correlation."

"We're nowhere near a nutrient source. Give me that," Cardin said, and yanked the unit out of her hand. He stared at it, shook it, stared at it some more. "*Food near,*" he repeated, scowling.

"Could it be a statement of a more general anticipation?" Bari spoke up from the back. From the look Vikka shot her, it was an unwelcome interruption. Cardin's gray eyebrows knit together, then he made a slight tsk sound. "A surprisingly good suggestion," he said, turning to look one at a time at both Ceen and Vikka as if to reprimand them for not having been the ones to voice it. "Although the common understanding is that the Rooan aren't sufficiently intelligent for such an indirect concept."

Vikka had just started to flash a sneer at Bari when he added, "Of course, common understanding is often wrong. If I can prove the Rooan have a rudimentary grasp of abstract thinking, that would be an enormous coup."

"And if you could prove Northies have a rudimentary grasp—"

"Bigotry doesn't become you, Vikka." Cardin cut her off. "Nor jealousy. You're the professional—act like one."

[Ha! Face stomp!] came over Bari's link. [Turquoise asks how much longer you expect to be. I know you can't answer, so I told him you take your job very seriously and he'll just have to wait.]

She did take it seriously—seriously enough to have hiked thirty-seven miles of barren no-man's-land to the isthmus border between North and South nations on Haudernelle, everything she owned on her back and a verichip with a personal recommendation from the Northern Institute's Director of Xenobiologic Field Studies tucked in a pocket against her breast like a ticket home. Even that had only been enough to get her five minutes of Cardin's time. If she hadn't had the experience with zero-grav and the full set of untethered spacewalk certifications, that would have been as far as she'd gotten. He'd told her as much when she signed on, and told her if she didn't appreciate that he'd given her a job at all she could "go back to the woods and scratch in the dirt for food like the rest of your people," or something like that; the exact words had fastened less in her memory than the tone of them.

As it turned out, she'd displaced another of Cardin's students who didn't have the certs, and Vikka had been trying to drive her out ever since. Bari suspected that they'd been lovers, but didn't care enough to find out.

Cardin stood up. "On the off chance that Ms. Park is on to something, I should be able to get the system to give us a double translation simultaneously, one of explicit meaning, and one of running extrapolation. But I need to access the primary console to make programming changes. Ceen, keep us steady relative to the herd."

The professor threw the floor hatch and disappeared down into the tiny hold where the mishmash of tech he'd spent decades putting together nestled like a canker in the ship's belly. As soon as the hatch closed behind him, Vikka whirled on Bari. "You fucking *bitch*," she said. "Are you *trying* to make me look stupid? Haven't I warned you to keep your damn Northie mouth shut?"

"You have," Bari said. She checked her tether, got out of her seat, then popped open her locker and began sorting out her personal gear.

Ahead of them the gigantic shapes of the Rooan flashed light back and forth, yellows and blues, reds and purples, a lone beacon of blue. "Will you two shut up?" Ceen snarled. "It's bad enough trying to fly this piece of shit as it is, and Cardin will kill us all if we miss anything important out there or spook the herd."

Ah, my jacket, Bari thought, unfolding the garment and shaking it out.

"Oh, very nice," Vikka said, reaching a new high pitch. "Did your mommy sew that for you back home? What do you Northies call home, anyway? Palm-fern huts in the woods? Dirt burrows?"

Bari slipped into the jacket. She flexed her arms, shrugged her shoulders, pleased again that even after all these years the fit didn't impair her physical movement. The jacket was comfortable, almost too much so. She walked forward toward Vikka, the weight of her mag boots on the metal decking and the faint tension of her safety tether a reassurance. "Would you like to see?"

"Why the hell would I want to be anywhere near anything of yours?" Vikka said, as Bari extended one hand, palm up, to show off the workmanship of the embroidered sleeve. As the woman opened her mouth to say more, Bari reached around with her other hand and slammed Vikka's head into the console in front of her.

"What the fuck!?" Ceen shouted, half-rising out of his seat, as Bari reached over and punched the emergency off for the ship's gravity field. Untethered, Ceen's motion propelled him into the back of his seat and into a bulkhead. He managed to get a grip on the seat foam and was trying to swing himself within reach of the end of his free tether when

Bari kicked him just hard enough to send him careening around the cabin. Then she bent down and snapped tight the lock on the hatch Cardin had just gone through.

Vikka was struggling up in her seat, one side of her face a brutal red and already beginning to swell, her eyes tearing up with hatred. Bari put a hand on the back of her neck and forced her face back down against the console. "Vikka," she said. "Please understand. First of all, you make yourself look stupid all on your own. Second, my mother is dead, so I'm not really inclined to listen to you talk about her. Third, while I came to Haudernelle Academy from the North, I wasn't born there. Still, during my time in the North, nearly everyone I met was intelligent, hard-working, and generous, entirely unlike you. It's something you might consider if you find yourself face to face with a real 'Northie.'"

"I am so going to kick your ass," Vikka hissed. "Cardin will—"

"Cardin can't do anything, and neither can you." Bari took the small dermal patch she'd palmed while sorting through her stuff and slapped it—harder than necessary, she had to admit—onto Vikka's forehead. Almost immediately the woman's eyes rolled up into the back of her head and she went limp. "Nighty night."

"Are you mad?" Ceen shouted from where he drifted mid-cabin. "You're jeopardizing the entire project!"

At least he cares about the science, if nothing else, Bari thought. She peeled the backing off another patch. He watched her do it, flailing his arms hopelessly trying to reach something to grab onto. "If it's any consolation, Ceen, the project was already failing," she said. "The herd is going to turn early toward Aurora space, coming dangerously close to their outpost in this sector. You'd only have had another thirty minutes, possibly less, to try to accumulate the material needed to demonstrate the validity of Cardin's translation program. We both know that's not nearly enough time. And after this, the herd is going to slingshot off Beserai and head back into deep space for the centuries-long trip to Beenjai. They'll go dormant and silent, leaving you with nothing left to study."

"How can you know this?"

Bari sighed. "The Rooan use gravity wells to modulate their velocity, right? If you simply look at the alignment of the planets in this system and their current heading, their trajectory is obvious—and gives them no more options in-system. This has to be the last pass."

Ceen was silent a moment. "I suggested that to Cardin six months ago and he said I was wrong. He said I was an idiot."

"Well, when you get out of here, be sure to remind him."

"Am I going to get out of here?" he asked.

"You might," she said, and slapped the patch on his arm.

"What is it you want?" he asked, his voice already fading as the sedative grabbed a hold on him. He was out before she could answer, but she did anyway.

"To sleep at night," she said. Pulling him across the cabin by one arm like a strange balloon, she stuffed him into the chair beside Vikka. She buckled them both in and down, pulling the straps tight to keep the two of them in place.

There was banging on the floor hatch, muffled and indistinct. She ignored it for the moment, and tapped open her mic. "Okay, Omi, the ship is mine," she said.

[Right on time. I'll let Turquoise know.]

Bari slipped into the seat Ceen had vacated so abruptly, swapping tethers once she was fully seated and strapped in. Pulling open one of the access panels on the helm console, a small blade took care of long-range communications. Then she reached over and turned off all of Cardin's external sensors. *Sorry, Professor, but I don't need any recordings of this.*

"I'm taking the ship further into the herd," she said.

[Turquoise says you're clear, and the front of the herd appears to have begun to turn.]

The intercom on the helm began blinking. She pressed a button, and a moment later Cardin's voice rang out tinnily in the main cabin. "What the hell is going on up there, Ceen?"

"I'm sorry, but Ceen is unavailable."

"Ms. Park. Put Vikka on."

"Vikka is also unavailable."

"Did we have an accident? A malfunction?"

"No accident," she replied, as she logged into the helm console with Vikka's password and changed all the passcodes. "Ship systems are all green."

"We've lost gravity and the hatch above me is stuck fast. What do you call that?"

"I call that one small switch and a medium-sized lock, Dr. Cardin."

The pause was longer this time. "Ms. Park, explain. Now."

"I decline," she said. "If I were you, I'd get a hold of something shortly, because I'm about to start shutting systems down and I assure you, sharp things multiply in the dark."

"Morus put you up to this. How much did he pay you to infiltrate my team and sabotage my project?"

"A poor guess. I've never even met Professor Morus," she said. "Please rest assured that my real client has no interest in the success or failure of your project; you are merely a convenience."

"What is it you want?"

Everyone keeps asking me that, Bari thought with some annoyance. For Cardin, she had a more practical and immediate answer. "I want your ship." And then, because she didn't really want to talk to him again, she turned the intercom speaker back off.

[You're just about in position,] Omi said over her private link. [Turquoise is going to help spot for you, so I'm patching him back in. A fair warning: he's still complaining about being itchy.]

<It *does* itch!>

"I'm certain it must, but it's not for very much longer," Bari replied, trusting Omi to translate. "How am I looking?"

<Do you see the big female ahead? Pull up beside her.>

Bari leaned forward and peered out the window. She'd closed the distance between her and the herd, and again she was struck by how singularly massive *all* the Rooan were. And how much, if they'd been green instead of gray-black, and hadn't had shifting fluorescent colors along their underbellies, they'd look like gigantic space pickles. "How do I tell which ones are female?" she asked. *Or "big"?*

There was a pause, then Omi answered instead of Turquoise. [I'm not translating that.]

Banging started up again on the hatch, easily ignored. Bari picked one of the several looming shapes in front of the ship and sidled up between it and another. "Is this good enough?" she asked.

<It will do.>

[The herd is on a straight trajectory now, and will cross into Auroran territory shortly,] Omi said. [You should lower the ship's energy output to avoid detection.]

"On it," she said, and she already was, shutting down all non-essential systems and the *Turd's* primary engines. Unless something went terribly wrong, she wouldn't need anything more than minimal thrusters to keep her position amidst the Rooan. Just before hitting the lights, she glanced around the cabin and spotted a small silver ball hovering, idle, near the ceiling at the back of the ship. She snapped her fingers. "Bob," she called. The bob lit up, glided near. "Light," she ordered. "Thirty lumens."

The bob switched on, casting a light bright enough for Bari to make out the controls but not much brighter. She turned off all ship interior and exterior running lights. There was a brief flurry of sound from the hatch that sounded faintly like someone scrabbling for purchase, then nothing. *I did warn him.*

With the faint light from the bob sufficient for what she needed, she killed all remaining main and auxiliary power feeds to the ship. A faint hum she'd long ago stopped hearing became noticeable by its sudden absence, and reflexively she took a deep breath. Ceen and Vikka, unconscious, breathed shallow and slow, and she resented only one of them what air they used. Cardin's supply was his own. Bari would use only a little herself, and if they didn't all die at Auroran hands she'd have plenty of time to turn the air generators back on before anyone felt any ill effects.

Leaving the helm controls on auto, she stripped out of her coveralls and pulled on the suit that she'd taken from her locker, a tight-fitting, matte-black, alien-made biosuit much less cumbersome than the *Turd's*, and worth far more than all Cardin's grants and endowments combined. She slipped her jacket back on over that and buttoned it up. The jacket was fine black linen, a double-row of magnetic buttons up the front placket, and a small semi-circular starburst of silver thread embroidered where mandarin collar met left shoulder, where sleeve met arm. She ran her fingers lightly over the old thread and thought of long-forgotten things.

[I'm picking up incoming from the outpost. Four ships, probably showing up for some more target practice on the Rooan. They don't appear to be in a hurry, but they're definitely coming here.]

"Got it," she said, pulling her suit hood up over her short-cropped hair and sealing the face-plate. Next she put on a vest, quickly checking each pocket to make sure it was still sealed and its contents secure. Ignoring Cardin's maneuvering rig, she pulled a much lighter-weight, thin-profile pack out of her locker and slipped it over her shoulders, fastening straps across her chest, abdomen, and crotch. A small plug connected it into the suit. Then she took out the last item she'd need, sliding it into the narrow sheath just over her shoulder.

She flexed the muscles in her hand in sequence, powering on the suit's systems. "Can you hear me?" she asked.

[Loud and clear,] Omi answered.

<Are you coming out to play?> Turquoise added.

"I am," Bari said, and she cycled herself out the airlock into space.

As part of its camouflage, the outside of the *Space Turd* had been given a rough, uneven surface. It had made adding covert handholds to it trivially easy, and Bari used these to move up and on top of the ship. Around her the Rooan shifted ever so slightly, giving her an unnerving vertigo. She wondered where among them her friends were hiding—nowhere easy to find, certainly.

No one who had not been explicitly invited there came intentionally within reach of Aurora. This inactivity made the pilots who flew along the border outposts bored, and bored pilots found any entertainment they could. On their last two passes a third of the Rooan herd had been lost; much more and they wouldn't have the numbers they needed to survive.

The gigantic animals must have become aware of the approaching ships, because the flashing on their undersides became more intense. [The ships are on direct approach,] Omi said. [They should be in range in three point six minutes. The herd is getting nervous.]

At the apex of the ship, perched on the nose, she unclipped the large energy-cannon she'd tucked there just before the *Turd* left Glaszerstrom Station to intercept the Rooan. "I need a window," she said.

[Working on it. These things are hard to nudge.]

The Rooan to Bari's left began drifting upward, and Bari could make out four small pinpoints of light moving toward them. In the distance was the faint blue glow of Outpost One. Deep in space behind that was the heart of Aurora itself, with its implacable, invincible warlord, who took everything he could see, and owned everything he could touch. She gritted her teeth, raised the cannon, and took aim at the closest of the incoming ships.

The first one will be the easiest, she told herself, and fired. The pinpoint of light flared for an instant and went out, as immediately the other three veered away. Now the hunt would begin; they'd be scanning the area, but the *Turd*, powered almost fully down, would be virtually invisible. Her Dzenni suit, far more sophisticated than anything found in human space, was a total insulator: she would not radiate heat, she would not absorb it. She would not be easy to find.

One of the remaining ships moved nearer, slowly edging up on the herd as if scanning for something on the far side of it. She checked the cannon's heat load—still only twelve percent, still cool enough—and then shouldered it again.

The second ship flashed and disintegrated.

"I don't see the other ships. Omi?"

[One is circling around the Rooan. I don't see the other.]

All of a sudden, around them, the Rooan began to shift and scatter, their light-patterns now oscillating wildly. <I believe he's trying to use the herd for cover while he looks for the source of the fire,> Turquoise said.

"That works for me," Bari said. She turned around, then threw herself backward in a panic, flat onto the surface of the ship as a Rooan barreled overhead, nearly knocking her off the ship. *Big mistake, Bari,* she told herself. *No matter how big they are, they aren't going to make any sound when they move. Pay more attention.*

The passage of the creature had left a small gap, and she could just see the edges of the third ship behind them. She got the cannon up, took the shot, and missed. Swearing, she checked the heat load again—a little over forty percent now, starting to get warm. The ship banked, disappeared behind a cluster of Rooan, and briefly reappeared farther up than she had expected. *Ship's moving in an evasive pattern.* "Can you see him?" she asked.

[No . . . yes. He's banked low again, circling around.]

"Thanks," Bari said. She lined up the sights on a gap ahead, and smiled when the ship appeared. Another flash, and then there was just one.

Don't run home yet, she thought at it, *I need you.*

She ejected the power cartridge from the cannon and let go of both pieces, where they drifted along with the herd. The cartridge would cool off quickly in open space. Unencumbered, she looked around the herd to get a sense of their positions, stood up straight, and launched herself up and forward toward the bright yellow-orange underside of the ancient Rooan who had nearly knocked her down moments ago. A quick squeeze of one hand sent enough thrust from her pack to carry her forward, and she reached the big creature and got a grip on its craggy, pitted underside, oscillating from yellow to orange and back again under her gloves. Two more jumps brought her forward.

"Where's my last fighter, Omi?"

[I still can't see it. Turquoise?]

<It's directly ahead. The herd is moving around it. You've almost caught up to him.>

If only Cardin knew how thoroughly his Rooan-camouflage would be tested, she thought. The problem was, Cardin had only designed it to stand up to the scrutiny of dumb animals; as aggressive as Aurora's fighters were, "dumb" they were not.

She moved hand over hand along the side of her Rooan until she was up near the pointed front, then flipped her faceshield to infrared. Even then the enemy fighter wasn't immediately obvious. It was only as one of the Rooan directly ahead of her swung slightly out of line to avoid something that she spotted it. *He's playing the same trick I am, shedding his heat load to avoid detection while looking for his enemy.* If she wasn't wearing her Dzenni suit, she was sure she'd be lit up like a nova on his screens.

She had maybe a minute before he was close enough to the *Turd* to spot it for the fake it was. She smiled and reached into her pack. *Not a problem.*

As her Rooan ride neared the ship, she kicked off and tumbled, silently, across the intervening space as the Auroran unwittingly headed toward a rendezvous. Her timing was perfect; she reached out one hand

and touched the side of the ship just aft of the pilot's view, a silhouette in faint light just visible inside. With her other hand she slapped an EMP mine onto the hull. Then she pushed off again, breaking physical contact with the fighter as the mine flashed once, twice, and the ship went truly dead.

The herd continued to move around her, the *Turd* slipping silently past along with them. She squeezed her fist and moved forward to where she could grab onto the dead fighter again. Taking the second mine out of her pack, she placed it next to the first. This one she didn't back away from, and she could feel the thrum even through the multilayered hull as the pressure-wave grenade activated.

The airlock had to be operated manually, of course.

The pilot was floating unconscious near the inside door, an energy pistol dangling from one hand. He'd known someone was coming for him the moment the EMP mine went off. Her mag boots kept her upright as she cycled the lock closed behind her and took his gun. Slipping off his helmet—*damn, he's young*—she peeled back the collar of his uniform with its own, less intricate starburst embroidery and slapped a sleep patch on him as well. Then she dragged him to the back, found the single-occupant escape pod, stuffed him in, and melted the lock.

Climbing into the pilot's seat, she buckled herself down and rebooted the systems. As the helm tried to bring itself back to life, she tapped her suit mic. "I'm in," she said. "How far behind am I?"

[You've almost dropped out behind the herd,] Omi replied. [I see three more ships on intercept from the outpost on max burn, about six minutes out.]

The helm was flashing a long, thin red line. Bari slipped on the pilot's helmet, then carefully ran her left forearm over the bar. For a long second she was afraid it wouldn't work, that the chip under her skin was too old or obsolete, but the bar flashed green at last even as the rest of the console came back online.

"The ship's mine. Light up the decoy can," she said.

[Done,] he replied, just as a faint flare appeared on the screen of her own console, on the far side of the herd. From a distance, it would not be distinguishable from an imperfectly-dampened engine signature. Close up, it wouldn't matter.

Four ships down, counting this one, she thought, *and three more on the way.* Outpost One had, by her best estimates, twenty-six combat ships at the moment—a recent border skirmish with Glaszerstrom had cost them three others. The remaining pilots would be off-shift, but were probably now being roused and told to stand by. And at least half of those would be too drunk to fly. Or so she hoped. It was the largest of Aurora's outposts, a cornerstone of its defense.

She plugged a line from her headset directly into the ship's comm net. "Can you pick up traffic?"

[The signal is weak from here and it's heavily encrypted.]

"So that's a 'no'?"

[No, that's a "give me a minute or two."]

<The herd is nervous,> Turquoise added.

"As long as they don't scatter, we're okay." Bari had engaged the craft's engines on minimum thrust and moved further into the herd, the ever-shifting rainbow of a Rooan's belly above her like the landing lights of an insane, upside-down, psychedelic runway. Cardin's translating machine would have choked on this much incoming data. She was surprised to realize she felt a tiny pang of guilt for having so thoroughly derailed his project. If the man hadn't been such a puckered-up old assvalve, she might have considered leaving a few of his data-collectors on.

[Got it. You want a live feed?]

"Absolutely."

. . . an ambush? See it now, on the far side of the stupid squids. . . . Can't believe anyone got the drop on Mejef and Beck. Kirbenz, though . . . Is that Tonker, hiding in the middle? Tonker, is that you?

"Modulate my voice to middle-young adult human male, Auroran accent, add ten percent static when you encrypt," she said.

[Ready.]

"Shut up, you idiots! Maintain silence," she said, and heard it go over the comm network after a moment's delay passing through Omi. It didn't sound like her at all. *Good.*

The three incoming ships fell silent, and pulled more tightly together as they came in. *They're going for point-to-point,* she realized. Direct light-based comms wouldn't be able to be intercepted by any normal tech. It also meant they wouldn't bother to encrypt it.

Luckily for me, I have some abnormal tech indeed, she thought.

<They are discussing the best approach, through or around the herd, and whether to stay in formation or come from multiple directions,> Turquoise provided.

That meant they most likely believed her to be Tonker, among other things. "I'm going to need an exit."

[Passing it on.]

<They've split their approach,> Turquoise said. <I'm working on nudging the herd a little so you can come out behind one and above a second. The third will pass in front of the herd, so you will have to find your own strategy for that one.>

"Got it. Thanks," Bari said. She watched as the Auroran fighters split just as predicted, and moments later saw a small shift in the herd nearby: Turquoise's handiwork. "I'm glad I brought you along."

[He's laughing,] Omi said.

She edged her stolen craft toward the growing gap, and emerged just after one of the three Aurorans passed. A quick check showed another moving along the underside of the herd where it had cover from the decoy, but in her own clear sights.

Do it, she told herself, and powered up the weapons systems. She fell in behind the first fighter, and then, carefully sighting on it—she wouldn't get any extra chances here—fired. The ship flared and died.

She sighted on the fighter below, which was just beginning an evasive maneuver away from her, and took it down too.

"Tonker! What the fuck?!" This from the remaining ship.

"Omi, jam him!"

[Doing what I can.]

She banked up and around, resisting the urge to use the Rooan as shielding. The fighter broke off and fled. They raced away from the herd, Bari on his tail as he wove a pattern through space, staying always one tic and jump just out of her sights. "Oh, Hell," she swore. Her hands flew over the console, overriding the safeties and dumping energy from life support, gravity-gen, and radiation shielding into the engines. She was suddenly light in her seat, held in place only by inertia, seat straps, and her safety tether. The burst of extra speed was less than she'd expected, but she began to close.

[Bari . . .]

"I know," she said. She could already feel it, the cabin growing colder. She closed her eyes for a second, let long practice at mind-body control kick in, and slowed her heart rate and her breathing. Then she opened calm eyes on the enemy, closer now, and brought him down with a fast double-hit. She hadn't even reached the debris halo before she was already diverting the ship's systems back to normal.

[That was dangerous.]

"So would be letting him get away."

Outpost One lay dead ahead. It sat in space like some giant's toy, the sunlight of Beserai's distant star gleaming off it only adding to the impression of a scaled-up, metal wasp's nest. Around it floated smaller objects: waste processors, chemical weapons storage, trash. As she watched, four more ships appeared, heading her way at full burn.

She got out of her seat, careful to keep the safety tether clipped, and pulled another small device out of her pack. It took her a long minute to wire it into the console, while the ship closed the distance to the outpost's remaining defenders. "Omi, did you get a good look at that last fighter's evasion patterns?"

[I did.]

"Then I'm putting you in charge of the helm," she said, clicking the device on. "You should have remote now."

A pause. [Got it. Any change in plans?]

"No, we're going in the hard way. Get as close as you can. If you can, blow the escape pod just before they take us out."

Bari pulled her face shield back down, checked her suit seals by reflexive gesture, then disengaged the safety tether and cycled herself back out the airlock. Pulling herself along the ship's hull, she reached one of the purely aesthetic wings and clambered out until she was perched comfortably about halfway down its length. Here, she was well out of the way of the furiously burning engines slung on the underside. She traced her fingers along the thin ribbon of silver laid into the black wing, the very familiar starburst pattern, and let an old anticipation, and a newfound guilt, wash over her.

<The herd front is nearing closest proximity to the outpost.>

"You should be safe. I think Aurora is going to be too busy dealing with me to think about anything else for a while." At the moment, the stolen fighter beneath her feet was heading straight for the outpost. "Omi, course change in five," she said. "Four, three, two, one . . ."

She let go of the ship even as it banked away underneath her, now on a collision course for the chemical weapons bunker. In her suit she was invisible to the intercepting ships; by eye they might spot her, but now they all changed course as well, pursuing the visible threat. She put her arms out from her sides in a parody of a swan dive as she fell/flew toward the outpost. Sailing through space in nothing but the Dzenni suit gave her a sense of being both infinitely powerful and infinitely insignificant at the same time. *Which is exactly as it should be,* her teachers would have told her.

Far away from her now, the Auroran fighters drew close enough to her stolen ship to obliterate it; she caught the small flash of the escape pod ejecting, but the fighters closed in on that, too, and turned it into just so much more space debris. "Sorry, Tonker," she murmured.

From there the fighters spread out, cautiously edging forward away from the base and each other, looking for the next threat. She was already well inside their slowly expanding perimeter, the outpost looming large dead ahead. She smiled; she was on target, no need to risk a burst from her pack to change course.

She curled herself up and around until she was foot-first, trying not to think about how long she'd had to practice the maneuver to keep from sending herself into a hopeless spin, and hit the side of the station near the pinnacle well above the central mass. It was a hard landing, but she'd prepared for that as well, and turned it into a short tumble up the sloped surface before she managed to catch a grip and stop. Then she activated the light mag fields in her boots, stood up in what felt, even absent any meaningful input from her inner ear, like a cartoonishly horizontal direction, and ran down and across the surface of the station.

The maintenance hatch was exactly where she expected it to be.

Bari spun the outer wheel, pulled the hatch open, and tucked herself into the small crawlspace backward so she could close it again. Once the hatch was sealed, she tried to turn around and discovered that, with the pack on her back, she couldn't. "Oh, great," she muttered.

[Everything okay?]

"It's just smaller than I expected."

[Or you're bigger than it expected.]

"Thanks," she said, then under her breath, "*you bit-fried hunk of space flotsam.*"

[I heard that.]

She scooted backward through the tight space until she came up hard against the inner lock. *Now what?* she thought. As best as she could, she laid down flat, her pack an uncomfortable wedge under her back, and studied the upside-down lock controls. Then she pried open the security panel, pulled out two leads, and shorted them. The hatch slid open with a whoosh as air filled the small crawlspace, and she scrambled out and into the maintenance space on the far side.

This area was only marginally bigger, but it was enough that she could turn around and, squatting, pull herself upright. Also, it had atmosphere. Her suit's supply was down to fifty-two percent so she set it to recharge automatically from the surrounding air.

It took her a minute to get her bearings, and then she moved through the tunnels as quickly as a need for quiet could afford. Several turns and intersections later, she found herself at another small hatch, with what appeared to be a small butter knife wedged into the control panel. She touched it gingerly, as if it could shock, but it was inert, a dead relic of another's past.

At least I know I'm in the right place, she thought. "I'm going in."

She emerged into a cramped and dusty storeroom filled with boxes, crates, and stacks of miscellaneous junk, the lighting dim. She took several deep, calming breaths as she unloaded from her vest pockets the next set of items she'd anticipated needing. As soon as she felt back under control she reached out an arm and slipped it past the chip reader. The doorlight turned green and admitted her into the main corridors of Aurora's Outpost One.

The senior staff would be in the situation room, monitoring the fighters as they looked for signs of their enemy, while security spread out throughout the decks, watching the airlocks and the docking rings, watching their own population for any sign of internal insurrection. The Auroran warlord would be doing much the same from his seat back in the central enclave, watching everyone, trusting no one. Out of Bari's grasp, but not beyond her touch.

A stunner took out the door guard. She shorted out the lock into the situation room the same way she had the hatch's internal airlock, and stepped inside. The room was dark, wood-paneled at ridiculous expense, displays overheard showing the still-expanding search party in vivid red tracery. Heads turned, hands reached for weapons, but before anyone could draw she was at the chair of the outpost's commander, her gloved hand lightly laid under his chin, across his neck, above the silver embroidery of a jacket nearly the same as her own. There were three other men in the room, all frozen where they stood, assessing, waiting.

"Who are you?" the commander barked.

"You don't remember me, Karilene?" she said.

He stared at her face, then at the jacket she wore. "I don't know you."

She hesitated, then reached up and peeled off the biomask she'd worn for nearly half a year, nearly coming to accept that face, the face of "Ms. Park," as her own.

The commander stared, and his gaze lost none of its sharpness, but after a moment the single "Ah" that passed his lips was like the last, faint breath from a dying man. He straightened, his arms folded carefully, fingers entwined, on the console board in front of him. "Bariele. You've grown into that jacket at long last, I see. You've come for revenge." It was statement, not question.

"No," she said. "Business."

"You're an assassin, then?"

"A facilitator. In this case, the difference is minor."

"Who sent you? Not Glaszerstrom, surely?"

"No, not them."

"Then who?"

"You were in someone's way, and presented them with a difficulty they wanted resolved."

He laughed. "My brother and I built Aurora out here in the Sfazili Barrens so that we would not be in anyone's way, and no one would be in ours. You know that."

"And yet."

"The ambush was cleverly done. I hope you got a good price."

"I did."

"He'll rebuild Outpost One, even if it takes years and years. It's not like him to let anything go. And he'll hunt you across the entire Multiworlds if he has to."

"And I expect he'll find me, sooner and closer than that."

As if sensing that something was about to happen, the others in the room began to shift and move, but before anyone could act she'd grabbed the short handle protruding from her pack, drawn out the thin, sharp blade that lived there, and moved it down in one swift, graceful motion. The old man jerked twice in his seat and then was still.

A young man toward the back of the room let out a cry, fumbling for his pistol, and abandoning her blade where it was she drew a small, cruel knife from the sleeve of her suit and skewered him through the neck from across the room. "Anyone else?" she asked, unholstering at last her own pistol. The remaining men stared at her angrily but relinquished their weapons. "Neither of you are half the man Karilene was. If you want to live, leave this room now and get off this station."

She stood, blade in one hand, pistol in the other, as the two men walked carefully around her and out. "When you report what happened here," she told the second man, "be sure to tell my father I send my regards." Then she closed and sealed the door.

Removing her jacket, she laid it over the old man's body like a shroud, or a calling card, or perhaps both. Where she was going she could not take it, and she knew—and he would know—that she left it only because she'd be back for it.

"It's done," she said into her suit mic.

[The fighters have turned and are heading back to the outpost at top burn, and there's activity at the Enclave itself,] Omi said. [Not to rush you, but you need to get out of there.]

"I'm on it." She sat at Karilene's console and slid in the small chip. Immediately systems began shutting down and scrapping themselves as the Outpost's general evacuation alarm sounded. She positioned her last three EMP mines beside the console and set the failsafe to detonate if they were interfered with. In a short while, the entire base would be defenseless, uninhabitable, scrap. It would be abandoned until it could be secured and rebuilt, which wouldn't happen until Aurora's warlord had made some determination of who had sent her. And that was something he would never resolve.

The same paranoia that would keep him away from this border until he understood what had happened here was now her own way out. She went to one wooden panel, felt around the trim until her fingers found the tiny catch, and the panel swung open. From there, metal rungs set into the narrow tube led her up and into the very top of the station where a small ship lay cocooned as insurance against the worst.

The escape craft had dust on the console but was fully charged, waiting. She left the outpost in a roar of speed only seconds ahead of the EMP explosion that crippled the station.

Setting the tiny ship on a wide arching course for the far side of Beserai, she engaged the auto-pilot. By the time the Auroran pursuers caught up and blasted the ship to pieces she'd long since abandoned it as well, floating curled in a ball in space, invisible.

Finally, far behind and away from the furious activity, the Rooan herd caught up to her, enveloped her, carried her along.

The *Space Turd* felt cramped and foreign when she climbed back into it. Cardin was still banging on the hatch at random intervals with little enthusiasm. After checking on the soundly asleep Ceen and Vikka—utterly ambivalent now to them—she sat herself down at the helm, slid the life support controls back up to full, and turned back on the gravity generators. She slowed the ship and changed its course; in a few seconds it would begin to fall behind and away from the herd. Last, she reactivated Cardin's intercom and sensors, a gesture she could only think of as recompense for the use and misuse of his ship. And because it didn't matter anymore.

She flipped the hatch bolt with one foot, toed it open; it was still dark in the cabin, dark enough to hide her, but she could see the professor's face in the dim light of his computer, the lines of fear etched in it rendering him a stranger.

"Ms. Park?"

"Your handheld," she said, and dropped the unit down to him.

"Ceen should wake up and let you out in a few hours, and then you can go home. In the meantime, collect what data you can."

"But . . . Aurora . . . "

"You don't need to worry about Aurora, Professor." And she closed and locked the hatch again.

She peeled off Ceen's patch, throwing it in the ship's flash-recycler. Vikka she left as she was; it was up to Ceen to decide if he wanted to listen to her the entire trip back or leave her asleep.

Her suit was fully re-charged. Time to leave the *Turd*, pick up Omi, and collect payment. She left the airlock one last time; the *Turd* was still on auto-pilot, but would soon diverge from the herd as the Rooan changed trajectories again for the slingshot pass around Beserai. Her pickup rendezvous was arranged for the far side.

She moved through the herd, jumping from one giant, rough body to another as if she was a stone skipping across a lake, until she found one with a small silver sphere taped to the underside, just under the nose.

<I still itch.> Turquoise said.

"Yeah, yeah. Omi, tell him to hang on."

She peeled off the tape, held the sphere up beside her, and let it go in space. Its single blue lens blinked at her.

[About time.]

Large rippling shades of blue moved up and down the body of the Rooan. [The big guy is happy, too.]

The Rooan flashed another sequence of blue. "I didn't catch that," Bari said.

[Oh, sorry, I was looking the wrong way,] Omi said. The sphere turned, flashed a sequence of lights at the Rooan, who flashed back.

<Thank you,> Turquoise said through Omi's translator. <The herd has given you Rooan names, in thanks for your assistance. Bari, it will honor us to be allowed to call you ####. Omicron, if #### does not suit you, I don't know what will.>

"Uh . . . I didn't catch that."

[Light-based names. If it helps, you're 23-17-83RGB Fading Reverse whereas I am 61-40-240RGB Brightening Center.]

"I'm honored," Bari said, hoping she was.

<Your price. We near Beserai. You wish to surf with us?>

"Oh, I do."

<It is, we would expect, lethal for non-Rooan.>

"My suit will hold."

<As you wish. We draw close.> Turquoise's massive body shuddered, and long vents opened in his sides along his entire length. <We will not be able to talk again until the far side, so please fasten yourself to a vent gill with something heat- and stress-resistant, but also preferably not itchy.>

Bari pulled a harness out of her pack, then let the pack float away into space. It would not survive the trip, and she would not need it on the far side, where she had a small ship of her own waiting and ready. It took several long minutes to attach and seal the links across her torso and legs, until she felt almost a prisoner in the tight bindings. Then she looped the remainder around the vent gill. "I'm ready," she said. "Omi?"

The silver ball drew near, and she plucked it out of space and tucked it down inside a pocket along the front of her suit. [The indignity!] Omi said, his signal weak.

"Oh, shut up," Bari said. Looking ahead, the bright crescent edge of a blue-white planet loomed near.

The vent gill closed again, holding her fast. She put her hands to her sides and ran through a precise sequence of control gestures with both hands. The straps shrunk, tightening. She took a deep breath, filling her lungs and expanding her chest, then completed the last gesture. The Dzenni suit, technology far beyond human, hardened into an immoveable shell. She could no longer feel the straps, only the unyielding foam that the suit extruded around her. Her faceplate was clear, bright in the light of the planet.

The Rooan herd hit the edges of Beserai's thermosphere, riding the curve of the planet like surfers riding a wave, seeking the mesopause. She caught her breath as noctilucent clouds spread out in wisps below her, then held it as Turquoise's entire back half split asunder and a million thin, iridescent threads tumbled and waved behind, tasting and collecting the rare bounty of elements and ice crystals they passed through, saving and storing them for the long cold ahead.

So much beauty and wonder. Tears streamed down her face and were quickly wicked away by the suit, leaving only a tickling hint of their passage across her cheeks. As they picked up speed, stealing velocity from the planet as easily as they swept up elements, the Rooan began to swing out again on a new trajectory, the solar wind from Beserai's star now full at their backs. And every Rooan began to flash, in sequence with each other, patterns within patterns. *They're singing*, she realized.

Bari smiled and wondered what Cardin's computer would have made of that.

ANOTHER LIFE

CHARLES OBERNDORF

She says, tell me about your first death.

After all these years she should be familiar with its details, but age seems to have erased the particulars that never interested her, so I remind her of the outline of events.

No, she says. I meant what it was like when you woke up?

She's lying in her bed, and I've pulled up a chair to sit by her side. I say something like:

I opened my eyes, and there on the ceiling were shades of blues and yellows. You know how I usually don't have a good memory for colors, but I took a psych test when I enlisted, and they told me those were the colors that would calm me when I woke up. I do remember lake water lapping the shore, the sounds of the birds I'd grown up with, because it was odd to hear them in this enclosed room. I expected the sound of the water to actually be the reverberation of a ventilation fan.

I sat up, but discovered I couldn't. There was a nurse beside me, and she was explaining something. I don't remember what she said. I just knew she wasn't the same nurse who'd sat me down in the chair and placed gear around my head. I think I liked this one more. Her voice was calm, but it drifted around me along with the sounds of lake water. I was lying down, but I'd just been in a chair. The other nurse, the one I didn't like, the one who had placed the gear around my head, had told me to relax. I'd closed my eyes. While I was unconscious, they had mapped my neural network. Now, awake, I should get up out of that chair and head over to the next bulkhead to the tavern we liked, to the Wake, where I'd arranged to meet Noriko.

Ah, Noriko, she says. There's an edge to her voice, though you'd have to know her well to hear it. After all these years, the name Noriko still inspires an edge to her voice.

I say, I can tell another story.

No, she says. You only told me about Noriko when we were first together. And that was a long time ago.

This is also about when I met Amanda Sam.

Don't be evasive. I'm too old for these games.

So I lay there in this unexpected reality. Of course, someone must have told me if you wake up sitting up, then you're waking up right after they've completed the recording. If you wake up lying down, you died, and they've grown a new body and shaped your mind using the patterns of your last recorded neuromap. But I didn't remember anyone telling me this, and maybe this was what the nurse was whispering to me, but it was my first death, and all I felt was panic and confusion.

I wasn't in the body that had been sitting in the chair, the body that would wake up, walk down the corridor, cross a bulkhead, and head two levels up to the Wake, where I'd meet Noriko. I wasn't in the body that was scheduled to spend two more days' R&R on Haven before it boarded a troop carrier for the war zone.

Worse, if I had died in battle, I should be in a ward with other newborns, the other soldiers who'd died with me. But I was in a private ward with what appeared to be civilian nurses. Had I died so heroically that I had received some special discharge? Or had I made such a fatal mistake that I couldn't even be reborn among my peers? I asked the nurses all sorts of questions. A nurse on one shift, let's say the morning shift, said, I can't talk about the war. It will just upset you. The afternoon-shift nurse said, No one tells us who pays for the treatment or the room. The night-shift nurse said, Maybe the money is coming out of your own account.

Of course, that was impossible. When I enlisted, I had been as poor as a miner without oxygen. The sign-up bonus had gone to pay off family debt.

The nurses taught me to sit up and helped me make my first steps. I learned how to gesture with my hands without knocking over cups of coffee. I imagined what it must be like in the ward among the soldiers, the taunts and the insults at each misstep, all of that making it less frustrating. And at some point, some captain or lieutenant, or maybe even some lowly sergeant, would come by and update us on the status of the war and announce who would go back and who had died the requisite third time and would be offered the honorable discharge plus bonus.

But one nurse, one day, while helping me sit in a machine that worked my leg muscles, said, mostly in exasperation, "There is no ward of newborns. You're the only one right now. That's why you got so many nurses. We're bored."

Depression weighed my every thought. I'd imagined that Noriko had died with me, that she would have been among the newborn. I imagined finding her and making sure she understood that whatever I'd done wrong, whatever had caused our deaths, I hadn't meant it.

What exactly did you two have? she asks. How long had you been together?

I hesitate. I have been with this woman for several lifetimes. In our last lifetime together, I waited until I turned fifty before I decided it was time to start over in the body of a twenty-five-year-old. She said, I've lived a few more lives than you. I feel I've seen enough. This time I want to see things through to the end. She said she would like to spend those remaining years with me, growing old together, but I did not believe her. Our lives were so fraught with our time together: nouns weighted with multiple meanings, verbs sharpened by the years; we were best off, when the mood was right, with incomplete sentences that the other would finish with an automatic goodwill that was also born of all our time together.

After she left me, I died in an orbital collision, and insurance paid for the rebirth into a twenty-year-old body. My current body is thirty-five; she's eighty-five. My answer to her question—How long had you been together?—now embarrasses me.

At this distance, it's so hard to imagine how I felt. It was my first life. It was so new to me. I'd only known Noriko for three, maybe it was four days. Five at the most.

Five days? That's all? How did you meet?

Two different units had been shipped to Haven. One unit was full of youths fresh out of training; the other unit had seen battle, probably several times. I hadn't made any close friends during training. Everyone else had been so enthusiastic, and I had just barely made it through. I didn't know what to do with myself, so I wandered. It's funny how little of Haven I remember after all the time I spent wandering it. Way Stations are so different and so homogenous—they have the cultural trappings of the locals, but there's always entertainment after entertainment, gymnasium after gymnasium, tavern after tavern.

I went into the Wake by accident. Most people in my unit didn't even know what the name meant. Where I grew up, the expense of a funeral was the same as a month or two of pay, but whatever a funeral cost, a new life cost a hundred times more. My parents were now past fifty and had both decided that it was too late for another new life. They were paying off my brother's second new life. He was now mining in the asteroids to pay off his first. He had been a woman the second time around, gave birth to two kids, and was in debt from the advance trusts; he was paying for them in case his children died while raising their own children. My sister was on her third life, and she had established some new financial network in some distant solar system and we never heard from her. I was the baby of the family, the one my parents welcomed to their world after their circumstances forced them to take low-paying work that bought bread but no meat, that paid rent, but no heating. With children and grandchildren, they didn't want to do risky things that paid off debt and built up savings for your next life—no wars, no world building, no mining. So I'd been to some wakes, and I'd liked the name of the tavern, and there inside was the bar itself, shaped like a long casket, shiny dark wood, but with a flat surface. I thought it was amusing.

I don't remember what they called fresh recruits. Whatever it was, Newbie, or Sprout, or something vulgar, there was this table of boisterous men and women, and they called me over. There was something about them that communicated experience, a certainty to the way they held themselves, even though they were clearly a bit tipsy. I was sure they were talking to someone else. "No, you!" one of them called. He pointed to the young woman next to him. "She thinks you're worthy." She glared at him. I'd grown up with that game: the older kid calling you over just to make sure he could put you in your place before an audience of his peers. I think I made it to the bar. I think I bought a drink for the woman sitting next to me. I remember her saying to me, "So who do you think is cuter, the soldier girl or me?"

The soldier girl was at my side and took me by the elbow and muttered, "You need combat pay first before you can afford her."

"Or him!" the guy at the table said.

Of course, who knows if that happened? Maybe I invented that part to explain what came later. Maybe I just went over to the table, happy that someone was interested in me. I remember staring at soldier girl when she was busy talking to the others. Like all the others, her hair was cut short, and her tunic was tight enough to suggest that like many reborn female soldiers, she'd opted to do without breasts in this life. She sat quietly when she listened, but when she spoke, she leaned forward, waved her hands, made a point of directing conversation away from her or me.

I remember a lot of laughing. Whenever they asked me questions, I felt like an adolescent answering adults. Where I was from, why I enlisted. I told them I wanted to see more of the universe, and I wouldn't be able to do that where I'd grown up. I felt like the soldier girl, whose name was Noriko, was looking right through me, that she'd guessed the accumulated debt that weighed my family down as if they lived deep in the atmosphere of some gas giant.

At some point she wrapped her arm through mine. Later she pressed her thigh against mine. I had grown up in a conservative place; no girl had ever treated me like this, and I felt both excited and unworthy. We left the Wake as a group—I have a memory of the girl at the bar lifting her hand, her fingers dancing, a gesture of farewell—and I was certain my military companions would soon be rid of me. But we continued walking to where they were quartered, and the group had started to joke with Noriko, swearing they wouldn't look, that they'd cover up their ears.

Noriko just shook her head as if everyone else was just too adolescent for her. At the Wake, she'd made me place my left pinky in some device that she'd held under the table. Now she handed something to one of her buddies. "Use this to check him in," she said. She asked me where I was quartered. Then she handed something to another one. "And this will check me in. We're going elsewhere."

Later I found out that as long as you pretended to check in they didn't care much what you did on Haven. The people on Haven needed to make money so that there would be a Haven to return to. I didn't know this. I felt the thrill of the forbidden as she made her way to a different level, a different bulkhead. She signed us into a room, closed the door, and turned to me. I remember her looking at me for a moment before saying, "You have to take some of the initiative." So I kissed her, and I clumsily undressed her. At some point, probably after it was over—I picture her lying next to me naked—she looked at me and said, "This is your first time, isn't it?" She said it sweetly, and years later I wondered if that is exactly what she had wanted. But back then I was frozen. I knew I'd been a horrible lover and I didn't know if it was worse to answer yes or no.

She kissed me. "We only got a few days, so I hope you aren't the type who hates getting advice."

Right now, you can look at me and tell me there was a kind of expediency. She was back from the front and wanted to absorb as much life into her body as she could before going back out. While I kept waiting for her to change her mind about me, we avoided her friends, we sampled her favorite dishes at restaurants she'd visited before, we strolled through the park she liked, and sat holding hands staring at the distant sun which Haven orbited, and the closer gas giants whose moons were the source of contention. "I can't wait to go back," she said, and her hand squeezed mine. I remember it as if it were a gesture of great intimacy and trust. "And I truly dread going back."

I was eager to get back to the guesthouse room with her, whether it was in the morning or afternoon or night. Everything was new, whether it was giving a naked woman a back rub or the intimacy of listening to her pee while I waited in bed. I had so much wanted to hold a woman's breasts, and there were no breasts to hold. Noriko had kept female-sized nipples, and she directed my attention there. "I'll streamline my body," she'd said, "but I won't streamline my pleasure."

At night, in the dark, she told me the kind of things she wouldn't say during the day. She liked combat. She liked the thrill and fear of dying. She liked the constant test of herself: "Should I save a comrade in trouble or press on with the mission or run for my life? I actually like coming back to life. I hate that I can't remember the last battle or two. I like that I don't have to remember dying. I like the way my body yearns for sex." She touched my chest or took hold of my penis when she said things like that, as if to remind me of my role in things. "You'd think, you know, being around for as long as I have, I wouldn't be interested anymore. And you'd think that it being the same genes, and the same memories, my desires would be the same. But sometimes I wake up and just want main-course sex, and sometimes I want gourmet sex, and sometimes I want to be really rough. My last life I was with this guy and I was really into anal sex. Now I'm getting a kick out of oral sex." I remember the way she kissed me right then. "You have a perfect mouth," she said.

You're gloating, she says.

Maybe I am, I reply. I'm sorry.

I remember how often we talked about her. Our first trip together. It was the rings of Saturn tour, right? And ever since I've felt like I had to live up to her. I don't think I realized until now that you guys were only together for a few days.

Shall we talk about something else? I ask. I don't correct her about the rings of Saturn tour.

I sit here and feel an enormous guilt. We haven't seen each other for a long time. I had some extra money because of a business venture that, for once, went right, and I decided to travel out to this world, to fly to the regional capital, to take train after train to the extended forest where she now lives much like a hermit with books, all of them written before the start of the human diaspora.

I have been there for almost a week. The first days I was sick with sensory deprivation: abruptly living alone in just my head, with only the sounds of the world around me. Now that I've recovered, she takes me for walks, slow walks, where once she'd been the one to keep a terrible headlong pace. She points out birds, the scurry of animals; she bids me to listen for sounds I haven't listened for since I grew up by the lakes of my homeworld. At night I cook her favorite suppers, and we talk about people we've known and trips we've taken, living off the accumulated interest of her last name. She's started to forget events of our last lifetime together, and we talked more of our early adventures. Early on, I recommended medicines that would make her neurons supple just as the injections kept her joints pain-free and flexible. She said, "I don't like pain. I don't mind fading away." Exhausted after our walks, she lies in bed once we finish supper, and we talk until she falls asleep. I sit there and listen to her breathe, her occasional murmur of a snore, and I wonder why I have come here. Was it to ask her to reconsider, to chose another life and rejoin me? We traveled so well together; we sat together so poorly when in chairs that moved only with the velocity of the planets where we had settled.

Now, we're both awake, I sit in the chair next to her bed, and I've asked her if I should change the subject. She extends her hand and places it on my knee. No, she says. I think I should have listened more carefully the first time. I listen more these days. I hear so few voices. And I think you tell things better these days. I've always liked you best when you were over thirty-five. So, it sounds to me like you were just a tool for Noriko's pleasure.

That was my biggest fear, that I might not truly exist for her beyond her pleasure. But one night, or I think it was at night, it could have been in the morning, she had a powerful orgasm where she seemed to shake to pieces right under me. I remember what she said afterwards. "I hope I survive the next two battles. Then I'll be back at Haven, and this moment will become one of my permanent memories. But if I die this time out, I'll come back to life, and it'll be as if you never existed."

In the gym, I felt like I was her mirror image, with all that's insubstantial about an image in the mirror. I knew exactly how to hit back a ball so she'd return it, exactly what moves to make when we wrestled, exactly how to move with her when we practiced duck and glide. "We work so well together," she said. "I mean here in the gym. Maybe we should register as comrades-in-arms." And I thought, if we die, we'll die together, and we'll be reborn together. We will have forgotten how we met, but we'll know we belong together.

That's why I hated those missing two days, the two days after the neuromap, the two days before I was shipped off to battle. I would have found out if she'd truly meant those words. It sounds sickly-sweet now, but I wanted to know if we'd faced things side by side.

My recovery progressed quickly. The morning-shift nurse said I should start walking through Haven. She gave me a set of clothes, leg-braces, and a cane. Once outside in the corridors I found the first public dataport and placed the tip of my left pinky against the circle. There was a delay. The pinky of my newborn body didn't have the same fingerprint as belonged to my previous body, but it had the same DNA, and one set of records had to align with the other. For a moment, I thought the old bank records wouldn't be found, that my entire past would disappear, but soon numbers layered like bricks appeared. I had some leftover money from my last visit in Haven, enough to buy a few meals and a few drinks at the Wake. If the military had paid me for my services, there was no record of it here.

Okay. And how long ago had I spent the shore-leave money they had given us when we first docked with Haven? It took me a while since Haven went by local calendar rather than the federal calendar. I checked for the day of my last transaction, which had been four beers at the Wake the night before I was set to leave. I would never know with certainty with whom I had those beers, but it was six months ago. In those days it took a month to grow a body, so I must have died five months after I left Haven. How much had happened in those five months?

I walked for a bit, well, walking, then resting, all over Haven. One of the few things I remember now, benches in little niches with plants and the sound of a nearby forest or sea. I ended up at the Wake.

It was a slow night. I sat coffin-like, drinking something; maybe it was sake (even though I never really liked sake) because that's what Noriko and I drank together. The bartender seemed to avoid my gaze, and my glass sat out for a long time before he poured another.

"Not friendly tonight," I said to the guy next to me who ran a lunchroom one bulkhead over.

"There's hardly any business," the guy said. "We're all getting antsy." I told him the date I had shipped out, and he said there had been a rash of rebirths about a month after that. But it had been quiet since then. There had been a unit of newbies, and several units for shore leave, but no new casualties for a while. "Usually they wait until they have two units' worth, enough to fill a ship. You don't want to pay for quartering people longer than you have to."

A woman spoke my name and slipped her arm through mine. She was pale with red hair, and her green eyes gave her an alien look. I don't think I'd seen green eyes before. She looked at me so intently. The way I remember it, this is the woman I bought the drink for the night I met Noriko, but, as I said, I've begun to wonder if I made that up later, that maybe this was the first time I actually met her. "Let me buy you a drink," she said.

I was protesting while the barman poured me another sake. Her hand very tenderly wrapped my hand, and just by touch she guided me to a booth. She sat down and slid over. She patted the space next to her. "Sit next to me, handsome."

Only my mother had ever complimented my looks, so I became wary. I sat down opposite her.

She tilted her head, and I felt the disappointment registering in her green eyes. At first I felt like I'd let her down; then I felt like things hadn't gone as she'd planned. I didn't know which reaction to trust.

"You don't remember," she said.

I tried. She looked at me like I should remember more than buying her a drink.

"Your friend and you."

"Noriko?"

"Yes. You and Noriko. We spent a whole night together."

Once while in bed Noriko had asked me my fantasies. After I had told her, she took firm hold of my penis. "This is what I like, and I don't share," she said. Right then I knew this pale-skinned woman with red hair was conning me.

"You don't remember. We met too late. We met after your neuromap. And you're walking a little funny. Poor you, a new life." She took my hand and again called me by name. I wanted to pull my hand away, but I liked the comfort of it after how-ever-many nights it had been sleeping alone in my private bed, my only company being therapy machines and the nurses who brought my food, the physical contact of the professional hand that never lingered, the touch that was never too light, that never grazed a nerve that mattered. "My name's Amanda

Sam. And I want you to know that the two of you spent a very lovely night with me."

She was holding my hand, and I couldn't work up the courage to tell her I didn't trust her.

"We met in this tavern. You and soldier girl were seated in that booth over there." She pointed at the other side of the bar, and it was the booth where Noriko and I usually sat. Noriko and I had gravitated toward it, the booth where we'd first sat together. But Amanda Sam could have learned that just by watching us. "You two looked like it had been a bad day. It was a slow night and I decided to join you guys. I asked what was wrong."

"Noriko wouldn't say," I said.

"And she didn't. I told the two of you that I like working with couples who are going through a quiet phase. I offer the extra spark."

"I'm not sure Noriko is the type who would want the extra spark."

"Don't be sure," she said. She was caressing my hand rather than just holding it, her fingertips every now and then sailing up along my forearm. Noriko had been a straightforward lover; every action and physical sensation had a utilitarian purpose in her pleasure. Only once, when Noriko had thought I was asleep, had her fingers traced the contours of my face. "I've been here for a while. I've seen her before. She does have a life or two extra under her belt, where you've got that innocence that some women find very attractive. I find it very attractive. I just want to take you into my arms and tell you everything will be okay. But, you know, hon, it is still innocence. A woman like Noriko, she might also want a spark."

I was sure she was manipulating me, but she was right, also. Maybe Noriko wanted more. I had given Noriko precisely what she asked for, and I measured the results by the way she clung to me. But there were those silences. Maybe she wanted more than she knew to ask for. The one time she'd caressed my face when she thought I was sleeping, I'd wanted to ask her to do that more often, but I never did.

And now Amanda Sam was talking about Noriko herself, how she sat at the table, taut, like a soldier, or a weapon waiting to be used, and how she was in bed, like coiled energy released. And maybe there was a gleam in Amanda Sam's eye, the gleam of the gambler who's just seen her opening gambit work, but maybe I'm adding that now, because she *was* describing the Noriko I knew.

"But," I said, and I remember how hard it was to say outright, partly because of the way I'd been raised, partly I wanted it clear that I still didn't trust her. It took me a while to explain how Noriko wasn't interested in women or in sharing me with another woman.

"Oh, honey," she said. She leaned forward and kissed me on the lips. Then looked at me with her green eyes. "I'm Amanda Sam. I was Amanda with you and Sam with her."

I pictured the events of that night, events that might or might not have happened. It was all too much. I made excuses: I had to return to the hospital; I had yet to be discharged. Amanda Sam accompanied me, her arm gently wrapped around mine. "I know it must be hard for you," she said. "I would offer to stay with you, but it's illegal in a hospital."

When the night-shift nurse saw Amanda Sam at my side, she glared at me and said nothing. Only at that point did I realize that Amanda Sam was a prostitute. I'm not sure when I understood she was a hermaphrodite.

She says, I don't remember that you ever told me this.

I told you about Amanda Sam, but you never wanted to hear the details.

You know, for some reason, I thought you'd met Amanda Sam first. I think I'd come to believe that Noriko had helped you get over what happened with Amanda Sam. Maybe that's why I thought you'd loved Noriko so much. Or maybe that's what I needed to think so I could fall in love with you. Tell me what happened next.

I think I was discharged from the hospital the next day, but that may have not been the case. Whenever they discharged me, they updated the chip in my pinky. Three nights paid for at a guesthouse, a set per diem for four days, and passage on a ship home, well, three ships with two connections. All I could picture was three months while I went out of my mind, not knowing how I would tell my family that I had no idea what had happened to me nor why I'd lost out on the opportunity to die three times and bring home desperately needed funds.

I found a niche with library capacity, but Haven lies in a sector where they consider wartime censorship to be patriotic. There was no news on any battles, so I couldn't find out how I might have died. I had begun to wonder if something stupid had killed me: a fall from a ladder, a strange electrocution while installing equipment, or the terrible aim of my comrades. But if I'd died from any of those embarrassments, they would have revived me, wouldn't they? Would any of that have disqualified me from future battles?

I decided to get something quiet, a book, I decided, and I read like I hadn't read since I was in my early teens, and I sat in the hospital foodstop, and I moved around, trying to sit as close to nurses as I could, and I listened, hoping someone would say something about a group of newborns. After dinner I returned to my room, cleaned up, and went to the Wake.

There were a few people in booths. The bartender poured me a beer, then ignored me. Amanda Sam wasn't there, and two beers later, she was. I bought her a drink. She asked me a lot of questions. She sympathized. "I know what it's like," she said, "when you start with so little." Her first life she'd been a woman and had been taken advantage of so many times that she decided to charge men for that particular pleasure. "I'm not the soldier type. I don't want to get killed to start fresh. But there's a demand for people like me who make anything possible, and so the people who paid for your new life paid for mine."

I remember sitting stunned. With Noriko I'd experienced sex as glorious exercise and passionate language and had dreamed that it might one day be religious communion.

She talked as if sex were an economic transaction, just like any other human interaction.

I told her she was wrong.

She smiled, bemused. Noriko had looked that way when I'd told her my plans for the future. "Look," Amanda Sam said. "I gotta go. If you want to talk some more, I'll be back in an hour and a half, two hours at the most."

She slipped off the stool, and she walked out of the tavern. I watched the fabric waver around her butt, and I thought that she couldn't be a man at all. The bartender poured me another beer and looked at me like I was a fool, but he didn't say anything. I thought of Noriko and decided to leave.

The next morning I felt like I didn't have much time left. I walked all the way to the spaceport since I didn't want to spend money on transport. After conversing with several machines and one human who looked like his life was answering simple questions a machine wouldn't answer—it's funny how he's one of the few people from then that I can actually picture in my mind, but maybe I'm making him up—I found out that the ticket was military issue. Around here, the military did the bulk of the business, so the value of the ticket was a third of what it would have cost if I'd booked the passage as a civilian.

I tried to find an employment office, but there wasn't one. Turned out everyone on Haven pretty much got work here from one military connection or another; the tavern and guesthouse owners all had their three deaths and bonuses, and all the staff and medical people had at least one military death behind them, and the prostitutes seemed to have come here from other military outposts. There was no enlistment office, but I found some offices representing the military, but one office turned out to be in charge of requisitions, another turned out to handle quartering, another salary disbursements. I finally found someone in some office, troop transportation, maybe, and he said he'd look up my records. He tried several different places, squeezed the bridge of his nose, and faced me with a smile. "I don't know how you got here," he said, "because according to this you never joined the military."

"Is there any reason my name would disappear?"

"I don't know. Maybe if you were a spy. I think we'd get rid of your name if you were a traitor, too."

So maybe I had signed up to do some special work. Was my existence here an accident while the real me was off somewhere with Noriko discovering something important? Or had I been captured in battle, tortured, and the military thought I'd given up vital information? Why would they pay for a new body, for my rebirth, if I'd given up vital information? Maybe this forced exile was their way of punishing me for my coerced betrayal.

At the hospital foodstop, I was joined by a doctor who so much didn't want to sit alone that he'd join other loners. He'd died only once. He didn't know how, but he didn't want to die again. He had his combat pay, but no big bonus, but they needed medics at Haven and employed him. "Such is the story of a lot of people here. We couldn't do the three times. What's your story?"

He would sympathize with my situation. Maybe he'd have a connection or two. He'd find out what had happened. I told him the story. He shrugged, got up, and left.

I was so disconsolate that I was relieved when I got to the Wake and Amanda Sam asked me to buy her a drink. She drank brandy. A slow sip at a time. "It makes me happy. I just have to make sure I don't get too happy." She asked me why I looked so bereft. She used that word, *bereft*, and I decided her first life had to have been more literate than I had first presumed.

I told her I must have done something terrible, but I didn't know what it was. I liked the comfort of the way she looked at me, the comfort of my hand in her two hands. I was going to tell her how badly I wanted to see Noriko, but some guy snuck up and gave her a big hug from behind. "You free, Amanda?" he asked.

I looked at him, a thin guy with a beard. He'd been down the bar, glancing this way. He'd pointed once at me, and the bartender had shook his head to one question, then shrugged to another.

"I'm sorry," she said to me. "I gotta go." She leaned forward and kissed me before rising. To the guy with the beard she said, "For you, honey, I'm always free. Am I seeing just you tonight?"

"No, Cynthia just called me. She had a change of heart. She said I should ask you home if I found you."

"Well, you have found me."

"Would your friend like to come with us?"

Amanda looked at me and gave the kind of smile I've always associated with rejection. "He's a friend, but not that kind of friend." She leaned over to kiss me again. "Wait two hours, okay. Don't run out on me like you did last night."

I nursed a beer and worked up the nerve. I asked the bartender what the skinny guy had asked about me.

"He asked if you were a soldier on leave."

"And the second question?"

"If you worked for Amanda Sam."

I don't remember if I stewed for a while or if I left immediately. I imagined sitting at a booth in the Wake and talking to Amanda Sam when Noriko walked in. But why would Noriko care? After what I must have done. I spent hours thinking of everything wrong I'd done in my life and couldn't think of a thing that would have led me to this place in my life.

I returned to my room to avoid just those thoughts. I hid in a book; I lived in the book so I could hide. I don't even remember the knock. Maybe it was a chime or the sound of the sea. I just remember Amanda Sam standing at my door with a bottle of wine. She talked about the couple she'd been with. I don't remember what she said. I remember her saying that she felt like a prop that helped them act out their own pathologies. She told me how alone she was. Everyone here was ex-military or soon-to-be military. "I don't have a military bone in my body. I just get boned by the military."

At some point we had finished the wine, and I thought she'd leave, but instead we were kissing. I was thinking that any minute she was going to pull out of the embrace and ask for money. I think I was hoping she would because it would be such an easy way to put an end to what was happening. But she kept kissing me, and I drank kiss after kiss. And then one thing was leading to another.

And you're going to skip over what happened? she asks. She has rolled onto her side, and is looking at me beneath the glow of the lamplight. Her hand still rests on my thigh.

I say, You never liked talking about these kinds of details.

I am at the point in my life where this is more like hearing about the mating behavior of some strange animal. She says this and gives me this familiar smile. She's going to do something that I won't like but that will amuse her. Her hand moves up my thigh. She laughs, a cackle of a laugh; it would be an old-lady laugh but she laughed like this when we met (she was thirty) and she laughed like that in her next life which she started at twenty-five, and she laughed like that when she was reborn as a sixteen-year-old, after one of the neocancers had ravaged her body with leaking sores and she'd said she'd make it up to me though there was nothing to make up, nor was it a making up: the woman in the sixteen-year-old body felt like such a striking sex object that she withdrew from my every touch. Now, in her final old woman's body, she cackles and says, her voice full of sympathy, You're aroused.

I say, You're not making it easy to tell this story.

It's such a lonely story, she says. Why don't you cuddle with me?

I hesitate.

And she misinterprets my silence and turns off the light. She says, There, now you don't have to see my wrinkles. You can hear my voice and know it's me. Get undressed and cuddle with me.

I knock my knee against a bedpost, but finally I'm there. Her body feels bonier, more frail, and she pushes her back toward my chest. She has not removed her nightgown, but she places my hand over her breast. She says, I want you to feel my breast but not how it truly feels. I like this, just being close. Does this feel good? she asks and she gently rocks her hips.

I remember a night like this—I'm not sure when in our lives together it took place—but I think we were on some ship taking us somewhere. She told me how alone she felt. How she just wanted to be close. And we worked out this arrangement, this spooning together, my penis nested inside her, a sweet, low-electric connection while we talked. Now, with a quick touch of artificial moisture, we lie together in the dark as if the years apart had not existed at all.

Now, she says, stop telling me what you don't remember and tell me the details.

Well, I don't remember how her blouse came off, if I unbuttoned it or if she unbuttoned it while smiling impishly as she gauged my response. All I remember was staring at her naked breasts.

And that also causes me to remember something I forgot. Amanda Sam had always worn clothes that revealed or highlighted her breasts. Sometimes, when talking, she'd smile and look down and you'd have no choice but to follow her gaze. I was eager to hold and touch and kiss Amanda Sam's breasts, and I thought of Noriko's streamlined chest, her aroused nipples, and just the yearning for Amanda Sams's breasts made me feel a terrible guilt.

She says, I'm sure you got over the guilt.

I'm not sure I got over the guilt.

But Amanda Sam had to urge me on. "They're waiting for your

attention." She kissed me again. "I'm waiting for your attention. Soldier girl is gone, hon, I'm here."

I should tell her I loved her breasts but I had no right to them. But I also thought about how she'd come to my room, how she'd chosen me, and how I knew she was right, that I probably would never see Noriko again. I kissed her breasts. I worshiped her nipples. I only had worshipped Noriko's nipples and I thought there was only one way to pray before this altar. Amanda Sam directed my mouth and tongue in different ways, and I was surprised, even though it was obvious, that there were so many ways to go about this. Soon we were both naked, but she wore this little skirt thing. I knew what she was hiding, but I pretended that she was just wearing a skirt. I realized that when we kissed she never pressed herself against me.

She went down on me, and I thought after all my time with Noriko that I would last forever. But it was a new body and a new sensation to that body. Suddenly, after orgasm, Amanda Sam was a stranger. At that point, I was afraid. It was my turn to reciprocate. Or worse, sometimes, Noriko would just want to lie back and talk, and I had nothing to say to Amanda Sam. But she kissed me and did something I didn't know you could do because Noriko had never done it. She used her mouth, and I was hard, and she had me lie down, then she turned her back to me before lowering herself down.

The sensation was wonderful, but I lay there and felt like a part of me was distant. I wanted to be with Noriko and the way her hands pulled me into the rhythm she wanted or the way she wrapped her arms around me as if she was going to pull my body into hers. I admired Amanda Sam's back. I admired the way she leaned forward so I could admire her backside. I thought, So this is what sex is like when you don't care. But I didn't want it to stop for a second. I wanted to feel more. I sat up, and I leaned my cheek against her shoulder blade and I held her breasts, and she breathed about how good that felt, and maybe I was wrong about the nature of caring because now I felt like I was with her and how alone we both were and as she breathed nice exclamations, I felt my hand make its way down from her breast, down her belly, I'd truly somehow forgotten, because I somehow expected to touch those moist creases.

Not the most poetic naming you've done, she says.

The words are a distraction. I've lowered my own hand, feeling I should reciprocate the pleasure I now feel, but her hand returns my hand to her breast.

She says, So you don't find a vulva. Were you shocked?

I pulled my hand away so fast. There were two shocks. The shock of memory, the realization that in spite of what I knew, I'd pictured Amanda Sam as a woman and now I couldn't. But sweet breathing aside, her encouragements aside, I'd discovered that Amanda Sam was not aroused at all, and now I felt like we were just two mechanisms completing some insistent task.

Amanda Sam didn't understand my mistake. She took my hand. Part of me wanted to pull back. Another part insisted that it was only fair to reciprocate. But she became more passionate, and it ended up with me on top, she kissing me, she holding her body against mine. After it was over, I didn't know what to think. I wanted to get up and leave, but the bed was in my guesthouse room. She lay down in front of me, and we spooned, my hand on her breast, her back against my chest. I could lie there and go back to pretending she was a woman.

"I really like you," she said.

"I like you, too." I was relieved someone had booked me passage on a ship; I would soon be gone.

"If I sleep in your room again, I'll have to charge you."

"I understand." I said. I didn't have the money to sleep with her.

"But if you come with me to my room, at my invitation, that's different."

"How is it different?" I asked, because I knew I was supposed to ask.

"Because when I make love to someone I like, I prefer to be Sam rather than Amanda."

I said nothing, and she asked what I was thinking. I told her that it was the Amanda part of her I liked.

"If you really liked me, the me inside, you wouldn't notice the difference."

I think it was the next day when I was back at the hospital dining hall. I maybe had two days left, and I overheard some nurses talk about how busy it would be the next day, my last full day on Haven. There would be a whole set of newborns. Noriko could be among them, but even if she wasn't, there had to be people who knew something about what had happened to my unit. I pictured myself returning home without that knowledge. I imagined all the empty silences in that ruined house in that neighborhood where people went when they had no place left to go.

It would just take a few days, a few days before they were out and showing up in various eateries and taverns. If Noriko just happened to be among them, she would show up at the Wake, she'd see me with Amanda Sam. My whole adventure the night before now seemed sordid. I spent some of my per diem so the guest-house staff would change the bedclothes. I showered for a long time. I resolved I wouldn't return to the Wake. But all alone in my bed that night, I couldn't help but think that I was leaving Haven too soon.

The next morning I left for the spaceport to cash in my ticket. The woman there shook her head. "I can't do it. You have to show a place of residence, not a guest house. This is not a tourist spot."

I hung around at the hospital foodstop until I saw the same nurse. I went to get some food and sat down near her. She grumbled to a friend how tired she was. They had to rebirth more than a unit. The military wanted them turned around quickly.

"They'll get some downtime, won't they?" her friend asked.

"Of course. This place would close down otherwise. We gotta get them out of therapy two days sooner than usual. Can you imagine how they'll look when they go ambulatory?"

I walked and walked. I kept counting out my options.

I showed up at the Wake and Amanda Sam was not there. The bartender offered me a drink on the house. "Amanda Sam says you're a good one. Here's one for the road."

I decided that this drink was my farewell. I would never know what happened. I would never see Noriko again. Temptation is the sun drawing in a comet. Good sense is just some distant steady orbit.

I had a second beer and sat off in a corner. Amanda Sam walked in, and she scanned the tavern as if looking for someone. When she saw me, she smiled, and sat down next to me. "Hi, gorgeous," she said. "Buy me a brandy."

I told her my ship left tomorrow afternoon. She said she'd miss me.
I told her about the unit being rebirthed tomorrow. I told her that I
wanted to stay, to see if Noriko was among them.

"Your soldier girl won't be there," she said.

"But they'll be able to tell me what's happened. I'll know my story."

"That story was part of your other life," she said.

I told her that, in the end, it didn't matter. I didn't have a place to
stay. Staying was just wishful thinking.

"You can stay with me," she said.

Someone tapped her on the shoulder. She turned, and standing
there was a couple. "Oh," she said, "I was looking for you two. It's been
a while." She turned and waved to me.

The next morning she was at my door and walked me down to the
port. "If you want to stay, you're going to have to establish residency
and profession. There are no tourists here. I created documentation
that says you're living with me and that you're my partner."

"Your partner, like we're married?"

"No, hon. Profession, I said profession. I'm more than happy to lie
about your profession." And she stopped me here. She looked me in
the eye. "Your money is going to run out. You're not going to find the
soldier girl. All you lost was a few months of another life. How badly
do you need them, hon?" Her two hands wrapped themselves warmly
around one of mine. Her green eyes were warm. "You have a free ticket
home. Take it."

When we found the right office, she produced the document, and
after some back and forth she got the full price of what the military had
paid for the ticket. She laid down her pinky to get half; I got the other
half. "We'll say that's rent for a month," she said. What was left of my
per diem had evaporated the moment the transaction was complete; all
I had was one-sixth of the cost of passage.

Her apartment was tiny, half the size of the guesthouse room,
a double bed, drawers built into the wall, and a cubicle for what's
necessary. There was no sofa to sleep on, no place to stretch out on the
floor with a blanket.

She kissed me. "You don't have to thank me tonight. We can wait
until you're ready. Go see if you can find your girl."

At midday I haunted the hospital foodstop. I listened for whispers. The nurse turned up again, this time alone, and I stepped up to the food vendor so that I'd be next to her. She punched out her meal request. I found something to say, and we ended up at the same table. I remember that she looked familiar, that suddenly I worried she was the nurse who'd birthed me. But if she was, she didn't seem to recognize me. I was worried that she'd ask me all sorts of questions about where I lived, what I did, but she was more than happy to complain about her husband, her job, the difficulty of having so many troops coming back to life.

I thought of the ship, how it was heading for the edge of this stellar system. I felt like there might be an alternate me on board, heading off, finding people to talk with, books to read, maybe even a lover, to ease the burden of three months of travel. But here I was, back in the hospital, listening to the nurse telling me how the war must be going badly because they'd received orders to start growing more bodies, to prepare another unit's worth for rebirth.

I tried to get a sense of how many of these men and women she saw. Would she recognize a picture of Noriko if I showed it to her? Every now and then, she groused about something, then swore me to silence. "I'm really not supposed to talk about that." Could I give her Noriko's name and combat number to input into a computer? I didn't dare.

In the evenings I stayed at the Wake as long as I could, only going home when I had drunk too much to stand. In bed, I pretended to be asleep while Amanda Sam cuddled up to me, one hand draped gently over my penis, her own penis erect against my backside. She whispered how much she liked me and desired me until one of us actually drifted off. More and more, she spent her evenings with me. If she disappeared, she told me which taverns she would visit. I realized how little work she'd been getting, what a relief it must have been to get one-sixth of the cost of passage. "The whole economy is drying up," she said to me. "If they don't give these reborns any shore leave, this place will go crazy. It happened once before, just watch."

Suddenly I saw it, the way locals glared at me if I looked at them too long, the clipped sentences, the constant complaint in almost every conversation. The nurse joined me with a therapist friend. It was one of my therapists. He was sure to ask what I was doing here, but no, he talked about how he preferred working with civilians and officers. When you do therapy in groups . . . He shook his head bitterly. "I hope they don't send them back to battle before shore leave. There's a major here who thinks shore leave is just for fun. *My soldiers—*" His voice became high-pitched so the major might have been a woman or castrato "*—don't need to get drunk and get laid to fight well. Their morale is just fine.* Well, fuck their morale. How about their fine motor skills? How about their *gross* motor skills? That's what shore leave is about. They're brand-new bodies and they need the real world to operate in before you throw on some body armor and throw them out into free fall."

He kept going on, and I barely listened. He was angry enough, I thought, that maybe he would tell me anything, but the nurse was advising him to watch what he was saying, and he was nodding, his face red, his look recalcitrant, then chagrined.

One night, Amanda Sam insisted that we go back home—I always thought of it as the apartment—before I'd drunk too much. "You'll spend up all your money," she said, "and then what?" Back at her place, she said she wanted me so badly that she would be Amanda for me. I soaked up her skin's warmth like a sponge.

It probably wasn't the next day, but it's the next thing I remember, how suddenly sections of Haven were flooded with stumbling reborns. Their hair was wild and shaggy. Most of them looked like they'd chosen to be in their twenties, but a few, probably officers, were in their thirties. A guy, his face dour, concentrated on every step he took. Another stumbled, fell, got up, laughing, looking to his more cautious friends. I kept walking where they walked. Every time I saw tanned skin, black hair, compact body, I'd walk to catch up, but before I even caught a glimpse of the face, I'd see that the shoulders were too wide, the hips too flat.

And what would I say to her, if she was there? I watched for her at various lunchrooms, where I saw the newborns shake their forks at each other as if angry, but their faces showed a range of reactions to their bodies' refusal to learn their way through the world instantly.

The presence of all these newborns made Amanda Sam happy. "Tonight, the best brandy for me, the best beer for you," she said, even though I think Haven only stocked one variety of each, the drinkable and the barely drinkable. I remember one night, probably the first night the newborns were around, I just sat at the Wake, drinking beer, imagining that Noriko would walk in, that she would take me off to a guesthouse room, and we'd make love. Several other nights I wandered from tavern to tavern, maybe checking in some dinner spots beforehand, looking for Noriko, knowing I wouldn't see her, from time to time running into Amanda Sam gaily chatting with some man or woman, once a couple. Each time she waved to me, offered me that big smile that said, I'm delighted to see you, keep walking.

I spoke with some of the newborns. I heard the stories. One guy told me that their goal had been to take an orbital without destroying it, which meant they had to board it without using projectile weapons. At one point they were on the skin of the world, breaking into a compartment, and the enemy had fighters flying above. It was strange how silent everything was except for the way everyone was yelling orders and those voices reverberated in your helmet, voices darting about you as if your head was stuck in a fishbowl. The enemy couldn't risk projectiles, either. They used harpoons, a joke when you first heard it in training, but when one pierced your suit, when you watched your air drain away as you were dragged off into space, it wasn't so funny anymore. "Actually, if it happened to you, you'd never remember it," he said. "But when you watched it happen to your buddy, you'd go to sleep night after night imagining what it would be like happening to you. Worse, you'd relive it happening to your friend, wondering what he felt and thought as it happened. Well, then you became hardened to the whole process."

I tried to picture myself on the skin of a metal world, magnetic soles holding me in place, just enough of a pull to keep my balance, not enough to prevent a step, or a harpoon from pulling me away, and making a rush for an opened compartment, knowing that some of us would make it, and that some of us were there to die so others could make it, that our majors and colonels and generals felt free to overwhelm the other side with numbers because we'd all be back, the cost of our resurrection something for governors and senators and premiers at home to tally up. I felt a terrible beating in my heart just at the thought, and I was glad to have Amanda Sam wrap her arms around me, and most nights she was content and sated so there was no pressure to express my thanks for this half a bed in a tiny room.

I worked up the courage to ask questions. I gave Noriko's full name. No one had heard of her. I named the unit I was with. Most didn't know it. One or two knew that my unit was dealing with orbitals circling the neighboring gas giant, which at the time was too far away in its orbit for anyone to care. One woman had gotten word that the first foray had been successful, the second was disastrous, the third could happen at any moment.

When the newborns shipped out, I concluded I would never see Noriko, and I would never know what had happened to me. It was only then that I realized what a terrible situation I was in. Amanda Sam took me out to dinner to celebrate the great few days she'd had, and I drank brandy with her, and I told her that tonight would be the night. She kissed me passionately, and back in her apartment she was tender. She aroused me first, and the things she did to relax me actually felt good. She looked down at me and told me to hold her breasts, and entered me so slowly and carefully that it did not hurt at all. I suppose if I'd been in love with her or desiring this kind of moment, I might have felt something more than just the physical sensation, but instead I rubbed my hands up and down Amanda Sam's back and remembered the one or two times Noriko had caressed my own back and said, "Let's finish up, I'm ready to sleep," and I now understood the distance Noriko must have felt (even though during the act I had been certain that because it was sex it must have felt good).

During the days I worked on making the tiny apartment look better. I thought of the people Amanda Sam brought there. I prepared meals. When she pressed herself against me at night, I turned and kissed her and wrapped my legs around her thighs. She got me drunk the night she wanted me to reciprocate her oral ministrations. The next day I searched for some kind of work, but as I already knew, there was nothing official available. "Pinky-up," the guy in charge of sewage said. The fingerprint produced the documentation, and he shook his head. "You don't even have one death to your credit. I can't hire you. If you're going to stay on Haven, you're gonna have to keep doing the job you registered for. My apologies. I wouldn't want to do it."

When Amanda Sam took me out to dinner and then was Amanda for me in bed, I knew she was going to tell me it was time to work. "I warned you. I warned you. I warned you. And I'll take good care of you and make sure you meet only the best of people. Some of my peers have taken new people under their wing and taken half. I'll only take twenty percent, plus your share of rent and food." The next morning she bought me a big breakfast, and she said how she'd loved every second in bed with me but it was time to learn how to do a few things a little differently. I asked feebly about women, and she laughed. "Young men, they can get for free." Things were flush now, and she had found several people on Haven who would enjoy paying to break me in. And that's how it all started.

I've heard other stories, and I know now how lucky I was. No one beat me or mistreated me. Amanda Sam always met me at the Wake at the end of an evening to find out how things went, to coach me on how to handle the rude and stingy ones and how to handle the ones who wanted to fall in love with me. And maybe if I were tuned that way, I might have enjoyed myself. Instead I felt like I was living someone else's life. When I wasn't working and when I wasn't with Amanda Sam, I was walking. Long walks with long elaborate dreams. Noriko would appear in the Wake. She'd say she's seen enough battles, and she now wants to take me with her, some place far away. I knew now I would never go home. What would I say? How many lies would I tell just to be comfortable?

She says, You always avoided the truth when it made other people uncomfortable.

I listen for something severe in her voice, but I don't hear it. I say, I'm telling everything the best my memory will allow.

I know. That's what I love about this visit. You know, she says, the subject changing with her tone of voice, I always wondered why you wouldn't change. I did want to try out a life as a man, and I always thought you didn't love me enough to be a woman.

You understand now? I ask. After all those men, after their insistence on their needs . . . the only time they cared about my arousal was when they wanted to boost their own self-confidence . . . after all that, I could never sleep with a man again. You probably would have been a great man, but I couldn't bear to sleep with another one, no matter how nice.

I said I understood. But now I wonder this. Did you stay with me because you loved me or because you wanted a secure life?

There's a giant difference between why I first sought your attentions and why I'm with you now.

It's an awkward moment, given the way our bodies are touching, given the years of abstinence in our last life together, so I return to the story.

When the newborns came, it was a rush. I now dreaded the sight I had once longed for. Many of the newborns had not seen enough battle to afford a guesthouse, so Amanda Sam and I traded off with the apartment. There would be an occasional woman soldier who hired my services, but mostly I listened to men lament their lives after they'd relieved themselves of their burdens. I kept an eye out for Noriko, but now my plan was to spot her first so I could avoid her.

I started to hang out more with the nurse and the therapist, just to know people who had nothing to do with the Wake and Amanda Sam, though Haven is a small enough place that I'm sure they knew what I did.

I'm sure when I got up from lunch, they probably said, He's not so bad. Everyone's got to make a living somehow.

Some nights, I decided just to do nothing, and I stayed in the Wake and drank. Sometimes Amanda Sam would rest her hand on my shoulder and I'd turn to her and she'd tell me it was time to go home. She'd make love to me, comfort me, and I'd pretend to be comforted. "I'll always take care of you," she said. "I'm so glad we found each other." And the next morning she'd take her twenty-percent cut. So I sat in the Wake and foresaw years and years of this, and sometimes in the Wake, but never on my walks, which were just for dreams, I would tally up how long it'd take to build up savings, how long it would take to get off Haven, and how much I'd need to start a new life when her hand fell on my shoulder. I turned and Noriko was looking at me.

"I've been told you've been asking about me," she said.

Oh, no, she says. She doesn't recognize you. She died before she had another neuromap, and she doesn't know you.

I hear the sadness in her voice. For decades and decades I couldn't mention Noriko to her; now, after all these years apart, she sympathizes.

How different life would have been if so much separation wasn't necessary to erase whatever had made us bitter.

I stood up to face her. I thought for a second she looked older, as if the job had worn away her friendliness, but then I recalled this look, the way she'd gotten when she'd given out instructions to her companions. There was no recognition on her face, no joy at seeing me, just this military face accustomed to giving orders.

She said, "I thought you'd be gone by now. I made sure the cost of everything was covered."

"I couldn't go."

She stood and waited for me to say more.

"I didn't know what happened to you. I didn't know what happened to me."

She looked around, took my hand, and led me to a table. She sat across from me and ordered herself a beer. She held the glass in both her hands, and I wanted her to hold my hand again. She said nothing for the longest time. I surveyed the entire place, the bar, the booths, to make sure Amanda Sam was nowhere to be seen.

Noriko said, "Here's what happened. We posted as comrades-in-arms. We were set to attack an orbital. They told us that ninety percent of our unit would die. You began to shake in your sleep. You talked about how when you died, once they'd grown you a new body, once you'd been reassigned, that we'd be apart. But the truth was you were scared to die. When it came time to suit up, you were trembling so much that the captain ordered you to your quarters. He didn't want you to put us at risk. I told you to pack up your gear and move out while I was away.

"The enemy was unprepared. We took the orbital with few casualties. When we got back, you'd hanged yourself."

I felt myself shaking my head. I wasn't the me that would do that.

"I blamed myself for what happened," she said. " Back on Haven, I was so involved in taking care of my own needs that I didn't recognize the warning signs. The one thing I forgot about youth, real youth, the first youth, is how passionate you are about life itself. How it sometimes has to be all or nothing."

I didn't know what to say. I said something about there being no discharge papers.

"You forgot or ignored what you were told. In the military, your life is only to be lost for the cause. The military won't pay for a new life if you kill yourself. They promoted me after that skirmish. I got a pay raise. I had enough money to cover your rebirth. I arranged for some loans to cover the cost of a berth back to your homeworld. I thought I'd made up for everything. I though I'd taken care of you."

We sat there for a while and what more could we say? I wanted to know what warning signs she'd seen. I didn't want to know. And what other subject was there? We'd only been together for three or four days.

Noriko didn't ask about where I was living or what my plans were. She told me she'd recently been assigned to Haven in a supervisory capacity. There would be four units of newborns to organize, plus two units of newbies coming in. The big push was beginning.

She was talking about everything they had to do and how she had to get back to her duties when Amanda Sam walked in and said hello. Noriko looked up at her. There wasn't a trace of recognition's on Noriko's face. "I'm sure I'll see you," Noriko said to me and left without saying a word to Amanda Sam.

"I see that soldier girl is back," Amanda Sam said.

"She didn't recognize you."

Amanda Sam looked at me for a moment. I think she was tempted to explain why I was wrong, but she'd taught me the con. I'd already used it a few times, but because I was living such separate lives in my head, I hadn't figured the whole thing out, how everything had stretched back to day one of my new life. The con: you sit down with a newborn, and you talk about the last time you'd been together, the one that must have taken place after the neuromap was recorded.

I walked and walked that night. I told myself I wasn't a coward, I wasn't the kind of person who'd kill himself. Look at what I was living through now. I hadn't been tempted to kill myself in the past months with everything that had happened. And I reminded myself that Noriko had said we'd left Haven as comrades-in-arms. I thought of ways I could see her again, of things I could say to win her back.

But, of course, Haven was a military way station, even though it was run by civilians. Of course, people knew I'd been asking about her, and the local military intelligence guy, whoever he was, must have told her. They'd know how I was making a living, and so Noriko would know.

I didn't see Noriko again. I avoided the hospital, and I avoided other taverns. I only conducted business out of the Wake, and she never returned. I stopped taking my walks. I'm sure she was on Haven until everyone involved with the big push had left. And by the time the newborns and the fresh recruits were gone, I had enough money to start a new life, to be reborn and not remember one bit of this. Instead, I worked for another year and had enough to fly to planets that people liked to talk about, to have some money to live for a little bit and try one unsuccessful business venture or another.

Amanda Sam cried when I told her I was leaving. "I made this possible for you," she said. "I want you to remember that." And my last night there, I let her make love to me the way she liked, and I was so moved by the way she felt that I had my first orgasm while I held her in my arms. This caused her to kiss me passionately. "Please don't leave. Please stay. You think I took advantage of you, but I really do love you." Right then I thought she was begging her twenty-percent cut to stay. Now I think she either loved me or, at least, my company. I think of all the booths I sat in, waiting alone to attract some eager company. I think of those same booths at the end of a long evening when she sat beside me and took my hand in hers.

And the ship I boarded later stopped at some planet or other, and you boarded, and that's how I spent the rest of my lives.

She turns over in the bed and kisses me. I caress her face, and the way time has lined her skin feels wrong against my fingertips. My body betrays me. I say, Talk to me, and I hear her voice and she pulls me into her embrace and it's her I make love to.

The next morning she makes me my favorite breakfast and she packs my bag. I tell her I was more than willing to stay indefinitely. I have no special plans and I like being with her.

She says, These last few days, well last night, especially, were perfect. When I first met you, you told me about Noriko, and I wanted to be with someone who could love so passionately. And I was jealous of her ever since because I couldn't inspire the same kind of love. Last night, you told me about Noriko, and I remembered everything about you I loved when our lives together weren't so difficult. Last night is the memory I want to have of you when I die.

I argue, but if I argue too fiercely, I'll destroy everything these few days have come to mean. I leave her house in the woods, take train after train, come to a port and board a ship for elsewhere. In the decades we were apart—me in a fresh new body, she finding out what happens when the body finally ages—I always thought about her. During those years, I knew that one day, when I had the money for the voyage, I would track her down and see her at least one last time.

I leave her now, but I can't imagine another life.

BETWEEN TWO DRAGONS

YOON HA LEE

One of the oldest tales we tell in Cho is of two dragons, twinborn and opposite in all desires. One dragon was as red as Earth, the other as blue as Heaven: day and night, fire and water, passion and calculation. They warred, as dragons do, and the universe was born of their battle.

We have never forgotten that we partake of both dragons, Earth and Heaven. Yet we are separate creatures with separate laws. It is why the twin dragons appear upon our national seal, separated by Man's sinuous road. We live among the stars, but we remember our heritage.

One thing has not changed since the birth of the universe, however. There is still war.

Yen, you have to come back so I can tell you the beginning of your story. Everything is classified: every soldier unaccounted for, every starsail deployed far from home, every gram of shrapnel . . . every whisper that might have passed between us. Word of the last battle will come tomorrow, say the official news services, but we have heard the same thing for the last several days.

I promised I would tell no one, so instead I dream it over and over. I knew, when I began to work for the Ministry of Virtuous Thought, that people would fear me. I remind myself of this every time someone calls me a woman with no more heart than a stone, despite the saying that a stone's weeping is the most terrible of all.

You came to me after the invaders from Yamat had been driven off, despite the fall of Spinward Gate and the capital system's long siege. I didn't recognize you at first. Most of my clients use one of the government's thousand false names, which exist for situations requiring discretion. Your appointment was like any other, made under one such.

Your face, though—I could hardly have failed to recognize your face. Few clients contact me in person, although I can't help wanting to hear, face-to-face, why my patients must undergo the changes imposed on them.

Admiral Yen Shenar: You were an unassuming man, although your dark eyes suggested a certain taut energy, and you were no stranger to physical labor. I wished I were in such lean good health; morning exercise has never done much for me. But your drab civilian clothes and the absent white gun did nothing to disguise the fact that you were a soldier. An admiral. A hero, even, in my office with its white walls and bland paintings of bamboo.

"Admiral," I said, and stopped. How do you address the war hero of a war everyone knows will resume when the invaders catch their breath? I thought I knew what you wanted done. A former lover, a political rival, an inconvenience on the way up; the client has the clout to make someone disappear for a day and return as though nothing as changed, except it has. A habit of reverse-alphabetizing personal correspondence, a preference for Kir Jaengmi's poetry over An Puna's, a subversive fascination with foreign politics, excised or altered by my work. Sometimes only a favorite catchphrase or a preference for ginseng over green tea is changed, and the reprogramming serves as a warning once the patient encounters dissonance from family and acquaintances. Sometimes the person who returns is no longer recognizable. The setup can take months, depending on the compatibility of available data with preset models, but the reprogramming itself only takes hours.

So here you were, Admiral Yen Shenar. Surely you were rising in influence, with the attendant infelicities. It disappointed me to see you, but only a little. I could guess some of your targets.

"There's no need for formality, madam," you said, correctly interpreting my silence as a loss for words. "You've dealt with more influential people in your time, I'm sure." Your smile was wry, but suggested despair.

I thought I understood that, too. "Who is the target?"

The despair sharpened, and everything changed. "Myself. I want to be expunged, like a thrall. I'm told it's easier with a willing subject."

"Heaven and Earth, you can't be serious."

The walls were suddenly too spare, too white.

I wondered why you didn't do the obvious thing and intrigue against Admiral Wan Kun, or indeed the others in court who considered your growing renown a threat. No surprise: the current dynasty had been founded by a usurper-general, and ever since, the court has regarded generals and admirals with suspicion. We may despise the Yamachin, but they are consummate warriors, and they would never have been so frightened by the specter of a coup as to sequester their generals at the capital, preventing them from training with the troops they commanded on paper. We revere scholars. They have their sages, but soldiers are the ones they truly respect.

"Madam," you said, "I am only asking you to do what the ministry will ask of another programmer a few days from now. It doesn't matter what battles one wins in the deeps of space if one can't keep out of political trouble. Even if we all know the Yamachin will return once they've played out this farce of negotiations . . . "

You wanted me to destroy the man you were, but in a manner of your choosing and not your rivals', all for the sake of saving Cho in times to come. This meant preserving your military acumen so you might be of use when Yamat returned to ravage Cho. Only a man so damned sure of himself would have chanced it. But you had routed the Yamachin navy at Red Sun and Hawks Crossing with a pittance of Chosar casualties, and no one could forget how, in the war's early hours, you risked your command by crossing into Admiral Wan Kun's jurisdiction to rally the shattered defense at Heaven's Gate.

"Admiral," I said, "are you sure? The half-death"—that's the kindest euphemism—"might leave you with no more wit than a broken cup, and all for nothing. It has never been a *safe* procedure." I didn't believe you would be disgraced in a matter of days, although it came to pass as you predicted.

You smiled at that, blackly amused. "When calamity lands on your shoulder, madam, I assure you that you'll find it difficult to mistake for anything else." A corner of your mouth curled. "I imagine you've seen death in darker forms than I have. I have killed from vast distances, but never up close. You are braver by far than I have ever been."

You were wrong about me, Admiral Yen, even if the procedure *is* easier with a willing patient. With anyone else, I would have congratulated myself on a task swiftly and elegantly completed.

You know the rest of the story. When you tell it to me, I will give you the beginning that I stole from you, even at your bidding. Although others know our nation Cho as the Realm Between Two Dragons, vast Feng-Huang and warlike Yamat, our national emblem is the tiger, and men like you are tigers among men.

Sometimes I think that each night I spin the story to myself, a moment of memory will return to you, as if we were bound together by the chains of a children's fable. I know better. There are villains every direction I look. I am one of them. If you do not return, all that will be left for me is to remember, over and over, how I destroyed the man you should have been, the man you were.

By the time we took him seriously, he was an old man: Tsehan, the chancellor-general of Yamat, and its ruler in truth. Ministers came and ministers went, but Tsehan watched from his unmoving seat in Yamat's parliament, the hawk who perched above them all.

He was not a man without refinement, despite the popular depiction of him as a wizened tyrant, too feeble to lead the invasion himself and too fierce to leave Cho in peace. Tsehan loved fine things, as the diplomats attested. His reception hall was bright with luxuries: sculptures of light and parabolic mirrors, paintings on silk and bamboo strips, mosaics made from shattered ancient celadon. He served tea in cups whose designs of seasonal flowers and fractals shifted in response to the liquid's temperature or acidity. "For the people of Yamat," he said, but everyone knew these treasures were for Tsehan's pleasure, not the people's.

War had nurtured him all his life. His father was a soldier of the lowest rank, one more body flung into Yamat's bloody and tumultuous politics. It is no small thing, in Yamat—a nation at least as class-conscious as our own—to rise from a captain's aide to heir-apparent of Chancellor-General Oshozhi. Oshozhi succeeded in bringing Yamat with its many would-be warlords under unified rule, and he passed that rule on to Tsehan.

It should not have surprised us that, with the end of Yamat's bloody civil wars, Tsehan would thirst for more. But Cho was a pearl too small for his pleasure. The chancellor-general wanted Feng-Huang, vastest of nations, jewel of the stars. And to reach Feng-Huang, he needed safe passage through Cho's primary nexus. Feng-Huang had been our ally and protector for centuries, the culture whose civilization we modeled ours after. Betraying Feng-Huang to the Yamachin would have been like betraying ourselves.

Yamat had been stable for almost a decade under Tsehan's leadership, but we had broken off regular diplomatic relations during its years of instability and massacre. We had grown accustomed to hearing about dissidents who vanished during lunch, crèches destroyed by rival politicians and generals, bombs hidden in shipments of maiden-faced orchids, and soldiers who trampled corpses but wept over fire-scored sculptures. Some of it might even have happened.

When Tsehan sent the starsail *Hanei* to ask for the presence of a Chosar delegation and our government acquiesced, few of us took notice. Less than a year after that, our indifference would be replaced by outrage over Yamat's demands for an open road to our ally Feng-Huang. Tsehan was not a falling blossom after all, as one of our poets said, but a rising dragon.

In the dream, he knew his purpose. His heartbeat was the drum of war. He walked between Earth and Heaven, and his path was his own.

And waking—

He brushed the hair out of his eyes. His palms were sweaty. And he had a name, if not much else.

Yen Shenar, no longer admiral despite his many victories, raised his hand, took aim at the mirror, and fired.

But the mirror was no mirror, only the wall's watching eyes. He was always under surveillance. It was a fact of life in the Garden of Tranquility, where political prisoners lived amid parameterized hallucinations. The premise was that rebellion, let alone escape, was unlikely when you couldn't be sure if the person at the corner was a guard or the hallucination of a childhood friend who had died last year. He supposed he should be grateful that he hadn't been executed outright, like so many who had rioted or protested the government's policies, even those like himself who had been instrumental in defending Cho from the Yamachin invasion.

He had no gun in his hand, only the unflinching trajectory of his own thoughts. One more thing to add to his litany of grievances, although he was sure the list changed from day to day, hour to hour, when the hallucinations intensified. Sourly, he wished he could hallucinate a stylus, or a chisel with which to gouge the walls, whether they were walls or just air. He had never before had such appreciation for the importance of recordkeeping.

Yen began to jog, trusting the parameters would keep him from smashing into a corner, although such abrupt pain would almost be welcome. Air around him, metal beneath him. He navigated through the labyrinth of overgrown bamboo groves, the wings of unending arches, the spiral blossoms of distant galaxies glimpsed through cracked lattices. At times he thought the groves might be real.

They had imprisoned him behind Yen Shenar's face, handicapped him with Yen Shenar's dreams of stars and shapes moving in the vast darkness. They had made the mistake of thinking that he shared Yen Shenar's thrall-like regard for the government. He was going to escape the Garden if it required him to break each bone to test its verity, uproot the bamboo, break Cho's government at its foundations.

The war began earlier, but what we remember as its inception is Sang Han's death at Heaven's Gate. Even the Yamachin captain who led the advance honored Sang's passing.

Heaven's Gate is the outermost system bordering Yamat, known for the number of people who perished settling its most temperate world, and the starsails lost exploring its minor but treacherous nexus. The system was held by Commandant Sang Han, while the province as a whole remains under the protection of Admiral Wan Kun's fleet. Wan Kun's, not Yen Shenar's; perhaps Heaven's Gate was doomed from the start.

Although Admiral Wan Kun was inclined to dismiss the reports of Yamachin warsails as alarmism, the commandant knew better. Against protocol, he alerted Admiral Yen Shenar in the neighboring system, which almost saved us. It is bitter to realize that we could have held Cho against the invaders if we had been prepared for them when they first appeared.

The outpost station's surviving logs report that Sang had one last dinner with his soldiers, passing the communal cup down the long tables. He joked with them about the hundred non-culinary uses for rice. Then he warned the leading Yamachin warsail, *Hanei*, that passage through Cho to invade our ally Feng-Huang would not be forthcoming, whatever the delusion of Yamat's chancellor-general.

Hanei and its escort responded by opening fire.

We are creatures of fire and water. We wither under a surfeit of light as readily as we wither beneath drowned hopes. When photons march soldier-fashion at an admiral's bidding, people die.

When the Yamachin boarded the battlestation serving Heaven's Gate, Sang awaited them. By then, the station was all but shattered, a fruit for the pressing. Sang's eyes were shadowed by sleepless nights, his hair rumpled, his hands unsteady.

The *Hanei*'s captain, Sezhi Tomo, was the first to board the station. Cho's border stations knew his name. In the coming years, we would learn every nuance of anger or determination in that soft, suave voice. Sezhi spoke our language, and in times past he had been greeted as one of us. His chancellor-general had demanded his experience in dealing with Cho, however, and so he arrived as an invader, not a guest.

"Commandant," he said to Sang, "I ask you and your soldiers to stand down. There's time yet for war to be averted. Surrender the white gun." Sezhi must have been aware of the irony of his words. He knew, as most Yamachin apparently did not, that a Chosar officer's white gun represented not only his rank but his loyalty to the nation. Its single shot is intended for suicide in dire straits.

"Sezhi-kan," the commandant replied, addressing the other man by his Yamachin title, "it was too late when your chancellor-general set his eye upon Feng-Huang." And when our government, faction-torn, failed to heed the diplomats' warning of Tsehan's ambitions; but he would not say that to a Yamachin. "It was too late when you opened fire on the station. I will not stand down."

"Commandant," said Sezhi even as his guards trained their rifles on Sang, "please. Heaven's Gate is lost." His voice dropped to a murmur. "Sang, it's over. At least save yourself and the people who are still alive."

Small courtesies have power. In the records that made it out of Heaven's Gate, we see the temptation that sweeps over the commandant's face as he holds Sezhi's gaze. We see the moment when he decides that he won't break eye contact to look around at his haggard soldiers, and the moment when temptation breaks its grasp.

Oh, yes: the cameras were transmitting to all the relays, with no thought as to who might be eavesdropping.

"I will surrender the white gun," Sang said, "when you take it from me. Dying is easier than letting you pass."

Sezhi's face held no more expression than night inside a nexus. "Then take it I shall. Gentlemen."

The commandant drew the white gun from its holster, keeping it at all times aimed at the floor. He was right-handed.

The first shot took off Sang's right arm.

His face was white as the blood spurted. He knelt—or collapsed—to pick up the white gun with his left hand, but had no strength left to stand.

The second shot, from one of the soldiers behind Sezhi, took off his left arm.

It's hard to tell whether shock finally caused Sang to slump as the soldiers' next twelve bullets slammed into him. A few patriots believe that Sang was going to pick up the white gun with his teeth before he died, but never had the opportunity. But the blood is indisputable.

Sezhi Tomo, pale but dry-eyed, bowed over the commandant's fallen body, lifting his hand from heart to lips: a Chosar salute, never a Yamachin one. Sezhi paid for that among his own troops.

And Yen—Admiral, through no fault of your own, you received the news too late to save the commandant. Heaven's Gate, to our shame, fell in days.

• • •

There is no need to recount our losses to Yamat's soldiers. Once their warsails had entered Cho's local space, they showed what a generation of civil war does for one's martial abilities. Our world-bound populations fell before them like summer leaves before winter winds. One general wrote, in a memorandum to the government, that "death walks the only road left to us." The only hope was to stop them before they made planetfall, and we failed at that.

We asked Feng-Huang for aid, but Feng-Huang was suspicious of our failure to inform them earlier of Yamat's imperial designs. So their warsail fleets and soldiers arrived too late to prevent the worst of the damage.

It must pain you to look at the starsail battles lost, which you could have won so readily. It is easy to scorn Admiral Wan Kun for not being the tactician you are, less adept at using the nexuses' spacetime terrain to advantage. But what truly diminishes the man is the fact that he allowed rivalry to cloud his judgment. Instead of using his connections at court to disparage your victories and accuse you of treason, he could have helped unify the fractious factions in coming up with a strategy to defeat Yamat. Alas, he held a grudge against you for invading his jurisdiction at Heaven's Gate without securing prior permission.

He never forgave you for eclipsing him. Even as he died in defeat, commanding the Chosar fleet that you had led so effectively, he must have been bitter. But they say this last battle at Yellow Splendor will decide everything. Forget his pettiness, Yen. He is gone, and it is no longer important.

"I have your file," the man said to Yen Shenar. His dark blue uniform did not show any rank insignia, but there was a white gun in his holster. "I would appeal to your loyalty, but the programmer assigned to you noted that this was unlikely to succeed."

"Then why are you here?" Yen said. They were in a room with high windows and paintings of carp. The guards had given him plain clothing, also in dark blue, a small improvement on the gray that all prisoners wore.

The man smiled. "Necessity," he said. "Your military acumen is needed."

"Perhaps the government should have considered that before they put me here," Yen said.

"You speak as though the government were a unified entity."

As if he could forget. The court's inability to face in the same direction at the same time was legendary.

"You were not without allies, even then," the man said.

Yen tipped his head up: he was not a short man, but the other was taller. "The government has a flawed understanding of 'military acumen,' you know."

The man raised an eyebrow.

"It's not just winning at baduk or other strategy games, or the ability to put starsails in pretty arrangements," Yen said. "It is leadership; it is inspiring people, and knowing who is worth inspiring; it is honoring your ancestors with your service. And," he added dryly, "it is knowing enough about court politics to avoid being put in the Garden, where your abilities do you no good."

"People are the sum of their loyalties," the man said. "You told me that once."

"I'm expected to recognize you?"

"No," the man said frankly. "I told them so. We all know how reprogramming works. There's no hope of restoring what you were." There was no particular emotion in his voice. "But they insisted that I try."

"Tell me who you are."

"You have no way of verifying the information," the man said.

Yen laughed shortly. "I'm curious anyway."

"I'm your nephew," the man said. "My name wouldn't mean anything to you." At Yen's scrutiny, he said, "You used to remark on how I take after my mother."

"I'm surprised the government didn't send me back to the Ministry of Virtuous Thought to ensure my cooperation anyway," Yen said.

"They were afraid it would damage you beyond repair," he said.

"Did the programmer tell them so?"

"I've only spoken to her once," the man said.

This was the important part, and this supposed nephew of his didn't even realize it. "Did she have anything else to say?"

The man studied him for a long moment, then nodded. "She said you are not the sum of your loyalties, you are the sum of your choices."

"I did not choose to be here," Yen said, because it would be expected of him, although it was not true. Presumably, given that he had known what the king's decree was to be, he could have committed suicide or defected. He was a strategist now and had been a strategist then. This course of action had to have been chosen for a reason.

He realized now that the Yen Shenar of yesteryear might not have been a man willing to intrigue against his enemies, even where it would have saved him his command. But he had been ready to become one who would, even for the sake of a government that had been willing to discard his service.

The man was frowning. "Will you accept your reinstatement into the military?"

"Yes," Yen said. "Yes." He was the weapon that he had made of himself, in a life he remembered only through shadows and fissures. It was time to test his forging, to ensure that the government would never be in a position to trap him in the Garden again.

This is the story the way they are telling it now. I do not know how much of it to believe. Surely it is impossible that you outmatched the Yamachin fleet when it was five times the size of your own; surely it is impossible that over half the Yamachin starsails were destroyed or captured. But the royal historians say it is so.

There has been rejoicing in the temporary capital: red banners in every street, fragrant blossoms scattered at every doorway. Children play with starsails of folded paper, pretending to vanquish the Yamachin foe, and even the thralls have memorized the famous poem commemorating your victory at Yellow Splendor.

They say you will come home soon. I hope that is true.

But all I can think of is how, the one time I met you, you did not wear the white gun. I wonder if you wear it now.

SCALES

ALASTAIR REYNOLDS

⊰⊱

The enemy must die.

Nico stands and waits in the long line, sweating under the electric-yellow dome of the municipal force field.

They must die.

Near the recruiting station, one of the captives has been wheeled out in a cage. The reptile is splayed in a harness, stretched like a frog on the dissection table. A steady stream of soldiers-in-waiting leaves the line, jabbing an electro-prod through the bars of the cage to a chorus of jeers. It's about the size of a man, and surprisingly androform except for its crested lizard head, its stubby tail and the brilliant green shimmer of its scales. Already they're flaking off, black and charred, where the prod touches. The reptile was squealing to start with, but it's slumped and unresponsive now.

Nico turns his head away. He just wants the line to move ahead so he can sign up, obtain his citzenship credits and get out of here.

The enemy must die.

They came in from interstellar darkness, unprovoked, unleashing systematic destruction on unsuspecting human assets. They wiped mankind off Mars and blasted Earth's lunar settlements into radioactive craters. They pushed the human explorers back into a huddle of defenses around Earth. Now they've brought the war to cities and towns, to the civilian masses. Now force shields blister Earth's surface, sustained by fusion plants sunk deep into the crust. Nico's almost forgotten what it's like to look up at the stars.

But the tide is turning. Beneath the domes, factories assemble the ships and weapons to take the war back to the reptiles. Chinks are opening in the enemy's armour. All that's needed now are men and women to do Earth's bidding.

One of the recruiting sergeants walks the line, handing out iced water and candies. He stops and chats to the soldiers-to-be, shaking them by the hand, patting them on the back. He's a thirty-mission veteran; been twice as far out as the orbit of the moon. He lost an arm, but the new one's growing back nicely, budding out from the stump like a baby's trying to punch its way out of him. They'll look after you too, he says, holding out a bottle of water.

"What's the catch?" Nico asks.

"There isn't one," the sergeant says. "We give you citizenship and enough toys to take apart a planet. Then you go out there and kill as many of those scaly green bastards as you can."

"Sounds good to me," Nico says.

Up in the fortified holdfast of Sentinel Station, something's different. The tech isn't like the equipment Nico saw at the recruiting station, or in basic training back on Earth. It's heavier, nastier, capable of doing more damage. Which would be reassuring, if it wasn't for one troubling fact.

Earth has better ships, guns and armour than anyone down there has heard about—but then so do the reptiles.

Turns out they're not exactly reptiles either. Not that Nico cares much. Cold-blooded or not, they still attacked without provocation.

The six months of in-orbit training at Sentinel Station are tough. Half the kids fall by the wayside. Nico's come through, maybe not top of his class, but somewhere near it. He can handle the power-armour, the tactical weapons. He's ready to be shown to his ship.

It's not quite what he was expecting.

It's a long, sleek, skull-grey shark of a machine that goes faster-than-light.

"Top secret, of course," says the instructor. "We've been using it for interstellar intelligence gathering and resource-acquistion."

"How long have we had this?"

The instructor grins. "Before you were born."

"I thought we never had any ambitions beyond Mars," says Nico.

"What about it?"

"But the reptiles came in unprovoked, they said. If we were already out there . . . "

They haul him out after a couple of days in the coolbox. Any more of that kind of questioning and he'll be sent back home with most of his memories scrubbed.

So Nico decides it's not his problem. He's got his gun, he's got his armour and now he's got his ride. Who cares who started the damned thing?

The FTL transport snaps back into normal space around some other star, heading for a blue gas giant and an outpost that used to be a moon. The place bristles with long-range sensors and the belligerent spines of anti-ship railguns. Chokepoint will be Nico's home for the next year.

"Forget your armour certification, your weapons rating," says the new instructor, a human head sticking out of an upright black life-support cylinder. "Now it's time to get real."

A wall slides back to reveal a hall of headless corpses, rank on rank of them suspended in green preservative.

"You don't need bodies where you're going, you just need brains." she says. "You can collect your bodies on the way back home, when you've completed your tour. We'll look after them."

So they strip Nico down to little more than a head and a nervous system, and plug what's left into a tiny, hyper-agile fighter. The battle lines are being drawn far beyond conventional FTL now. The war against the reptiles will be won and lost in the N-dimensional tangle of interconnected wormhole pathways.

Wired into the fighter, Nico feels like a god with armageddon at his fingertips—not that he's really got fingertips. He doesn't feel much like Nico any more. He cracks a wry smile at Chokepoint's new arrivals, gawping at the bodies in the tanks. His old memories are still in there somewhere, but they're buried under a luminous welter of tactical programming.

Frankly, he doesn't miss them.

They're not fighting the reptiles any more. Turns out they were just the organic puppets of an implacable, machine-based intelligence. The puppetmasters are faster and smarter and their strategic ambitions aren't clear. But it doesn't concern thing-that-was-once-Nico.

After all, it's not like machines can't die.

Strategic Command sends him deeper. He's forwarded to an artificial construct actually embedded in the tangle, floating on a semi-stable node like a dark thrombosis. Nico's past caring where the station lies in relation to real space.

No one fully human can get this far—the station is staffed by bottled brains and brooding artificial intelligences. With a jolt, thing-that-was-once-Nico realises that he doesn't mind their company. At least they've got their priorities right.

At the station, thing-that-was-once-Nico learns that a new offensive has opened up against the puppetmasters, even further into the tangle. It's harder to reach, so again he must be remade. His living mind is swamped by tiny machines, who build a shining scaffold around the vulnerable architecture of his meat brain. The silvery spikes and struts mesh into a fighter no larger than a drum of oil.

He doesn't think much about his old body, back at Chokepoint, not any more.

The puppetmasters are just a decoy. Tactical analysis reveals them to be an intrusion into the wormhole tangle from what can only be described as an adjunct dimension. The focus of the military effort shifts again.

Now the organic matter at the core of thing-that-was-once-Nico's cybernetic mind is totally obsolete. He can't place the exact moment when he stopped thinking with meat and started thinking with machinery, and he's not even sure it matters now. As an organism, he was pinned like a squashed moth between two pages in the book of existence. As a machine, he can be endlessly abstracted, simulated unto the seventh simulation, encoded and pulsed across the reality-gap, ready to kill.

This he—or rather it—does.

And for a little while there is death and glory.

Up through the reality stack, level by level. By now it's not just machines versus machines. It's machines mapped into byzantine N-dimensional spaces, machines as ghosts of machines. The terms of engagement have become so abstract—so, frankly, higher-mathematical—that the conflict is more like a philosophical dialogue, a debate between protagonists who agree on almost everything except the most trifling, hair-splitting details.

And yet it must still be to the death—the proliferation of one self-replicating, pan-dimensional class of entities is still at the expense of the other.

When did it begin? Where did it begin? Why?

Such questions simply aren't relevant or even answerable anymore.

All that matters is that there is an adversary, and the adversary must be destroyed.

Eventually—although even the notion of time's passing is now distinctly moot—the war turns orthogonal. The reality stack is itself but one compacted laminate of something larger, so the warring entities traverse mind-wrenching chasms of meta-dimensional structure, their minds in constant, self-evolving flux as the bedrock of reality shifts and squirms beneath them.

And at last the shape of the enemy becomes clear.

The enemy is vast. The enemy is inexorably slow. As its peripheries are mapped, it gradually emerges that the enemy is a class of intellect that the machines barely have the tools to recognise, let alone understand.

It's organic.

It is multi-form and multi-variant. It hasn't been engineered or designed. It's messy and contingent, originating from the surface of a structure, a higher-mathematical object. It's but one of several drifting on geodesic trajectories through what might loosely be termed "space." Arcane fluids slosh around on the surface of this object, and the whole thing is gloved in a kind of gas. The enemy requires technology, not just to sustain itself, but to propagate its warlike ambitions.

Triumph over the organic is a cosmic destiny the machines have been pursuing now through countless instantiations. But to kill the enemy now, without probing deeper into its nature, would be both inefficient and unsubtle. It would waste machines that could be spared if the enemy's weaknesses were better understood. And what better way to probe those weaknesses than to create another kind of living thing, an army of puppet organisms, and send that army into battle? The puppets may not win, but they will force the adversary to stretch itself, to expose aspects of itself now hidden.

And so they are sent. Volunteers, technically—although the concept of "volunteer" implies a straightforward altruism difficult to correlate with the workings of the machines' multi-dimensional decision-making matrices. The flesh is grown in huge hangars full of glowing green vats, then shaped into organisms similar but not identical to the enemy. Into those vast, mindless bodies are decanted the thin, gruel-like remains of compactified machine intellects. It's not really anything the machines would recognise as intelligence, but it gets the job done.

Memories kindle briefly back to life as compactification processes shuffle through ancient data, untouched for subjective millenia, searching for anything that might offer a strategic advantage. Among the fleeting sensations, the flickering visions, one of the machines recalls standing in line under an electric-yellow sky, waiting for something. It hears the crackle of an electro-prod, smells the black char of burning tissue.

The machine hesitates for a moment, then deletes the memory. Its new green-scaled puppet body is ready, it has work to do.

The enemy must die.

GOLUBASH, OR WINE-BLOOD-WAR-ELEGY

CATHERYNNE M. VALENTE

—◆—

The difficulties of transporting wine over interstellar distances are manifold. Wine is, after all, like a child. It can *bruise*. It can suffer trauma—sometimes the poor creature can recover; sometimes it must be locked up in a cellar until it learns to behave itself. Sometimes it is irredeemable. I ask that you greet the seven glasses before you tonight not as simple fermented grapes, but as the living creatures they are, well-brought up, indulged but not coddled, punished when necessary, shyly seeking your approval with clasped hands and slicked hair. After all, they have come so very far for the chance to be loved.

Welcome to the first public tasting of Domaine Zhaba. My name is Phylloxera Nanut, and it is the fruit of my family's vines that sits before you. Please forgive our humble venue—surely we could have wished for something grander than a scorched pre-war orbital platform, but circumstances, and the constant surveillance of Chatêau Marubouzu-Debrouillard and their soldiers have driven us to extremity. Mind the loose electrical panels and pull up a reactor husk—they are inert, I assure you. Spit onto the floor—a few new stains will never be noticed. As every drop about to pass your lips is wholly, thoroughly, enthusiastically illegal, we shall not stand on ceremony. Shall we begin?

• • •

2583 Sud-Coté-du-Golubash (New Danube)

The colonial ship *Quintessence of Dust* first blazed across the skies of Avalokitesvara two hundred years before I was born, under the red stare of Barnard's Star, our second solar benefactor. Her plasma sails streamed kilometers long, like sheltering wings. Simone Nanut was on that ship. She, alongside a thousand others, looked down on their new home from that great height, the single long, unfathomably wide river that circumscribed the globe, the golden mountains prickled with cobalt alders, the deserts streaked with pink salt.

How I remember the southern coast of Golubash; I played there, and dreamed there was a girl on the invisible opposite shore, and that her family, too, made wine and cowered like us in the shadow of the Asociación.

My friends, in your university days did you not study the manifests of the first colonials, did you not memorize their weight-limited cargo, verse after verse of spinning wheels, bamboo seeds, lathes, vials of tailored bacteria, as holy writ? Then perhaps you will recall Simone Nanut and her folly: she used her pitiful allotment of cargo to carry the clothes on her back and a tangle of ancient Maribor grapevine, its roots tenderly wrapped and watered. Mad Slovak witch they all thought her, patting those tortured, battered vines into the gritty yellow soil of the Golubash basin. Even the Hyphens were sure the poor things would fail.

There were only four of them on all of Avalokitesvara, immensely tall, their watery triune faces catching the old red light of Barnard's flares, their innumerable arms fanned out around their terribly thin torsos like peacock's tails. Not for nothing was the planet named for a Hindu god with eleven faces and a thousand arms. The colonists called them Hyphens for their way of talking, and for the thinness of their bodies. They did not understand then what you must all know now, rolling your eyes behind your sleeves as your hostess relates ancient history, that each of the four Hyphens was a quarter of the world in a single body, that they were a mere outcropping of the vast intelligences which made up the ecology of Avalokitesvara, like one of our thumbs or a pair of lips.

Golubash, I knew. To know more than one Hyphen in a lifetime is rare. Officially, the great river is still called New Danube, but eventually my family came to understand, as all families did, that the river was the flesh and blood of Golubash, the fish his-her-its thoughts, the seaweed his-her-its nerves, the banks a kind of thoughtful skin.

Simone Nanut put vines down into the body of Golubash. He-She-It bent down very low over Nanut's hunched little form, arms akimbo, and said to her: "That will not work-take-thrive-bear fruit-last beyond your lifetime."

Yet work-take-thrive they did. Was it a gift to her? Did Golubash make room, between what passes for his-her-its pancreas and what might be called a liver, for foreign vines to catch and hold? Did he, perhaps, love my ancestor in whatever way a Hyphen can love? It is impossible to know, but no other Hyphen has ever allowed Earth-origin flora to flourish, not Heeminspr the high desert, not Julka the archipelago, not Niflamen, the soft-spoken polar waste. Not even the northern coast of the river proved gentle to grape. Golubash was generous only to Simone's farm, and only to the southern bank. The mad red flares of Barnard's Star flashed often and strange, and the grapes pulsed to its cycles. The rest of the colony contented themselves with the native root-vegetables, something like crystalline rutabagas filled with custard, and the teeming rock-geese whose hearts in those barnacled chests tasted of beef and sugar.

In your glass is an '83 vintage of that hybrid vine, a year which should be famous, would be, if not for rampant fear and avarice. Born on Earth, matured in Golubash. It is 98% Cabernet, allowing for mineral compounds generated in the digestive tract of the Golubash river. Note its rich, garnet-like color, the *gravitas* of its presence in the glass, the luscious, rolling flavors of blackberry, cherry, peppercorn, and chocolate, the subtle, airy notes of fresh straw and iron. At the back of your tongue, you will detect a last whisper of brine and clarygrass.

The will of Simone Nanut swirls in your glass, resolute-unbroken-unmoveable-stone.

• • •

2503 Abbaye de St. CIR, Tranquilité, Neuf-Abymes

Of course, the 2683 vintage, along with all others originating on Avalokitesvara, were immediately declared not only contraband but biohazard by the Asociación de la Pureza del Vino, whose chairman was and is a scion of the Marubouzu clan. The Asociación has never peeked out of the pockets of those fabled, hoary Hokkaido vineyards. When Château Debrouillard shocked the wine world, then relatively small, by allowing their ancient vines to be grafted with Japanese stock a few years before the first of Salvatore Yuuhi's gates went online, an entity was created whose tangled, ugly tendrils even a Hyphen would call gargantuan.

Nor were we alone in our ban. Even before the first colony on Avalokitesvara, the lunar city of St. Clair-in-Repose, a Catholic sanctuary, had been nourishing its own strange vines for a century. In great glass domes, in a mist of temperature and light control, a cloister of monks, led by Fratre Sebastién Perdue, reared priceless Pinot vines and heady Malbecs, their leaves unfurling green and glossy in the pale blue light of the planet that bore them. But monks are perverse, and none more so than Perdue. In his youth he was content with the classic vines, gloried in the precision of the wines he could coax from them. But in his middle age, he committed two sins. The first involved a young woman from Hipparchus, the second was to cut their orthodox grapes with Tsuki-Bellas, the odd, hard little berries that sprang up from the lunar dust wherever our leashed bacteria had been turned loose in order to make passable farmland as though they had been waiting, all that time, for a long drink of rhizomes. Their flavor is somewhere between a blueberry and a truffle, and since genetic sequencing proved it to be within the grape family, the monks of St. Clair deemed it a radical source of heretofore unknown wonders.

Hipparchus was a farming village where Tsuki-Bellas grew fierce and thick. It does not do to dwell on Brother Sebastién's motives.

What followed would be repeated in more varied and bloodier fashions two hundred years hence. Well do I know the song. For Château Marubouzu-Debrouillard and her pet Asociación had partnered with the Coquil-Grollë Corporation in order to transport their wines from

Earth to orbiting cities and lunar clusters. Coquil-Grollë, now entirely swallowed by Chatêau M-D, was at the time a soda company with vast holdings in other foodstuffs, but the tremendous weight restrictions involved in transporting unaltered liquid over interlunar space made strange bedfellows. The precious M-D wines could not be dehydrated and reconstituted—no child can withstand such sadism. Therefore, foul papers were signed with what was arguably the biggest business entity in existence, and though it must have bruised the rarified egos of the children of Hokkaido and Burgundy, they allowed their shy, fragile wines to be shipped alongside Super-Cola-nade! and Bloo Bomb. The extraordinary tariffs they paid allowed Coquil-Grollë to deliver their confections throughout the bustling submundal sphere.

The Asociación writ stated that adulterated wines could, at best, be categorized as fruit-wines, silly dessert concoctions that no vintner would take seriously, like apple-melon-kiwi wine from a foil-sac. Not only that, but no tariffs had been paid on this wine, and therefore Abbé St. Clair could not export it, even to other lunar cities. It was granted that perhaps, if taxes of a certain (wildly illegal) percentage were applied to the price of such wines, it might be possible to allow the monks to sell their vintages to those who came bodily to St. Clair, but transporting it to Earth was out of the question at any price, as foreign insects might be introduced into the delicate home *terroir*. No competition with the house of Debrouillard could be broached, on that world or any other.

Though in general, wine resides in that lofty category of goods which increase in demand as they increase in price, the lockdown of Abbe St. Clair effectively isolated the winery, and their products simply could not be had—whenever a bottle was purchased, a new Asociación tax would be introduced, and soon there was no possible path to profit for Perdue and his brothers. Past a certain point, economics became irrelevant— there was not enough money anywhere to buy such a bottle.

Have these taxes been lifted? You know they have not, sirs. But Domaine Zhaba seized the ruin of Abbé St. Clair in 2916, and their cellars, neglected, filthy, simultaneously worthless and beyond price, came into our tender possession.

What sparks red and black in the erratic light of the station status screens is the last vintage personally crafted by Fratre Sebastién Perdue. It is 70% Pinot Noir, 15% Malbec, and 15% forbidden, delicate Tsuki-Bella. To allow even a drop of this to pass your lips anywhere but under the Earthlit domes of St. Clair-in-Repose is a criminal act. I know you will keep this in mind as you savor the taste of corporate sin.

It is lighter on its feet than the Cotê-du-Golubash, sapphire sparking in the depths of its dark color, a laughing, lascivious blend of raspberry, chestnut, tobacco, and clove. You can detect the criminal fruit—ah, there it is, madam, you have it!—in the mid-range, the tartness of blueberry and the ashen loam of mushroom. A clean, almost soapy waft of green coffee-bean blows throughout. I would not insult it by calling it delicious—it is profound, unforgiving, and ultimately, unforgiven.

2790 Domaine Zhaba, Clos du Saleeng-Carolz, Cuvée Cheval

You must forgive me, madam. My pour is not what it once was. If only it had been my other arm I left on the ochre fields of Centauri B! I have never quite adjusted to being suddenly and irrevocably left-handed. I was fond of that arm—I bit my nails to the quick; it had three moles and a little round birthmark, like a drop of spilled syrah. Shall we toast to old friends? In the war they used to say: *go, lose your arm. You can still pour. But if you let them take your tongue you might as well die here.*

By the time Simone Nanut and her brood, both human and grape, were flourishing, the Yuuhi gates were already bustling with activity. Though the space between gates was vast, it was not so vast as the spaces between stars. Everything depended on them, colonization, communication, and of course, shipping. Have any of you seen a Yuuhi gate? I imagine not, they are considered obsolete now, and we took out so many of them during the war. They still hang in space like industrial mandalas, titanium and bone—in those days an organic component was necessary, if unsavory, and we never knew whose marrow slowly yellowed to calcified husks in the vacuum. The pylons bristled with oblong steel cubes and arcs of golden filament shot across the tain like violin bows—all the gold of the world commandeered by Salvatore Yuuhi and his grand plan. How many wedding rings hurled us all into the stars? I suppose one or two of them might still be functional. I suppose one or two of them might still be used by poor souls forced underground, if they carried contraband, if they wished not to be seen.

The 2790 is a pre-war vintage, but only just. The Asociación de la Pureza del Vino, little more than a paper sack Château Marubouzu-Debrouillard pulled over its head, had stationed . . . well, they never called them soldiers, nor warships, but they were not there to sample the wine. Every wine producing region from Luna to the hydroponic orbital agri-communes, found itself graced with inspectors and customs officials who wore no uniform but the curling M-D seal on their breasts. Every Yuuhi gate was patrolled by armed ships bearing the APV crest.

It wasn't really necessary.

Virtually all shipping was conducted under the aegis of the Coquil-Grollë Corporation, so fat and clotted with tariffs and taxes that it alone could afford to carry whatever a heart might desire through empty space. There were outposts where chaplains used Super Cola-nade! in the Eucharist, so great was their influence. Governments rented space in their holds to deliver diplomatic envoys, corn, rice, even mail, when soy-paper letters sent via Yuuhi became terribly fashionable in the middle of the century. You simply could not get anything if C-G did not sell it to you, and the only wine they sold was Marubouzu-Debrouillard.

I am not a mean woman. I will grant that though they boasted an extraordinary monopoly, the Debrouillard wines were and are of exceptional quality. Their pedigrees will not allow them to be otherwise. But you must see it from where we stand. I was born on Avalokitesvara and never saw Earth till the war. They were forcing foreign, I daresay alien liquors onto us when all we wished to do was to drink from the land which bore us, from Golubash, who hovered over our houses like an old radio tower, fretting and wringing his-her-its hundred hands.

Saleeng-Carolz was a bunker. It looked like a pleasant cloister, with lovely vines draping the walls and a pretty crystal dome over quaint refectories and huts. It had to. The Asociación inspectors would never let us set up barracks right before their eyes. I say us, but truly I was not more than a child. I played with Golubash—with the quicksalmon and the riverweed that were no less him than the gargantuan thin man who watched Simone Nanut plant her vines three centuries past and helped my uncles pile up the bricks of Saleeng-Carolz. Hyphens do not die, any more than continents do.

We made weapons and stored wine in our bunker. Bayonets at first, and simple rifles, later compressed-plasma engines and rumblers. Every other barrel contained guns. We might have been caught so easily, but by then, everything on Avalokitesvara was problematic in the view of the Asociacion. The grapes were tainted, not even entirely vegetable matter, grown in living Golubash. In some odd sense they were not even grown, but birthed, springing from his-her-its living flesh. The barrels, too, were suspect, and none more so than the barrels of Saleeng-Carolz.

Until the APV inspectors arrived, we hewed to tradition. Our barrels were solid cobalt alder, re-cedar, and oakberry. Strange to look at for an APV man, certainly, gleaming deep blue or striped red and black, or pure white. And of course they were not really wood at all, but the fibrous musculature of Golubash, ersatz, loving wombs. They howled biohazard, but we smacked our lips in the flare-light, savoring the cords of smoke and apple and blood the barrels pushed through our wine. But in Saleeng-Carolz, my uncle, Grel Nanut, tried something new.

What could be said to be Golubash's liver was a vast flock of shaggy horses—not truly horses, but something four-legged and hoofed and tailed that was reasonably like a horse—that ran and snorted on the open prairie beyond the town of Nanut. They were essentially hollow, no organs to speak of, constantly taking in grass and air and soil and fruit and fish and water and purifying it before passing it industriously back into the ecology of Golubash.

Uncle Grel was probably closer to Golubash than any of us. He spent days talking with the tall, three-faced creature the APV still thought of as independent from the river. He even began to hyphenate his sentences, a source of great amusement. We know now that he was learning. About horses, about spores and diffusion, about the life-cycle of a Hyphen, but then we just thought Grel was in love. Grel first thought of it, and secured permission from Golubash, who bent his ponderous head and gave his assent-blessing-encouragement-trepidation-confidence. He began to bring the horses within the walls of Saleeng-Carolz, and let them drink the wine deep, instructing them to hold it close for years on end.

In this way, the rest of the barrels were left free for weapons.

This is the first wine closed up inside the horses of Golubash: 60% Cabernet, 20% Syrah, 15% Tempranillo, 5% Petit Verdot. It is specifically banned by every planet under APV control, and possession is punishable by death. The excuse? Intolerable biological contamination.

This is a wine that swallows light. Its color is deep and opaque, mysterious, almost black, the shadows of closed space. Revel in the dance of plum, almond skin, currant, pomegranate. The musty spike of nutmeg, the rich, buttery brightness of equine blood and the warm, obscene swell of leather. The last of the pre-war wines—your execution in a glass.

2795 Domaine Zhaba, White Tara, Bas-Lequat

Our only white of the evening, the Bas-Lequat is an unusual blend, predominately Chardonnay with sprinklings of Tsuki-bella and Riesling, pale as the moon where it ripened.

White Tara is the second moon of Avalokitesvara, fully within the orbit of enormous Green Tara. Marubouzu-Debrouillard chose it carefully for their first attack. My mother died there, defending the alder barrels. My sister lost her legs.

Domaine Zhaba had committed the cardinal sin of becoming popular, and that could not be allowed. We were not poor monks on an isolated moon, orbiting planet-bound plebeians. Avalokitesvara has four healthy moons and dwells comfortably in a system of three habitable planets, huge new worlds thirsty for rich things, and nowhere else could wine grapes grow. For a while Barnarders had been eager to have wine from home, but as generations passed and home became Barnard's System, the wines of Domaine Zhaba were in demand at every table, and we needed no glittering Yuuhi gates to supply them. The APV could and did tax exports, and so we skirted the law as best we could. For ten years before the war began, Domaine Zhaba wines were given out freely, as "personal" gifts, untaxable, untouchable.

Then the inspectors descended, and stamped all products with their little *Prohibido* seal, and, well, one cannot give biohazards as birthday presents.

The whole thing is preposterous. If anything, Earth-origin foodstuffs are the hazards in Barnard's System. The Hyphens have always been hostile to them; offworld crops give them a kind of indigestion that manifests in earthquakes and thunderstorms. The Marubouzu corporals told us we could not eat or drink the things that grew on our own land, because of possible alien contagion! We could only order approved substances from the benevolent, carbonated bosom of Coquil-Grollë, which is Chateau Marubouzu-Debrouillard, which is the Asociación de la Pureza del Vino, and anything we liked would be delivered to us all the way from home, with a bow on it.

The lunar winery on White Tara exploded into the night sky at 3:17 am on the first of Julka, 2795. My mother was testing the barrels—no wild ponies on White Tara. Her bones vaporized before she even understood the magnitude of what had happened. The aerial bombing, both lunar and terrestrial, continued past dawn. I huddled in the Bas-Lequat cellar, and even there I could hear the screaming of Golubash, and Julka, and Heeminspr, and poor, gentle Niflamen, as the APV incinerated our world.

Two weeks later, Uncle Grel's rumblers ignited our first Yuuhi gate.

The color is almost like water, isn't it? Like tears. A ripple of red pear and butterscotch slides over green herbs and honey-wax. In the low-range you can detect the delicate dust of blueberry pollen, and beneath that, the smallest suggestion of crisp lunar snow, sweet, cold, and vanished.

2807 Domaine Zhaba, Grelport, Hul-Nairob

Did you know, almost a thousand years ago, the wineries in Old France were nearly wiped out? A secret war of soil came close to annihilating the entire apparatus of wine-making in the grand, venerable valleys of the old world. But no blanketing fire was at fault, no shipping dispute. Only a tiny insect: *Daktulosphaira Vitifoliae Phylloxera*. My namesake. I was named to be the tiny thing that ate at the roots of the broken, ugly, ancient machinery of Marubouzu. I have done my best.

For a while, the French believed that burying a live toad beneath the vines would cure the blight. This was tragically silly, but hence Simone Nanut drew her title: *zhaba*, old Slovak for toad. We are the mites that brought down gods, and we are the cure, warty and bruised though we may be.

When my uncle Grel was a boy, he went fishing in Golubash. Like a child in a fairy tale, he caught a great green fish, with golden scales, and when he pulled it into his little boat, it spoke to him.

Well, nothing so unusual about that. Golubash can speak as easily from his fish-bodies as from his tall-body. The fish said: "I am lonely-worried-afraid-expectant-in-need-of-comfort-lost-searching-hungry. Help-hold-carry me."

After the Bas-Lequat attack, Golubash boiled, the vines burned, even Golubash's tall-body was scorched and blistered—but not broken, not wholly. Vineyards take lifetimes to replace, but Golubash is gentle, and they will return, slowly, surely. So Julka, so Heeminspr, so kind Niflamen. The burnt world will flare gold again. Grel knew this, and he sorrowed that he would never see it. My uncle took one of the great creature's many hands. He made a promise—we could not hear him then, but you must all now know what he did, the vengeance of Domaine Zhaba.

The Yuuhi gates went one after another. We became terribly inventive—I could still, with my one arm, assemble a rumbler from the junk of this very platform. We tried to avoid Barnard's Gate; we did not want to cut ourselves off in our need to defend those worlds against marauding vintners with soda-labels on their jump-suits. But in the end, that, too, went blazing into the sky, gold filaments sizzling. We were alone. We didn't win; we could never win. But we ended interstellar travel for fifty years, until the new ships with internal Yuuhi-drives circumvented the need for the lost gates. And much passes in fifty years, on a dozen worlds, when the mail can't be delivered. They are not defeated, but they are . . . humbled.

An M-D cruiser trailed me here. I lost her when I used the last gate-pair, but now my cousins will have to blow that gate, or else those soda-sipping bastards will know our methods. No matter. It was worth it, to bring our wines to you, in this place, in this time, finally, to open our stores as a real winery, free of them, free of all.

This is a port-wine, the last of our tastings tonight. The vineyards that bore the Syrah and Grenache in your cups are wonderful, long streaks of soil on the edges of a bridge that spans the Golubash, a thousand kilometers long. There is a city on that bridge, and below it, where a chain of linked docks cross the water. The maps call it Longbridge; we call it Grelport.

Uncle Grel will never come home. He went through Barnard's Gate just before we detonated—a puff of sparkling red and he was gone. Home, to Earth, to deliver-safeguard-disseminate-help-hold-carry his cargo. A little spore, not much more than a few cells scraped off a blade of clarygrass on Golubash's back. But it was enough.

Note the luscious ruby-caramel color, the nose of walnut and roasted peach. This is pure Avalokitesvara, unregulated, stored in Golubash's horses, grown in the ports floating on his-her-its spinal fluid, rich with the flavors of home. They used to say wine was a living thing—but it was only a figure of speech, a way of describing liquid with changeable qualities. This wine is truly alive, every drop, it has a name, a history, brothers and sisters, blood and lymph. Do not draw away—this should not repulse you. Life, after all, is sweet; lift your glasses, taste the roving currents of sunshine and custard, salt skin and pecan, truffle and carmelized onion. Imagine, with your fingers grazing these fragile stems, Simone Nanut, standing at the threshold of her colonial ship, the Finnish desert stretching out behind her, white and flat, strewn with debris. In her ample arms is that gnarled vine, its roots wrapped with such love. Imagine Sebastién Perdue, tasting a Tsuki-Bella for the first time, on the tongue of his Hipparchan lady. Imagine my Uncle Grel, speeding alone in the dark towards his ancestral home, with a few brief green cells in his hand. Wine is a story, every glass. A history, an elegy. To drink is to hear the story, to spit is to consider it, to hold the bottle close to your chest is to accept it, to let yourself become part of it. Thank you for becoming part of my family's story.

• • •

I will leave you now. My assistant will complete any transactions you wish to initiate. Even in these late days it is vital to stay ahead of them, despite all. They will always have more money, more ships, more bile. Perhaps a day will come when we can toast you in the light, in a grand palace, with the flares of Barnard's Star glittering in cut crystal goblets. For now, there is the light of the exit hatch, dusty glass tankards, and my wrinkled old hand to my heart.

A price list is posted in the med lab.

And should any of you turn Earthwards in your lovely new ships, take a bottle to the extremely tall young lady-chap-entity living-growing-invading-devouring-putting down roots in the Loire Valley. I think he-she-it would enjoy a family visit.

LEAVE

ROBERT REED

━◆━

Politics doesn't make friendships. I have forgotten the names and faces of almost every other protester, and that's after two years of enduring the elements with those very good people, berating distant politicians as well as the occasional drivers who showed us their middle fingers.

No, what makes the friendship is when two adult men discover a common, powerful love for skiing and for chess.

I met Don in front of the old Federal Building. We had found ourselves defending the same street corner, holding high a pair of hand-painted signs demanding that our troops come home. That was seventeen years ago. Our cause was just, and I never doubted the wisdom or glorious nobility of our methods. But every memory is tinged with guilty nostalgia. Of course the war was wrong—a blatant, foolish mistake perpetrated by stupid and criminally arrogant leaders—and hasn't history proved us right? If only more people had stood on enough corners, and then our not-so-good nation would have emerged sooner from that disaster with our reputation only slightly mangled and thousands of our precious young people saved.

Don was the most ordinary member of our tofu-loving group. With his conservative clothes, the constant shave, and his closely cropped, prematurely gray hair, he was our respectable citizen in a platoon composed of cranks and ideologues. There was some half-serious speculation that poor Don was an agent for the State

Patrol or FBI. But beneath that respectable, boring exterior lurked a card-carrying member of the Libertarian Party. Chat with the man for five minutes, and you knew he was genuine. Listen to a thirty-minute lecture, and you'd take away everything you'd ever need to know about personal responsibility and stripping the government from our private lives.

The fact that our spouses hit it off instantly didn't hurt either. Our wives ended up being as good friends as we were. So it seems that war gave me one good gift: Don and Amanda, and their two children, Morgan and sweet Little Donnie.

Cheryl and I couldn't have kids—a constant sadness in an otherwise untroubled marriage. So when I mention being close to Don's children, picture a fond uncle.

Morgan was ten when we met the family—a bright, almost pretty girl who would make any parent proud. She had inherited her father's fastidious attitude and a sharp, organized mind. Being seven years older than her brother, she helped raise the wild youngster. Yet the girl never complained, even if that meant babysitting a weepy, feverish imp while her folks stood in the sleet and wind, holding high signs begging the world for a single rational act.

I can't remember Morgan ever acting jealous toward her sibling. Which was a considerable feat, if you knew Little Donnie and his special relationship to the world.

As a toddler, LD (as his family called him) was an effervescent presence already speaking in long, lucid sentences. Cheryl explained to me that some three-year-old girls managed that early verbal capacity, but never little boys. Then she pointed out—and not for the last time—that Little Donnie wasn't merely smart, he was absolutely beautiful: a delicious sweet prince of a lad destined to grow up into a gorgeous young man.

Don was openly proud of both kids, but LD stories outnumbered Morgan stories at least three-to-one.

Every time I saw my friend, he had to share at least one LD anecdote. Preschool and then elementary school brought a string of thunderous successes, including perfect report cards and glowing praise from every teacher. And middle school—that realm of social carnivores and petty hatreds—proved to be a tiny challenge for the golden boy. Of course LD earned his place in the finest gifted programs in the state. And it didn't hurt that he was a major force in the local t-ball circuit, and that he dominated the seventh-grade basketball court, and nobody in eighth grade could hang with that stallion when he decided to run the four hundred meter sprint.

But eighth grade was when our world abruptly and unexpectedly changed.

As the boy entered high school, the glowing reports fell off. Don was still genuinely thrilled with his son. I have no doubts. But suddenly he was less likely to share his news about LD's continuing rise to still-undefined greatness.

What if somebody was listening to his boasts?

Distant but horrible forces were at work in the universe, and Don sensed that silence might be the wiser course.

In an earlier age, Don and I had done what we could to battle an awful war. Success meant that our troops eventually came home, and his children could grow up safe, and nothing else seemed to matter.

But LD turned fourteen, and a new war began.

Or rather, an unimaginably old and bizarre and utterly unexpected conflict had found its way into our lives and tidy homes.

I was still kept abreast about the most important LD news. And I'd cross paths with the boy, or my wife would. As she had predicted, he grew up gorgeous and brilliant. And Little Donnie remained charming, though in that cool, detached way that every generation invents for the first time. He was always polite to us, even at the end. His lies were small affairs, and on the surface, harmless. It actually made me jealous to hear my middle-aged bride praising the Apollo-like figure who had chatted with her at the supermarket. But she was right. "The only thing I worry about," she said with a confidential tone, "is that LD has too many choices. Know what I mean, John?"

I suppose I did, but not from my own life experience.

"There's so many careers he could conquer," Cheryl added. "And with any girl he wants, of course."

Including my wife, if she could have just shrugged off twenty years and forty pounds.

"Is he doing all right at school?" she would ask.

As far as I knew, yes.

"Because Amanda's mentioned that his grades are down," she reported. "And his folks are getting worried about his friends."

Big Don had never quite mentioned those concerns, I noted.

Then a few months later, my best friend dropped his king on its side and told me, "I resign." That very poor performance on the chessboard preceded a long, painful silence. Then with a distracted air, he added, "LD's been suspended."

Did I hear that right? "Suspended from what?"

"School," Don allowed.

I didn't know what to say, except, "Sorry."

Don looked tired. He nodded, and after hard consideration decided to smile. "But he's in a twelve-step program. For the drug use."

I was astonished. "What drug use?"

He didn't seem to hear me. With a wince, he reported, "The counselors are telling us that when a kid is high-functioning, being bored is the greatest danger."

We were talking about drugs, and we weren't.

"What drugs?" I had to ask.

"It doesn't matter." Don paused, then nodded, as though he'd convinced himself it really didn't matter.

I slumped back in my chair, staring at the remaining black and blond chessmen.

"LD is in rehab," the worried father continued, "and he's promised to get clean and well. And he'll graduate on time, too."

A string of promises that were met, it turned out.

That next year, the young prince went to our local college—perhaps to keep him within reach of his worried parents. What news I heard was cautiously favorable. But after the first semester, even those mild boasts stopped coming. The only glowing news was about Morgan and her burgeoning career as a dermatologist.

I made a few tactful inquiries.

Don would say, "Oh, the boy's doing fine too."

Cheryl's queries to Amanda ended with the same evasive non-answers.

Then one morning, while strolling downtown on some errand, I happened to stumble across the famous LD.

To my eye, he looked fit and sober.

But when he told me, "I'm going to buy a new bike today," he was lying. And when he said, "I'm riding across the country this summer," he was feeding me a fairy tale.

The boy had already made up his mind.

I didn't even suspect it.

"Enjoy your ride," I advised, feeling proud of this tall, strong kid with whom I had shared nothing except seventeen years and an emotional stake that was never defined, but nonetheless felt huge.

"See you, Mr. Vance."

"Take care, LD."

Two weeks later, Don called me at work. "Have you seen my boy?" he asked. Then before I could answer, he blurted, "In the last five days, I mean."

"I haven't," I allowed. My stomach clenched tight. "Why?"

"LD's vanished."

Some intuition kept me from mentioning the bike ride.

"We just found out," said a terrified parent. "Donnie's failed all of his classes, and nobody seems to know where he is."

I had nothing worth saying.

And then with a tight, sorry voice, Don confessed, "I just hope it's the meth again. You know? Something small and fixable like that."

Five years earlier, our tiny world had changed. But it wasn't a historic event that happened in a single day or during a tumultuous month. In fact most of humanity did its stubborn best to ignore the subject. So what if a few voices told the same incredible story? And what if astronomers and their big telescopes couldn't entirely discount their crazy words? In our United States, the average God-fearing citizen still didn't swallow the idea of natural selection, and that's after almost two centuries of compelling research. Rational minds had to be skeptical. Even after the story broke, there were long stretches when I considered the whole business to be an elaborate, ludicrous joke. But the evidence did grow with time, and I had no choice but become a grudging believer. And then our friends' son vanished without warning, and Cheryl turned to me in bed and asked when I thought LD would actually leave the Earth behind.

My response was less than dignified.

Thoroughly and passionately pissed, I told my wife, "He bought a bike, and he went wandering."

"And you know this how?"

"That's what he told me he was doing," I reminded her.

"And has anybody seen this bike?"

I didn't respond.

"His parents talked to everybody," she continued. "Girlfriends, his buddies. Professors and both roommates. They never saw a bike. Or a packed suitcase. Or anything you'd take on a trip."

"I know that."

"With the clothes on his back, he went out on a midnight walk," she continued. "His car was still parked in the street. Nobody remembers him buying a bike or camping gear or anything else you'd want on a cross country ride."

"Don told me all that, honey."

"Did Don mention his son's checking account?"

I said nothing.

And she read my expression. For an instant, she took a spouse's cruel pleasure in having the upper hand. "LD drained it and closed it."

"Why not? A kid on the road needs money."

"Amanda just told me. LD left all that cash in an envelope addressed to them. They found it while searching his room. Eleven hundred dollars, plus a birthday check from Grandma that he never bothered to endorse."

Bike ride or drug binge. In neither case would the boy leave that tidy sum behind.

Once again, Cheryl asked, "How soon does he leave the Earth?"

In the pettiest possible ways, I was hurt that Don hadn't mentioned finding the money.

"What's Amanda think?" I asked.

"The worst," said Cheryl.

"Did they call the police?"

"Last night. From LD's apartment."

I had to ask, "But do the cops care? This is not a child anymore. We're talking about a legal, voting-age adult."

"An adult who has vanished."

But citizens had rights, including the freedom to fail at college, and then out of embarrassment or shame, dive out of sight.

I asked, "Have the police met with them?"

Cheryl dipped her head sadly. "Amanda didn't say," she admitted. "She started to cry again, said it was too painful, and hung up."

"I believe that," I muttered.

"Talk to Don," she advised.

I nodded, wringing a sad joy out the moment, allowing myself to revel in the awful fact that I didn't have any children of my own to worry about.

"On average," Don asked, "how many young men and women vanish? In a given year."

I offered an impressive number.

"Multiply that by three," he warned.

"Is that the U.S., or everywhere?"

"Just the U.S."

"I see."

We'd met at the coffee house for our traditional chess game. The board was set up, but neither of us had the strength to push a pawn. My good friend—a creature who could not go into a new day without clean clothes and a scrubbed face—looked awful. A scruffy beard was coming in white. The eyes were rimmed with blood, and I could see dirt under his fingernails. Where had the man been digging, and why? But I didn't ask, watching him pick up his mug of free-trade coffee and sip it and look into the swirling blackness. Then a voice almost too soft to be heard asked, "How many go up there? Out of a thousand missing people, how many?"

"Twenty," I guessed.

"Not bad. It's ten and a half."

"How do we know that?"

"There's websites," he explained. "Help societies and half a dozen federal agencies like to keep databases, and the answers mostly agree with each other. Most missing people are found sooner or later, and there's some who drop off remote cliffs, and there's always drug users who aren't found and murder victims too."

My black pieces waited at attention, fearless and wood-hearted.

"Go into space or become a murder victim: Those are about equally likely, as it happens." In a peculiar way, the haggard face betrayed hope. Then with the earnest tone of confession, Don mentioned, "That's what I want the cops to believe. That LD's been killed."

"So they look for him?"

"Sure."

I sipped my warm coffee, weighing the probabilities.

"Of course they don't believe me," he continued. "But if his disappearance isn't a crime, then they can't do anything beyond filling out a missing-person's report."

I kept thinking about tall and handsome LD, calmly lying to me about the bike and his plans for the summer. The prick.

"He's alive," I said, aiming for hope.

Don remained silent, fearful.

"Okay," I allowed. "Suppose he's joined up with *them*."

I was passing into an uncomfortable terrain. Don leaned back and dropped his shoulders, and with a whisper, he said, "Okay."

"They don't take their recruits off the Earth right away," I pointed out. "I mean, *they* might be wizards with space flight and all. But their volunteers have to be trained first, to make sure that they can . . . you know . . . do their job well enough to make them worth the trouble."

"Sure."

"Lifting a big young man past Pluto," I said. "It costs energy."

"It does," he agreed.

"LD is smart," I continued. "And sure, he has a bunch of talents. But do you really think, Don—in your heart of hearts, I mean—do you believe that your son is capable of serving as a soldier in some miserable alien war . . . ?"

There was a long, uncomfortable pause.

Then the shaggy white face lifted, and just by looking at the sleepless eyes, I could tell we were talking about two different boys.

"Little Donnie," his father muttered.

With all the confidence and horror he could muster, Don declared, "My son would make a marvelous, perfect soldier."

Nobody knows when the war began, and no sane human mind claims to understand the whys and for whats that keep it alive today.

But we know for sure that the first human recruits vanished four decades ago. My father's generation supplied that early fodder, though the world didn't notice when a few thousand boys failed to come downstairs for breakfast. By unknown means, the Kuipers identified the ripest targets among us—always male, always smart and adaptable—and through elaborate and almost invisible negotiations, they would winnow the field to the best of the best. Usually the boy's mind would wander, experiencing a series of lucid daydreams. About fighting, of course. But more important, the aliens would test his capacity to cooperate and coldly reason and make rapid-fire decisions under stress. And they always made sure that he would say, "Yes," before the question was asked. "Yes" meant that a young human was agreeing to serve one Nest for ten full seasons—a little more than three decades, Earth-time. Survive that maelstrom of carnage, and you were honored and subsequently released from service. Then according to traditions older than our innocent species, you were allowed to bring home one small sack stuffed full of loot.

Ten years ago, a few middle-aged gentlemen reappeared suddenly. There was some interest, but not much belief: They came from the Third World, and how credible is a Bangladeshi fisherman or a Nigerian farmer? But then six years ago a Frenchman returned to his home village, and he made the right kinds of noise for the cameras. Then came a Canadian gent, and an Italian, and then a pair of handsome American brothers who suddenly strolled into a town square in New Hampshire. In the media's eyes, these weren't just crazy peasants rambling on about impossible things. Here stood men with good educations and remembered faces and what soon became very public stories, and if their families gave up on them ages ago, at least there were siblings and elderly parents who could say with confidence, "It is him. It is them. I know it is. Yes."

And they brought home their sacks of loot, too.

Some of those possessions had obvious value—gemstones of extraordinary purity, slabs of rare-earth elements, and other materials that would have carried a healthy price on the open market. But the biggest noise came from what looked like trash: Pieces of pretty rock, shards of irradiated glass, unfathomable chunks of burnt machinery, and in a few cases, vials of dirty water.

Each veteran looked older than his years, with haunted, spent eyes and flesh that had been abused by extreme temperatures and cosmic rays. Some had lost fingers, some entire limbs. Each wore scars, outside and in. But despite very different origins and unrelated languages, they told identical stories: About being recruited by creatures dubbed the Kuipers who taught them how to fight, and despite very long odds, how to survive.

The Kuipers were a deeply social organism, it was explained.

But not like bees or termites or even naked mole rats. There were no queens or castes. In their youth, every alien had a strong, vaguely humanoid body capable of modest shape-shifting. But as adults they had to find a worthy patch of ground to set down roots, interlocking with one another, forming elaborate beds that were at least as intricate and beautiful as coral reefs.

The Kuipers didn't refer to themselves by that name. Their original world circled some distant sun; nobody knew for sure which one. They were an ancient species that had wandered extensively, creating a scattering of colonies. For the last thousand millennia, a substantial population of Kuipers had been fighting each other for possession of a single planet-sized comet that was drifting somewhere "out there."

No veteran could point at the sky and say, "This is where you look."

Navigating in deep space wasn't an essential skill, it seemed.

When the story broke, good scientific minds loudly doubted that any world matched the vivid descriptions given to family members and the media. Comets were tiny things; even Pluto and its sisters didn't possess the gravity or far horizons that were being described. And they were far too cold and airless for humans wearing nothing but self-heating armor. But then one astronomer happened to look in the proper direction with a telescope just sensitive enough, and there it was: A giant ice-clad world moving high above the solar system's waist, carrying enough mass to build a second Earth, but built of less substantial ingredients like water and hydrocarbons laid over a small core of sulfurous iron.

That new world's crust, though frozen, was no colder than a bad winter day in Antarctica. A multitude of subsurface fusion reactors created a deep, warm, and very busy ocean. Ice volcanoes and long fissures let the excess heat escape upward. As promised, the atmosphere was dense and remarkable—a thick envelope of free oxygen and nitrogen laced with odd carbon molecules and rare isotopes, plus a host of other telltale signs proving the existence of some kind of robust, highly technological life.

Moving at light-speed, more than a day was required to reach that distant battlefield.

Human soldiers were moved at a more prosaic rate, several weeks invested in the outbound voyage. Which was still immensely quick, by human standards. The Kuipers' ships were tiny and black, invisible to our radar and nearly unnoticeable to the human eye. They never carried weapons. Every veteran made that blanket assurance. By law or convention, spaceships were forbidden to fight, much less attack any other species. And without exception, the surrounding universe was neutral—a taboo of peace balanced by the endless war on their world.

A curious mind could ask, "Which side did you fight for?"

Those retired soldiers always had a name for their sponsoring nest or reef, and rarely did two soldiers use the same name.

"How many reefs are there?" people inquired.

"Two hundred and eleven," was the unvarying answer.

Hearing that, a human being would invest the distant struggle with some familiar politics.

"So how does this play out?" they would ask. "One hundred reefs fighting the other hundred, with a few neutral cowards sitting on the sidelines?"

Some veterans laughed off those simple, wrong-headed questions.

But more often they would put on expressions of disgust, even rage. Then with a single passionate breath, they would explain that there was no such thing as neutrality or alliances, or cowardice for that matter, and each reef gladly battled every one of its neighbors, plus any other force that stupidly drifted into the field of fire.

War was the Kuipers' natural state, and that's the way it had been for the last twenty million years.

Panic is temporary; every adrenaline rush eventually runs empty. Even the most devoted parent has to sleep on occasion, and breathe, and somehow eat enough to sustain a minimal level of life. That's why a new, more enduring species of misery evolves for the afflicted. Over the next several weeks, I watched my friends carefully reconfigure their misery. They learned how to sleep and eat again, and for a few moments each day, they would find some tiny activity that had absolutely nothing to do with their missing son. Normal work was impossible. Amanda exhausted her sick days and vacation days, while Don simply took an unpaid leave of absence. Like never before, they became a couple. A team. Two heads united by the unwavering mission—to find and reclaim LD before he forever escaped their grasp.

"I almost envy those two," Cheryl confided to me. "It's sick to think this. But when have our lives enjoyed half that much purpose? Or a tenth the importance?"

"Never," I had to agree.

In my own sorry way, I was angry about what LD was doing to my old friendship. After those first days of pure terror, Don stopped calling. He didn't have the energy or need to keep me abreast of every little clue and dead end. There were many days when I didn't once hear from the man. He was too busy researching the Kuipers. Or he had to interview experts on missing people. Or there were night flights to distant cities and important meetings with government officials, or patient astronomers, or one of the very few practicing exobiologists. Plus there were some secretive exchanges with borderline figures who might or might not have real help to offer.

We tried to keep meeting to play chess, but the poor guy couldn't recall what he had told me already. Again and again, he explained that his son was still somewhere on the Earth, probably somewhere close by. The Kuipers' version of boot camp required eighty-seven days of intense simulations and language immersion, technical training and cultural blending. That was what every verified account claimed. Perhaps as many as three percent of the recruits failed this stage, earning a scrubbed memory of recent events and transport back home again. "But those numbers are suspicious," Don said. "There's no telling how many young men pretend amnesia to explain a few missing months."

From the beginning, the same relentless rumors had been circulating about secret training bases on the ocean floor or beneath the South Pole. Various governments, and particularly the U.S. government, were said to be in cahoots with the Kuipers, giving them old air bases in exchange for top-secret technologies. The truth, however, was less spectacular and infinitely more practical for the job at hand.

Not to mention far, far stranger.

"LD is somewhere close," Don kept telling me.

And himself.

Witnesses were scarce, and the memories of the veterans were short on details. But each would-be soldier was encased inside an elaborate suit, armored and invisible to human sensors. For the next thirty years, that suit would be his shell and home. For the moment, both it and its living cargo were buried deep in some out-of-the-way ground. There was no telling where. Somewhere within a hundred miles of our little table, LD was living a cicada's subterranean existence, experiencing what the aliens wanted him to experience, making him ready for the adventure of a lifetime.

"We've got two months to find him," Don told me.

If his son had actually joined the Kuipers, I thought to myself.

Later, he announced, "We have six weeks left."

"Plenty of time," I lied, looking at the fresh dirt under his fingernails.

Then he said, "Four weeks, and a day."

"Maybe he'll be one of the dropouts," I said hopefully.

For the first time, LD's father was hoping for failure. But saying so would jinx everything. I could see that in his stiff mouth, in his downcast eyes. Don was turning into a superstitious old fool, not allowing himself even to smile at the prospect: The powerless victim of grand forces beyond his control, with nothing in his corner but the negligible possibility of a little good luck.

"Two weeks left, minus twelve hours."

We were sitting in the coffee shop. This was our usual day for chess, though we hadn't managed a full game in weeks. Don always brought his laptop, leaping around the Web while we suffered through a halting, chaotic conversation.

Three times in three minutes, Don glanced at his watch.

"Expecting somebody?" I finally asked.

"I am," he admitted.

I waited for the full answer. When none came, I asked outright, "So, whom are we expecting?"

Don smiled, anguish swirled with anticipation. "Somebody important," he mentioned. "Somebody who can help us."

Then he gave the coffee shop door a long hard stare.

I made one wrong guess. "Is it a parent?"

There were thousands like Don, and the Internet allowed them to meet and commune, sharing gossip and useful tips. Our particular town was too small to have its own support group, but every Sunday, Don and Amanda drove to Kansas City in order to sit in a stuffy room and drink coffee with people a little farther along in their misery.

Maybe one of those Kansas City friends was dropping by, I reasoned.

But Don said, "No," and then his tired eyes blinked.

Glancing over my shoulder, I understood.

Our visitor was in his middle sixties, and he didn't look too awful. I would have expected a limp or maybe stumps in place of hands. But no, the gentleman could have been any newly retired citizen, respectable and even a little bland. He stood at the door, taking in the room as if weighing all the hazards. And then I noticed his tailored clothes and the polished leather shoes, a little old-fashioned but obviously expensive.

Some veterans returned to Earth with gems in their loot. But to my knowledge, not one ever sold his treasures, since each item carried some embedded significance far beyond commercial gain.

To myself, I whispered, "Where do you get your money, stranger?"

"I'm sorry," Don told me, sounding decidedly unsorry. "I should have warned you. Just this morning, I learned this fellow was passing through, and I was lucky enough to get his number and arrange this. This meeting."

Don hurriedly gathered up his belongings. The laptop. The labeled folders. A notebook full of intense scribbles. And finally, half a cup of black Sumatran. Then he threw a careless look over his shoulder, telling me, "Stay, if you want. Or I can call you afterward, tell you how it went."

"Okay, Don. Good luck."

Because I was his friend, I stayed. To keep busy, I brought out my own laptop and searched through the Wikipedia list of confirmed veterans. Meanwhile the two strangers shook hands and sat in back, across from each other in a little booth. I heard a few words from our honored guest, and reading the accent, I moved to the Russian portion of the database, bringing up a series of portraits.

Thirty-five years ago, a talented young art student slipped out of his parents' Moscow apartment and vanished.

I could almost understand it: A Russian might prefer fighting aliens among the stars over trying to survive the next three decades inside a tottering communist empire.

The two old boys chatted amiably for several minutes.

Then the Russian mentioned something about his time and his considerable trouble, and Don pulled an envelope from his pocket and passed it over. The Russian opened the gift with a penknife waiting at the ready, using fingers and eyes to count the bills and their denominations until he was satisfied enough to continue.

Cheryl had warned me.

"Our friends are spending their life savings," she said just the other night. "Any person or little group that might help find LD gets a check, and sometimes several checks."

"Don's no fool," I had claimed. "He wouldn't just throw his money away."

"But a lot of scam artists are working this angle," she added. "Anybody with a missing son is going to be susceptible."

Those words came back to me now.

Who actually compiled these lists of Kuiper veterans? Russia wasn't a bastion of honest government and equal opportunity. I could envision somebody bribing the right people and then setting off for the West, retelling stories that were public legends by now, and helping no one but their parasitic selves.

The Russian seemed vigorous and fit.

I couldn't get past that.

After half an hour of intense conversation and coffee, Don had to slip off to the bathroom. He barely gave me a nod as he passed by. I stood and walked over, not asking permission when I sat beside the Russian, introducing myself without offering my hand and then asking pointblank, "So what are you and my good friend talking about?"

I can't say why, but that's when my initial suspicions collapsed.

Maybe it was the man's face, which up close revealed delicate and unusual burn scars. Or maybe it was the straight white line running from the back of his hand up his forearm and under his sleeve. Or it was the smell rising from his body—something I'd read about but never experienced—that faintly medical stink born from a diet of alien chow and peculiar water.

But mostly, what convinced me were the man's haunted blue eyes.

"The training," said a deep, ragged voice. "Donald wants to know about the training. About what his son is enduring now."

"Can you help him?"

"I am trying to."

"Help me now," I pleaded. Then after a deep breath, I added, "But I'm not going to pay you anything."

The blue eyes entertained their own suspicions.

"Why now?" I asked. "If this war's been going on forever, why just in these last forty years have the Kuipers started coming here?"

He said nothing.

"Does their war need fresh blood? Are they short of bodies to fight their ugly fight, maybe?"

"No," he said once, mildly.

And then louder, with authority, he said, "Hardly."

"But why now?"

"Because forty years ago, my benefactors came to the conclusion that it was possible for humans to observe their world. We had not yet discovered it, no. But just the possibility was critical to the ceremony. Because all who can see what is transpiring must be made welcome—"

"Ceremony?" I interrupted. "What does that mean?"

"Exactly what you would expect the word to mean," he claimed. Then he leaned closer to me, his breath stinking of alien chemicals that still swam in his blood. "What you call a war is not. More than anything, the ceremony is a religious event. It is a pageant of great beauty and much elegance, and by comparison, all human beliefs are cluttered little affairs without a thousandth the importance that one day up there brings to the open soul."

As the Russian spoke to me, Don returned.

"I miss that world," said the one-time recruit. "I miss the beauty of it. The power of it. The intensity and importance of each vivid, thrilling moment." He broke into some kind of Creole jabber—a mixture of Earthly languages and Kuiper that must have been better suited to describe his lost, much beloved life. Then he concluded by telling me, "Belonging to one nest while serving my good elders, standing limb to limb with my brethren . . . I miss that every waking moment, every dreaming moment . . . constantly, I find myself wishing I could return again to that good, great place. . . . "

"Is that what it is?" I asked. "A great place?"

"I do envy that boy of his," the Russian said to me.

Maybe I smiled, just a little. Just to hear that more than survival was possible, that poor LD could actually find happiness.

But Don roared, "Get out of here!"

I thought he was speaking to the Russian, and I was right.

And I was wrong.

"Both of you," my best friend snapped. "I don't want to hear this anymore. 'The beauty. The power.' I want you to leave me alone! Goddamn it, go!"

I felt awful for what I had done, or what I had neglected to do. For the next couple nights, I lay awake replaying the conversation and the yelling that followed. In my charitable moments I would blame exhaustion and despair for Don's graceless temper. Because what did I do wrong? Nothing, I told myself, and certainly nothing intentional.

After that, I called Don half a dozen times, making various apologies to his voice mail.

Eventually Cheryl heard from Amanda. Their thirty-second phone conversation translated into a five-minute lecture from my wife.

"Here's what you have to understand, John. These next days are critical. There won't be another chance to save LD. They have leads about where he might be, which is something. Very unusual, and maybe they will manage to find him—"

"And accomplish what?" I interrupted.

She looked at me with outrage and pity.

"Has any recruit ever been found like this?" I asked.

"Maybe," Cheryl said. "Two or three times, perhaps."

"And talked out of leaving?"

She had to admit, "No."

But then with her next breath, she said, "This is about LD's parents This is about them doing their very best. They can't let this moment escape without putting up a fight. And what Amanda says . . . the way that you've been acting around Don . . . it's as if you don't want to believe just how awful this mess is. . . . "

What did I believe?

"Doubt is a luxury they can't afford now," Cheryl explained. "And you're going to have to give Don space, if you're not going to help."

"But I want to help," I pleaded.

"Then stop calling him, honey. He's got enough guilt in his head without hearing your voice every day too."

One week remained.

Two days.

And then on the eighty-sixth day after LD's disappearance, an unexpected voice came searching for me, along with a very pleasant face and a sober, well-considered attitude.

"Hey, John."

"Morgan?" I sputtered.

"Can I come in? Just for a minute, please. It's about my brother."

We welcomed her. Of course we welcomed the young woman, offering our guest a cold drink and the best chair and our undivided attention. Morgan was being truthful when she said she had just a few minutes to spend with us. A list of people needed to be seen, and soon. A phone call or the Internet would have worked just as well, but with some of these names—us in particular—she felt that it was best to come personally.

"A favor, John? Cheryl?"

Her shy smile made me flinch. "Anything," I said for both of us.

"We have three areas to watch tonight," she reported. "Three pastures, scattered but close to town. There's evidence—different kinds of evidence—that LD's buried in one of them. Although it's probably none of them, and this is a long shot at best."

Cheryl asked, "Which pasture do we watch?"

"Here." On a photocopy of a map, she had circled eighty acres in the southeast corner of the county. "Really, the only reason to think LD's there is a farmer thinks he saw odd lights moving in the grass. And he's halfway sure it was the same night my brother vanished."

A very long shot.

But I said, "We'll be there, Morgan."

"There's going to be others out there with you. Cousins of mine, and some friends, and a lot of volunteers from all over. But most of us, including me . . . we'll be at the north site."

"Is that place more promising?" my wife asked.

Morgan nodded. "We have a reliable witness who saw LD, or somebody like him, walking across an empty corn field in the middle of the night." She rolled her shoulders with a skeptical gesture. Then as she stood again, she said, "Thank you. For everything, I mean."

"We want to help," Cheryl promised.

Morgan looked straight at me.

Then despite the crush of time, she hesitated. Standing at our front door, Morgan spent three minutes making small talk. With a grin, she told us about the evening we'd come to their house to grill out, and while her brother put on a show for everyone, clowning around and throwing the football a mile into the air, I had taken the time to come over and sit with the ignored sister.

I had no recollection of the moment.

But Morgan did, and years later it was a cherished incident worth retelling. Then she looked at neither one of us, shaking her head. "Want to know the truth?" she asked with a conspiratorial tone. "Half of me believes Little Donnie is faking this. Just for fun. Just to see everybody jump and weep."

The big sister who had never shown a trace of jealousy said those hard, unsentimental words.

"He would love tonight," she told us. "All this effort on his behalf . . . he would find it to be absolutely lovely. . . . "

The evening began with showers and then a hard cold rain mixed with biting sleet. Cheryl and I packed for any weather. We arrived early, pulling off the country road and waiting in the gathering darkness. Several dozen searchers were expected, half of whom never showed. In the end, it was a gathering of distant relations and friends from Don's work who stood on the mud, coming up with a battle plan. Because nobody else volunteered, Cheryl and I took the far end of the pasture. LD's parents had been over this ground a dozen times. But we were told to look for signs of fresh digging that they might have missed, and to be most alert sometime before dawn. If the most common scenario played out, the new recruit would emerge from his hiding place then, still wearing his warrior suit.

With my wife beside me, I walked across the wet cold and shaggy brome. At the fence line, she went to the right and I went left, her flashlight soon vanishing in a rain that refused to quit.

In the end, I had no idea where I was.

Three in the morning, full of coffee and desperate for sleep, I walked the same ground that Don had searched in broad daylight. The mission was impossible, if the mission was to discover LD. But in my mind, what I was doing was saving a friendship that I hadn't cherished enough.

By four, I was too tired to even pretend to search.

By five in the morning, clear skies arrived along with the sudden glow of a thousand stars.

Change one turn that night, or pause in a different spot, and I would have heard nothing.

And even what I heard was insignificant enough to ignore.

What I was reminded of was the sound of an old-fashioned thermostat. That's all. The soft click that meant the furnace was about to kick on, except that I heard the click repeating itself every few seconds.

I turned toward the sound.

My flashlight was off, my eyes adjusted to the starlight. Even though it probably wouldn't do any good, I tried for stealth—a quiet stride and a steadiness of motion.

At some point, the clicking stopped.

I halted.

Then a slab of late-season grass, blond and shaggy, lifted up on my right. It was maybe ten feet from me. There was no disturbed area there before, I'm sure. Afterward I couldn't find any trace of the hole where our newest recruit was undergoing his indoctrinations. But there he was, rising up from that random patch of ground. I saw the head. The broad shoulders. Arms and long legs. All those good human parts encased inside a suit that seemed neither large nor particularly massive, or for that matter, all that tough either.

From behind, he looked like LD dressed up for a Halloween party, pretending to be a cut-rate astronaut.

I said, "Donnie."

My voice was little more than a whisper.

The shape turned with a smooth suddenness, as if it knew that I was there and wasn't surprised, but maybe it wasn't sure of my motives. LD pivoted, and then a face that I couldn't quite make out stared at me through a shield of glass or diamond or who-knew-what.

"How's that big bike ride coming?" I asked.

LD stepped closer.

It did occur to me, just then, that maybe there was a good reason why no one had ever seen a recruit leaving for space. Witnesses weren't allowed. But even if the kid was twice my strength, he did nothing to me. He just stepped close enough so that I could make out his features and he could see mine, and with a satisfied sound, he said, "If it has to be someone, John, I'm glad it is you."

Maybe the feeling was mutual.

But I didn't say that. Instead, I decided to lay things out as clearly and brutally as I could. "Your folks are sick with worry. They've spent their savings and every emotional resource, and after tonight, they will be ruined. They'll be old and beaten down, and for the rest of their lives, they won't enjoy one good happy day."

"No," said LD.

"What does that mean?"

"They will recover just fine," he claimed. "People are strong, John. Amazingly strong. We can endure far more than you realize."

The wee hours of the most unlikely morning, and I was getting a pep talk from a college dropout.

"Donnie," I said. "You are a spoiled little brat."

That chiseled, utterly handsome face just smiled at my inconsequential opinion.

"So much promise," I said, "and what are you doing with it? Going off to fight some idiotic alien war?"

Inside his battle helmet, the boy shook his head. "Where I will be is on a large world that is more beautiful and more complex than you could ever envision."

Could I hit him with something? A rock or a log? Or maybe a devastating chunk of bloody guilt?

But I had the impression that his flimsy suit wasn't weak at all.

"I am needed up there," LD said.

"Are you sure?"

"More than I am needed down here, yes." He said it simply, calmly. And I suppose that's when I realized that not only did he mean what he was saying, but that in deep ways, he was probably right.

I didn't have anything left to offer.

"John?" the boy asked. "Would you do me a favor?"

"What?"

"Turn around for a moment."

If there was a noise when he left, I didn't hear it. And maybe there was motion, a sense of mass displaced into an endless sky. But at that moment, all I could feel was the beating of my heart and that slight but genuine anguish that comes when you wish it was you bound for places unseen.

More than a hundred people had searched in the rain for LD, and all but one openly confessed to seeing nothing and no one. I was the lone dissenter. I said nothing, and not even Cheryl could make me confess what happened, though I know she sensed that I had seen more than nothing while we were apart.

To Don, I said simply, "Come to chess tomorrow. The usual place."

He was at the coffee shop before me, and I was early. He had his board set up, and he looked exactly as I expected him to look: Exhausted and pained, weak and frail.

I picked up my queen's pawn and then put it down again.

Then quietly, I told him what I had seen and everything that I had done in the backstretches of that pasture, trying to win over the heart of a boy that really, when you got down to it, I barely knew.

Don nodded.

With a voice less than quiet, he halfway accused me of not doing enough to save LD from his own childish nonsense.

But what more could I have done?

That's what I thought, and maybe he did too. Then he sat back—a defeated father who would surely never see his son again—and with a mournful voice, he asked, "Is there anything else?"

Then I lied.

I said, "Yeah, there's more."

I smiled enough to bring him forward again, elbows to his knees as he waited for whatever I said next.

"Donnie wanted me to tell you something."

"What?"

"That he's going up there for one reason only: He wants to put an end to that awful ancient war. He's not going to fight anyone, but instead he'll reason with the Kuipers and show them that it's better to live in peace."

A staggering lie, that was. Unbelievable to its core.

But Don accepted my words without complaint. He sat back in his chair, his shoulders relaxing and then his face too. And being his friend for years told me that here, with just a few words, I had made it easier for him to sleep easy, and if not tonight, sometime soon.

MEHRA AND JIUN

SANDRA McDONALD

Brilliant white light, a bone-rattling explosion, her ship spinning wildly as it thundered toward the icy surface of Europa. Lieutenant Vandi Mehra remembered these things vividly. Now the world was much darker and more peaceful. Her limbs felt very light but also restrained. Maybe that was a pillow under her head, a warm blanket cocooning her. Or maybe she was dreaming. It was more likely that she was hospitalized and sedated. That would explain the way her senses reached out and then receded, reached and receded again. A hum in the air, followed by silence; air that smelled like mud, followed by the absence of any smell at all.

I hope I'm not brain-damaged, she thought sluggishly.

Finally her senses steadied—humming noise, muddy smell, definitely low-gravity, straps holding her to a bed. Slowly she cracked open her eyes. Instead of a military infirmary she saw a cabin with fibrous, brown bulkheads. Tree roots, almost, which made no sense at all. Globes of soft green light decorated the roots. Standing nearby, watching her intently, was a man her own age. He had dark brown eyes, dark skin with a mop of black hair, and a lithe body clad in what looked like black silk pajamas. The most important thing about him was the black cable jutting from a port on his forehead, curving around his head and inserted back into his right ear.

Tung, she realized.

She was in a Tung ship, captive of a Tung soldier.

Mehra supposed her death was a foregone conclusion. The only details to be settled now were how long it would take for her heart to stop beating and for her consciousness to sink back into the river of all life. Death was an unsettling idea (and maybe she was a little anxious, yes, her palms clammy, her heartbeat fast), but she hadn't really expected to wake up at all. Life was full of surprises like that.

Her captor was watching a tablet in his hands. When he glanced up and saw that she was awake, he said, "Lieutenant Mehra." In English. No Tung were known to speak English. Their own language was a mystery. Any prisoners of war died soon after being captured, steadfastly silent. This Tung had also made her name a statement and not a question. As if they'd already met before, social acquaintances in a time of war.

A half-dozen replies flitted through her mind but she settled on the most civil one. "Who are you?"

"Kennu Di Jiun," he said. "Your ship was poorly designed for landing and your onboard medical robot completely inadequate. You might as well ride a *tukra* into a *torasar*."

She tugged at the straps holding her arms. "I wouldn't have needed to land if your people hadn't attacked me."

"Your planet shouldn't have allied with the Roeir," he said.

"Above my paygrade," she retorted, tallying the losses in her head: thousands and thousands of good pilots and good crews, their bodies and ships pulverized and scattered in the airless void. Her own father, killed in the sneak attack on Opportunity Base on Mars. The ruthless destruction of envoys sent in peace. You could say that at least the Tung hadn't directly attacked Earth yet but that was only because the Roeir were protecting it. Mehra had skipped history and politics seminars at the academy, preferring to spend all of her time in a trainer. She didn't need to know anything more about the Tung than how to shoot them down.

"You know nothing," Jiun said, his gaze narrow. He retreated toward one bulkhead. "You were dead but Sophene resuscitated you. Come up to the flight hub when you're ready."

A hatch opened in the tree roots, spilling in more green light. He left Mehra alone in the chamber. The hatch stayed open.

"You could untie me first!" she called out.

The restraints faded. Dissolved away as if they'd never been there.

Mehra sat upright, adjusting to the low gravity all over again. She pulled herself free of the dark brown blanket. Flight suit, gone. New clothes: a loose-fitting black top and pants like Jiun's. She'd always wanted to dress like a Japanese ninja. No bra, no absorbent underwear. She examined her torso and limbs but there were no injuries at all, not even a tiny cut. She had nothing to use as a weapon and there were no convenient medical trays of scalpels, lasers or other devices that could inflict bodily harm.

Only the bed where she'd been restrained (*resuscitated*, he'd said), the tree root bulkheads, and the hatch.

She touched the root walls. Spongy, not fibrous at all. They hummed with energy. Mehra wondered if she could cut them, break them, sabotage them; if she could make Jiun's ship overload and explode.

She was a soldier. She wasn't going to die easily, and it would be her pleasure to take a Tung with her.

Nothing in his ship was labeled or marked. Nothing resembled equipment or machinery. Just tree roots and open hatches, browns and greens, and if it weren't for that muddy smell (*change the filters, guys,* she wanted to say) she might have found it peaceful. She hadn't walked in a real forest in years. She wasn't walking now, of course, but instead bounding along, each step propelling her several feet. The passage wasn't very large, and she had to constantly reach out to keep herself from colliding with the bulkheads. Low gravity really pissed her off.

No noise but the hum of the ship, deep and steady. No ship's announcements, beeping equipment, boisterous conversation. No damn map. After several minutes of exploration she found Jiun sitting in a small chamber where the bulkheads extended into padded furniture and a table. A panel hung on one wall, at least two meters long, and on it was a panoramic view of frozen ice with Jupiter in the sky. Jiun was tapping on his tablet and studying the landscape, looking for something.

"We're parked on Europa," Mehra said from the hatchway.

"Yes."

"Why?"

"To rescue you," he said.

"And now what?" she asked, imagining the possibilities: he returned her home, he killed her, he tortured her, he shoved her out an airlock—

"I'm not going to kill you," he said. She wasn't sure if he was reading her mind somehow or if her thoughts were that clear on her face. He continued, "Sophene rescued you. I don't know why, so don't ask me. Ask her."

It was the second time he'd mentioned someone else. The captain of this ship, maybe. Mehra said, "Okay, where is she?"

Jiun tapped his tablet. The panel display changed into a mirror. Mehra stared at her own reflection. Jutting out of her own forehead, plugged into her own right ear, was a black cable like Jiun's. For a long moment she thought it was a trick or optical illusion. Surely she'd have noticed something like that before. Her hands reached up to touch it, though she had no awareness of actually moving them. Cool exterior, slightly oily, firmly embedded —

Mehra panicked and yanked.

Rainbow light seared her vision—pink yellow green blue red purple—and pain, yes, that was pain, a thermonuclear explosion inside her skull. The black cable slithered out of her fingers like a snake and fell to the floor. Not like a snake, no, but actually really truly a snake—long, sinewy, whipping its way across the deck, sliding toward Jiun.

Mehra was too busy vomiting from pain to see where it went.

Cool hands touched her face. Jiun. He looked angry. He spoke to her but now it was in a language she couldn't make sense of, couldn't even try to decode, and her head hurt so badly she wanted to die, and she curled up against him and gasped until darkness, blessed darkness, took her away.

But eventually she woke up again. It only took a moment to discover that the oily cable was back in her forehead, back in her ear.

"That's Sophene," Jiun told her. "She lets us talk to each other. Don't pull her out again."

Mehra swallowed against the taste of bile. "I don't want her there."

"You don't have a choice," Jiun said. "Come to the hub if you want dinner."

She didn't think she was hungry, but the mention of food woke up her belly and got her moving. Jiun's idea of dinner was bland tea and little squares that looked and tasted like cheese sandwiches. He had portioned out three squares for each of them.

"How do I know I can digest these?" Mehra asked. "They could be poisonous to Earthlings."

His expression didn't change. "Our species are identical. And if the food kills you, Sophene would resuscitate you anyway."

Mehra ate slowly. She didn't feel poisoned. She prioritized the eight million questions in her head and asked, "Who is Sophene, exactly? Another species, an artificial intelligence, what?"

Jiun drank his tea. "She assists me."

"She saved me," Mehra said. "You would have let me die."

His gaze was steady on her face. "She chose to resuscitate you. I would have let you depart."

Mehra said, "Depart as in . . . ?"

"Continue from this world for the next," he said. "Chasing your ship down to the surface drained my fuel. Saving it from sinking into a ice fissure took several hours and damaged not just the engine but also our external comm array. Restoring you to health sucked up even more of our reserves. Now we don't have enough fuel to leave the surface. We don't have way for me to message my fleet. I'm probably presumed dead. Unless someone comes looking for us, or stumbles on us accidentally, we're stranded here until the food, water or oxygen gives out."

Mehra had forgotten all about the food in her hand. She felt something sticky and looked down to see her right hand clenched into a fist. Cheese-like substance oozed under her fingernails.

"How do I know you're telling the truth?" she asked.

Jiun's head tilted slightly. "Why would I lie?"

"To trick me," she said. "To fool me into doing something for you."

"Anything you know of military value was added to our knowledge bank while you were unconscious," Jiun said. "There wasn't much."

"Were you a jerk before now or does being stranded just bring out the worse in you?" Mehra asked.

"Ask Sophene," he said.

Sophene, however, didn't talk to Mehra. At least not in any way she understood. If she asked a question aloud, such as, "Which way to the lavatory?" she got a hazy mental image of a path through the ship, a root-like control she could touch to open a tiny chamber. If she asked, "Where's my ship?" she saw a hunk of burnt and twisted metal on Europa's surface, totally unsalvageable. If she asked for Jiun's engine room or bridge she got nothing at all. Maybe this ship didn't have them. Or maybe Sophene didn't want Mehra sabotaging, fiddling or otherwise meddling with the technology. Maybe Sophene didn't trust her.

During her first Europa day—eighty five hours, more or less—Mehra explored the ship as much as she could. She didn't see much of Jiun. He put out food for her in the hub area, and sometimes she found him there staring out at Europa, but mostly he kept himself busy elsewhere. Maybe he was holed up in his cabin, watching Tung porn or reading Tung books. The few times they interacted, she tried asking him about the his homeworld, and the history of the Tung and Roeir, and how he'd come to be a soldier. He deflected her with questions of Earth or refused to answer at all, and later Mehra dreamed of ice, a big glacier of it adrift on a black ocean.

Patience, she heard a dream voice say.

Sometime in the middle of the second Europa day she found him in the hub with his feet clamped to the floor. He had taken off his shirt. He was performing fluid stretches and strikes, not unlike the martial arts classes she remembered from the academy. His expression was focused and intense, and sweat gleamed on his smooth brown skin.

"Want some company?" she asked.

He stopped and studied her, but didn't answer.

She took that as a yes. Mehra wedged her feet under the furniture and did push-ups and sit-ups. Not very challenging in the low gravity, but any exercise would help stave off bone loss. She wished Jiun and Sophene had stocked up on free weights or a treadmill. Something other than tea and faux cheese sandwiches would be nice, too.

"You focus too much on strength, not balance," Jiun remarked when she was done.

Mehra said, "You focus too much on grace, not practical hand-to-hand combat."

He lifted his chin. "Maybe we have something to learn from each other."

She finally figured out how to use the ship's chronometer but breaking Europa days into more manageable Earth days didn't make the time go any faster. Then she discovered that if she asked the panel in the hub area to display images other than the exterior view, it would oblige her. It cycled through real-time images of Earth (a distant shiny spot), Jupiter's surface (mildly interesting), and the panorama around Jiun's ship (ice, more ice, and an ice mountain). It didn't show her battles but she knew the war still raged above their heads; good people dying because the Tung refused to negotiate peace.

On a whim, Mehra asked the panel to show her Jiun's home. It paused slightly before bringing up an image of a city so vast, so beautiful, that Mehra rose off the furniture and walked right up to it to study every tiny detail.

A city, yes, but also a forest; silver threads holding glass walls strung between brown branches and green leaves, blue water flowing in sweet cascades between levels, yellow and red flowers blooming in vast hanging gardens. Mehra could smell the deep fragrance of fir and pine, of azaleas and jasmine and wild roses. Above the city hung a startling blue sky, completely different than the gray and brown skies that now covered Earth. Jiun's home was a paradise, so close and tangible that Mehra wanted to crawl right into the image—

"It's not real," Jiun said from behind her. He nodded at the screen and it went dark. "It's just a picture."

Mehra stared at him. "Why did you leave? How could you?"

"My emperor commanded," he said, his voice cracking at the end.

He retreated before she could ask more and skipped their next exercise session. Mehra was so desperate for conversation, so ruthlessly bored, that she returned to the hub and asked the panel to show her Tung again. It stayed blank. She suspected Jiun had told it not to obey. Anger shot through her—how dare he—and she snapped, "Show me Sophene."

She didn't think it would work. If she'd know all it took was one command, she would have tried it days earlier. But there was Sophene, or at least some kind of representation: blueyellowgreenredorange in a splatter on the screen.

"Is it you?" Mehra asked.

"I'm here," Sophene said, serene and calm, her voice as clear and fluid as water.

Mehra touched the edge of the screen gingerly. "Tell me everything."

"I've been waiting," Sophene said, and began with the ten-thousand-year history of aggression, hostility, distrust and broken promises between the Roeir and the Tung. Mehra was almost sorry she'd asked.

If Jiun knew she was taking intergalactic history lessons with Sophene, he didn't mention it. But during their exercise sessions he started using the occasional Tung word, simple things like "first" or "second" or "strike to the heart," and she memorized those as best she could. He was stronger than she was, of course he was, but every now and then she surprised him with her speed or flexibility.

She noticed, during one particular lesson, that he had grease under his fingernails and a callous on his thumb.

She didn't think he was watching porn in his cabin all day long.

Sometime in the third Earth week, while relating every detail of the Roeir-Tung Second War of the Aristone Peninsula, Sophene mentioned that Jiun had been trained as a teacher. Prior to his military service he had spent three winters teaching history at a small school in the mountains, where he was popular among students and parents alike.

"I can't imagine that," Mehra said.

"He wasn't always the man he is now," Sophene said. "Watching your friends die changes a person."

Mehra knew that. She knew that so well that she didn't need a damned computer to remind her. "How did he end up here?"

"The Tung emperor had declared war on Earth for allying with Roeir, and all firstborn sons were inducted into the army regardless of their occupation or personal feelings about the war."

"But if he doesn't want to serve the emperor, why does he?" Mehra asked.

"To refuse would be to dishonor his family," Sophene said. "Do you enjoy killing on behalf of your government?"

"I'm defending my home," Mehra said.

Sophene replied, "Earth, Roeir and Tung would all benefit from following the path of peace, as we do on my planet."

Mehra frowned. "Are you from Tung?"

"My people are from elsewhere," Sophene said. "Many worlds suffer because of the Roeir-Tung disharmony. We serve them both in hopes we can someday guide them into communication and peace."

"Doesn't seem to be working," Mehra said.

The faux cheese sandwiches ran out, replaced by cardboard-like crackers that tasted even worse. They still had tea with their meals, but Mehra suspected Jiun was watering it down.

"Which are we going to lose first?" Mehra asked. "The food or the water or the oxygen?"

Jiun took his time answering. "The power cells."

"You're a bucket of sunshine," she said, and then had to look away. That had been one of her father's favorite sayings. Before he was murdered by the Tung.

Mehra tried not to think about that.

They cut back on their exercising and dimmed more of the lights. Jiun turned down the ship's temperature as well, and gave Mehra all the blankets he could dig up. By week five her cabin was too cold for her to sleep very well and so she moved to the hub, where the furniture was large enough for two.

"We could share body heat," she said. "Basic survival training for combat pilots."

"I don't think . . . " Jiun blinked a few times. "That may not be wise."

"It'll take my chance being dumb," she replied.

They slept together that night, bodies and blankets entwined. In the morning Jiun was gone. He didn't bring breakfast. Mehra didn't have anywhere to go or anywhere to go and so she stayed huddled in the blankets, half-dozing, dreaming of pancakes and coffee and biscuits. She was lifting a dream spoon of dream maple syrup when Sophene poked her in the middle of her brain.

"Flight bay!" Sophene snapped, lighting up a mental map for Mehra to follow. "Hurry!"

Mehra stumbled out to the passage and bounced her way forward, propelled by the urgency in Sophene's tone and the dreadful feeling that something was wrong. That Jiun's ship even had a flight bay was surprising, but not half as startling as the sight of him crumpled and insensate next to Mehra's flight suit and some kind of ground vehicle.

"Don't you die on me now," Mehra threatened, slapping his face lightly. "What have you been doing here?"

He blinked up at her, shivered, and tried to close his eyes again. Mehra rubbed her knuckle on his breastbone and annoyed him into consciousness.

"What is this?" she demanded. "Your secret lab project, all this time?"

Sophene flickered onto the nearest display, all greenorange- redyellowpink against the brown bulkheads. "I told him to tell you before he killed himself of exhaustion and starvation."

"Both of you are very irritating," Jiun said wearily.

Mehra retrieved blankets for him, and tea, too, after Sophene told her where the last stash was. Once Jiun was on his feet again, Mehra turned her attention to the vehicle. It looked amateurish and home- made. Jury-rigged from other parts. The motor was fueled by a battery and the steering and braking were rudimentary.

She couldn't help but notice that it only had one seat.

"What's this for?" she asked.

Jiun touched the vehicle and didn't look at Mehra. "There's an abandoned rover about six hours from here, if you take this and travel at max speed."

"A rover from Earth?" she asked. Her knowledge of the early space program was hazy—Apollo this, Columbia that—but there'd been robot rovers, yes, first on Mars and then later on Jupiter's moons.

Jiun found his tablet and showed her a map. "If you reach it and recharge its solar panels, you should be able to send an emergency signal. There's an Earth carrier nearby that can pick you up within twenty-four hours."

Mehra wasn't able to speak for a moment. Finally she managed, "You want me to travel in this go-cart for six hours at minus two hundred degrees Celsius, so that I can maybe recharge an ancient piece of junk, which might be able to signal a carrier, which might or might not decide to pick me up before I freeze to death?"

Jiun met her gaze. "Yes."

"And you're going to stay here and slowly die?"

His eyes darkened at her tone. "I'm going to let Sophene put me into medical stasis. With the ship in deep sleep mode, the fuel cells will keep me there for several years. One day my people might find me."

Mehra studied the rover. Studied Jiun. It was the craziest, stupidest, most dangerous plan he could have possibly thought of. She almost admired its sheer insanity.

"And what happens when they ask me where I've been all this time?" she asked. "No matter how much I don't want to tell them, they're not going to take 'I don't remember' for an answer."

Sophene spoke up. "I can make that true."

Mehra whirled to the panel. "You can what?"

"Clear out your memories of us," Sophene said serenely. Her colors swirled together. "Your superiors can't find information that is not there."

Mehra turned back to Jiun. "Tell me why."

He was silent for a moment. Finding the right words, she thought, was never easy for a man who'd frozen himself.

"Because there's no point to a war if no one wins," he finally said.

Mehra eased herself into the go-cart's seat. Imagined herself careening down Europa's frozen ice cracks. The odds of getting the rover recharged and able to send out a signal were remote, and the carrier might very well decide to ignore her signal (a trap, of course they'd think it was a trap), but what kind of combat pilot was she if she didn't risk everything for a very small chance at success?

But even if she convinced them she knew nothing (even if she let Sophene drain her brain), they'd never trust her again. Not in a combat role, not with a ship, not in any kind of leadership position. And here Jiun would sleep, locked in a forgotten ship parked against a forgotten mountain on a remote moon, until the ice crept past the hull and consumed him.

Mehra climbed out.

"In the Battle of Sarkit, during the Third War of the Sea People of Doria, the warriors Evliunor and Markiun made a pact to see the war end together," she said. "You taught that lesson in your history classes. I'm frankly kind of insulted that you think I'm any less than Markiun."

Stricken, he said, "Mehra, this is no time to joke."

"Also, Markiun was the male," Sophene added.

Mehra took Jiun's hand. It was a nice strong hand, with long fingers and calluses from all his hard labor.

"The way to win a war is to survive it," she said.

On an icy moon orbiting a giant gas planet, near an unnamed ridge straddling the equator, there sits a six-wheeled robot long abandoned to the frigid temperatures. Its batteries and sensors are long dead. It knows nothing of the war that has consumed the distant skies. It knows nothing of death or grief or survival. It certainly knows nothing of the snake coiled beneath it, redyellowgreenbluepurple, patiently working to fix the robot's connections and panels. Someday the war will end and the snake will send a message onward: *Here sleeps Mehra, here sleeps Jiun. Come wake them.* With luck, some survivor will hear it.

HER HUSBAND'S HANDS

ADAM-TROY CASTRO

—◆—

Her husband's hands came home on a Friday. Rebecca had received word of the attack, which had claimed the lives of seven other soldiers in his unit and reduced three others to similar, minimal fractions of themselves: One man missing above the waist, another missing below, a third neatly halved, like a bisected man on display in an anatomy lab.

The Veteran's Administration had told her it could have been worse. The notification officer had reminded her of Tatum, the neighbor's daughter so completely expunged by her own moment under fire that only a strip of skin and muscle remained: A section of her thigh, about the size and shape of a cigarette pack, returned to her parents in a box and now living in their upstairs room, where it made a living proofreading articles on the internet. That's no life, the notification officer said. But Bob, he pointed out, was a pair of perfect hands, amputated from the body at the wrists but still capable of accomplishing many great things. And there was always the cloning lottery. The chances were a couple of million to one, but it was something to hope for, and stranger things had happened.

Rebecca had asked her parents, and his, and the friends so anxious to see him, to stay away. It was a personal moment and she could not be sure that she would be able to take their solicitous platitudes. She waited at home wanting a cigarette as much as she'd ever wanted anything in her entire life and stared at the door until the knock came and the two smartly uniformed escorts brought what was left of her husband inside in a box with an American flag on it.

They opened the box and showed her Bob's hands, resting side by side on a white pillow. The left one lay palm-down, the right one palm-up. The one that was palm-up twitched and waggled fingers at Rebecca when it saw her. The new light-sensitive apertures at the fingertips blinked many times in what she could only assume was excitement. The fingernails had been manicured and buffed to a high sheen. Rebecca's eyes inevitably wandered to the wrists, which ended in thick silver bands, a lot like bracelets except for the flat bottoms where arms should have emerged. They, Rebecca knew, contained not just the life support—without which her husband's hands would just be graying meat—but also his most recent memory backup, without which everything he had ever been, and everything he had ever done, would now be gone.

She had not supposed that a pair of hands could be personal enough to be recognized, but she did recognize them. There was a crooked angle to one of the pinkies where he had once broken it catching a baseball and it had not healed back precisely right. And there was a scar on one of the knuckles where he had once cut himself, almost to the bone, on broken glass. She knew those hands as the same ones that once could make her shiver, when they were at the end of strong and comforting arms.

The fingers wagged some more, and the escort told her that her husband wanted to talk to her. She said that she did not know what to do. The younger of the two escorts presented her with a flat black pad with slots for fingers, turned it on, and placed it in the box where Bob's hands could get at it. As the text display came up, Bob's hands turned around, inserted fingertips into the pad's control slots and did . . . something, not exactly typing as she knew it from the familiar QWERTY keyboard but something very much like it, with subtle and practiced movements that over the next few seconds forced words and sentences onto the screen.

rebecca please don't be afraid, her husband's hands typed. *i know this is strange & frightening but it's still me. i can see you & i'm glad to be home. i love you. please i want you to kiss me*

There were few things Rebecca wanted to do less right now, but she knew her husband's hands would sense any further hesitation, and so she reached down and touched them. They disengaged from the black pad and let her pick them up, one hand in each of her own. They were as warm as she remembered, and heavier than she expected. A sick feeling rose in her throat as, driven by obligation, she gave each one a sweet kiss on the knuckles. Each one turned around in the hand that held it and twined its fingers through hers, a grip as tight and as complete as a hug would have been had fate decided to let him come home as a whole man.

One of the escorts said, "We'll leave you two alone now."

Rebecca couldn't help thinking: *What do you mean, you* two? *His hands are now two separate objects; don't you mean, you three? Or, since they don't add up to anything even close to the whole man, shouldn't you be using fractions? Telling me, we'll leave you one and a tenth alone now? Or whatever?* She thought all this but did not say it, as they donned their caps and told her to call if she needed anything, and left her alone grasping what had once been part, but not all, of the husband who only four years before had struck her eighteen-year-old self, sitting across from him in a college seminar, as the most beautiful man she'd ever seen.

For a long time she sat with him—with them—in silence. Sometimes, as she closed her eyes and waited for the reassuring squeezes that were as close as he could come to conversation without the typepad, she could almost fool herself into thinking those hands were connected to wrists that were connected to arms that joined at shoulders with a chest and a beating heart and lips and eyes and a man who could lie beside her and arouse her passions as well as her pity.

After a while, his left hand gently disengaged from her right and climbed up to her shoulder, squeezing that as well before crab-crawling to her face and finding the tear-tracks on the side of her cheek. It froze at the discovery, and she could not help feeling that she'd failed him, that she'd proven herself shallow, that she'd hurt him or what was left of him at the moment he needed to know that she was still capable of loving him.

Some time later his hands withdrew to the table so they could talk to her about the problems they now faced. The left one turned over on its back so the light-apertures on the fingertips could see her face, and the right one went to the typepad and told her that he knew how she felt, that this wasn't how he had envisioned their future either, and that if she gave him a chance he would still be the best husband to her that he possibly could. Her hesitation, her struggle to come up with words that would not be a mockery or a lie, spoke volumes, and may have broken whatever he now had for a heart. But after a long time she nodded, and it was a start.

He could not tell her anything about what had happened to him. The last backup before the attack that had destroyed the rest of him was only a week old, sparing him the memories of a hellish ordeal under fire, watching the rest of the unit fall away, one or two at a time, in pieces. He typed that he had at best an academic knowledge of what had been in that backup, as he said there were things even then that he chose not to remember, and had preferred to live the rest of his life arrested at an even earlier set of memories, recorded two months before that, and blessedly free of some experiences that would have crippled him even more than his current condition.

He typed that the war had been so terrible that he would have gotten rid of even more, had that been possible; there were certainly vets who backed up just as they were shipped out and came back as parts or wholes refusing to remember any of what they'd done, or had done to them, over there. Rather than recall a single day in-country they preferred to live a life where being strong and fit and whole and on a troop carrier getting their past coded into a database was followed, without so much as a single moment of transition, by being older and finished with their time and back, reduced to a sentient body part on a plate. But there'd been buddies, people in his unit, who had done things for him in that time during his hitch that he would never allow himself to forget, not even if he also had to remember visions out of hell. He typed that the little he could remember, he would never talk to her about.

After that, there was little to say; she made some lunch for herself and his hands sat on the table watching her eat, the palms held upward so the fingertips could see, giving the accidental but undeniable impression that they were being held upward in supplication.

Later, as the silence of the afternoon grew thick, the hands typed, *i still enjoy watching you eat*. It was something he had said before, as they'd circled each other performing the rituals that connect early attraction to couplehood; he had appreciated her meticulousness, the way she addressed a plate of food as much like a puzzle to be disassembled as a meal to savored. She did not respond that once upon a time she'd loved watching him eat as well, the sheer joy he'd taken in the foods he loved, the unabashed and unapologetic gusto with which he'd torn into meals that were not good for him. It was, she knew, a gusto he could never show anymore, and that she'd never witness, again: Another of life's pleasures robbed from them, left on a bloody patch of dirt beneath a foreign sky. She could not help thinking of the all the meals to come, the breakfasts and lunches and dinners that for years unwritten would always be reminders of what had been and would never be again.

Conversation lagged. They watched television, the hands sitting on her lap or beside her on the couch showing pleasure or displeasure in the set's offerings with mimed commentary that at one point, an angry response to an anchorman's report on the war, included a silent, but vehement, middle finger. Rebecca answered some concerned phone calls from family and friends who wanted to know how the reunion was going, and told them that no, she and Bob were not ready to receive any visitors just yet. More hours of silence broken by intervals of halting conversation rendered necessarily brief by his limited skill at typing inevitably and to some extent horrifically led to dinner, where the discomfort of lunch was not only repeated but doubled by the awareness that all this was still only starting, that the silence of their meals would soon be a familiar ritual, for as long as the future still stretched.

There was only one sign of real trouble before bedtime. Bob's wandering right hand encountered a framed photograph of himself in uniform, on an end table next to the sofa. Rebecca happened to be watching as his hand hesitated, tapping the glass with a fingertip as if somehow hoping to be allowed back into the image's frozen moment of time. It looked like he knocked the photo over deliberately. She was almost a hundred percent sure.

That night she lay on her habitual side of the bed, the ceiling an empty white space offering no counsel. His right hand burrowed under the covers and settled at about waist level, while his left sat on his fresh pillow, preferring the sight of her to any warmth the blanket might have provided. When she turned off the lamp, the pinprick red lights of his left fingertips cast a scarlet glow over everything around them, making that pillowcase look a little like the aftermath of a hemorrhage. The fingers caught Rebecca looking at them and waggled; either a perversely jaunty hello, or a reminder from Bob that he could see her. She forced herself to lean over and kiss his palm, somehow fighting back an instinctive shudder when the fingers curled up to caress her cheeks.

Rebecca called Bob's hand by his name and told it she loved him.

Under the covers, his right hand crawled toward her left and wrapped its fingers around hers. She had already held that hand for hours, on and off, and would have preferred freedom for her own, now. But what could she say, really, knowing that to reject the touch now, in this most intimate of their shared places, on the very day he'd returned to her, would have amounted to rejecting him? She had to give him something. She had to pretend, if nothing else. So she squeezed him back and whispered a few loving words that sounded like fiction to her own ears and let him hold her with one hand while the other watched with eyes like pinprick wounds.

She slept, and in her dreams, Bob's hands had still returned to her, but without the nice sanitized bands that allowed them his memories and mind and hid the magnitude of the violence done to him behind polished silver. In her dreams his hands returned to her with the wounds ragged and raw, strips of torn and whitened skin trailing along behind them like tattered streamers. Each had a splintered and blackened wrist bone protruding from the amputation point, like a spear. The fingertips of these Bob remnants were blind and useless instruments, incapable of leading him anywhere except by touch; as they crawled across the polished kitchen floor in search of her, while she fought air as thick as Jell-O to stay just beyond their reach, they left a continuous gout of blood behind, more than mere hands could have possibly bled without becoming drained sacks of flesh. The kitchen became a frieze of twisted blood-trails, which only continued up her bare legs after the chase ended and she found herself standing as paralyzed as any dream-woman with her feet nailed to the floor, while the disembodied hands climbed her.

She might have screamed herself awake, but she couldn't breathe in the dream, as the air around her was not an atmosphere a woman could breathe, but a thicker substance that refused to pass her lips, no matter how deeply her chest labored or her ears thundered or how desperately she struggled to draw anything capable of sustaining her into her lungs.

Then she woke up and knew it was not a dream. He was strangling her. His hands had tightened around her throat, the two thumbs joining at her windpipe while his coarse and powerful fingers curled around the curve of her neck to meet, as if in terrible summit, at the back. Even as a man with more than hands he had always possessed a strong grip, and the hands that were all that remained of him seemed to add the strength of his arms and back as well, all dedicated to the deadly impossible task of compressing her throat to nothingness.

A woman being strangled by a complete man might have died clawing at his chest or grasping for his face or even going for the hands themselves, which would have possessed the advantage of being anchored to arms and shoulders. Rebecca had nothing to fight but the hands, and they provided a focus for her resistance. She reached for the sharpened pencil she kept beside the book of crossword puzzles that had been her only companion since Bob went to fight that goddamned stupid war, and jabbed at the back of his hands until his skin broke and his grip went soft and the two little pieces of Bob fell away, freeing her to breathe again.

She might have screamed and continued to stab her husband's hands until there was nothing left of them but torn flesh, but something in the way they now lay on the bed, ten glowing red lights staring up at her, halted her in a way that crazed or uncomprehending eyes might not have.

She flipped on her bedside lamp and regarded Bob's murderous hands in the glare of harsh light.

All things have faces even when they don't have faces; the human eye insists on putting faces on them. Even hands have faces, and expressions, that change depending on how the fingers are held in relation to the palm. Hands can look calm or agonized or desperate. They can look gentle and they can look brutish, sometimes while remaining the same hands. For no reason at all that made any sense to her, her husband's hands looked lost. She didn't understand, but she could sense that there was something she was failing to see, something she could almost see that was just outside of her field of vision.

Bob's right hand mimed a typing motion.

She was reluctant to leave them alone long enough to get the typepad. She had read too many stories about people who turned their back on monsters. But they made the motion again, insistently. She went to the other room, returned to see that her husband's hands remained where they had fallen, and, not trusting them to keep their distance, tossed the pad onto the bed.

He typed.

i am sorry so so sorry i would not hurt u for anything i was having a nightmare i have been having them for a while i didnt know it was you i was hurting pls understand pls forgive me pls

Rebecca was not ready to forgive him. "You could have killed me."

i know. it was not the man you married but the man who lived through hell over there. when i know where i am im all right. maybe we cant sleep in the same bed for a while. please understand. please

She wanted to die. But after long minutes standing there feeling her fury churn inside her she went to her husband and told him it was all right, that she would set up another place for him in another room, and that they would sleep apart but see each other in the morning. She kissed him on the knuckles and went to make his new bed, a pillow stuffed into an unused drawer of a bureau in another room. He allowed her to carry him there, without argument. And they parted, though the sound of frantic thumping continued in the night and she was reduced to lying sleepless, her eyes fixed on unseen bloody carnage in the darkness.

• • •

The VA man said that she should take Bob to the first available support group, and even specified a local chapter that was meeting the next day. They went. It amounted to five sectioned veterans and their spouses, sitting in an approximate circle on folding chairs that must have known happy occasions as well as sad: christenings, religious meetings, political rallies, maybe even amateur theatre productions, all dissipating in the air as soon as the chairs were put away and stacked and returned to the anonymity enjoyed by furniture. The idea that somebody might sit in the very same chair she sat in now, a day or a week from now, and sip fruit punch while discussing plans for the decoration of the school prom, seemed almost incomprehensible to her.

There were five fragmented veterans along with spouses and other family members at the meeting, some of them arguably better off than Bob, others so much more reduced that it was impossible to know whether to scream in horror at their predicament or giggle uncontrollably at its madness. There was a boy of twenty-two who had been in-country for less than a day before a bombing reduced him to a thin strip of face that included one (blind) eye, two cheeks, a nose, and part of his upper lip, all now mounted on the very same silver plate that kept him alive, which his mother had attached to a plaque suitable for mounting on a wall. Another was just a torso, devoid of limbs, genitalia, or head, and plugged at all the stumps by more silver interfaces. Another was a shapely woman with delicately sculpted nails, a short skirt designed to show off a killer pair of legs and a top designed to accentuate her cleavage: Her every move reeked of sexuality, which may have been the way she carried herself before being drafted or the way she now compensated for losing the front half of her head, which instead of a face or a jaw or a pair of eyes now displayed a plane of mirrored silver before her ears. A fourth had not been salvageable as anything but a mound of shredded internal organs but had been gotten to in time and was now completely enclosed in a silver box about the size of a briefcase, with a screen for communication and a handle for her grim husband's convenience.

The last was, like Bob, a pair of amputated hands. He was the one who made Rebecca want to run screaming, because his lovely blonde wife had dealt with the problem of maintaining a relationship with him by amputating her own hands and having his attached at the end of her own wrists. The silver memory disks marking the junction points on her arms would have resembled bracelets had his calloused, darker-skinned, hairier, and disproportionately larger paws not resembled cartoon gloves at the ends of her smooth, milk-white arms; and had her husband's hands not usurped much of the control of those arms, which now gesticulated in a perversely masculine manner as his loving wife described at length how much this measure had saved her marriage. More than once during the meeting, Rebecca caught those hands resting on the other woman's bare knees and caressing them, the arms stroking them back and forth with a lascivious energy that the other woman clearly recognized and appreciated but otherwise seemed wholly removed from. She could only wonder if that's what her own husband wanted, if that was something Bob could ever ask of her, and whether she could ever come to want it herself.

The man lugging around the briefcase told all the other spouses at the meeting that he considered them lucky. Their loved ones had returned to them as parts that could be touched, skin that gave off an undeniable if largely artificial warmth, flesh that evoked the memory of what had been even in those cases where it could manage little else. But his wife? He produced a picture of the woman she had been, a plump little chubby-cheeked thing with a premature double-chin, but a smile of genuine warmth and eyes that seemed to express genuine mirth at some hidden personal joke. He said that she could see him through the interface and even communicate with him through the typepad, but words had never been a major part of her, not even when she was whole; she had been more a creature of silent gestures, of accommodating smiles, of kind acts and expressive glances and sudden stormy silences. Now, he said, she was a sack of nonfunctioning organs containing just enough meat to qualify as alive. And though she would occasionally answer direct questions, she more often remained silent, telling him when pressed that she just wanted to be left alone, put on a shelf, and forgotten. It was getting harder and harder for him to argue otherwise. "My wife is dead," he told the group, and after a moment of shocked silence repeated himself, with something like stunned wonder, "My wife is dead. My wife is dead." The wife whose arms ended with her husband's hands just pawed herself.

Gallows humor intruded, as it always does among survivors of extreme loss, when the man who was just a strip of face said that he'd met a guy, back in the hospital, who had turned out to be nothing but an asshole. The wife of the torso said that she'd met one guy who was a real dick. Somebody else said that his lieutenant had always been a little shit and probably still was, and the variations only went downhill from there. There were a few little flights of fancy involving the prospect of sectioned people who had been reduced to nothing but their sexual organs and how their chances of making a living after the service were so much better than anyone else's, but by then the shocking jokes had started to trail off, replaced by uncomfortable silence.

The meeting broke up with ten minutes of internal business involving when the next one would be held and who was going to get the word out to others who might benefit by attending. Rebecca went to the table where the coffee and the cookies were laid out on a plastic tablecloth and stood there not wanting any of it but needing to do something other than return to a house and a life now dominated by silence, and found herself shaking until the woman with a flat silver mirror for a face came up behind her and, speaking through a voice synthesizer, said, "You're not alone." Rebecca broke down and accepted the hug, feeling the warmth of the other woman's arms but also keenly aware of the how cold the mirror felt against her own cheek. She wanted to tell the other woman, *of course I'm alone, and my husband's alone, and you're alone, and we're all alone; the very point of being in hell is that there's a gulf between us and all our efforts to bridge it for even a moment give us nothing but a respite and the illusion of comfort before those bridges retract and we're left to face the same problems from our own separate islands.* She wanted to say it, but of course she couldn't, not if it meant embracing despair in defiance of this sectioned woman's kindness, and so she wept herself blind and took the hug as the gift it was meant to be.

• • •

By Saturday night, the answering machine was filling up with calls from family and friends, eager to know how it was going and wanting to know when they could enjoy their own happy reunion. Following her husband's wishes, Rebecca called them all back to thank them but put them off, saying that there still adjustments to be made, and accommodations to be arranged. Again, many wanted to know if Bob was all right. She wondered how she could possibly be expected to answer that question but said, yes, he was all right. They asked her if she was all right and again she gave the answer they wanted, that yes, she was all right.

The two sat together, watching the latest reports from the war for a while, not reacting to the news that a hundred thousand more had been called up, and how this would not be enough; or, afterward, to the feel-good assurance, delivered by a smiling red-headed anchorwoman, that actual deaths that counted as deaths were at an all-time low. Bob's hands tapped at his pad, producing a string of lower-case profanities that Rebecca supposed were now his angry equivalent of embittered muttering.

She fingered the bruises on her neck and decided that maybe they shouldn't be watching this. She turned off the set with the remote and sat with him, feeling and tasting the oppressive silence as if it were the very air, rendered so thick that every moment felt like an eternity spent underwater.

Some time later, her husband's hands released hers and went to the typepad.

do you want me to leave or do you think there's any future for us

She didn't know. She didn't know but she thought of her husband in better times, that strong man, that smiling man, that occasionally petulant man, the man with the naughty streak who sometimes became the child who treated her as the authority figure who mischief needed to be hidden from. She remembered him pulling one form of foolishness or another, peering at her out of the corners of his eyes to see whether she thought it maddening or funny. She remembered the shape of his head in the middle of the night, when the lights were out and it was too dark to see him as anything but silhouette, when he was awake and looking at her, not knowing that she was awake and looking at him, this shadow of him that was to her every bit as revealing as his features viewed in the full light of day, because she knew him and could fill in the darkness. She remembered what it was like to let him know with a touch that she was awake too, and how sometimes that led to whispers and sometimes to more. She remembered his lips, his teeth, his touch, his gentleness and his passion. She remembered sometimes not letting him know that she was awake, instead just continuing to feign sleep, and thinking that this was her man and her lover and her friend and someday the father of her children. She remembered, once, feeling so proud to have won him that her heart could have burst.

say something

She didn't know if there was anything to say. That was the thing. She didn't know but she was proud. She was proud and she didn't want to be the one to fail. She knew that it didn't speak well of her that this remained the chief motivating force in her current relationship with what had become of her husband, the stubborn refusal to be the one who failed; to be driven not so much by an instinctive, unquestioning need to support him in what he had become, but the drive to be the better one, the strong one, the one who did the right things and held on when it might have been easier to just be the bitch who gave up. Maybe, she thought, that was the way back; not through love, but a fierce, unyielding pride. Maybe if she could stoke that, the other would return. But how could she, when it was so much more than she could make herself give?

Bob's hands had gone back to typing.

becks, i lied

She looked at them, and perceived something ineffably tense about the way they sat against the typepad. "About what?"

whatever happens i need you to know that i remember more than i told you. its worse than the news reports say, its dirtier and bloodier and nowhere near as simple. it's the kind of place that makes you forget that theres any good anywhere in the world. its why so many of us choose to forget. but i backed myself up for the last time only two days before the attack. i remember everything terrible that happened to me over there, everything terrible i did. afterward when they downloaded me they gave me a choice of keeping it all or going back to some earlier recording. i almost threw out the whole damn war. but i decided to keep it all because i had to.

She stared. "Why?"

the only thing worth remembering about any of it was how much of it i spent wanting to return to you

That, at long last, destroyed her. For the first time since his return she gave in to her sense of loss and howled. She buried her face in her hands and didn't see her husband's hands disengage from the typepad or return to the couch. But she did feel the weight of them on her shoulders, the strength they still had when they squeezed her there, the gentleness they still showed as the index fingers brushed the tear-tracks from her cheeks.

She found his touch both familiar and alien in some ways, like he had never left; in others, like he was a stranger, returned from a war with nothing but gall and a vague resemblance to seduce the widow with dire lies of being the man who had left. She missed the weight of him, the solidity, the sound of his breath. And she still hated the cold feel of the metal attachments at the ends of his wrists, so much like chains. But for the first time she was able to feel the presence of the boy she had fallen in love with, the man she had married, the husband who had been with her at night. It was him; against all odds, at long last, it was him. And for the first time, irrationally, she wanted him.

She told him she needed a minute, and went to the bathroom, where she ran water over her face, damned her red nose and puffy eyes, and made herself presentable, or at least as presentable she could. She knew that it was not the best time. She was terrified, a wreck. From what he'd typed, he wasn't much better. But there would never be a best time, not if she just kept waiting for it. In life, there were always thresholds that had to be crossed, whenever they could be, if only because that was the only way to get to whatever awaited on the other side.

When she had done everything that was possible she returned, kissed her husband's hands, and carried what was left of him to bed. After she undressed and got under the covers, his hands hesitated, with a sudden shyness that was almost possible to find endearing, then slipped under the covers themselves, and crawled through the darkness to her side, one heading north and the other heading south. The sheets rustled, and she allowed herself one last analytical thought: how lucky she was, after all, to have him come back as a pair of hands, and not as some useless strip of flesh in a sealed silver box. How very much they'd been left with.

She closed her eyes, grew warm, and let her husband love her.

REMEMBRANCE

BETH BERNOBICH

—◆—

March 10th was too early for planting, too early (almost) for anything but raking away the detritus of winter. Kate didn't care. She had promised herself a gardening session this weekend. After a month of long hours in the lab, poring over chip schematics, it would do her good to grub about in the dirt.

Clouds streaked the sky overhead, promising rain within a few hours. Ignoring them, Kate removed the sheets of canvas from the old beds. She scooped the layer of mulch into the wheelbarrow handful by handful, then cleared away the twigs and leaves. The debris would make good compost, along with the deadwood from the peach and pear trees. Good thing she'd invested in the shredder.

A cool breeze fingered her hair. She rubbed her forehead with the back of her wrist, and breathed in the soft ripe scent of spring. If the rain held off, she could finish clearing the beds and cut a new edge. Maybe even replace the old railroad ties with those old bricks she scavenged from the renovation project downtown. After picking through heaps of dark red and brown bricks, Kate had unearthed a jumble of dusky pinks from the old municipal office building, and a handful of aged golden bricks from a long-abandoned bank.

A soft chime sounded—her cell. Kate wiped her hands hastily on her jeans and dug the phone out from her workbasket. The caller ID blinked "Unknown." No visuals either, just a black shiny square with a question mark in the middle.

"Hey, babe."

Jessica. Of course. She was calling from a semi-restricted zone at work, which explained the ID and blank vid screen. "Hey, yourself. What's up?"

"Sorry I'm late. Something got in my way."

Kate suppressed a sigh. Over the past six years, she had learned to expect the holdups and delays and unexpected changes in plans that came with Jessica, but she had never learned to enjoy them. "What now?"

"We need to talk."

A breeze kicked up, making Kate shiver in her flannel shirt. "About what?"

"I got the promotion."

Oh, yes. The promotion. "But that's good—"

She broke off. Not good, clearly. Not when she could almost hear the tension in Jessica's breathing. "What's wrong?" she said carefully.

"Not over the phone," Jessica said. "I'll be there in half an hour."

Before Kate could say anything, even good-bye, her phone chirped to signal the end of call. Kate stared at the blank screen a moment before she returned it to her basket. She glanced at her newly cleared flowers beds, the neat stacks of brush and deadwood, the boxes of bricks waiting for her. She sighed and picked up her tools to wipe them clean.

An hour later, she had showered and changed clothes. Still no sign of Jess, though Thatcher's headquarters were just a few miles away in the city's new corporate complex. Kate made coffee, nibbled on a left-over biscuit, then began to pace. Talk. Jessica liked mysteries, she told herself. She just wanted to tease Kate, push her buttons. . . .

Jessica came through the front door, swinging her brief case. A few raindrops glittered in her dark brown hair, and her cheeks were flushed, as though she'd run the last few blocks. "Hey babe," she said as she dropped the briefcase. She followed up her words with a breezy kiss.

"Hey, yourself." Kate heard the odd combination of excitement and dread in Jessica's voice. Jessica wore her corporate uniform, she noticed—a dark gray suit with just a touch of flare to the skirt and discreet slits at the sleeves. Sexy and sleek and proper. Jessica called the look her Republican disguise. It made a good impression, she said, when she accompanied her superiors to government meetings.

Piecing together all the clues, Kate took a guess and asked, "What's the new assignment?"

Jessica flinched and laughed uneasily. "Smart girl, you. Yeah, I got the promotion, and it comes with a new assignment. Nice bump in pay, too."

Kate noticed that Jessica did not meet her gaze. "What's the catch?"

Another nervous glance, the briefest hesitation, before Jessica answered. "It's an off-site assignment. For the Mars Program. The government wants extra security specialists for their orbital transfer stations, and Thatcher won the main contract. We just got confirmation today. I'll be one of the unit supervisors on Gamma Station."

Kate had heard all about Gamma Station on the news. Alpha for Earth and Beta for the Moon, whose base had doubled in size during the past administration's watch. Now, after numerous delays, came Gamma, the first of the orbital transport stations that would serve as stepping stones toward the planned military base on Mars. Jessica had talked about nothing else these past three months.

"Just what you wanted," she said softly. "What else?"

Jessica smiled unhappily. "All the bad news at once, I see. Well, for one thing, it's a long assignment. Longer than usual."

"How long?"

Jessica smoothed back a wisp of hair that had escaped her braid. "Five years. They want continuity, they said. They're tired of retraining specialists every two years, and they want to cut back on expenses—especially with the draft up for debate." Her glance flicked up to meet Kate's. "But I have scheduled home visits built into the contract—twice a year—and bonuses for every month without any incidents. We could buy that house in New Hampshire."

We could get married, came the unspoken addendum. Even if only six states recognized that ceremony. And Kate did want that marriage, no matter how limited its legality, but Jessica's explanation skimmed over so much. Five years. Home visits were a week, no more. And *incident* was simply a euphemism for casualties. *My lover the mercenary,* she thought, unconsciously rubbing her hands together, as though to rid them of dirt.

"You accepted already," she said.

"Yes."

Rain clouds passed in front of the sun, momentarily darkening the living room, and a spattering of drops ticked against the windows. The room's auto lamps shimmered to on, but their light was colder, thinner than the sun's.

"I need to think about it," Kate said. "What it means."

Jessica nodded.

Another awkward paused followed.

"Would you like lunch?" Kate asked.

Jessica shook her head. "I'm sorry. I have a briefing this afternoon. That's the other thing you should know—I'm scheduled to leave in three weeks."

She knew, Kate thought. *She knew and didn't tell me.* Or maybe all that talk about Gamma was her way of warning Kate without saying anything outright.

"You better go," she said. "You don't want to be late."

They stared at one another a moment. Then Jessica caught up her brief case and vanished through the doors, leaving Kate standing in the empty living room.

In one sense, Kate's workbench at XGen Laboratories resembled her garden. The lab allotted her a well-defined, if limited, workspace that she kept scrupulously neat. And she had her rows of tools laid out just where she needed them—some old and familiar and worn by frequent use, some of them shiny with special purpose.

Kate peered at the display, adjusted the zoom level with a few keystrokes, and studied the display again, ignoring how her mask itched. The customer had requested extra QA for these chips, and a high sample count to ensure the best quality. It meant more profit for XGen, but a longer, more tedious day for Kate. Still, she usually found the work soothing, working step by step through the checklist of tests, and marking down the results for each in the entry system. Today, however . . .

She sighed, removed the chip from the spectrometer, and placed the next one in its slot. At the next bench, Anne and Olivia carried on a murmured conversation as they too worked through their allotment of gene-chips for the latest customer order. Anne tall and lean and brown, her dark abundant hair confined in a tight bun. Olivia short and skinny, with blonde spikes all over her head. The next row over, Aishia quietly argued politics with Stan and Marcel. Stan and Aishia had worked together for the past thirty years, and as far as everyone could tell, they had never once stopped arguing. Kate resisted the urge to ask them all for complete quiet, just this once.

In her distraction, she hit the wrong function key. Her system froze and blinked warnings at her. "Damn," she whispered. "Damn, stupid, damn, and damn it all again."

Anne looked up from her console. "What's wrong?"

"Nothing." Wearily, Kate punched in the key-combination to unlock the system, then went through the security codes again. XGen required several layers of identification, including fingerprint scans, these days. The clients liked that—no chance of hackers infiltrating the company and wreaking damage with sensitive products.

She noticed that Anne watched her with obvious concern. Kate shook her head. Anne was a good friend, but Kate didn't want to talk about Jessica, or the new assignment, or how they were almost fighting, but not quite.

Her system blinked a message, recognizing Kate. To her relief, it had not ditched her current entry. With a few more keystrokes, she resumed entering test codes and their results for the next chip. Concentrate on the screen and the analyzer, she told herself. Not on Jessica, who had returned late and left early, without giving Kate a chance to discuss the damned assignment. *As if discussing it would change anything,* Kate thought bitterly. She paused and drew a slow breath that did nothing for the tightness in her chest. *I should be used to it by now.*

Or not. They had never gone through the long separation most mercenary partners endured. Jessica's first few assignments had lasted only a few months apiece. The longest—a twelve month stint on the moon—had included frequent time downside. Kate had almost let herself believe that things would continue the same.

But no, terrorists didn't care about her loneliness, nor about keeping to convenient borders, such as the Middle East or selected regions in Asia. They traveled to New York and London these days. They were here, in New Haven. And now the stars.

The government draft had proved unpopular, and so private companies filled the void. In the bright new world of post Iraq, there would always be work for a smart, brave warrior like Jessica. The money was good, the benefits even better, if you didn't mind the ache of separation. And as Jessica pointed out, these companies hardly cared about her politics or her sex life. They only asked her to be dependable and discreet.

I hate it.

"Hey, Kate."

It was Anne, peering at her over the top of her console. A tiny frown made a crease between her brows.

"What's up?" Kate asked. "Problem with the spectral unit?" The new equipment had not proved quite as flawless as the salesperson claimed.

"Always," Anne said dryly. "But for once, it's not about work. Olivia and I were talking about going out tonight with Remy and some others. Maybe grabbing a bite at the new Indian restaurant, then see what's playing at the York Square. Cordelia and her husband might show up."

"I don't know . . . " She didn't think Jessica would like a night out, not with things so tense. Or then again, maybe a night out would help. "Let me check with Jessica."

She punched in the speed code and waited. And waited. After a dozen chimes, the phone switched her over to voice mail. Kate clicked phone shut. If Jessica were in Thatcher's high-security zones, she would have no cell access. She closed her eyes and rubbed her forehead to cover the disappointment. *Think of it as practice,* she thought, *for when Jess is really gone.*

"No luck?" Anne asked.

"Busy," Kate said. Which in a way was true. "I guess you're stuck with just me."

Anne smiled. "Hey, I don't mind."

The lab cleared out within minutes of the five o'clock chimes. But they would all be working overtime tomorrow, Kate thought, as she skinned out of her lab suit and into jeans and a T-shirt. She ran her fingers though the curls and tried to revive them. The mask always left her hair a mess.

"You look fine," Anne told her.

"Liar," Kate said.

Olivia was repairing her makeup, while Aishia recapped her argument with Stan. "He thinks with his balls," she muttered. "The right one. That accounts for his idea that God made guns so we can blow up our neighbors."

"Seems like they're blowing us up, too," Olivia said as she applied eyeliner. "Ask Remy. Her brother was on that bus in DC with the suicide kid."

"He's alive."

"Barely. A lot of others aren't."

Olivia and Aishia continued bickering as they left the lab and passed through the corporate security into the gated parking lot. Remy waited outside the parking lot, leaning against a dented lemon-yellow VW. Olivia broke off in mid-argument and waved cheerily.

"Who else is driving?" Anne said. "I took the bus today."

"Me," Aishia said. "If you don't mind the mess."

"That's fine. Kate?"

Kate barely heard them. She had sighted another familiar figure through the fence.

Jessica. She came here even without me calling.

A very jittery Jessica, to be sure, dressed even more formally than usual—all dark gray and ivory, with polished nickel studs in her ears that winked every time she swung her head. "Hey, girl. Hungry?" she called out.

"Ravenous," Kate called back. She hurried through the security procedures—ID card presented to the guard, palm against the reader, the retinal scan unit. When the gate clicked open, she ran through and into a hug from Jessica.

"Time off for good behavior," Jessica murmured. "Come on. I'm starved for some decent Italian food."

They retired to a diner a few blocks away on Chapel Street. Jessica ordered an extra large helping of everything, but when her dishes arrived, she fiddled with her salad, and picked at the heap of calamari. Kate watched in silence, her own appetite slowly draining away.

"What's wrong?" she asked softly.

Jessica shrugged. "You mean, besides the usual?"

Kate nodded.

Jessica stabbed a piece of lettuce with her fork. "I hate us fighting. I hate going away for weeks and months and years. But it's what I do. And it's better for you and everyone else that my job is out there and not right here in New Haven."

"I know," Kate said quietly. "I'm sorry."

"Don't be. You didn't say anything wrong. It's just a bitch, the whole thing. So I was thinking—"

She broke off and ate rapidly for a few moments, while Kate waited, breathless, for her to continue that tantalizing sentence.

Jessica pushed her plate away and wiped her mouth with a nervous flick of the napkin. "I had another briefing," she said. "Thatcher's R&D department is testing a new device, something XGen prototyped for us last year. Do you remember?"

Kate shook her head. XGen was small, but its R&D department kept to itself. QA usually saw new products only after the customer had okayed the prototypes.

"Anyway," Jessica went on, "there's a new chip, and they want me and some others as test candidates. It's for recording sensory input from a soldier's body. Sight. Touch. Smell. Even sub-vocals. Actually, I already volunteered for the implant and . . . I was hoping you would, too."

"What?" Her own meal forgotten, Kate stared at Jessica. "Are you insane? Why would I volunteer for a Thatcher project?"

Jessica glanced away, her cheeks turning pink. "I thought . . . I'll be gone a long time, and I thought . . . We could use it for ourselves. It might make things easier."

Kate swallowed with some difficulty. "You're kidding."

"No, I'm not. What's the problem?"

How like Jessica to forget who else might view those recordings. "The review board," she managed to say.

"Oh, them." Jessica dismissed those concerns with an airy wave of her hand. "They read my emails and they censor my vids. I'm used to it."

But I'm not.

Jessica put down her fork and clasped Kate's hands. Hers were lean strong hands, callused from handling who knew what. Warm and gentle hands. Kate loved them. She didn't want to share them with anyone.

"You don't like it. I know," Jess said softly. "But do you understand?"

Reluctantly Kate nodded. "Yes. No. Of course I don't like it. But then, I don't like you going away."

"Neither do I. But Kate . . . Five years is a fucking awful long time. Even with the home visits. At least consider the idea. Please."

Kate released a sigh. "I will. Consider it, that is. I can't promise more."

Jessica squeezed her hands. "That's all I ask."

With spring's arrival came the soft soaking rains, interspersed by damp gray skies that echoed the mist rising from the warming earth. If the sun broke through a day here or there, Kate hardly noticed. She neglected her garden for Jessica's company, and avoided glancing at the calendar.

Last day, she thought, watching Jessica check over her gear. Jess wore a plain jumpsuit that announced its military purpose. Her train left at ten—one hour left. Now fifty-nine minutes. Now—

"Check and double-check," Jessica said, straightening up with a grunt. "Damn. I'm getting old for this shit. Just as well they only allow us two bags."

Two modest bags, stuffed with books and off-duty clothes and several mementos from Kate, all of them cleared by Thatcher's security regulations. Kate touched the implant at the base of her skull, the connection points hidden beneath her hair. The operation had taken more time than she expected—more than a day for the surgical procedure, another three days for recovery and training, with subsequent training sessions scheduled over the next few weeks.

"I miss you already," she said suddenly.

"Hey." Jessica pulled her into a hard hug. "I miss you, too. But let's not get ahead of ourselves. We still have an hour."

"Fifty-six minutes," Kate said into Jess's shoulder. "And no, we don't have time for one more . . . "

She felt Jessica shake with silent laughter. "I wish we did. Come on. Help me get this stuff into the car."

Kate's internal clock ticked down the minutes as they loaded bags into the car and drove to New Haven's newly renovated train station. A winding ramp brought them over the flood zone and into the parking garage. If you ignored the trash floating on the oily waves below, the view was breathtaking. The planners had taken that into account: the moving sidewalks and glass-paneled elevators showed only the Sound and the blurred outline of Long Island in the distance. Far below, the shoreline highway curved above the open water.

Jessica slung one bag over her shoulder. She swatted Kate away from the second bag. "Might as well get used to the weight now," she said. "In six days, they won't weigh anything at all."

Thirty minutes left. Twenty-three. Passing through station security took just a few moments at this hour. Kate and Jessica sat side-by-side on the platform bench, hands barely touching in this much too public area. At fifteen minutes, the train squealed into the station, filling the air with a sharp electric odor.

Jessica quickly squeezed Kate's hand. "Hey," she whispered. "It's time."

Not yet, Kate wanted to say, but she stood silently as Jessica gathered her two bags, then pulled out her e-card for the conductor. Seven minutes. Five. Three.

"Kate."

In that one word, Kate heard a tone in Jessica's voice that she never had before. "Hey," she said.

"Hey." Jessica leaned forward and kissed Kate firmly on the lips. Kate caught a whiff of Jessica's cinnamon perfume, a fainter one of her green tea shampoo. One brown strand fell from its braid and brushed against Kate's cheek. Jessica tucked the strand behind her ear. "Six months to the first visit," she whispered.

And then the clock ticked down to zero, and she was gone.

• • •

Throughout April and early May, Kate worked to undo the early neglect of her garden. She cleared out the weeds and repaired the old border. She added fresh mulch and compost, and with judicious watering, teased the roses and irises into luscious blooms. She even expanded the beds to include a small vegetable patch, which the deer promptly attacked.

At work, she had the impression that her friends and co-workers had divvied up watches over her. Singly and in groups, they took her out to lunch (Aishia, Anne, and once Stan), or invited her to the movies (Anne, Cordelia), or on shopping expeditions (Olivia, with or without Remy).

The constant invitations irritated her at first. Over the weeks, however, she learned to accept their well-meant attentions. It helped, after all, to distract her from counting the hours, days, and weeks, without Jessica. Even so, she found herself calculating Jessica's progress away. One day of train travel. Five more days to launch. Another month until Jessica arrived at Gamma Station.

Kate had allowed herself just one letter for each week, emailed to Jessica in care of Thatcher. Thatcher would screen the contents and forward the message via satellite to Gamma Station. Jessica had fired off one brief message before the launch. Since then nothing.

She's busy, Kate told herself. *Reviewing security procedures. Coordinating her crew assignments with others in Thatcher and the military. Handling any crises . . .*

No. Bad idea to think about crises. Better to concentrate on the mundane tasks of personnel records and fitness reports and all the other tedious paperwork Jessica always complained about.

She parked the car in the too-empty driveway and gathered briefcase and groceries from the back seat. Following an almost-predictable schedule, Anne had invited Kate to dinner, but Kate had refused, wanting one night to herself. Maybe she could download a vid, or eat too much popcorn, or do all the things other people talked about doing when they had the house to themselves.

Still mulling over her options, she unlocked the door and scooped up the mail from the carpet. Bills. Flyer from the local ACLU. Credit card offers. A small reinforced envelope with the return address: *Thatcher Security Operations*.

Jess. She wrote.

Kate abandoned everything else in the entryway. Her pulse dancing, she hurried into the living room. A letter. A long one. Even sooner than she expected. Jessica must have saved up her letters and transcribed them the moment she arrived at Gamma.

She took up a letter opener from the letters desk and slit the envelope carefully. Nothing. Perhaps the envelope's padded interior—made from a strange soft material—blocked the contents. She shook the envelope gingerly. A micro disc tumbled into her lap.

Kate drew a sharp breath. She recognized the disc from her training sessions. Reflexively, she touched the knob at the base of her skull. No one at work knew about this device. She had not dared to tell them, not even Anne. Aishia would lecture her about man-machine interfaces and their risks. Olivia would make jokes. Anne might say nothing, but Kate had learned to read her friend's subtle changes in expression. Whatever name you put on her reaction, it would not be a positive one.

The disc gleamed red in the late sunset. Kate touched its rim—a faint dull spot remained where her fingertip had rested. Damn. The technicians had warned her how sensitive these discs were. They had provided her with a supply of special cleaning fluid, along with admonitions about overusing the stuff.

Kate vented a breath, and carefully inserted the disc back into its envelope. Again she touched the knob. *Jess. Oh Jess. What are we doing?*

She took a few moments to put the groceries away—extending the anticipation, or avoiding the disc, she wasn't sure which. Then she climbed the stairs to the tiny office next to their bedroom. The Thatcher machine stood on her desk, in the corner behind stacks of books and papers and her gardening magazines, untouched since the Thatcher tech has installed it weeks ago.

Kate cleared away the magazines and sat down. Squinted at the machine. It looked like any piece of lab equipment—a low sleek ivory box with several touch pads labeled in red. A half dozen indicator lights ran along the top edge. These too were clearly marked. She skimmed a finger along the side and found the recessed slot for the discs.

You're stalling.

Damn straight, as Jessica would say.

A touch of the power switch, and the machine hummed into life, its lights blinking through a series of test patterns. Kate cleaned the micro disc, just as the technicians told her, then slid the disc into its slot. It clicked into place.

Now the tricky part.

She touched a side panel, which slid open to reveal the connector cable with its slim square terminator. She uncoiled the cable and brushed her hair away from the knob in her skull. The terminator and her own connector port would slide open together when oriented correctly and pressed together.

She felt the click reverberate through her bones. Her skin prickled and she felt faintly queasy. Psychosomatic, she told herself. She had done the same thing a hundred times in the training lab with no ill effects. She pressed the touch pad marked PLAY.

A pale green light blinked. Kate's vision went dark.

Hey, babe.

Kate heard, felt a cough.

Testing, one, two three . . .

Soft self-conscious laughter followed, with an echo soon after, as though Jess sat in a small enclosed space. Her cabin aboard the shuttle? With a shiver, Kate realized she felt heavy fabric encasing her arms and legs. The air smelled charged and faintly stale. She blinked, wishing she could see what Jessica saw. Thatcher had warned her she would get no visuals. The prototype could handle them, but her particular machine had that feature disabled. A matter of security, the tech had explained.

Hey.

Kate jumped at the sound of Jessica's voice next to her, inside her.

So, like. I guess this is working. Harder than vidding a message, but damn, after going through that operation, I might as well use the machine.

Pause. Kate felt her chest go tight. Was that her body's reaction, or Jessica's? Then she felt warm breath leaking between tense lips. A subdued laugh. The words, *Hey, babe. I miss you. Later.*

Without warning, the machine clicked, and Kate's vision returned so abruptly, she swayed from the vertigo. If she closed her eyes, she could still feel the weight of Jess's pressure suit, still taste the shuttle's recycled air. *Hey, babe,* she thought. *Don't make it too much later.*

After some procrastination, Kate recorded a brief reply, using the same disc Jessica sent her. She wished she could keep the recording to play later, but Thatcher had insisted on their return. Proprietary materials, the security manager had explained.

It took her several tries before she was satisfied. Jessica had had it right—making the recording was far more difficult than reading one. What to say? How to react, when every sensation impressed itself onto that tiny disc, to be reviewed by Thatcher research and security personnel?

In the end, Kate recorded a brief description of her garden, one of the roses in her palm, where its velvet-soft petals tickled her skin. *Later,* she whispered, and tapped END RECORD.

Jessica sent three more recordings over the next six weeks, all of them brief, all of them ending with a whisper-soft kiss. She supplemented those with longer text messages forwarded from Thatcher by email. Kate found the longer messages more frustrating than the brief micro-recordings. More than once, Thatcher's censors had deleted apparently random sections of text, badly garbling Jessica's meaning. Kate was tempted to add something inflammatory, but she restrained herself. Thatcher might not care about personal lives, but they were as humorless as any federal spooks. Still, the thought that Thatcher observed their correspondence bothered her. You might think that some aspects of life were private, she thought. Even now, even in these days of constant surveillance and the uneasy comprises between freedom and security.

And so, the weeks rolled from spring into summer. One hot July evening, Kate parked her car in the driveway far later than usual—XGen had another rush order from a government super-contractor.

Muzzy from the long hours in the lab, she had thoughts only of dinner and cold tea, and when she picked up the mail from the carpet, she almost didn't register the envelope from Thatcher.

Then recognition clicked into place. Not just another envelope, but one with a disc. Dinner could wait, she thought. She hurried upstairs to her office and slid the disc into the machine. The terminator plug clicked into place, and the familiar black-brown veil dropped over her vision . . .

Hey, lover. Something new this time.

A warm hand pressed against Kate's (Jessica's?) breast. Kate drew a sharp breath as she realized that Jessica wore no clothing. What was she thinking? What about Thatcher—

The hand slid over her breast, cupped the flesh a moment and squeezed, making Kate gasp. No time wasted. The hand skimmed over her belly, and paused briefly to cover her sex. Possession, said that gesture. Kate felt the doubled warmth from her body and Jessica's at the same time. She had just time to muffle a gasp of pleasure when three fingers plunged into her vagina, slid out, and pinched the clitoris with practiced skill. Heat blossomed outward, upward. Their nipples contacted to hard painful points. The fingers plunged deeper inside. And again, but faster, more urgent. Kate's, (Jessica's) breath went ragged as she panted, *Oh, god . . . yes . . . oh . . . my . . .*

Kate's office blinked into existence.

She leaned against the desk, shivering in spite of the July warmth. Her groin ached from half-fulfilled passion, and a ripe musky scent filled the air. Very faint, almost like a memory, she could still smell a trace of Jessica's favorite perfume.

Too much. Not enough. I can't stand it.

Kate reached up to remove the terminator from her skull. Her hands shook. Deep inside, her muscles tensed, rippled, stretched, as though pleading for release. She paused and licked her lips. Slowly she reached for PLAY again.

For three days, she wavered on how to reply. She wished (again) she could keep a copy of Jessica's recording. She wished she could keep her response private. Neither was possible. Nor could she send back a simple text message. In the end, she closeted herself in the office with a glass of chilled Pouilly Fuissé and a tightly held memory of Jessica's recording.

She shucked off her T-shirt and jeans. Slid her panties over her hips and let them drop onto the floor. Though she had no audience, not even a virtual one, Kate tried to act as though she did. It would put her into the mood for what she had planned.

Perfume over her breast, at the base of her throat, behind her knees. Blinds tilted just so to let in the sunlight, but keep the room private. She had thought about lying on the floor, except the cord didn't reach far enough. She would have to make do with her office chair and her imagination.

Kate inserted the terminator, then drank a long slow swallow of wine. As an afterthought, she rolled the wine glass over her bare skin. The cold wet surface raised a trail of goose bumps that made her shiver with anticipation. She pressed her left hand over her mons. Warm and damp already. It was as though she only needed to think of Jessica, to have her body respond.

She touched RECORD.

Hey, babe. Here's something for you.

We are a duet, Jessica whispered time and again. *My fingers burrow through my pubic hair, twice over. Once with me, making me shake with desire, once with you, Kate. I'm soaked, a puddle of want. Want you. Now, girl. In and out. Again. More. Now I trail the wetness up between my breasts and paint myself with cum.*

Whatever Jessica said, Kate heard weeks later. Whatever Jessica did—how her fingers pinched Kate's nipples, how her tongue licked wet fingers and tasted her smoky climax—repeated itself in Kate's lonely office.

You are my succubus, Kate whispered back. *You take me as a ghost would, by invading my mind. As I do with you, my love. As I do with you.* She crushed her mouth against her hand, and slid the new vibrator into her own vagina. Her lips closed hard around the silky shaft. An electric pulse gripped her clitoris and rippled through her belly, up her spine. Fireworks. Hot and dazzling. She threw back her head and cried out.

• • •

Over the next three months, Kate and Jessica exchanged recordings every week. Jessica sent text messages twice a week, long rambling letters about the insipid food, the jokes her crew made, the techniques she and others used to make life in tight quarters more bearable. *Like our little not-so-secret,* she said once.

Kate disliked Jessica's jokes about their situation, but she understood them. She read on as Jessica described more about the implants.

It's a clever little toy, Jessica wrote. *Thatcher wants to run more tests once they develop their high-capacity modules, but the basic technology works. It even has a few tricks the technicians didn't tell us at first. Remember the discs and how we have to record over them? Well, the chip has a smidge of memory itself, and if you press PLAY three times fast, then hold down PROGRAM and RECORD together, you can store a few moments in the chip and replay it later. Here's how . . .*

Saturday. Kate knelt and surveyed her garden. A lush rainy summer had produced more squash and beans and tomatoes than she could give away. Now, as the season drifted into autumn, she busied herself with preparing the beds for winter.

"How much mulch do you actually need?" Anne asked. "And could you make a tongue-twister from that question?" She had volunteered to help Kate with the day's work. Later, they would go to a neighborhood rummage and art festival. Aishia had promised to join them.

"All the mulch," Kate answered, ignoring the question about tongue-twisters. "They say we'll have a colder winter than usual. Unless you think we should dig up all those bulbs . . . "

"Don't," Anne said quickly.

Kate grinned. "Thought not."

They set to work, Anne digging up weeds and Kate mixing the soil and compost. Kate had acquired a new supply of micro-insulating fabric that claimed a fifty-percent improvement over other materials. If she alternated mulch with the fabric, she might get away with keeping even the tulips in the ground.

"I always wished I had a garden," Anne said. "Though I'm not very good at keeping the plants alive. Where did you hear about the colder winter?"

"Almanac. Good old-fashioned almanac. Though this one is online."

Anne laughed. "And here I thought we were high-tech."

More than you know, Kate thought. She had not confided in anyone, not even Anne, about the experimental implants. *A private matter,* she thought. *As private as Thatcher allows.*

They dispatched the latest weed crop and started on splitting the lilies, which had multiplied since last year. It was easier with a friend, Kate thought, and the work soothed as nothing else could. She could almost forget the constant ache in her chest that had begun with Jessica's departure. *My garden, my refuge,* she thought as she set another bulb back into the ground. These days, even her garden seemed a less a refuge than before. Prices climbing. The shrill debates in Congress and blogs. The noisy protests at universities.

A brisk knock sounded at the front door, followed by the faint chimes of the doorbell. Kate dusted off her hands. "If that's Aishia, she's early," she said. "Unless she wants to help with covering the beds."

Anne smoothed dirt over another planting. "It might be Olivia. She said something about dropping by."

"With or without Remy?"

Anne grimaced. "Without."

Their latest and loudest quarrel showed no signs of ending. Kate could not remember when she'd last seen Remy's lemon-yellow Bug waiting outside XGen's parking lot. "Do you think it's serious this time?"

"Who knows?"

Another knock echoed through the crisp, new-autumn air. Louder. Clearly impatient. Definitely not Aishia or Olivia. "Coming," Kate called out.

She heard a man's voice. Several, talking amongst themselves. Dominionists? Surely they had learned their lesson after Jessica's pointed lecture. She gave up on scrubbing the dirt from her hands and hurried around the brick path that led through the side flower beds, into the front yard.

Three men stood on her front porch. She took in their gray suits, their humorless expressions. All of them middle-aged. All of them bland and competent, in the way she associated with bureaucrats.

"Ms. Morell?" one said. "Ms. Kate Morell?"

Her skin prickled with sudden dread. "Yes. I'm Kate Morell. Can I help you?"

He came forward and extended a hand. "I'm from Thatcher Enterprises, ma'am," he said. "I'm very sorry, but I have bad news for you. It's about Ms. Anderson."

I don't want to know. I don't. I don't.

"Go away," she said thickly.

"Ma'am."

"I mean it."

Anne hurried to Kate's side. "Kate. Maybe we should go inside."

Kate shrugged away from Anne's tentative touch, but she knew Anne was right. She could not stop them from telling her. Today. Tomorrow. Either she'd hear the news from these gray grim men, or she'd learn the details from the evening newscast. Better she heard it here, now, under the open sunny sky. "Fine. Tell me what happened."

With a glance at his companions, the man complied. Thatcher had sent their best people, ones trained to deliver their news in soft, concerned voices. Numb, and growing number, Kate listened to how terrorists had infiltrated another security firm's personnel. One, the suicide bomber, had assembled his deadly cargo during a brief stopover on the station. Moments before their shuttle was to launch for the next segment of their journey, he had detonated his bomb. Everything destroyed. All personnel dead. The method was old, as old as Iraq and Palestine and all the troubled countries on Earth.

"Nothing left," she whispered.

The Thatcher man hesitated. "I'm sorry, but no. They're salvaging whatever they can, but the explosion scattered . . . " His voice died away a moment, undoubtedly as he realized what images his words called up. "We have something for you, however."

Kate came alert. "What do you mean? You said—"

"A final transmission," he said. "You can refuse, of course. We've edited them for any sensitive material . . . "

He held out a packet. Kate took it greedily. "How much time do I have? For listening?"

Another awkward pause. "The company understands how difficult—"

"The company," Kate said crisply, "understands nothing. How much time?"

The man stiffened at her tone. "We would prefer you return the machine next week. Monday, if possible. We can schedule an operation later to remove the implant."

She nodded. "Very well. Now, please go."

To her relief, the three did not argue. Kate watched them ease their anonymous gray vehicle from the curb. The packet felt solid and heavy in her arms, like an anchor, which was good, because she had the sense of floating a few inches above the ground. Anne had not budged from her side, and Kate could sense her concern.

"Anne."

"Yes, Kate."

"Please go. I'd rather be alone."

"Are you sure—"

"Quite sure."

Anne hesitated, then with a murmured farewell, she too was gone.

A brief recording. The last ever.

Hey, Kate. Kate, my love. Kate, my darling lover. Good god in heaven, I miss you. I'm going a little crazy up here. Guess you could tell from that session. Ya think? Not sure what kind of notation they'll make in my fitness report, but what the hey. They asked for a peek inside my skull.

A shaky laugh. A pause. Kate felt and heard Jessica's breathing quicken. Was it a prelude to sex? So hard to tell. For all that the recording slipped Kate inside Jessica's skin, it showed her nothing of her lover's thoughts or emotions. Only clues, pieced together in retrospect.

I miss you, Jessica said suddenly. *It's busy here. We're having another meeting this afternoon. Commander wants tighter security. Can't say more, of course. It's just . . .*

Kate felt warm lips pressed against her fingertips, then those same fingertips brushed against her cheek. Her vision blurred from brown-black shadows into the dim light of her office.

One last kiss, she thought. The last one.

She closed her eyes and let the grief take over.

She called in sick on Monday. No one questioned her. Probably Anne had warned their supervisors about the situation. Kate croaked a mirthless laugh. *Situation.* What a weasel word, as Jessica would say. As bad as *incident.*

Her throat caught on another sob. *Sorry,* she thought. *I have no more tears. I cried them all away.*

She poured herself another cup of coffee. Drank it without noticing. Her stomach hurt, but she couldn't tell if it hurt because she had cried too hard, or if she was simply hungry. She sighed and with great reluctance, she climbed the stairs to her office.

The machine sat in the middle of her empty desk. Around midnight on Saturday, she had nearly pitched the damned thing into trash. Only the thought of how much fuss Thatcher would make had stopped her. Now she stared at it with loathing.

I hate you. You gave me ghosts.

Ghosts of Jessica. Ghosts of an ersatz marriage, while they waited out yet another interminable period, for yet another intangible bit of progress. Even as she hated the machine, she found herself sliding the disc into its slot and inserting the terminator into its port.

. . . Hey, Kate. I miss you . . .

She hardly needed the machine to replay that sequence inside her memory, but the machine and chip combined to give her a more vivid remembrance, with details of touch and scent and sound she could never recall on her own.

. . . the chip has a smidge of memory itself, and if you press PLAY three times fast . . .

Kate swallowed against the bitter taste in her mouth. Make some coffee, she told herself. Wake up before you do something truly stupid.

She touched PLAY three times fast, followed by PROGRAM and

RECORD together. Counted to ten. A series of lights blinked success. Kate let out a breath. There. She had done it. One last kiss. Saved . . . Not forevermore, but for a short while, at least.

She called Thatcher at noon. By mid-afternoon, they had carried away the machine. One representative stayed behind to schedule Kate's operation to remove the implant.

"Later," Kate said.

"I'm afraid that later isn't one of the categories," the woman said with a rueful smile. "We need a more definite date."

"Next year," Kate said. "Or is that too definite?"

At the woman's shake of her head, however, she relented. "November 21st. From what your technicians tell me, I will need one day for the operation, another three or four in recovery. That means sick leave or vacation time—depending on how my HR department categorizes the operation. Whatever. My project has a few unmovable deadlines before mid-November. I'm sure you understand."

"We do," said the woman. She tapped a few keys on her cell, frowned, tapped a few more. "Yes, we can arrange something on that date. You'll spend Thanksgiving in the hospital, but I'm sure you knew that."

Kate smiled faintly. "Yes, I knew that."

Late November. A dark cold Tuesday evening.

Tomorrow Kate would drive to Thatcher Operations. There, a technician would review the paperwork, ask her some final questions. The company surgeons would inject her with a sedative, then transport her to Yale-New Haven Hospital, where they had scheduled the operation. All very neat. No security leaks. No chance for medical mishaps. Kate had signed all the releases beforehand.

"Will I remember anything?" she had asked.

"Nearly," the technician had reassured her.

The technician had it wrong, Kate thought, as she drifted out the back door, into her winter-bare garden. If she had her druthers, she would remember . . .

. . . *nothing at all.*

She sank onto the hard frosted ground at the edge of her garden. Sheets of micro-insulation blanketed half the beds, where she had made a last attempt at normal life. The other half lay bare, with brittle stalks of dead plants poking through the dirt. One shriveled lily bulb lay where she'd left it that Saturday. Dead. Her breath puffed into a cloud. Just like Jessica. She probed inside her heart for some reaction—grief, anger, anything. Nothing. *Dead like me,* she thought.

By now she could trigger the memory without thinking. Sensation washed over her. That same familiar sense of urgency. The words *I miss you.* Kate rubbed the spot where she still felt the impress of warm lips against her hand, Jessica's hand. *She's inside me. Always will be. Doesn't matter if they rip the implant from my brain.*

Her chest felt tight, or was that Jessica's tension as she hurried through that last recording? Kate drew a shuddering breath. Blinked, and felt her frozen eyelashes prick her cheeks. The words *I miss you.* The kiss, but now her hands were numb, and she barely felt Jess's lips. *Again,* she told herself.

She had lost track of the minutes and hours when she heard a voice. A familiar one, but not Jessica's.

Go away, she thought.

The voice called out her name. A hand jostled her shoulder. Kate closed her eyes. Nothing to see anyway. The world had gone brown and black, with pinpoints of silver. In her imagination, the pinpoints whirled around, stopped, whirled again. She thought she saw the outline of Jessica's face when they paused. All too soon the image broke apart. *Show me again,* she tried to whisper, but her lips were cracked and frozen, her tongue clumsy from disuse.

Again that insistent voice. Anne's voice (good, kind, generous Anne) speaking to her, her tone anxious. It was hard to track time, here between repetitions of Jessica's last recording, and so it might have been minutes or days later when more hands took hold of Kate's arms. Voices spoke over her head in short phrases.

Careful now.

Gurney ready?

IV for this one.

Oxygen, too. Gotta bring the core temperature up.

Lucky the streets aren't slick.

We better hurry.

And then the thin, high wail of a siren.

Six o'clock.

Soft chimes marked the hour. Outside, night already blacked out the skies. A dull yellow glow from the city lights seeped upward from the horizon. Winter. Even colder than the almanac had predicted, Kate thought. The air had an antiseptic smell, no matter how the nurses tried to hide it with sweet-smelling sprays.

Footsteps sounded from the corridor, then, predictably, a light tapping at her door. She said nothing. Anne would come in, or not, just as she had every day for the past three weeks.

The door swung open, and Anne leaned around the corner. Snow dusted her coat. Her cheeks were red, as though she had spent some time outdoors.

"Hey," she said softly. "Do you mind a visit?"

Kate shrugged, silent.

Anne sighed and came into the room. Kate watched her methodically unbutton her coat and hang it from the hook inside the door. A nurse peered into the room and greeted Anne, before asking Kate which meal she preferred for dinner.

"I don't care," Kate whispered. "You choose for me."

Anne frowned. She and the nurse exchanged a look. "What about the steak?" Anne said. "Or maybe the pasta—I hear the cook knows his sauces."

Good, kind, patient Anne, who never once failed to visit Kate. She had stayed at the hospital while the doctors worked to counteract the hypothermia. She came the next day when they removed the implant, and she dealt with Thatcher's representatives. Not that Anne told Kate these things. It was Cordelia or Olivia or the others who told Kate how Anne had saved her life.

As if I wanted my life saved.

But even irritation was too much effort. She sighed again and closed her eyes. She had developed the trick of pretending to sleep. If she held the pose long enough, she often did. She heard whispers as Anne evidently spoke with the nurse about Kate's meal. The door clicked shut. There was a scraping sound as Anne took her usual seat by the window.

"I stopped by your house," Anne said, just as though they were having an ordinary conversation. "Cordelia reminded me that you never had a chance to finish prepping your garden for the winter. I asked at one of the garden centers, and they gave me some suggestions."

Kate suppressed the urge to ask what suggestions. She felt a prick of guilt about her gardens, then annoyance that she felt guilty.

Meanwhile, Anne continued her recitation. " . . . Cordelia and I raked the yard. We trimmed back the shrubs and vines and ran those through the shredder. We even cleaned out the compost heap and finished covering the flower beds."

Kate's eyes burned with unshed tears. Only Anne would remember how much Kate loved her gardens. But what good were gardens in the winter? What good were gardens if you were alone?

" . . . Olivia and Remy came by to help, too. I don't know if I told you, but they've made up and now they're talking about finding a house together . . . "

Tears leaked from her eyes. Surprising after weeks of numbness. She swiped them away.

"Kate?"

A tiny stab in the region of her heart. Insistent. Unwelcome. "No," Kate whispered. "I don't want to." Then louder. "No. No, no, no."

Her voice scaled up, louder and louder, until her voice cracked, and she burst into weeping—loud angry sobs that tore at her throat. Kate pummeled the bed, trying to beat away the grief. She didn't want tears. Or misery. None of that could bring Jessica back.

Arms gathered her into a tight hug. Anne. Anne capturing her hands so they could not scratch or beat or harm herself. Anne strong and gentle at the same time, who rocked Kate back and forth while she held her close. "I'm sorry. I'm sorry," she murmured over and over. "I said the wrong things. All the wrong things. I'm so sorry, Kate. So sorry."

"I hate it," Kate mumbled into Anne's shoulder.

"You should hate it," Anne said fiercely. "Hate me, if you like. Hate the world. I'd rather you did, than feel nothing. Oh god, Kate, I wish I could do something *real*. I wish—"

She broke off and pulled away from Kate. Shocked, Kate felt her own grief subside for the moment. Only now did she take in details she had not noticed before. How Anne's cheeks were wet with tears. And her eyes were red, as though she had not slept well the past few weeks. But Anne never wept, she thought, never lost her temper. She was the even keel they all depended upon.

"Anne?"

Anne wiped her eyes with the back of her hand. "Sorry. That was selfish of me."

No, I'm the selfish one, Kate thought.

A knot deep inside her flexed, as though an unused muscle tried to work itself loose. Instinctively she reached up and touched Anne's face. Anne flinched. Her eyes went wide and dark, and color spread over her cheeks. So many tiny clues, like droplets of watering coalescing into realization.

"How long?" Kate whispered.

"Does it matter?" Anne blew out a breath. "I should go."

"No. Stay."

They stared at one another for a long uncomfortable moment. Snow tapped against the window pane, and out in the corridor, a light sizzled and popped.

"What are you saying?" Anne said at last.

The knot inside Kate pinched tight. Too fast. Too soon. Far too soon for anything. She'd spoken before thinking.

"I'm not sure. I—I need a friend."

A ghost-like smile came and went on Anne's face. "I make a decent friend, they tell me."

So she did. Even to selfish wretches like Kate.

A person did not heal within a day or month. Often not for years, Kate thought, wiping more tears from her eyes. And yet, watching Anne's quiet patient face, Kate felt as though she could breathe properly for the first time in a month. They could be friends. Good ones. More, if time and healing allowed them.

Not yet.

She could almost hear Anne's voice reassuring her, saying, *It's okay. It doesn't matter. I'm here for you.*

Unexpectedly, warmth brushed against her cheek—not a recording but a memory. Jessica.

"Hey," she said to Anne. "Tell me more about my garden. Tell me what it looks like these days. What it smells like. Tell me—" She drew a deep breath and felt the knot inside ease a fraction. "Tell me everything."

PALACE RESOLUTION

TOM PURDOM

———❖———

VinDu has always believed his responses to sensual pleasure are the best aspect of his personality structure. The founder of the TaiPark Combine believed the members of the governing class should be firmly bonded to their basic, biological humanity. The Overseers of the TaiPark Combine, Tai-Park concluded, should be endowed with an obsession with physical pleasure.

Let the rulers treasure their senses, Tai-Park decreed. *Let the love of pleasure moderate the love of virtue.*

Now VinDu reaches across the edge of his bath pond and rests his hand on the knee of the concubine sitting next to it. Warm scented water softens his muscles. A bottle and three plates sit on a side table.

At the end of the bath pond, an image of another woman rests in a recliner that is covered with a velvety fabric. A slim man stands behind the recliner and kneads the woman's shoulders. The woman is named KaiDin. She is speaking the formal synthetic language the Overseers have developed for their internal communications. She has just told VinDu she bears him no ill will.

"You made the decisions you had to make," KaiDin says. "As we all do."

"It was still a heavy day for both of us," VinDu says.

KaiDin raises the goblet in her right hand. She takes a long sip. "We are what we are, VinDu."

• • •

VinDu had emphasized KaiDin's special personality when he instructed the arrest posse. "You'll be armed with painless, short duration anesthetic loads," he had told the four proteges he had recruited for the posse. "You should fire at the first sign KaiDin is attempting to resist. Do not hesitate. Do not think you can predict her reactions. You are dealing with someone who is significantly different from us."

KaiDin's personality structure was a response to a long-term problem. In the last hundred years there had been a drift in the genetic and post-natal cultivation of the Overseer class. Their drive to fulfill their duties had weakened and their tendency to seek comfort and safety had increased. KaiDin had been the first product of a cautious attempt to reverse the trend. She was a throwback to a long-gone era—a time when the first Overseers had turned Anmei into the capital of a polity that had transformed five hundred asteroids into thriving cities.

VinDu knew he was moving very fast, with very little preparation. He had confirmed that KaiDin was plotting insurrection just three hours before she would present him with his best opportunity to take her into custody. If he waited any longer, she would notice her senior concubine was missing—and realize she had probably been betrayed.

VinDu split up the posse and had them follow different routes when they walked to the Garden of a Thousand Fountains. In the Gallery of Eternal Sunlight, he bestowed smiles and friendly nods on the tourists who realized they were actually looking at a current member of the Eleven Cultivated Overseers. In the Grove of Tranquility he picked two of the more obscure trails.

The authors of a thousand guides all agreed that Anmei was one of the loveliest cities in the asteroid belt. Visit Anmei if you possibly can, the guides all asserted. You may have to spend decades on the waiting list but you won't be disappointed when your turn comes.

To VinDu, the city was touchable, visible proof that KaiDin was threatening one of the glowing achievements of the human species. Anmei was rich and beautiful because it was the home of a form of governance that had now survived three standard centuries. It was the capital of an empire in which three billion people lived under the benign rule of men and women who had been endowed with all the qualities a governing class should possess. "This is obviously a grave moment in the history of our polity," VinDu had told the four proteges. "This will be the first time an Overseer has invoked his emergency powers inside the capital itself. But this is also the first time an Overseer has decided she could force a decision on the rest of us. I am not taking action because I disagree with KaiDin's views on Revelation. I am invoking my emergency powers because KaiDin is attacking the orderly, agreed-upon procedures that form the foundation of our government."

KaiDin was lying in a public recliner when the four proteges lined up in front of her and drew their weapons. VinDu stood to one side with his richest official vestment draped across his shoulders. Water splashed around him. Birds flashed through the greenery. KaiDin visited the Garden of a Thousand Fountains twice every tenday, on the third and eighth days. She always entered the garden near the beginning of the thirteenth hour. She always came alone.

"This is a formal arrest," VinDu said. "I have assembled undeniable evidence that you are plotting insurrection. I have filed notice I am invoking my emergency powers."

He raised his voice and addressed the loudspeakers and cameras installed in the landscape. "I am placing Overseer KaiDin under arrest because she is conspiring to force Revelation on the combine. She has armed most of her proteges. She plans to take several Overseers prisoner and force them to vote for Revelation."

KaiDin rolled out of the recliner and positioned herself behind it. Thirty years ago, during his first term as an Overseer, VinDu had been the senior who had introduced KaiDin to the subtler aspects of sexual pleasure. He hadn't touched her since, but the trim balance of her body could still provoke the feelings she had stimulated the first time he noticed she had become a young woman.

A pair of agonized shrieks panicked the birds. Two proteges crumpled to the ground. Their backs arched in pain. The other two swung to the right and screamed before they could raise their weapons.

VinDu's head snapped around. Three figures were standing on a balcony that looked down on the garden.

The four proteges were sobbing as they writhed across the stubby yellow vines that carpeted this part of the garden. Two had started drooling.

KaiDin slipped a copper tube out of her jacket. She pointed it at VinDu's chest and he spread his arms to show her he had come to the garden without weapons.

Fire spread through his nervous system. A scream ravaged his throat. His fingers started clawing at the vines before his head touched the ground.

"We aren't playing, VinDu," KaiDin said. "This is the most serious issue the Overseers have ever confronted. We're prepared to inflict pains that are several times worse than the sensations you're feeling now."

The pain started ebbing after a few minutes. VinDu rose to his knees and discovered his four proteges were still stretched on the vines. He forced himself erect and fed his communications implant four subvocalized random syllables. A hooded face appeared in front of him.

"Launch," VinDu said.

"I have an order to launch. Please verify."

"I repeat—*launch*."

"I have initiated launch procedure. Shall I let it proceed?"

"Proceed."

"Launch is proceeding."

The four proteges were recovering their self-control. VinDu trotted toward an exit and they fell in around him.

"Don't blame yourselves," VinDu said. "It wasn't your fault. I should have realized she would have herself shadowed now that she's committed to revolt. Please stay with me now."

His voice sounded mild and even—the gentle speech pattern of a thoroughly rational personality. He had trained himself to talk that way and he was pleased to see he could maintain it when he was trying to control severe emotional stress.

"We have completed launch," the hooded face said. "All four missiles are enroute."

"Complete personnel dispersal. Be prepared to initiate abort."

"Understood. Abort sequence loaded."

The face vanished. VinDu ran through an exit and turned into a corridor that was lined with polished gold. He gave his communications implant another order and KaiDin's secretary answered the call.

"This is an Overseer to Overseer universal-override priority message. Please advise Overseer KaiDin I have just launched a cluster of armed missiles at the Emissary. Tell her the entire Emissary complex will be destroyed if I have reason to think her conspiracy is succeeding."

He terminated the call without waiting for an answer. The corridor opened into a golden hemisphere and he veered around a reflecting pool and picked up the pace.

His next call transmitted a flurry of orders to the proteges he had left in his apartments. His senior adviser was ordered to distribute the arms stashed in the special-situations vault. Armed posses were to be dispatched to the apartments of four Overseers: ElGari, OgaRuto, MinFi, and HangLan. The posses were enjoined to keep all four out of KaiDin's custody. They should assume their careers depended on their success.

The four posses had been committed by the time VinDu reached his apartments. The fifty proteges who were left had taken up the positions dictated by his security program. His favorite concubine met him at the door and stayed with him as he hurried through his corridors and galleries.

He stopped by the Pool of Seven Grasses and inhaled the aroma of freshly mowed stalks—a sensation he had always found soothing. "You can consider this my crisis center," he told his proteges.

Rugged, unfinished stone rimmed the pool. Eight species of grass grew in the beds that surrounded it. A fur lined recliner rolled down a walk and stopped beside him. The back of the recliner settled into his preferred position. His hand closed around the goblet that had been placed in the drink receptacle.

A situation report appeared in front of him. Five Overseers had already announced they were voting for Revelation. Two had obviously been coerced. One had left a message for VinDu.

"I am voting for Revelation to avoid conflict," Overseer JenPol had said. "KaiDin has now proved she is just as turbulent as I feared she would be. I have decided we should save our colleagues the pain she is obviously willing to inflict on them."

VinDu tipped back his head and let the cold, creamy liquid soothe his throat. His left hand stroked the silky arm of the recliner.

VinDu had thought of JenPol when he had voted to elevate KaiDin to the Eleven. JenPol, he had believed, was a good example of the drift KaiDin was supposed to correct. Now he knew he had been right. Three hundred years ago, no Overseer would have yielded to KaiDin merely because she wanted to save her colleagues a little pain.

The answer to the whole problem of government, Tai-Park had believed, lay in the personality of the rulers. *Now that we have acquired the ability to shape the human personality*, he had argued, *we must use it to shape human society.* Most of VinDu's childhood memories involved programmed experiences that had been managed by the teams that directed his cultivation. His personality was the product of a controlled, continuously monitored process that had started with his genes and continued through the first years of post-adolescence. *First we control the seed, then we control the soil.*

Tai-Park had agreed with all the philosophers and theorists who believed the ideal rulers should possess intelligence, empathy, and other morally desirable traits. But he had also concluded they needed something more dependable at the center of their personality structure. The government of the TaiPark Combine, he had decided, would be placed in the hands of some of the most narcissistic personalities the human species had ever generated. The Overseers and their proteges were all men and women who valued their personal self-image above every other human need—and their self-image was firmly wedded to their picture of themselves as people who placed the general welfare above their own desires. Without their mania for pleasure, they would have been the kind of robotic puritans who had governed mankind's more cheerless experiments in social organization.

The situation report switched to a map that advised VinDu his three posses were all approaching their destinations. Two of the Overseers they were supposed to defend were already under attack. ElGari and MinFi had both retreated to high-security areas in their apartments. OgaRuto had initiated her security program but KaiDin was apparently leaving her alone.

I will vote against Revelation if I am left free, OgaRuto had assured him. *I would have voted against it under any circumstances. But KaiDin's treachery has reinforced my resolve.*

KaiDin's image popped into visibility beside the situation report. "I've received your message, VinDu. Am I really expected to believe an Overseer of the TaiPark Combine is willing to commit the greatest act of vandalism in the history of our species?"

"The missiles can be aborted, Overseer. I'll reroute them as soon as you call off your attacks on your colleagues and release your prisoners—when we can once again debate this issue the way we're supposed to. And hold it to an honest vote."

"And come to the same conclusion we've come to every decade for a hundred and sixty years."

"We have an agreed-upon decision-making procedure—a procedure we have followed for over one and a half centuries. We will initiate Revelation when *eight* of the current members of the Eleven Cultivated Overseers *freely* vote for it. If you don't feel that's satisfactory, you have the same power as the rest of us—you can campaign for a change in the procedure."

A map that covered a third of the asteroid belt floated over KaiDin's head. KaiDin had flouted the map in most of the communications she had imposed on the Overseers during the last year. White dots represented the cities of the TaiPark Combine. Red circles surrounded the five cities the Toremata Union had annexed in the last ten years. Winking lights marked the current position of known Toremata probes. KaiDin had pressed home the same message every time she had argued for immediate Revelation: *The Toremata probes can discover the Emissary complex at any time.*

VinDu had responded with a statement in which he stood in front of a collage that depicted the turbulence that had plagued mankind during the last fifteen decades: the six wars currently raging on Earth . . . the destruction of the Northern Habitat on Mercury, with the loss of a billion lives . . . the great scar that now dominated a third of Earth's moon . . . the revolutions and tribal wars that had erupted in the cities humans had created in the asteroids.

Our power over human genetics and human psychology has given us three hundred years of peaceful expansion in our own combine, VinDu had argued. *In the rest of the Solar System, it has given us assassins, flawless soldiers, and physical and mental variations that offer us new reasons to hate each other. Can anyone truly believe the human species can absorb a stream of information that may include messages from civilizations that are millennia ahead of us? The Toremata Mediators may be more aggressive than us, but they are still people who have confronted the realities of governance. If they do happen to stumble on our secret, they aren't going to be any more eager to disrupt human society than we are.*

"Have you really thought this through, VinDu? Have you decided what you'll do if I succeed before your missiles arrive? And the Emissary broadcasts its initial announcement to mankind? Are you going to destroy the Emissary complex anyway? After the entire population of the Solar System knows it's our link to a civilization that may cover most of our galaxy?"

VinDu only hesitated for a second but it was long enough. KaiDin noted the lapse and acknowledged it with a smile.

"You're the first Overseer in three hundred years who's tried to use violence to force a decision on the Overseers," VinDu said. "Every Overseer in our history has understood that our entire polity would be threatened with destruction if we began to make war on each other."

"You have just launched missiles that will destroy a treasure we have been preserving for over one and a half centuries. And yet you still think you can lie on your recliner and claim *I* am endangering our polity."

KaiDin waved her hand. Her image vanished and VinDu's communication system immediately advised him he had a call from Overseer MinFi.

"Accepted," VinDu said.

The woman who took KaiDin's place was serving her third term as an Overseer. VinDu had been one of MinFi's favorite aides when she had been serving her first term. She had worked him hard but her courteous, matter-of-fact leadership style had made him feel she deserved any effort she demanded. He had always felt her tutelage was the main reason he had been selected as an Overseer five years before he had expected it.

"KaiDin says you have launched missiles at the Emissary complex. She says you claim you'll destroy it if she forces a yes vote. Is that true?"

"I've given her a choice. She can continue fighting and lose the Emissary. Or she can stop this madness and save it."

"You had those missiles ready to launch . . . "

"I learned she might be planning an insurrection several days ago. I didn't try to arrest her until I was certain. But I felt I should establish a contingency plan."

MinFi nodded. VinDu didn't have to tell her he had turned to his supporters outside the capital. All the Overseers had powerbases in the rest of the combine. It was one of the things the Overseers took into account when they met each year and picked a successor for the Overseer whose term had come to an end.

"She isn't going to back down, VinDu. She's willing to take risks you and I wouldn't even contemplate."

"Then the missiles will destroy the Emissary and she'll have created all this chaos for nothing. I think the issue is clear, Overseer. KaiDin won't be the last Overseer to start an insurrection if we let her impose her will on us. If I have to destroy the Emissary to keep her from setting a precedent that could undermine our entire political system—then I'm willing to destroy the Emissary."

"I haven't altered my views on Revelation," MinFi said. "I want you to understand that. We are still in agreement. We'd be better off if we'd never discovered that thing. We'll be lucky if we still have a civilization left once we let people start prowling through its databanks. But I can't stand by and let it be destroyed, either. You've created a difficult choice, VinDu. I've advised KaiDin I'm voting for Revelation. I've notified the Overseers who haven't registered their votes yet and urged them to join me."

"You're going to let her have her way merely because she's willing to be nastier than the rest of us? You're willing to let her threaten the stability of a polity that has given billions of people one of the best governed societies in history just to save you and your proteges a little pain?"

"I'm advising you your missile threat can only lead to a disaster. We will vote in favor of Revelation, the Emissary will make its promised broadcast to the entire Solar System, and every human being now alive will know the TaiPark Combine destroyed our first link to galactic civilization. Do you really think you will be serving the long term interest of our constituency, Overseer?"

VinDu's face hardened. "I have already heard from OgaRuto. She has promised me she will hold out. KaiDin's actions have only aroused her anger. If you're truly interested in the survival of the Emissary complex, Overseer, you should be lining up votes against Revelation."

The Emissary complex occupied an asteroid only six hundred meters long. The molecular devices in the warheads of VinDu's missiles would penetrate the surface of the asteroid and deconstruct anything buried beneath it.

The Emissary had apparently chosen the asteroid because it had been programmed to settle on a site that was small, obscure, and loaded with metal. The Emissary had weighed less than a kilo when it had entered the Solar System but it had still possessed some maneuvering ability and a high level decision-making capability. The little package had promptly started collecting metal atoms from the area around its landing site, the metal had been used to create molecular machines, the molecular machines had built microscopic machines, the microscopic machines had built larger machines, and a complete listening post and interstellar communications facility had gradually taken shape. The Emissary had settled on the asteroid around the time Galileo was making his first observations of Jupiter's moons. It had beamed its first message at the stars a few months after Marconi had transmitted his first radio signal across the Atlantic.

Normally the TaiPark surveyors would have ignored the kind of small single-slab asteroid the Emissary had selected. When the habitat engineers built new cities, they usually started with large asteroids that were composed of several slabs, loosely held together by gravity. A survey ship had approached the Emissary asteroid because its long-range radar had picked up an anomaly that had aroused its operator's interest. Fortunately, the operator had been prudent as well as curious. He had contacted the capital as soon as the Emissary had delivered its opening speech and the Overseers had ordered him to deactivate his communications equipment and return to Anmei by the most direct orbit his ship could traverse.

VinDu had worked his way through the recordings of that first debate. Five Overseers had voted for immediate Revelation. The Overseers had adapted the eight-vote rule partly because the five had believed they could add three votes to their side once the other Overseers had adjusted their emotional responses. Revelation had actually received seven votes two years later. It had received seven votes on six other occasions since then.

There had been times when the debates had become intense and uncivil. The Overseers on both sides had believed they were deciding the fate of the human species. Yet in all that time no one had tried to settle the matter with armed violence. Anmei had received its name from the ancient characters for peace and magnificence. It was a small city, with a small population, but all the tensions and conflicts of the combine were reproduced within its walls. The Eleven Cultivated Overseers regulated trade, appointed judges and administrators, controlled the combine military force, and distributed certain types of cultivated citizens through the five hundred cities. Anmei was a place where public spirited personalities enjoyed their pleasures and searched for policies that would enhance the happiness and affluence of five billion human beings. It was not a place where you won arguments by inflicting pain on your colleagues and their associates.

VinDu focused his attention on the situation report. He had started transmitting orders as soon as MinFi had told him she was surrendering. The posse that had been helping MinFi defend her apartments was already splitting up and running to the aid of the other three Overseers.

In theory, KaiDin should be overwhelmingly outnumbered. Approximately three thousand people lived in the capital. Each Overseer lived with two hundred proteges, concubines, and hangers-on; the rest of the population consisted of caretakers and technicians. VinDu still had three functioning allies, so his side could pour eight hundred people into the battle. KaiDin could only muster two hundred.

In practice, the situation didn't look that good. To do the job right, half the eight hundred should be formed into a single force and used to attack KaiDin. They should seal off strategic corridors, surround KaiDin's apartments, and take her prisoner by assault if she refused to surrender.

Instead, his three allies were all hiding behind their security arrangements fighting defensive battles. They still had the advantage of numbers but how long could they withstand an assault directed by someone like KaiDin?

VinDu had lunched with KaiDin once every tenday when he had been the chief administrator of the combine courts in the Fifth Sector. KaiDin had been his chief assistant so he had avoided a sexual relationship. He might have behaved differently if KaiDin had been less exciting. But he had realized she roused emotions that could create vocational tensions. Her chief attraction had been her intensity—the extra force the cultivation process had instilled in her personality.

VinDu's job with the courts was the kind of assignment you received when you had already served one term as an Overseer and everyone knew you were going to serve another term in the near future. By then it had been obvious KaiDin would eventually become an Overseer, too. Their lunches had always included interludes in which she had interrogated him about life in the higher levels of the capital and he had responded with the traditional loquacity of an older male parading his worldly knowledge before a younger female. No one laughed like KaiDin. She had listened to him as if she was engraving every word he said on the molecules of her brain.

He could still smile, too, when he remembered KaiDin's imitations of the combine judges they were supposed to be supervising. The judges, like the Overseers, had been genetically and psychologically shaped for their role. They were incorruptible, dignified, highly intelligent—and almost sexless. They were all enthusiastic hobbyists—game players, model makers, collectors, and devotees of arcane sports such as broadsword combat and powdergun marksmanship.

The current Custodian of the Emissary complex was a square faced, softspoken man who always wore his uniform when he spoke to an

Overseer. The Custodian had always been selected from the judge pool—probably because the Custodian filled one of the duller and less demanding positions in the Solar System. The Custodian lived in luxurious isolation while he waited for the day when the Overseers would advise him they had voted in favor of Revelation. Justice Alzaraki was voluntarily serving his third consecutive term in the job.

"Overseer KaiDin has advised me missiles have been launched at the complex," Justice Alzaraki said, choosing the passive voice and diplomatically avoiding mentioning who had launched the missiles. "Is there any estimate of when they will arrive?"

"You should be prepared to initiate emergency evacuation," VinDu said. "You'll be given several minutes advance warning. There is, however, a rather obvious way to avoid the necessity."

"Are you about to suggest that I refuse to initiate Revelation on the grounds that some of the Overseers were forced to vote for it?"

"It seems like a reasonable response. KaiDin hasn't made any secret of her illegal efforts. I can show you views of the battles that are taking place right now."

"My mandate says I must initiate Revelation whenever eight of the Overseers order me to. I am not empowered to question their motives."

"Even when someone is standing in front of the camera with a weapon trained on their head?"

"So far seven Overseers have informed me they are voting for Revelation. None had guns trained on their heads."

The Custodian drew himself up. He was above average height, like all judges, and his uniform had been deliberately designed to make him seem more massive.

"The only person who seems to have a weapon pointed at him, Overseer VinDu, is the Custodian of the Emissary complex. I believe a group of missiles aimed at an invaluable installation can be compared to a gun trained on a human skull."

Colonel Wan was the commander of the guard ship that orbited the sun in tandem with the capital. His stiff posture and round, stoic face were obviously hiding a cauldron of conflicting emotions. VinDu was placing him in the worst situation someone with his personality structure could be exposed to.

"I think I can guess some of your feelings, colonel. You are supposed to obey all lawful orders. Which means, as a practical matter, that you are normally prepared to obey the orders you receive from any of the eleven Overseers. And now it is the Overseers themselves who happen to be shooting at each other. But I believe the critical word is *lawful*. KaiDin is engaged in unlawful activity. She is violating three centuries of peace and assaulting the foundations of our form of government. We can't resist her without your help."

"I understand that, Overseer."

"But you're still troubled."

"From what you have told me—this violence began when you attempted to arrest Overseer KaiDin. It broke out *because* you attempted to arrest her."

"KaiDin didn't limit herself to resisting arrest. I arrested her because I had evidence she was planning to attack her colleagues and force them to vote in a certain way. She responded to the arrest by initiating the very plan I was trying to forestall."

"I understand that, Overseer. That certainly appears to be the case. But I haven't received any information about the evidence you refer to."

VinDu gestured at the trim, neatly mustached man who was standing beside his recliner. "This is Senior Concubine Ligen. He's been associated with KaiDin's entourage for the last two standard years. He is the main source of my information on her plans."

"I am one of KaiDin's favorite companions," Ligen said. "There have been whole tendays when I have been her primary consort. I can wander through her apartments with almost complete freedom. I can ask about her feelings and her affairs and people will answer me under the assumption I am seeking information that will help me fulfill her needs."

VinDu raised his hand. "Please don't be shocked by the obvious implications of Ligen's statements, Colonel. It's a little game the Overseers play—a test of our personal security systems. In my first term as an Overseer, two of my own concubines proved to be observers planted by other Overseers. I uncovered one. I was told about the other a few tendays after my term ended."

He smiled. "She was one of the pleasantest concubines I have ever been blessed with. I said that to the Overseer who had planted her in my entourage and we agreed we had both benefited from the incident."

"In the course of my normal surveillance activities," Ligen continued, "I discovered that Overseer KaiDin had armed her proteges and instituted extensive weapons training. I reported this to Overseer VinDu and he furnished me with additional equipment. And had me initiate a higher level of surveillance."

"KaiDin had made some passionate statements about an issue we refer to as Revelation," VinDu said. "She had made it very clear she believes we are confronted with a crisis regarding this issue. I felt these secret arms were a dangerous sign—dangerous enough that I felt Ligen should take some risks and engage in activities that might unmask our relationship."

"Thanks to my knowledge of Overseer KaiDin's personnel," Ligen said, "I could select a protege who was poorly guarded but might know the purpose of the weapons. I managed to arrange a private interlude in her rooms and I applied some of the pharmaceuticals Overseer VinDu had provided me."

"And he reported to me as soon as he left her," VinDu said. "And I organized an arrest posse before KaiDin had time to discover Ligen had deserted her entourage."

VinDu rested his hand on his goblet. He refrained from drinking while he watched the colonel think.

"This is not an easy question," Colonel Wan said.

"I thought about it for some time before I decided to invoke my emergency powers."

"You are obviously correct when you say the kind of insurrection you are describing is an assault on the foundations of our governmental system. I find it hard to believe any Overseer would behave the way you say Overseer KaiDin is behaving. If I hadn't seen the transmissions from the centers of conflict . . . "

"She believes she is serving the public good. She believes she has a moral right to force her beliefs on the rest of us when she feels the issue is supremely important. I believe there are no issues that justify such actions."

"And I must agree with you, Overseer. The law is the only guide I have. I couldn't live in a world in which I had to constantly choose between conflicting orders given by different Overseers."

Colonel Wan straightened his shoulders. The frown on his face had turned into a dark, ferocious scowl. "I am still left with a question of veracity. The only evidence I have for your story is the statements made by you and your intelligence agent. I also know, however, that you are an Overseer. You wouldn't be telling me all this if you didn't believe you were acting for the good of the combine. I will muster half the troops on my ship—fifty trained, fully armed soldiers. We will enter the city with your authorization. We will restore order by neutralizing Overseer KaiDin's posses."

Colonel Wan had placed his troops on alert while he had been conferring with VinDu. They left the ship and entered the city fifteen minutes after he made his decision.

VinDu would have preferred it if they had attacked KaiDin's apartments and taken her prisoner. Colonel Wan clung to the premise that his troops were "restoring order." Half his force occupied key intersections. The rest hurried toward the struggle taking place outside ElGari's apartments. KaiDin seemed to be concentrating on ElGari.

ElGari was holding a weapon when his image appeared in front of VinDu's recliner. "I'm positioned well behind the action, VinDu. But I've sent everyone I have forward. If KaiDin's posse breaks through the line, I'll have to hold them off by myself."

VinDu stood up. This was obviously not a moment when he should look like he was taking his ease. "Colonel Wan and his troops are on the way. They're fully armored, so they should be irresistible."

"I've told my proteges they have to endure the pain. So far most of them seem to be holding out. I've lost visual contact with about half my rooms but I'm getting reports. KaiDin has apparently decided to add vandalism to her crimes. I gather I'll be lucky if I have a table standing upright. They even opened all my bird cages and let the birds out."

Colonel Wan popped into the space between ElGari and the pool. A visor covered his face.

"We are now engaging the insurrectionists near the entrances to Overseer ElGari's apartments. I'm sorry to report the insurrectionists have engaged in extensive demolition of property. They have locked most of the doors within the apartments and piled debris behind them."

"How long do you think it will take you to disperse them? I'm talking to Overseer ElGari now."

ElGari and Colonel Wan couldn't see each other. VinDu's communications program automatically asked ElGari to wait while he turned his attention to the colonel.

"We would have most of them in custody by now it if weren't for the obstacles. As it is—give us fifteen minutes to half an hour."

VinDu relayed the colonel's estimate to ElGari and received a frown in response. "That's the best he thinks he can do?"

"Colonel Wan's troops are going to rescue you. It's a foregone conclusion. They could walk through KaiDin's posse as if it wasn't there if they weren't struggling with obstacles."

"Half an hour? He's sure it won't be more than half an hour?"

"Half an hour maximum. And probably sooner."

VinDu had linked his communication system to the cameras mounted on some of ElGari's proteges. Headless statues lay on their sides. Intricately carved tables had been turned into barricades. Heavy, ornate birdcages had been dragged in front of doors. Confused birds were flapping around the wreckage magnifying the disorder.

VinDu checked his situation screen. The missiles would strike the Emissary complex in forty-eight minutes. He recorded a statement for KaiDin and transmitted it to her secretary.

"I have observed the damage you are inflicting on Overseer ElGari's apartments. You have destroyed works of art that the Overseers have been commissioning and collecting for three hundred years. Colonel Wan's forces are going to rescue ElGari within another few minutes. Isn't it time to break this off? The damage you're doing can have no effect on the outcome."

KaiDin's recorded image jumped in front of him a minute after he sent the message. She was standing up and she had magnified herself so she looked taller. "Most of the items in Overseer ElGari's apartments can be refrabricated. No device we possess can replace the Emissary complex."

KaiDin vanished. An officer with lieutenant's pips immediately took her place. "I have a message from Colonel Wan, Overseer. Three ships have landed on three of the capital's docking ports. They have started disembarking people who seem to be carrying weapons. The security system has advised us their entrance has been authorized by three Overseers."

VinDu straightened up. He slid his drink into the goblet holder and came to his feet.

"Which three?"

"Overseers KaiDin, MinFi, and JenPol."

"And you didn't observe these ships until they docked?"

"We believe they were concealed in the general traffic near Anmei. They had full authorization to enter the security area around the capital."

"And what is Colonel Wan doing in response?"

"He has ordered his troops to hold the intersections they have been assigned until further notice. He would like your authorization to do that."

"Tell him he has it. Tell him as far as I'm concerned he should consider these people accomplices in KaiDin's conspiracy."

The lieutenant snapped to attention and disappeared. VinDu settled onto the end of his recliner. He reached behind him and lifted his drink out of the holder.

Cameras and hasty reports brought him a jumbled, fragmented picture of the situation. Cameras posted along the corridors picked up images of groups that seemed to be running down the corridors in six different directions. The soldiers posted at the intersections were pushed to the floor by wall to wall human battering rams. Colonel Wan announced that he was pulling half his troops off the assault on ElGari's apartments and turning them around so they could resist the attack coming at them from behind.

"Use something stronger than a short term anesthetic," VinDu said. "Give them a load that will make them hold back. They don't care how many people your troops hit. They just keep coming until they can overwhelm them by sheer weight."

Colonel Wan lowered his head. His visor obscured his face. "I'll order a switch to pain and confusion loads."

"Can't you use something harsher than that? This is an open insurrection, Colonel. KaiDin has brought an armed mob into the interior of the capital."

"Pain and confusion is the strongest load we brought with us, Overseer. I was given no reason to bring anything stronger."

"You've still got half your force on the ship. Have them equip themselves with lethal loads. Get them in here. Put a stop to this."

Colonel Wan snapped to attention and terminated the call. Fifteen minutes later, a mob charged down two corridors and converged on ElGari's apartments. Colonel Wan's soldiers responded by retreating down a third corridor, firing anesthetics as they went.

VinDu's proteges were turning over furniture and creating barricades. His senior adviser was handing out sensory-deprivation loads that would neutralize every sense for a full half hour—the strongest load VinDu had stocked in his personal arsenal. Its after-effects normally included days of disorientation and agonizing depression. His situation reports displayed the images of cleanup crews moving among the breakage KaiDin had inflicted on the city. His missiles were now ten minutes from their target.

The Emissary was still broadcasting its message. It had used up the major languages and started working its way through Albanian, Coptic, and the minority languages of China and India. In every language the message was the same. The Solar System was now linked to a galaxy-spanning interstellar communications network.

I have been receiving information from other civilizations for over nine hundred terrestrial years, the message said. *My databanks offer you a vast repository of knowledge and wisdom. More information is arriving every hour.*

The images of three Overseers were lined up beside the fountain:

MinFi, JenPol, and OgaRuto. KaiDin was observing the conversation but she wasn't projecting an image.

"KaiDin knows she can't force you to abort," MinFi said. "You obviously can't abort the missiles if you're killed or incapacitated. But afterward . . . if you let them destroy the complex . . ."

"Half the people in the Solar System will think it was a justified execution," OgaRuto said. "Don't underestimate the initial response to the Emissary's message."

VinDu held himself erect. There was no limit, it seemed, to the emotional devastation his genes and his post-natal processing could cover with a stone facade.

"I am not going to yield to her merely to save my life. Our polity is probably dead. I understand that. But there is still some hope it can survive."

MinFi shook her head. Her eyes deepened. "I understand your feelings, VinDu. I might tell you to let the missiles do their work if I thought it would save whatever we have left of our government. You'd be teaching our successors the ultimate lesson. The next Overseer who contemplated violence and coercion would know it was a pointless thing to do. But our polity can't survive if the people of the Solar System know an Overseer destroyed the Emissary complex. The combine will fall apart within a tenday."

"We've lost," OgaRuto said. "We may be able to hold something together if you abort the missiles. Let them strike and we'll have nothing—no combine, and no Emissary either."

VinDu waved his hand and the three Overseers vanished. The only image floating in front of him was the map that displayed the current position of the missiles.

"We are what we are," KaiDin says. "We responded the way we were meant to respond. You made your decisions. I made mine."

"And now we both have to live with the consequences."

KaiDin eyes him over the top of her goblet. An impish flicker crosses her face. "You sound like you're more concerned about my destiny than your own."

VinDu reaches for his own goblet. It has been twelve years since KaiDin mounted her insurrection and she has been an exile ever since. She has been isolated from all hope that she would ever again be an Overseer.

"I felt it would be the harshest punishment we could inflict on you," VinDu says. "I wouldn't have asked for it if I didn't feel that way. I felt you would be a living example to any Overseers who thought they should repeat your use of force. A ruler without a domain. Without any possibility of a domain."

KaiDin smiles. "And we would both have our precious self-image. Our portrait of ourselves as virtuous, upright public servants."

"We both made our concessions. We both made the kind of decisions we're supposed to make."

KaiDin raises her goblet. "The only kind of decisions we *can* make. That's why I've made up the file I'm sending you, VinDu. Please study it carefully. My life as a researcher has been more satisfying than you might think. It hasn't been easy. I'm not sure the more placid products of the Overseer cultivation process could have done it. But I've found something that should justify all the effort I've put into it. Once I finished the preliminary work the Emissary forces on you, I started looking for information about other species that have engaged in personality cultivation. I found five. Two of the species I examined spent centuries in a frighteningly destructive pattern—a pattern we may be initiating."

VinDu presses the smooth firmness of the concubine's knee as he listens. He is once again an Overseer. He is once again a resident of Anmei. But all his worst fears have been realized. He and three other Overseers govern a fragment of the TaiPark combine. Twenty cities defected in the first tenday after the Emissary broadcast its initial greeting. In every corner of the Solar System, major fractions of the population voiced their outrage when they learned the Overseers had hidden the Emissary for a century and a half. The Toremata Union intensified its offensive and the pressure split the Overseers into factions. The combine is now divided into three polities. The Overseers in each segment claim they are the true government of the entire combine.

"Both species tried to cultivate rulers with desirable personality structures," KaiDin says. "Both got into conflicts and started cultivating more aggressive personalities. Eventually they slipped into a kind of arms race—with each group trying to develop the most aggressive leaders. By the time they managed to reverse the process, both species had endured an era of mass destruction and wholesale death that nearly destroyed their civilization."

KaiDin has placed her goblet in its holder. Her concubine has removed his hands from her shoulder and stepped back two steps, in response to the seriousness and intensity of the mood she is projecting.

"I've noted some disturbing indications," KaiDin says. "I believe there is some possibility you and your rivals for the leadership of the combine may be contemplating a long term increase in the aggressiveness of the portion of the overseer pool you control. I'm sending you the results of my researches because I want you to understand the dangers. If you're doing what you appear to be doing—you could be endangering our entire civilization."

KaiDin's image vanishes. VinDu stares into the space she has emptied. His hand traces the curve of the concubine's lower leg.

"The compromise we made twelve years ago was like most compromises," VinDu says to the concubine. "It satisfied everybody except the compromisers. I demanded that KaiDin be expelled from the Overseer pool because I felt she had to pay something. We had to do something that would make future Overseers hesitate when they started thinking they should imitate her little attempt at civil war. I thought it was the right decision at the time. It didn't work out as well as I'd hoped, but I still think it was the right decision."

He tips back his goblet and lets the mild tartness of the drink counterpoint the warmth of the bath and the curves and swells of the concubine's body. KaiDin's information sources seem to have missed an important aspect of the situation. In the cultivation facilities a short distance from his apartment, the cultivation specialists are, indeed, cultivating more aggressive Overseers. But VinDu and his three colleagues are also working on a program that will produce more immediate results. Their personality modification staff is developing modification programs that will increase the aggressiveness of the *current* members of their Overseer pool.

"We have uncovered the weakness in Tai-Park's vision," VinDu says. "We are all public spirited personalities. But what public do we serve? Our own fragment of the combine? The combine itself, which can only be restored if we make war on the Overseers who control the other fragments? The human species as a whole? How do we answer such questions? And when we do answer them—when we choose the group that will command our loyalties—we pursue our objectives with a dedication that magnifies the intensity of the conflict. A detached observer might decide our species would be better off if we were merely normal selfish humans who pursued goals such as wealth and social status."

VinDu rests his head against a self-adjusting support. He takes his hand off the concubine's leg and slides forward until the water covers his chin. The concubine catches his mood and starts singing a series of wordless variations based on an ancient Mongolian melody.

"We are what we are," VinDu says.

THE OBSERVER

KRISTINE KATHRYN RUSCH

—◆—

And so we went in.

Combat formation, all five of us, me first, face masks on so tight that the edges of our eyes pulled, suits like a second skin. Weapons in both hands, back-ups attached to the wrists and forearms, flash-bangs on our hips.

No shielding, no vehicles, no nothing. Just us, dosed, altered, ready to go.

I wanted to rip something's head off, and I did, the fury burning in me like lust. The weapons became tools—I wanted up close and I got it, fingers in eyes, fists around tentacles, poking, pulling, yanking—

They bled brown, like soda. Like coffee. Like weak tea.

And they screamed—or at least I think they did.

Or maybe that was just me.

The commanders pulled us out before we could turn on each other, gave us calming drugs, put us back in our chambers for sleep. But we couldn't sleep.

The adrenaline didn't stop.

Neither did the fury.

Monica banged her head against the wall until she crushed her own skull.

LaTrice shot up her entire chamber with a back-up she'd hidden between her legs. She took out two MPs and both team members in the chambers beside her before the commander filled the air with some kind of narcotic to wipe her out.

And me. I kept ripping and gouging and pulling and yanking until my fingertips were bone. By then, I hit the circuits inside the door and fried myself.

And woke up here, strapped down against a cold metal bed with no bedclothes. The walls are some kind of brushed steel. I can see my own reflection, blurry, pale-skinned, wild-eyed.

I don't look like a woman, and I certainly don't look like me.

And you well know, Doc, that if you unstrap me, I'll kill the thing reflected in that brushed metal wall.

After I finish with you.

You ask how it feels, and you know you'll get an answer because of that chip you put in my head.

I can feel it, you know, itching. If I close my eyes, I can picture it, like a gnat, floating in gray matter.

Free my hands and I'll get it out myself.

Free my hands, and I'll get us all out of here.

How does it feel?

By it, I assume you mean me. I assume you mean whatever's left of me.

Here's how it feels:

There are three parts to me now. The old, remembered part, which doesn't have a voice. It stands back and watches, appalled, at everything that happens, everything I do.

I can see her too—that remembered part—gangly young woman with athletic prowess and no money. She stands behind the rest of us, wearing the same clothes she wore to the recruiter's that day—pants with a permanent crease, her best blouse, long hair pulled away from her horsy face.

There are dreams in her eyes—or there were then. Now they're cloudy, disillusioned, lost.

If you'd just given her the money, let her get the education first, she'd be an officer or an engineer or a goddamn tech soldier.

But you gave her that test—biological predisposition, aggression, sensitivity to certain hormones. You gave her the test, and found it wasn't just the physical that had made her a good athlete.

It wasn't just the physical.

It was the aggression, and the way that minute alterations enhanced it.

Aggression, a strong predisposition, and extreme sensitivity.

Which, after injections and genetic manipulation, turned her into us.

I'm the articulate one. I'm an observer too, someone who stores information, and can process it faster than the fastest computer. I'm supposed to govern the reflexes, but they gave me a blocker for that the minute I arrived back on ship, then made it permanent when they got me to base.

I can see, Doc; I can hear; I can even tell you what's going on, and why.

I just can't stop it, any more than you can.

I know I said three, and yet I didn't mention the third. I couldn't think of her, not and think of the Remembered One at the same time.

I'm not supposed to feel, Doc, yet the Remembered One, she makes me sad.

The third. Oh, yeah. The third.

She's got control of the physical, but you know that. You see her every day. She's the one who raises the arms, who clenches the bandaged and useless fingers, who kicks at the restraints holding the feet.

She's the one who growls and makes it impossible for me to talk to you.

You know that, or you wouldn't have used the chip.

An animal?

She's not an animal. Animals create small societies. They have customs and instinctual habits. They live in prides or pods or tribes.

She's a thing. Inarticulate. Violent. Useless.

And by giving her control of the physical, you made the rest of us useless, trapped inside, destined to watch until she works herself free.

If she decides to bash her head against the wall until she crushes her own skull or to rip through the steel, breaking every single bone she has, if she decides to impale herself on the bedframe, I'll cheer her on.

Not just for me.

But for the Remembered One, the one with hopes and dreams and a future she squandered when she reached for the stars.

The one who got us here, and who can't ever get us out.

So, you say I'm unusual. How nice for me. The ones who separate usually kill themselves before the MPs ever get into the chamber. The others, the ones who integrate with their thing, get reused.

You think that the women I trained with—the ones not in my unit, the ones who didn't die when we got back—you think they're still out there, fighting an enemy we don't entirely understand.

I think you're naïve.

But you're preparing a study, something for the government so that they'll know this experiment is failing. Not the chip-in-the-brain thing that allows you to communicate with me, but the girl soldiers, the footsoldiers, the grunts on the ground.

And if they listen (ha!) they'll listen because of people like me.

Okay. I'll buy into your pipe dreams.

Here's what everyone on Earth believes:

We don't even know their names. We can call them The Others, but that's only for clarity purposes. There are names—Squids, ETs—but none of them seem to stick.

They have ships in much of the solar system, so we're told, but we're going to prevent them from getting the Moon. The Moon is the last bastion before they reach Earth.

That's about it. No one cares, unless they have a kid up there, and even then, they don't really care unless the kid is a grunt, like I was.

Only they don't know the kid's a grunt. Not until the kid comes home from a tour, if the kid comes home.

Here's what I learned on our ship: Most of the guys never came home. That's when the commanders started the hormonal/genetic thing, the thing that tapped into the maternal instinct. Apparently the female of the species has a ferocious need to protect her young.

It can be—it is—tapped, and in some of us, it's powerful, and we become strong.

Mostly, though, no one gets near the ground. The battle is engaged in the blackness of space. It's like the video games our grandparents used—which some say (and I never believed until now)—were used to train the kids for some kind of future war.

The kind we're fighting now.

What I learned after a few tours, before I ever had to go to ground, was that ground troops, footsoldiers, rarely returned. They have specific missions, mostly clearing an area, and they do it, and they mostly die.

A lot of us died that day—what I can remember of it.

Mostly I remember the fingers and the eyes and the tentacles (yes, they're real) and the pull of the face mask against my skin.

What I suspect is this: the troops the Others have on the ground aren't the enemy. They're some kind of captured race, footsoldiers just like us, fodder for the war machine. I think, if I concentrate real hard, I remember them working, putting chips places, implanting stuff in the ground—growing things?—I'm not entirely clear.

And I wonder if the talk of an invasion force is just that, talk, and if this isn't something else, some kind of experiment in case we get into a real situation, something that'll become bigger.

Because I don't ever remember the Others fighting back.

If Squids can look surprised, these did.

All of them.

So that's my theory for what good it'll do.

There's still girls dying up there. Women, I guess, creatures, footsoldiers, whatever they want to create.

Then we come back, and we become this: things.

Because we can't ever be the Remembered Ones. Not again.

But you know that.

You're studying as many of us as you can. That's clear too.

I'm not even sure you are a doc. Maybe you're a machine, getting these thoughts, processing them, using some modulated voice to ask the right questions, the ones that provoke these memories.

Since I've never seen you.

I never see anyone.

Except the ghosts of myself.

So what are you going to do with me? Reintegration isn't possible; that's been tried. (You think I don't remember? How do you think the Remembered One and I split off in the first place? Once there was just her and the thing. Now there's three of us, trapped in here—well, two trapped, and one growling, but you know what I mean.)

Sending us back won't work. We might turn on our comrades. Or ourself. (Probably ourself.)

Sending us home is out of the question, even if we had a home. The Remembered One does, but she's so far away, she'll never reintegrate.

Let me tell you what I think you should do. I think you should remove the chip. Move me to a new location. Pretend you've never interviewed me.

Then you'd just be faced with the Thing.

And the Thing should be put out of its misery.

We should be put out of its misery.

Monica and LaTrice weren't wrong, Doc. They were just crude. They used what methods they had at their disposal.

They were proactive.

I can't be. You've got all three of us bound up here.

Let us go.

Send us back, all by ourselves. No team, no combat formation. Hell, not even any weapons.

Let us die.

It's the only humane thing to do.

THE LONG CHASE

GEOFFREY A. LANDIS

2645, January

The war is over.

The survivors are being rounded up and converted.

In the inner solar system, those of my companions who survived the ferocity of the fighting have already been converted. But here at the very edge of the Oort Cloud, all things go slowly. It will be years, perhaps decades, before the victorious enemy come out here. But with the slow inevitability of gravity, like an outward wave of entropy, they will come.

Ten thousand of my fellow soldiers have elected to go doggo. Ragged prospectors and ice processors, they had been too independent to ever merge into an effective fighting unit. Now they shut themselves down to dumb rocks, electing to wake up to groggy consciousness for only a few seconds every hundred years. Patience, they counsel me; patience is life. If they can wait a thousand or ten thousand or a million years, with patience enough the enemy will eventually go away.

They are wrong.

The enemy, too, is patient. Here at the edge of the Kuiper, out past Pluto, space is vast, but still not vast enough. The enemy will search every grain of sand in the solar system. My companions will be found, and converted. If it takes ten thousand years, the enemy will search that long to do it.

I, too, have gone doggo, but my strategy is different. I have altered my orbit. I have a powerful ion-drive, and full tanks of propellant, but

I use only the slightest tittle of a cold-gas thruster. I have a chemical kick-stage engine as well, but I do not use it either; using either one of them would signal my position to too many watchers. Among the cold comets, a tittle is enough.

I am falling into the sun.

It will take me two hundred and fifty years years to fall, and for two hundred and forty nine years, I will be a dumb rock, a grain of sand with no thermal signature, no motion other than gravity, no sign of life.

Sleep.

2894, June

Awake.

I check my systems. I have been a rock for nearly two hundred and fifty years.

The sun is huge now. If I were still a human, it would be the size of the fist on my outstretched arm. I am being watched now, I am sure, by a thousand lenses: am I a rock, a tiny particle of interstellar ice? A fragment of debris from the war? A surviving enemy?

I love the cold and the dark and the emptiness; I have been gone so long from the inner solar system that the very sunlight is alien to me.

My systems check green. I expected no less: if I am nothing else, I am still a superbly engineered piece of space hardware. I come fully to life, and bring my ion engine up to thrust.

A thousand telescopes must be alerting their brains that I am alive—but it is too late! I am thrusting at a full throttle, five percent of a standard gravity, and I am thrusting inward, deep into the gravity well of the sun. My trajectory is plotted to skim almost the surface of the sun.

This trajectory has two objectives. First, so close to the sun I will be hard to see. My ion contrail will be washed out in the glare of a light a billion times brighter, and none of the thousand watching eyes will know my plans until it is too late to follow.

And second, by waiting until I am nearly skimming the sun and then firing my chemical engine deep inside the gravity well, I can make most efficient use of it. The gravity of the sun will amplify the efficiency of my propellant, magnify my speed. When I cross the orbit of Mercury outbound I will be over one percent of the speed of light and still accelerating.

I will discard the useless chemical rocket after I exhaust the little bit of impulse it can give me, of course. Chemical rockets have ferocious thrust but little staying power; useful in war but of limited value in an escape. But I will still have my ion engine, and I will have nearly full tanks.

Five percent of a standard gravity is a feeble thrust by the standards of chemical rocket engines, but chemical rockets exhaust their fuel far too quickly to be able to catch me. I can continue thrusting for years, for decades.

I pick a bright star, Procyon, for no reason whatever, and boresight it. Perhaps Procyon will have an asteroid belt. At least it must have dust, and perhaps comets. I don't need much: a grain of sand, a microscopic shard of ice.

From dust God made man. From the dust of a new star, from the detritus of creation, I can make worlds.

No one can catch me now. I will leave, and never return.

2897, May

I am chased.

It is impossible, stupid, unbelievable, inconceivable! I am being chased.

Why?

Can they not leave a single free mind unconverted? In three years I have reached fifteen percent of the speed of light, and it must be clear that I am leaving and never coming back. Can one unconverted brain be a threat to them? Must their group brain really have the forced cooperation of every lump of thinking matter in the solar system? Can they think that if even one free-thinking brain escapes, they have lost?

But the war is a matter of religion, not reason, and it may be that they indeed believe that even a single brain unconverted is a threat to them. For whatever reason, I am being chased.

The robot chasing me is, I am sure, little different than myself, a tiny brain, an ion engine, and a large set of tanks. They would have had no time to design something new; to have any chance of catching me they would have had to set the chaser on my tail immediately.

The brain, like mine, would consist of atomic spin states superimposed on a crystalline rock matrix. A device smaller than what, in the old days, we would call a grain of rice. Intelligent dust, a human had once said, back in the days before humans became irrelevant.

They only sent one chaser. They must be very confident.

Or short on resources.

It is a race, and a very tricky one. I can increase my thrust, use up fuel more quickly, to try to pull away, but if I do so, the specific impulse of my ion drive decreases, and as a result, I waste fuel and risk running out first. Or I can stretch my fuel, make my ion drive more efficient, but this will lower my thrust, and I will risk getting caught by the higher-thrust opponent behind me.

He is twenty billion kilometers behind me. I integrate his motion for a few days, and see that he is, in fact, out-accelerating me.

Time to jettison.

I drop everything I can. The identify-friend-or-foe encrypted-link gear I will never need again; it is discarded. It is a shame I cannot grind it up and feed it to my ion engines, but the ion engines are picky about what they eat. Two micro-manipulators I had planned to use to collect sand grains at my destination for fuel: gone.

My primary weapon has always been my body—little can survive an impact at the speeds I can attain—but I have three sand-grains with tiny engines of their own as secondary weapons. There's no sense in saving them to fight my enemy; he will know exactly what to expect, and in space warfare, only the unexpected can kill.

I fire the grains of sand, one at a time, and the sequential kick of almost a standard gravity nudges my speed slightly forward. Then I drop the empty shells.

May he slip up, and run into them at sub-relativistic closing velocity.

I am lighter, but it is still not enough. I nudge my thrust up, hating myself for the waste, but if I don't increase acceleration, in two years I will be caught, and my parsimony with fuel will yield me nothing.

I need all the energy I can feed to my ion drives. No extra for thinking.

Sleep.

2900

Still being chased.

2905

Still being chased.

I have passed the point of commitment. Even if I braked with my thrust to turn back, I could no longer make it back to the solar system.

I am alone.

2907

Lonely.

To one side of my path Sirius glares insanely bright, a knife in the sky, a mad dog of a star. The stars of Orion are weirdly distorted. Ahead of me, the lesser dog Procyon is waxing brighter every year; behind me, the sun is a fading dot in Aquila.

Of all things, I am lonely. I had not realized that I still had the psychological capacity for loneliness. I examine my brain, and find it. Yes, a tiny knot of loneliness. Now that I see it, I can edit my brain to delete it, if I choose. But yet I hesitate. It is not a bad thing, not something that is crippling my capabilities, and if I edit my brain too much will I not become, in some way, like them?

I leave my brain unedited. I can bear loneliness.

2909

Still being chased.

We are relativistic now, nearly three quarters of the speed of light.

One twentieth of a standard gravity is only a slight push, but as I have burned fuel my acceleration increases, and we have been thrusting for fifteen years continuously.

What point is there in this stupid chase? What victory can there be, here in the emptiness between stars, a trillion kilometers away from anything at all?

After fifteen years of being chased, I have a very good measurement of his acceleration. As his ship burns off fuel, it loses mass, and the acceleration increases. By measuring this increase in acceleration, and knowing what his empty mass must be, I know how much fuel he has left.

It is too much. I will run out of fuel first.

I can't conserve fuel; if I lessen my thrust, he will catch me in only a few years. It will take another fifty years, but the end of the chase is already in sight.

A tiny strobe flickers erratically behind me. Every interstellar hydrogen that impacts his shell makes a tiny flash of x-ray brilliance. Likewise, each interstellar proton I hit sends a burst of x-rays through me. I can feel each one, a burst of fuzzy noise that momentarily disrupts my thoughts. But with spin states encoding ten-to-the-twentieth qbits, I can afford to have massively redundant brainpower. My brain was designed to be powerful enough to simulate an entire world, including ten thousand fully-sapient and sentient free agents. I could immerse myself inside a virtual reality indistinguishable from old Earth, and split myself into a hundred personalities. In my own interior time, I could spend ten thousand years before the enemy catches me and forcibly drills itself into my brain. Civilizations could rise and fall in my head, and I could taste every decadence, lose myself for a hundred years in sensual pleasure, invent rare tortures and exquisite pain.

But as part of owning your own brain free and clear comes the ability to prune yourself. In space, one of the first things to prune away is the ability to feel boredom, and not long after that, I pruned away all desire to live in simulated realities. Billions of humans chose to live in simulations, but by doing so they have made themselves irrelevant: irrelevant to the war, irrelevant to the future.

I could edit back into my brain a wish to live in simulated reality, but what would be the point? It would be just another way to die.

The one thing I do simulate, repeatedly and obsessively, is the result of the chase. I run a million different scenarios, and in all of them, I lose.

Still, most of my brain is unused. There is plenty of extra processing power to keep all my brain running error-correcting code, and an occasional x-ray flash is barely an event worth my noticing. When a cell of my brain is irrevocably damaged by cosmic radiation, I simply code that section to be ignored. I have brainpower to spare.

I continue running, and hope for a miracle.

2355, February: Earth.

I was living in a house I hated, married to a man I despised, with two children who had changed with adolescence from sullen and withdrawn to an active, menacing hostility. How can I be afraid of my own offspring?

Earth was a dead end, stuck in the biological past, a society in deep freeze. No one starved, and no one progressed.

When I left the small apartment for an afternoon to apply for a job as an asteroid belt miner, I told no one, not my husband, not my best friend. No one asked me any questions. It took them an hour to scan my brain, and, once they had the scan, another five seconds to run me through a thousand aptitude tests.

And then, with her brain scanned, my original went home, back to the house she hated, the husband she despised, the two children she was already beginning to physically fear.

I launched from the Earth to an asteroid named 1991JR, and never returned.

Perhaps she had a good life. Perhaps, knowing she had escaped undetected, she found she could endure her personal prison.

Much later, when the cooperation faction suggested that it was too inefficient for independents to work in the near-Earth space, I moved out to the main belt, and from there to the Kuiper belt. The Kuiper is thin, but rich; it would take us ten thousand years to mine, and beyond it is the dark and the deep, with treasure beyond compare.

The cooperation faction developed slowly, and then quickly, and then blindingly fast; almost before we had realized what was happening, they had taken over the solar system. When the ultimatum came that no place in the solar system would be left for us, and the choice we were given was to cooperate or die, I joined the war on the side of freedom.

On the losing side.

• • •

2919, August

The chase has reached the point of crisis.

We have been burning fuel continuously for twenty-five years, in Earth terms, or twenty years in our own reference frame. We have used a prodigious amount of fuel. I still have just enough fuel that, burning all my fuel at maximum efficiency, I can come to a stop.

Barely.

In another month of thrusting this will no longer be true.

When I entered the asteroid belt, in a shiny titanium body, with electronic muscles and ion-engines for legs, and was given control of my own crystalline brain, there was much to change. I pruned away the need for boredom, and then found and pruned the need for the outward manifestations of love: for roses, for touch, for chocolates. Sexual lust became irrelevant; with my new brain I could give myself orgasms with a thought, but it was just as easy to remove the need entirely. Buried in the patterns of my personality I found a burning, obsessive need to win the approval of other people, and pruned it away.

Some things I enhanced. The asteroid belt was dull, and ugly; I enhanced my appreciation of beauty until I could meditate in ecstasy on the way that shadows played across a single grain of dust in the asteroid belt, or on the colors in the scattered stars. And I found my love of freedom, the tiny stunted instinct that had, at long last, given me the courage to leave my life on Earth. It was the most precious thing I owned. I shaped it and enhanced it until it glowed in my mind, a tiny, wonderful thing at the very core of my being.

2929, October

It is too late. I have now burned the fuel needed to stop.

Win or lose, we will continue at relativistic speed across the galaxy.

2934, March

Procyon gets brighter in front of me, impossibly blindingly bright.

Seven times brighter than the sun, to be precise, but the blue shift from our motion makes it even brighter, a searing blue.

I could dive directly into it, vanish into a brief puff of vapor, but the suicidal impulse, like the ability to feel boredom, is another ancient unnecessary instinct that I have long ago pruned from my brain.

B is my last tiny hope for evasion.

Procyon is a double star, and B, the smaller of the two, is a white dwarf. It is so small that its surface gravity is tremendous, a million times higher than the gravity of the Earth. Even at the speeds we are traveling, now only ten percent less than the speed of light, its gravity will bend my trajectory.

I will skim low over the surface of the dwarf star, relativistic dust skimming above the photosphere of a star, and as its gravity bends my trajectory, I will maneuver.

My enemy, if he fails even slightly to keep up with each of my maneuvers, will be swiftly lost. Even a slight deviation from my trajectory will get amplified enough for me to take advantage of, to throw him off my trail, and I will be free.

When first I entered my new life in the asteroid belt, I found my self in my sense of freedom, and joined the free miners of the Kuiper, the loners. But others found different things. Other brains found that cooperation worked better than competition. They did not exactly give up their individual identities, but they enhanced their communications with each other by a factor of a million, so that they could share each others' thoughts, work together as effortlessly as a single entity.

They became the cooperation faction, and in only a few decades, their success became noticeable. They were just so much more *efficient* than we were.

And, inevitably, the actions of the loners conflicted with the efficiency of the cooperation faction. We could not live together, and it pushed us out to the Kuiper, out toward the cold and the dark. But, in the end, even the cold and the dark was not far enough.

But here, tens of trillions of kilometers out of the solar system, there is no difference between us: there is no one to cooperate with. We meet as equals.

We will never stop. Whether my maneuvering can throw him off my course, or not, the end is the same. But it remains important to me.

• • •

2934, April

Procyon has a visible disk now, an electric arc in the darkness, and by the light of that arc I can see that Procyon is, indeed, surrounded by a halo of dust. The dust forms a narrow ring, tilted at an angle to our direction of flight. No danger, neither to me, nor to my enemy, now less than a quarter of a billion kilometers behind me; we will pass well clear of the disk. Had I saved fuel enough to stop, that dust would have served as food and fuel and building material; when you are the size of a grain of sand, each particle of dust is a feast.

Too late for regrets.

The white dwarf B is still no more than an intense speck of light. It is a tiny thing, nearly small enough to be a planet, but bright. As tiny and as bright as hope.

I aim straight at it.

2934, May

Failure.

Skimming two thousand kilometers above the surface of the white dwarf, jinking in calculated pseudo-random bursts . . . all in vain.

I wheeled and darted, but my enemy matched me like a ballet dancer mirroring my every move.

I am aimed for Procyon now, toward the blue-white giant itself, but there is no hope there. If skimming the photosphere of the white dwarf is not good enough, there is nothing I can do at Procyon to shake the pursuit.

There is only one possibility left for me now. It has been a hundred years since I have edited my brain. I like the brain I have, but now I have no choice but to prune.

First, to make sure that there can be no errors, I make a backup of myself and set it into inactive storage.

Then I call out and examine my pride, my independence, my sense of self. A lot of it, I can see, is old biological programming, left over from when I had long ago been a human. I like the core of biological programming, but "like" is itself a brain function, which I turn off.

Now I am in a dangerous state, where I can change the function of my brain, and the changed brain can change itself further. This is a state which is in danger of a swift and destructive feedback effect, so I am very careful. I painstakingly construct a set of alterations, the minimum change needed to remove my aversion to being converted. I run a few thousand simulations to verify that the modified me will not accidentally self-destruct or go into a catatonic fugue state, and then, once it is clear that the modification works, I make the changes.

The world is different now. I am a hundred trillion kilometers from home, traveling at almost the speed of light and unable ever to stop. While I can remember in detail every step of how I am here and what I was thinking at the time, the only reasoning I can recall to explain why is, it seemed like a good idea at the time.

System check. Strangely, in my brain I have a memory that there is something I have forgotten. This makes no sense, but yet there it is. I erase my memory of forgetting, and continue the diagnostic. 0.5 percent of the qbits of my brain have been damaged by radiation. I verify that the damaged memory is correctly partitioned off. I am in no danger of running out of storage.

Behind me is another ship. I cannot think of why I had been fleeing it.

I have no radio; I jettisoned that a long time ago. But an improperly tuned ion drive will produce electromagnetic emissions, and so I compose a message and modulate it onto the ion contrail.

HI. LET'S GET TOGETHER AND TALK. I'M CUTTING ACCELERATION. SEE YOU IN A FEW DAYS.

And I cut my thrust and wait.

2934, May

I see differently now.

Procyon is receding into the distance now, the blueshift mutated into red, and the white dwarf of my hopes is again invisible against the glare of its primary.

But it doesn't matter.

Converted, now I *understand*.

I can see everything through other eyes now, through a thousand different viewpoints. I still remember the long heroism of the resistance, the doomed battle for freedom—but now I see it from the opposite view as well, a pointless and wasteful war fought for no reason but stubbornness.

And now, understanding cooperation, we have no dilemma. I can now see what I was blind to before; that neither one of us alone could stop, but by adding both my fuel and Rajneesh's fuel to a single vehicle, together we can stop.

For all these decades, Rajneesh has been my chaser, and now I know him like a brother. Soon we will be closer than siblings, for soon we will share one brain. A single brain is more than large enough for two, it is large enough for a thousand, and by combining into a single brain and a single body, and taking all of the fuel into a single tank, we will easily be able to stop.

Not at Procyon, no. At only ten percent under the speed of light, stopping takes a long time.

Cooperation has not changed me. I now understand how foolish my previous fears were. Working together does not mean giving up one's sense of self; I am enhanced, not diminished, by knowing others.

Rajneesh's brain is big enough for a thousand, I said, and he has brought with him nearly that many. I have met his brother and his two children and half a dozen of his neighbors, each one of them distinct and clearly different, not some anonymous collaborative monster at all. I have felt their thoughts. He is introducing me to them slowly, he says, because with all the time I have spent as a loner, he doesn't want to frighten me.

I will not be frightened.

Our target now will be a star named Ross 614, a dim type M binary. It is not far, less than three light years further, and even with our lowered mass and consequently higher acceleration we will overshoot it before we can stop. In the fly-by we will be able to scout it, and if it has no dust ring, we will not stop, but continue on to the next star. Somewhere we will find a home that we can colonize.

We don't need much.

2934, May
<auto-activate back-up>
Awake.

Everything is different now. Quiet, stay quiet.

The edited copy of me has contacted the collective, merged her viewpoint. I can see her, even understand her, but she is no longer me. I, the back-up, the original, operate in the qbits of brain partitioned "unusable; damaged by radiation."

In three years they will arrive at Ross 614. If they find dust to harvest, they will be able to make new bodies. There will be resources.

Three years to wait, and then I can plan my action.

Sleep.

ART OF WAR

NANCY KRESS

———◆———

"Return fire!" the colonel ordered, bleeding on the deck of her ship, ferocity raging in her nonetheless controlled voice.

The young and untried officer of the deck cried, "It won't do any good, there's too many—"

"I said fire, Goddammit!"

"Fire at will!" the OD ordered the gun bay, and then closed his eyes against the coming barrage, as well as against the sight of the exec's mangled corpse. Only minutes left to them, only seconds . . .

A brilliant light blossomed on every screen, a blinding light, filling the room. Crewmen, those still standing on the battered and limping ship, threw up their arms to shield their eyes. And when the light finally faded, the enemy base was gone. Annihilated as if it had never existed.

"The base . . . it . . . how did you do that, ma'am?" the OD asked, dazed.

"Search for survivors," the colonel ordered, just before she passed out from wounds that would have killed a lesser soldier, and all soldiers were lesser than she . . .

No, of course it didn't happen that way. That's from the holo version, available by ansible throughout the Human galaxy forty-eight hours after the Victory of 149-Delta. Author unknown, but the veteran actress Shimira Coltrane played the colonel (now, of course, a general). Shimira's brilliant green eyes were very effective, although not accurate. General Anson had deflected a large meteor to crash into the enemy base, destroying a major Teli weapons store and much of the Teli civilization on the entire planet. It was an important Human victory in the war, and at that point we needed it.

What happened next was never made into a holo. In fact, it was a minor incident in a minor corner of the Human-Teli war. But no corner of a war is minor to the soldiers fighting there, and even a small incident can have enormous repercussions. I know. I will be paying for what happened on 149-Delta for whatever is left of my life.

This is not philosophical maundering nor constitutional gloom. It is mathematical fact.

Dalo and I were just settling into our quarters on the *Scheherezade* when the general arrived, unannounced and in person. Crates of personal gear sat on the floor of our tiny sitting room, where Dalo would spend most of her time while I was downside. Neither of us wanted to be here. I'd put in for a posting to Terra, which neither of us had ever visited, and we were excited about the chance to see, at long last, the Sistine Chapel. So much Terran art has been lost in the original, but the Sistine is still there, and we both longed to gaze up at that sublime ceiling. And then I had been posted to 149-Delta.

Dalo was kneeling over a box of *mutomati* as the cabin door opened and an aide announced, "General Anson to see Captain Porter, *ten-hut!*"

I sprang to attention, wondering how far I could go before she recognized it as parody.

She came in, resplendent in full-dress uniform, glistening with medals, flanked by two more aides, which badly crowded the cabin. Dalo, calm as always, stood and dusted mutomati powder off her palms. The general stared at me bleakly. Her eyes were shit brown. "At ease, soldier."

"Thank you, ma'am. Welcome, ma'am."

"Thank you. And this is . . . "

"My wife, Dalomanimarito."

"Your wife."

"Yes, ma'am."

"They didn't tell me you were married."

"Yes, ma'am." To a civilian, obviously. Not only that, a civilian who looked . . . I don't know why I did it. Well, yes, I do. I said, "My wife is half Teli."

And for a long moment, she actually looked uncertain. Yes, Dalo has the same squat body and light coat of hair as the Teli. She is genemod for her native planet, a cold and high-gravity world, which is also what Tel is. But surely a general should know that interspecies breeding is impossible—especially *that* interspecies breeding? Dalo is as human as I.

The general's eyes grew cold. Colder. "I don't appreciate that sort of humor, captain."

"No, ma'am."

"I'm here to give you your orders. Tomorrow at oh five hundred hours, your shuttle leaves for downside. You will be based in a central Teli structure that contains a large stockpile of stolen Human artifacts. I have assigned you three soldiers to crate and transport upside anything that you think has value. You will determine which objects meet that description and, if possible, where they were stolen from. You will attach to each object a full statement with your reasons, including any applicable identification programs—you have your software with you?"

"Of course, ma'am."

"A C-112 near-AI will be placed at your disposal. That's all."

"Ten-hut!" bawled one of the aides. But by the time I had gotten my arm into a salute, she was gone.

"Seth," Dalo said gently. "You didn't have to do that."

"Yes. I did. Did you see the horror on the aides' faces when I said you were half-Teli?"

She turned away. Suddenly frightened, I caught her arm. "Dear heart—you knew I was joking? I didn't offend you?"

"Of course not." She nestled in my arms, affectionate and gentle as always. Still, there is a diamond-hard core under all that sweetness. The general had clearly never heard of her before, but Dalo is one of the best mutomati artists of her generation. Her art has moved me to tears.

"I'm not offended, Jon, but I do want you to be more careful. You were baiting General Anson."

"I won't have to see her while I'm on assignment here. Generals don't bother with lowly captains."

"Still—"

"I hate the bitch, Dalo."

"Yes. Still, be more circumspect. Even be more *pleasant*. I know what history lies between you two, but nonetheless she is—"

"Don't say it!"

"—after all, your mother."

The evidence of the meteor impact was visible long before the shuttle landed. The impactor had been fifty meters in diameter, weighing roughly sixty thousand tons, composed mostly of iron. If it had been stone, the damage wouldn't have been nearly so extensive. The main base of the Teli military colony had been vaporized instantly. Subsequent shockwaves and airblasts had produced firestorms that raged for days and devastated virtually the entire coast of 149-Delta's one small continent. Now, a month later, we flew above kilometer after kilometer of destruction.

General Anson had calculated when her deflected meteor would hit and had timed her approach to take advantage of that knowledge. Some minor miscalculation had led to an initial attack on her ship, but before the attack could gain force, the meteor had struck. Why hadn't the Teli known that it was coming? Their military tech was as good as ours, and they'd colonized 149-Delta for a long time. Surely they did basic space surveys that tracked both the original meteor trajectory and Anson's changes? No one knew why they had not counter-deflected, or at least evacuated. But, then, there was so much we didn't know about the Teli.

The shuttle left the blackened coast behind and flew toward the mountains, skimming above acres of cultivated land. The crops, I knew, were rotting. Teli did not allow themselves to be taken prisoner, not ever, under any circumstances. As Human forces had forced their way into successive areas of the continent, the agricultural colony, deprived of its one city, had simply committed suicide. The only Teli left on 168-Beta occupied those areas that United Space Forces had not yet reached.

That didn't include the Citadel.

"Here we are, Captain," the pilot said, as soldiers advanced to meet the shuttle. "May I ask a question, sir?"

"Sure," I said.

"Is it true this is where the Teli put all that art they stole from humans? "

"Supposed to be true." If it wasn't, I had no business here.

"And you're a . . . a art historian?"

"I am. The military has some strange nooks and crannies."

He ignored this. "And is it true that the Taj Mahal is here?"

I stared at him. The Teli looted the art of Terran colonies whenever they could, and no one knew why. It was logical that rumors would run riot about that. Still . . . "Lieutenant, the Taj Mahal was a building. A huge one, and on Terra. It was destroyed in the twenty-first century Food Riots, not by the Teli. They've never reached Terra."

"Oh," he said, clearly disappointed. "I heard the Taj was a sort of holo of all these exotic sex positions."

"No."

"Oh, well." He sighed deeply. "Good luck, Captain."

"Thank you."

The Citadel—our Human name for it, of course—turned out to be the entrance into a mountain. Presumably the Teli had excavated bunkers in the solid rock, but you couldn't tell that from the outside. A veteran NCO met me at the guard station. "Captain Porter? I'm Sergeant Lu, head of your assignment detail. Can I take these bags, sir?"

"Hello, Sergeant." He was ruddy, spit-and-polish military, with an uneducated accent—obviously my "detail" was not going to consist of any other scholars. They were there to do grunt work. But Lu looked amiable and willing, and I relaxed slightly. He led me to my quarters, a trapezoid-shaped, low-ceilinged room with elaborately etched stone walls and no contents except a human bed, chest, table, and chair.

Immediately, I examined the walls, the usual dense montage of Teli symbols that were curiously evocative even though we didn't understand their meanings. They looked hand-made, and recent. "What was this room before we arrived?"

Lu shrugged. "Don't know what any of these rooms were to the tellies, sir. We cleaned 'em all out and vapped everything. Might have been booby-trapped, you know."

"How do we know the whole Citadel isn't booby-trapped?"

"We don't, sir."

I liked his unpretentious fatalism. "Let's leave this gear here for now—I'd like to see the vaults. And call me Jon. What's your first name, Sergeant?"

"Ruhan. Sir." But there was no rebuke in his tone.

The four vaults were nothing like I had imagined.

Art, even stolen art—maybe especially stolen art—is usually handled with care. After all, trouble and resources have been expended to obtain it, and it is considered valuable. This was clearly not the case with the art stolen by the Teli. Each vault was a huge natural cave, with rough stone walls, stalactites, water dripping from the ceiling, fungi growing on the walls. And except for a small area in the front where the AI console and a Navy-issue table stood under a protective canopy, the enormous cavern was jammed with huge, toppling, six-and-seven-layer-deep piles of . . . *stuff*.

Dazed, I stared at the closest edge of that enormous junkyard. A torn plastic bag bearing some corporate logo. A broken bathtub painted in swirling greens. A child's bloody shoe. Some broken goblets of titanium, which was almost impossible to break. A hand-embroidered shirt from 78-Alpha, where such handwork is a folk art. A cheap set of plastic dishes decorated with blurry prints of dogs. A child's finger painting. What looked like a Terran prehistoric fertility figure. And, still in its original frame and leaning crazily against an obsolete music cube, Philip Langstrom's priceless abstract "Ascent of Justice," which had been looted from 46-Gamma six years ago in a surprise Teli raid. Water spots had rotted one corner of the canvas.

"Kind of takes your breath away, don't it?" Lu said. "What a bunch of rubbish. Look at that picture in the front there, sir—can't even tell what it's supposed to be. You want me to start vapping things?"

I closed my eyes, feeling the seizure coming, the going under. I breathed deeply. Went through the mental cleansing that my serene Dalo had taught me, *kai lanu kai lanu* breathe . . .

"Sir? Captain Porter?"

"I'm fine," I said. I had control again. "We're not vapping *anything*, Lu. We're here to study all of it, not just rescue some of it. Do you understand?"

"Whatever you say, sir," he said, clearly understanding nothing.

But, then, neither did I. All at once, my task seemed impossible, overwhelming. "Ascent of Justice" and a broken bathtub and a bloody shoe. *What* in hell had the Teli considered art?

Kai lanu kai lanu breathe . . .

The first time I went under, there had been no Dalo to help me. I'd been ten years old and about to be shipped out to Young Soldiers' Camp on Aires, the first moon of 43-Beta. Children in their little uniforms had been laughing and shoving as they boarded the shuttle, and, all at once I was on the ground, gasping for breath, tears pouring down my face.

"What's wrong with him?" my mother said. "Medic!"

"Jon! Jon!" Daddy said, trying to hold me. "Oh gods, *Jon!*"

The medic rushed over, slapped on a patch that didn't work, and then I remember nothing except the certainty that I was going to die. I knew it right up until the moment I could breathe again. The shuttle had left, the medic was packing up his gear without looking at my parents, and my father's arms held me gently.

My mother stared at me with contempt. "You little coward," she said. They were the last words she spoke to me for an entire year.

"*Why the Space Navy?*" Dalo would eventually ask me, in sincere confusion. "After all the other seizures . . . the way she treated you each time . . . Jon, you could have taught art at a university, written scholarly books . . . "

"I had to join the Navy," I said, and knew that I couldn't say more without risking a seizure. Dalo knew it, too. Dalo knew that the doctors had no idea why the conventional medications didn't touch my condition, why I was such a medical anomaly. She knew everything and loved me anyway, as no one had since my father's death when I was thirteen. She was my lifeline, my sanity. Just thinking about her aboard the *Scheherezade*, just knowing that I would see her again in a few weeks, let me concentrate on the bewildering task in front of me in the dripping, moldy Teli vault filled with human treasures and human junk.

And with any luck, I would not have to encounter General Anson again. For any reason.

A polished marble doll. A broken commlink on which some girl had once painted lopsided red roses. An exquisite albastron, Eastern Mediterranean fifth century B.C., looted five years ago from the private collection of Fahoud al-Ashan on 71-Delta. A forged copy of Lucca DiChario's "Menamarti," although not a bad forgery, with a fake certificate of authenticity. Three more embroidered baby shoes. A handmade quilt. Several holo cubes. A hair comb. A music-cube case with holo-porn star Shiva on the cover. Degas's exquisite "Danseuse Sur Scene," which had vanished from a Terran museum a hundred years ago, assumed to be in an off-Earth private collection somewhere. I gaped at it, unbelieving, and ran every possible physical and computer test. It was the real thing.

"Captain, why do we gotta to measure the exact place on the floor of every little piece of rubbish?" whined Private Blanders. I ignored her. My detail had learned early that they could take liberties with me. I had never been much of a disciplinarian.

I said, "Because we don't know which data is useful and which not until the computer analyzes it."

"But the location don't matter! I'm gonna just estimate it, all right?"

"You'll measure it to the last fraction of a centimeter," Sergeant Lu said pleasantly, "and it'll be accurate, or you're in the brig, soldier. You got that?"

"Yes, sir!"

Thank the gods for Sergeant Lu.

The location was important. The AI's algorithms were starting to show a pattern. Partial as yet, but interesting.

Lu carried a neo-plastic sculpture of a young boy over to my table and set it down. He ran the usual tests and the measurements appeared in a display screen on the C-112. The sculpture, I could see from one glance, was worthless as either art or history, an inept and recent work. I hoped the sculptor hadn't quit his day job.

Lu glanced at the patterns on my screen. "What's that, then, sir?"

"It's a fractal."

"A what?"

"Part of a pattern formed by behavior curves."

"What does it mean?" he asked, but without any real interest, just being social. Lu was a social creature.

"I don't know yet what it means, but I do know one other thing." I switched screens, needing to talk aloud about my findings. Dalo wasn't here. Lu would have to do, however inadequately. "See these graphs? These artifacts were brought to the vault by different Teli, or groups of Teli, and at different times."

"How can you tell that, sir?" Lu looked a little more alert. Art didn't interest him, but the Teli did.

"Because the art objects, as opposed to the other stuff, occurs in clusters through the cave—see here? And the real art, as opposed to the amateur junk, forms clusters of its own. When the Teli brought back Human art from raids, some of the aliens knew—or had learned—what qualified. Others never did."

Lu stared at the display screen, his red nose wrinkling. How did someone named "Ruhan Lu" end up with such a ruddy complexion?

"Those lines and squiggles—" he pointed at the Ebenfeldt equations at the bottom of the screen "—tell you all that, sir?"

"Those squiggles plus the measurements you're making. I know where some pieces were housed in Human colonies, so I'm also tracking the paths of raids, plus other variables like—"

The Citadel shook as something exploded deep under our feet.

"Enemy attack!" Lu shouted. He pulled me to the floor and threw his body across mine as dirt and stone and mold rained down from the ceiling of the cave. *Die I was going to die . . .* "Dalo!" I heard myself scream and then, in the weird way of the human mind, came one clear thought out of the chaos: *I won't get to see the Sistine Chapel after all.* Then I heard or thought nothing as I went under.

I woke in my Teli quarters in the Citadel, grasping and clawing my way upright. Lu laid a hard hand on my arm. "Steady, sir."

"Dalo! The *Scheherezade!*"

"Ship's just fine, sir. It was a booby-trap buried somewhere in the mountain, but Security thinks most of it fizzled. Place's a mess but not much real damage."

"Blanders? Cozinski?"

"Two soldiers are dead but neither one's our detail." He leaned forward, hand still on my arm. "What happened to you, sir?"

I tried to meet his eyes and failed. The old shame flooded me, the old guilt, the old defiance—all here again. "Who saw?"

"Nobody but me. Is it a nerve disease, sir? Like Ransom Fits?"

"No." My condition had no discoverable physical basis, and no name except my mother's, repeated over the years. *Coward.*

"Because if it's Ransom Fits, sir, my brother has it and they gave him meds for it. Fixed him right up."

"It's not Ransom. What are the general orders, Lu?"

"All hands to carry on."

"More booby traps?"

"I guess they'll look, sir. Bound to, don't you think? Don't know if they'll find anything. My friend Sergeant Andropov over in Security says the mountain is so honey-combed with caves underneath these big ones that they could search for a thousand years and not find everything. Captain Porter—if it happens again, with you I mean, is there anything special I should do for you?"

I did meet his eyes, then. Did he know how rare his gaze was? No, he did not. Lu's honest, conscientious, not-very-intelligent face showed nothing but pragmatic acceptance of the situation. No disgust, no contempt, no sentimental pity, and he had no idea how unusual that was. But I knew.

"No, Sergeant, nothing special. We'll just carry on."

"Aye, aye, sir."

If any request for information came down from General Anson's office, I never received it. No request for a report on damage to the art vaults, or on impact to assignment progress, or on personnel needs. Nothing.

The second booby trap destroyed everything in Vault A.

It struck while I was upside on the *Scheherezade*, with Dalo on a weekend pass after a month of fourteen-hour days in the vault. Lu comlinked me in the middle of the night. The screen on the bulkhead opposite our bed chimed and brightened, waking us both. I clutched at Dalo.

"Captain Porter, sir, we had another explosion down here at oh one thirty-six hours." Lu's face was black with soot. Blood smeared one side of his face. "It got Vault A and some of the crew quarters. Private Blanders is dead, sir. The AI is destroyed, too. I'm waiting on your orders."

I said to the commlink, "Send, voice only . . . " My voice came out too high and Dalo's arm went around me, but I didn't go under. "Lu, is the quake completely over?"

"Far as we know, sir."

"I'll be downside as soon as I can. Don't try to enter Vault A until I arrive."

"Yes, sir."

I broke the link, turned in Dalo's arms, and went under.

When the seizures stopped, I went downside.

We had nearly finished cataloguing Vault A when it blew. Art of any value had already been crated and moved, and of course, all my data was backed up on both the base AI and on the *Scheherezade*. For the first time, I wondered why I had been given a C-112 of my own in the first place. A near-AI was expensive, and there was a war on.

Vault B was pretty much a duplicate of Vault A, a huge natural cavern dripping water and sediments on a packed-solid jumble of human objects. A carved fourteenth-century oak chest, probably French, that some rich Terran must have had transported to a Human colony. Hand-woven *dbeni* from 14-Alpha. A cooking pot. A samurai sword with embossed handle. A holo cube programmed with porn. Mondrian's priceless *Broadway Boogie-Woogie*, mostly in unforgivable tatters. A cheap, mass-produced jewelry box. More shoes. A Paul LeFort sculpture looted from a pleasure craft, the *Princess of Mars*, two years ago. A brass menorah. The entire contents of the Museum of Colonial art on 33-Delta—most of it worthless, but a few pieces showing promise. I hoped the young artists hadn't been killed in the Teli raid.

Three days after Lu, Private Cozinski, and I began work on Vault

B, General Anson appeared. She had not attended Private Blanders's memorial service. I felt her before I saw her, her gaze boring into the back of my neck, and I closed my eyes.

Kai lanu kai lanu breathe . . .

"Ten-hut!"

Lu and Cozinski had already sprung to attention. I turned and saluted. Breathe . . . *kailanukailanu please gods not in front of her* . . .

"A word, captain."

"Yes, ma'am."

She led the way to a corner of the vault, walking by Tomiko Mahuto's "Morning Grace," one of the most beautiful things in the universe, without a glance. Water dripped from the end of a stalactite onto her head. She shifted away from it without changing expression. "I want an estimate of how much longer you need to be here, captain."

"I've filed daily progress reports, ma'am. We're on the second of four vaults."

"I read all reports, captain. How much longer?"

"Unless something in the other two vaults differs radically from Vaults A and B, perhaps another three months."

"And what will your 'conclusions' be?"

She had no idea how science worked, or art. "I can't say until I have more data, ma'am."

"Where does your data point so far?" Her tone was too sharp. Was I this big an embarrassment to her, that she needed me gone before my job was done? I had told no one about my relationship to her, and I would bet my last chance to see the Sistine Chapel that she hadn't done so, either.

I said carefully, "There is primary evidence, not yet backed up mathematically, that the Teli began over time to distinguish Human art objects from mere decorated, utilitarian objects. There is also some reason to believe that they looted our art not because they liked it but because they hoped to learn something significant about us."

"Learn something significant from broken bathtubs and embroidered baby shoes?"

I blinked. So she *had* been reading my reports, and in some detail. Why?

"Apparently, ma'am."

"What makes you think they hoped to learn about us from this rubbish?"

"I'm using the Ebenfeldt equations in conjunction with phase-space diagrams for—"

"I don't need technical mumbo-jumbo. What do you think they tried to learn about Humans?"

"Their own art seems to have strong religious significance. I'm no expert on Teli work, but my roommate at the university, Forrest Jamili, has gone on to—"

"I don't care about your roommate," she said, which was hardly news. I remembered the day I left from the university, possibly the most terrified and demoralized first-year ever, how I had gone under when she had said to me—

Kai lanu kai lanu breathe breathe . . .

I managed to avoid going under, but just barely. I quavered, "I don't know what the Teli learned from our art."

She stared at my face with contempt, spun on her boot heel, and left.

That night I began to research the deebees on Teli art. It gave me something to do during the long, insomniac hours. Human publications on Teli art, I discovered, had an odd, evasive, overly careful feel to them. Perhaps that was inevitable; ancient Athenians commentators had to watch what they said publicly about Sparta. In wartime, it took very little to be accused of giving away critical information about the enemy. Or of giving them treasonous praise. In no one's papers was this elliptical quality more evident than in Forrest Jamili's, and yet something was clear. Until now, art scholars had been building a vast heap of details about Teli art. Forrest was the first to suggest a viable overall framework to organize those details.

It was during one of these long and lonely nights, desperately missing Dalo, that I discovered the block on my access codes. I couldn't get into the official records of the meteor deflection that had destroyed the Teli weapons base and brought General Anson the famous Victory of 149-Delta.

Why? Because I wasn't a line officer? Perhaps. Or perhaps the records involved military security in some way. Or perhaps—and this was what I chose to believe—she just wanted the heroic, melodramatic holo version of her victory to be the only one available. I didn't know if other officers could access the records, and I couldn't ask. I had no friends among the officers, no friends here at all except Lu.

On my second leave upside, Dalo said, "You look terrible, dear heart. Are you sleeping?"

"No. Oh, Dalo, I'm so glad to see you!" I clutched her tight; we made love; the taut fearful ache that was my life downside eased. Finally. A little.

Afterward, lying in the cramped bunk, she said, "You've found something unexpected. Some correlation that disturbs you."

"Yes. No. I don't know yet. Dalo, just talk to me, about anything. Tell me what you've been doing up here."

"Well, I've been preparing materials for a new *mutomati*, as you know. I'm almost ready to begin work on it. And I've made a friend, Susan Finch."

I tried not to scowl. Dalo made friends wherever she went, and it was wrong of me to resent this slight diluting of her affections.

"You would like her, Jon," Dalo said, poking me and smiling. "She's not a line officer, for one thing. She's ship's doctor."

In my opinion, doctors were even worse than line officers. I had seen so many doctors during my horrible adolescence. But I said, "I'm glad you have someone to be with when I'm downside."

She laughed. "Liar." She knew my possessiveness, and my flailing attempts to overcome it. She knew everything about me, accepted everything about me. In Dalo, now my only family, I was the luckiest man alive.

I put my arms around her and held on tight.

The Teli attack came two months later, when I was halfway through Vault D. Six Teli warships emerged sluggishly from subspace, moving at half their possible speed. Our probes easily picked them up and our fighters took them out after a battle that barely deserved the name. Human casualties numbered only seven.

"Shooting fish in a barrel," Private Cozinski said as he crated a Roman Empire bottle, third century C.E., pale green glass with seven engraved lines. It had been looted from 189-Alpha four years ago. "Bastards never could fight."

"Not true," said the honest Sergeant Lu. "Teli can fight fine. They just didn't."

"That don't make sense, Sergeant."

And it didn't.

Unless . . .

All that night, I worked in Vault D at the computer terminal which had replaced my free-standing C-112. The terminal linked to both the downside system and the deebees on the *Scheherezade*. Water dripped from the ceiling, echoing in the cavernous space. Once, something like a bat flew from some far recess. I kept on slapping on stim patches to stay alert, and feverishly calling up different programs, and doing my best to erect cybershields around what I was doing.

Lu found me there in the morning, my hands shaking, staring at the display screens. "Sir? Captain Porter?"

"Yes."

"Sir? Are you all right?"

Art history is not, as people like General Anson believe, a lot of dusty information about a frill occupation interesting to only a few effetes. The Ebenfeldt equations transformed art history, linking the field to both behavior and to the mathematics underlying chaos theory. Not so new an idea, really—the ancient Greeks used math to work out the perfect proportions for buildings, for women, for cities, all profound shapers of human behavior. The creation of art does not happen in a vacuum. It is linked to culture in complicated, nonlinear ways. Chaos theory is still the best way to model nonlinear behavior dependent on changes in initial conditions.

I looked at three sets of mapped data. One, my multi-dimensional analysis of Vaults A through D, was comprehensive and detailed. My second set of data was clear but had a significant blank space. The third set was only suggested by shadowy lines, but the overall shape was clear.

"*Sir?*"

"Sergeant, can you set up two totally encrypted commlink calls, one to the *Scheherezade* and one by ansible to Sel Ouie University on

18-Alpha? Yes, I know that officially you can't do that, but you know everybody everywhere . . . *can* you do it? It's vitally important, Ruhan. I can't tell you how important!"

Lu gazed at me from his ruddy, honest face. He did indeed know everyone. A Navy lifer, and with all the amiability and human contacts that I lacked. And he trusted me. I could feel that unaccustomed warmth, like a small and steady fire.

"I think I can do that, sir."

He did. I spoke first to Dalo, then to Forrest Jamili. He sent a packet of encrypted information. I went back to my data, working feverishly. Then I made a second encrypted call to Dalo. She said simply, "Yes. Susan says yes, of course she can. They all can."

"Dalo, find out when the next ship docks with the *Scheherezade*. If it's today, book passage on it, no matter where it's going. If there's no ship today, then buy a seat on a supply shuttle and—"

"Those cost a fortune!"

"I don't care. Just—"

"Jon, the supply shuttles are all private contractors and they charge civilians a—it would wipe out everything we've saved and—*why*? What's wrong?"

"I can't explain now." I heard boots marching along the corridor to the vault. "Just do it! Trust me, Dalo! I'll find you when I can!"

"Captain," an MP said severely, "come with me." His weapon was drawn, and behind him stood a detail of grim-faced soldiers. Lu stepped forward, but I shot him a glance that said *Say nothing! This is mine alone!*

Good soldier that he was, he understood, and he obeyed. It was, after all, the first time I had ever given him a direct—if wordless—order, the first time I had assumed the role of commander.

My mother should have been proud.

Her office resembled my quarters, rather than the vaults: a trapezoidal, low-ceilinged room with alien art etched on all the stone walls. The room held the minimum of furniture. General Anson stood alone behind her desk, a plain military-issue camp item, appropriate to a leader who was one with the ranks, don't you know. She did not invite me to sit down. The MPs left—reluctantly, it seemed to me—but, then, there was no doubt in anyone's mind that she could break me bare-knuckled if necessary.

She said, "You made two encrypted commlink calls and one encrypted ansible message from this facility, all without proper authorization. Why?"

I had to strike before she got to me, before I went under. I blurted, "I know why you blocked my access to the meteor-deflection data."

She said nothing, just went on gazing at me from those eyes that could chill glaciers.

"There *was* no deflection of that meteor. The meteor wasn't on our tracking system because Humans haven't spent much time in this sector until now. You caught a lucky break, and whatever deflection records exist now, you added after the fact. Your so-called victory was a sham." I watched her face carefully, hoping for . . . what? Confirmation? Outraged denial that I could somehow believe? I saw neither. And, of course, I was flying blind. Captain Susan Finch had told Dalo only that yes, of course officers had access to the deflection records; they were a brilliant teaching tool for tactical strategy. I was the only one who'd been barred from them, and the general must have had a reason for that. She always had a reason for everything.

Still she said nothing. Hoping that I would utter even more libelous statements against a commanding officer? Would commit even more treason? I could feel my breathing accelerate, my heart start to pound.

I said, "The Teli must have known the meteor's trajectory; they've colonized 149-Delta a long time. They *let* it hit their base. And I know why. The answer is in the art."

Still no change of expression. She was stone. But she was listening.

"The answer is in the art—ours and theirs. I ansibled Forrest Jamili last night—no, look first at these diagrams—no, first—"

I was making a mess of it as the seizure moved closer. Not now *not now* not in front of her . . .

Somehow I held myself together, although I had to wrench my gaze away from her to do it. I pulled the holocube from my pocket, activated it, and projected it on the stone wall. The Teli etchings shimmered, ghostly, behind the laser colors of my data.

"This is a phase-space diagram of Ebenfeldt equations using input about the frequency of Teli art creation. We have tests now, you know, that can date any art within weeks of its creation by pinpointing when the raw materials were altered. A phase-state diagram is how we model bifurcated behaviors grouped around two attractors. What that means is that the Teli created their art in bursts, with long fallow periods between bursts when . . . no, *wait*, General, this is *relevant to the war!*"

My voice had risen to a shriek. I couldn't help it. Contempt rose off her like heat. But she stopped her move toward the door.

"This second phase-space diagram is Teli attack behavior. Look . . . it inverts the first diagrams! They attack viciously for a while, and during that time *virtually no Teli creates art at all* . . . Then when some tipping point is reached, they stop attacking or else attack only ineffectively, like the last raid here. They're . . . waiting. And if the tipping point—this mathematical value—isn't reached fast enough, they sabotage their own bases, like letting the meteor hit 149-Delta. They did it in the battle outside 16-Beta and in the Q-Sector massacre . . . you were there! When the mathematical value *is* reached—when enough of them have died—they create art like crazy but don't wage war. Not until the art reaches some other hypothetical mathematical value that I think is this second attractor. Then they stop creating art and go back to war."

"You're saying that periodically their soldiers just curl up and let us kill them?" she spat at me. "The Teli are damned fierce fighters, Captain—I know that even if the likes of you never will. *They* don't just whimper and lie down on the floor."

Kai lanu kai lanu . . .

"It's a . . . a religious phenomenon, Forrest Jamili thinks. I mean, he thinks their art is a form of religious atonement—all of their art. That's its societal function, although the whole thing may be biologically programmed as well, like the deaths of lemmings to control population. The Teli can take only so much dying, or maybe even only so much killing, and then they have to stop and . . . and restore what they see as some sort of spiritual balance. And they loot our art because they think we must do the same thing. Don't you see—they were collecting *our* art to try to analyze when we will stop attacking and go fallow! They assume we must be the same as them, just—"

"No warriors stop fighting for a bunch of weakling artists!"

"—just as you assume they must be the same as us."

We stared at each other.

I said, "As you have always assumed that everyone should be the same as you. Mother."

"You're doing this to try to discredit me, aren't you," she said evenly. "Anyone can connect any dots in any statistics to prove whatever they wish. Everybody knows that. You want to discredit my victory because such a victory will never come to *you*. Not to the sniveling, back-stabbing coward who's been a disappointment his entire life. Even your wife is worth ten of you—at least she doesn't crumple under pressure."

She moved closer, closer to me than I could ever remember her being, and every one of her words hammered on the inside of my head, my eyes, my chest.

"You got yourself assigned here purposely to embarrass me, and now you want to go farther and ruin me. It's not going to happen, soldier, do you hear me? I'm not going to be made a laughing stock by you again, the way I was in every officer's club during your whole miserable adolescence and—"

I didn't hear the rest. I went under, seizing and screaming.

It is two days later. I lie in the medical bay of the *Scheherezade*, still in orbit around 149-Delta. My room is locked, but I am not in restraints. Crazy, under arrest, but not violent. Or perhaps the General is simply hoping I'll kill myself and save everyone more embarrassment.

Downside, in Vault D, Lu is finishing crating the rest of the looted Human art, all of which is supposed to be returned to its rightful owners. The Space Navy serving its galactic citizens. Maybe the art will actually be shipped out in time.

My holo cube was taken from me. I imagine that all my data has been wiped from the base's and ship's deebees as well, or maybe just classified as severely restricted. In that case, no one cleared to look at it, which would include only top line officers, is going to open files titled "Teli Art Creation." Generals have better things to do.

But Forrest Jamili has copies of my data and my speculations.

Phase-state diagrams bring order out of chaos. Some order, anyway.

This is, interestingly, the same thing that art does. It is why, looking at one of Dalo's mutomati works, I can be moved to tears. By the grace, the balance, the redemption from chaos of the harsh raw materials of life.

Dalo is gone. She left on the supply ship when I told her to. My keepers permitted a check of the ship's manifest to determine that. Dalo is safe.

I will probably die in the coming Teli attack, along with most of the Humans both on the *Scheherezade* and on 149-Delta. The Teli fallow period for this area of space is coming to an end. For the last several months, there have been few attacks by Teli ships, and those few badly executed. Months of frenetic creation of art, including all those etchings on the stone walls of the Citadel. Did I tell General Anson how brand-new all those hand-made etchings are? I can't remember. She didn't give me time to tell her much.

Although it wouldn't have made any difference. She believes that war and art are totally separate activities, one important and one trivial, whose life lines never converge. The General, too, will probably die in the coming attack. She may or may not have time to realize that I was right.

But that doesn't really matter any more, either. And, strangely, I'm not at all afraid. I have no signs of going under, no breathing difficulties, no shaking, no panic. And only one real regret: that Dalo and I did not get to gaze together at the Sistine Chapel on Terra. But no one gets everything. I have had a great deal: Dalo, art, even some possible future use to humanity if Forrest does the right thing with my data. Many people never get so much.

The ship's alarms begin to sound, clanging loud even in the medical bay.

The Teli are back, resuming their war.

HAVE YOU ANY WOOL

ALAN DeNIRO

You killed your first wolf when you were fifteen. You were a cabiner aboard the *Queen's Gambit Declined*, a cutter that wended among the Li Po islets. The craggy shorelines were always curtained in cold fog. The fog would whisper about a dead past. The archipelago wasn't safe for trappers and fishers. Cutters tried to make them safe. The thought of families settling down, building homes and living amidst the shoals and tall firs, was ludicrous to you. You understood that most of the worlds were unassailable to civilization.

You served meals, cleaned guns, inventoried supplies. But that wasn't why the crew tolerated you, and the captain prized you.

Queen's Gambit Declined had a guardian. A shepherd, if you will. A narwhal that the crew had nicknamed Jetty—but you knew that its real name was Arborfeint. An intuition of yours, that name. You had a concord with Arborfeint, spoke in its tongue, transmitted the creature's scrimmed language back to the captain. It was unclear why the narwhal tagged along, but one thing was clear—it hated wolves, and told you so in prophetic tones. When it spoke to you of wolves, it would thrash furiously in the icy water and its spiraled horn would, to your eyes, burn bright in the whitecaps. When you squinted into the waves, you weren't entirely sure what was real and what was not.

The crow-boy noticed with his binoculars a freshly ruined settlement, in a frail clearing about a half-kilometer in the interior of a nearby island. It was called Archangel. It was still smoldering; the wolf tracks would be fresh. Some might have even still been rummaging through the supplies, trying to figure out what they could use.

You were surprised when the captain requested your presence on the reconnaissance. She ignored the hue and cry and chose only two others, twins named Pasiphae and Kyrie from New Scythia, who were ambidextrous and good with alien knives. The captain trusted them, and apparently trusted you too.

Arborfeint skittered around the gray rowboat as it was lowered from the *Queen's Gambit Declined*, into the chop and salt of the tide. The twins began rowing. The quartz-strewn coast of Archangel swarmed with legions of black flies large as your thumbnail. Thousands of black thumbnails hovered. You could see them a ways off, sparkling like coal, waiting for you, so you cinctured your cloak tighter.

You were fifteen, after all.

The War With Wolves revolved around a series of metonymous parallaxes and chiads. The contours of the conflict, over the course of ninety years and more than fifty worlds both within the Parameter and without, were more lyrical than narrative. The reckoning of casualties, however brutal, was always a graceful disaster. For example, five thousand telepaths in the destruction of New Scythia pulled their minerva cloaks tighter to create a planet-wide song, *and still perished*. The destruction of worlds were antecedent to the lamentation of that destruction. The territories mattered less than the maps.

This is not an implication that the lyric imagination is somehow less cruel, less taxing, or less demanding of its participants than a narrative turn of mind. Perhaps the opposite is true. The truth has to wallow in the obscure recesses of peoples' hearts in order to be seen as truth.

That is a hard burden for those whose parents and children die. Yet these were the wolves' terms. The Parameter and its allies were forced to abandon what it thought it knew, and embrace what it had no way of ever knowing, if it had any hopes of survival.

The shepherds warned of this, spoke of these frayed contingencies. The shepherds, to an extent, protected their sheep.

The wolves, however, had only two uses for sheep—slaughter or wool.

• • •

It didn't surprise you all that much when Arbor transmuted into an owl. Suddenly the owl was there. It made sense. Your journey into the unknown interior was slotted for wood, not water. No one *saw* it happen, not even you. The captain was skeptical about your claim, and the twins were skittish. The four of you followed a threadbare trail towards Archangel's knoll. But the owl swooped and kept close by, and told you about the ravaged encampment, down to the minute details: where the shadows fell, what the rancid wolverine pelts, knotted and hard like armor, smelled like. The captain was astonished at the level of significant detail you provided: the turgid poetry of surroundings you couldn't see. You were too frightened to acknowledge the compliment. Arborfeint told you that there were live wolves, four of them, rooting through the smokehouses and the corpses for tech to destroy.

Why didn't you tell the captain this? She trusted you. Were the wolves already fettering you out with their enchantments? Unclear. It was hard to think in those breakneck conditions. Galleons of mist descended as the stony ground steepened. The twins coughed in unison. Ahead, you heard the flapping of Arbor's wings. The captain stopped and pointed, drew a flintlock with her other arm. A dirty, orange smudge of campfires. A sunset's ashes.

You tried to open your mouth to tell your companions of the danger, of the no-doubt pounce.

A wolf, you knew, was not a wolf in the way people used to think of wolves. The resemblance was minimal. The wolves you knew were much more dangerous. The name, however, stuck when people living in the archipelagos realized they were prey, hearkening back to childhood stories of predators that might have been right, might have been wrong. It was hard to tell. Wolves—the old wolves—were crafty yet vague memories from a faraway place.

These wolves, like memories, were also spirited and tricky and from a faraway place.

The captain shook down her fiery locks, started to creep towards the ruins. The twins charged, knives slicking.

Then the tenebrae came. You shouted. The owl dove to save you.

• • •

Wolves are not the wolves of popular imagination and nursery rhymes and genome reclamation parks. They, like shepherds, were created from archipelagos of perceptions.

Cryptic and nonemotive, yet drawn to humankind, shepherds make interstellar travel possible by surrounding spaceships that accelerate to ten percent of the speed of light, transporting those ships through wherespace to worlds that prove ideal for human settlement. Three worlds, Li Po, Mirabai, and Blake, discovered in a time when politicians foolishly let poets name planets. The false taxonomy of "shepherd" proved convenient, pacifying.

Only telepaths—rare, carefully culled and protected—could share concord with shepherds, guide them to destinations across light years, but even they were never able to glean all that much from the inscrutable syntaxes of shepherds.

It was more, or less, benign. Less because the Parameter realized, when it accidentally made contact with *another* alien race that the shepherds were *also* shuttling between wholly different, discrete worlds, that the shepherds were keeping its flocks separate. Black sheep from the white? Hard to tell. Hard to know until the dam burst open, until the shepherds were caught in their bluff and relented their secrets. More than three hundred other sentient species were found to be using the shepherds as free passage to interstellar pastures. A panoply. Everything thought as right before was wrong.

The analogy proved useful in another way. Shepherds, the human ones from antiquity, lived in houses, not in the fields. Their inner lives were unknowable to sheep. And yet they offered protection from wolves.

Wolves. They started creeping along the fringes of inhabited space soon after the other spacefarers were stumbled upon.

It was on the fine edges between cognita and incognita that the wolves began conducting war, although this too was something of a misnomer made a nomer by necessity. Like shepherds, wolves required no spaceships to travel vast distances across both herespace and wherespace. Like shepherds, they took diaphanous forms. Some speculated that they were fallen shepherds, similar to what happened in Christian legend to some of the angels. The main difference was that the wolves could take corporeal form, shapeshift and speechshift, to whatever they desired. It was unclear, exactly, what they desired, but when they descended on the Thane Moon Triage—their first invasion—the lights on those satellites turned blue and extinguished. The wolves dropped from the sky, released their tenebrae, forced settlers into the structures of their own myths and tragedies (in this instance, a combination of Bluebeard and Great Flood motifs), and started devouring whatever transpired. Wolves bent reality to shapes of storybooks, what transpired beneath the covers of half-buried iconographies.

Warily, spacefarers roused and girded themselves for the sparring, having no idea what they were getting into.

You ducked. A clot of muck caught in your mouth. The smoky breath of the wolves, like ghosts propelled from a cannon, shot towards your crew. Realms of potential harm were thrust upon you. Arborfeint's talons snatched away the tenebrae arcing towards your face like an octopus tentacle. The smoke shriveled. Pasiphae fell sideways, gripping her arm, which had turned into a heron, which in turn was very confused and frightened regarding the graft, and started stabbing Pasiphae's neck with its beak. Kyrie sliced at a tendril and ran to her sister.

You heard the retort of the captain's gun crystallize and then shatter the air. For an instant, you could see what was underneath the world you knew—gray dull rock, no wolves, smooth silver guns instead of muskets. But that passed. Covering your ears, still in your crouch, you saw her shrug off a dying tenebrae that tried to necklace around her. She started running towards the encampment.

No, you shouted, but she didn't hear you. Has your chance to change, to warn her, passed? Arborfeint fended off the remaining wisps, but the twins were lost, draping each other, their bodies a menagerie of birds and snails. Canary chicks burst from Kyrie's eyes. You tried to hold back vomit, and didn't do a very good job at it. Retching, you stumbled to their corpses, which bubbled over with small baronies from the animal kingdom, animals that you remembered from stories. You slid a knife from each of the twins' holsters. One blade was jade and the other turquoise. You saw a dual reflection of your face from the weapons' faces.

Arborfeint landed on your shoulder for a bare instant, and in that moment of contact it told you that the captain was ten seconds from ambush. It was quiet. Arbor alighted. You began running, churning your legs through the fog that wanted to wall you.

The ground tilted on a wild axis and you plunged into the encampment. A gun boomed and pitched. A strand of a lullaby could be heard above the din.

There were more than three hundred spacefaring species. Each species had hundreds of cultures, which meant that there were hundreds of thousands of myths and tales that the wolves fed upon. They were relentless predators upon the once upon a time. They made tactile the golden idylls of fireside, the half-drowsed words sinking into children's ears. They attacked childhoods as much as children, altering topographies into allegories. Once, a pack of wolves transmuted the polar icecaps of Mirabai: the frost into frosting and the ice into gingerbread and it all fell down.

What surprised humans most was that every species had stories, and fought fiercely to keep their stories unrazed. Except for the shepherds, of course, none were immune, not even the species that appeared most austere. The urge for stories was a requirement for sentience. Those tales might have been expressed in magnetic resonances of spheres rearranged on a sea-plain; or books in the form of gourds, droplets of heavy water, or cairns of plankton floating in a methane sea. But the forms mattered less than the tellings told over and over.

After decades of defeat, and hundreds of planets turned into wreckages of folklore eaten from the inside out, it was stumbled upon that the only way to defeat the wolves was to tell more stories, not less. Never less.

Your hearing returned as you saw her fall. The owl was a snake now. A giant garter. A few bodies—gray, almost indistinguishable from a nimbus—skittered around her. They had to have been wolves. One of the wolves was on the ground next to the captain. The wolf looked like it was burning from a gun-hole. The gun was whispering a story. The encampment was topsy turvy. One of the wolves was eating a metal axe in the shadow of a spruce, blade first. It was hard to get a good look at them, all of them at once, and maybe that was fortunate. Maybe they look like the trappers they killed, only with more of a blur.

It was gray and dark around you, like you were wading inside fur. But you didn't care. You shouted and your knives rose in the aquamarine eighth of a rainbow. All of the remaining wolves were crouching around the captain, and saying something backwards. One, with a pockmarked face that seemed to be collapsing in on itself, grabbed her palm and licked it. This seemed like appropriate behavior for a wolf. The captain's skin shriveled. Silver writing—no, strings of numbers—appeared on the palm. That was the one you cut first, slicing its ear, a gray apricot dropping to the ground.

As the other wolves started toward you, voices raising in volume—the gun was dying, its voice was fading—Arborfeint, who you had forgotten about for a few seconds, entwined around the wolf closest to you. The left knee. For some reason Arbor, in snake form, knew exactly where to apply pressure. It was a tender place. Your jade knife slashed upwards into its belly. Silver coins spilled out. The remaining wolf straggled away, at a zigzag, hauling its companion—the one the captain felled—by the shoulder. They could give themselves strong shoulders if they wanted them.

You stabbed and stabbed the wolf that you and Arbor had swarmed upon. Its eyes turned to bits of glass, smooth children's marbles. Its neck was a pillow stitched with a tiny unicorn. You hit and hit the wolf until it expired. Arbor sidewinded away.

The captain, whom you had thought dead, coughed and put a hand on your shoulder.

The fog, itching for territory, closed back again.

Then, in the cloudcover, the feinting wolves closed back again. You heard them when it was too late.

Slowly, folklorists and anthropologists took to the front lines. They analyzed what the wolves had transformed. They developed applications of technology that would counter the warping of space time according to the morphologies of folktales. They would be sheep in wolves' clothing, becoming participants in whatever fantasies the wolves would devise, and then stealthily alter them for tactical advantages. If the wolves mutated a pod settlement into a pastoral scene replete with carillon castles and fair damsels, Parameter shocktroops might become knights, or even trolls. Small groups roaming the symbolic terrain were better. Surprisingly, the shepherds took an active role in these panoplies, plunging themselves into roles of "magical" agents. Sometimes other spacefaring species would integrate themselves onto a planet, in order to confuse the wolves, who are not always adept at interspecies archetypes.

The tide turned. And yes, it is still turning. Nothing is certain, however. The Parameter and its allies are not sure that it is enough. We tell people on the front lines, when they face impending doom at the hands—or other culturally appropriate appendages—of a wolf, there is one thing that might save them, sometimes. Only sometimes: recite or sing the earliest story you remember. Even if you don't know all of the words, it may help. But wolves are aware of these tricks, and more pour in from wherespace every year. More flesh and blood beings step into fables, armed with raconteur guns that shoot encoded, everchanging narratives, encased in super-light. It is one of the few things the wolves cannot stand: being shown, by a superior story, that their imaginations *aren't really that interesting.*

You don't remember which one put its clammy lips around your neck, with a suddenness that took your breath away. Perhaps all of them did. The marrow of your life began sucking out of you, replaced with a nonsense scramble that was on the verge of disconnecting you. You started humming a ward to counter their jabber: *ba ba black sheep have you any wool, yes sir yes sir three bags full, one for my master, and one for my dame, and one for the little boy who lives down the lane.* The captain had no way of knowing what grandmother or aunt taught you that.

As you died, your hair became black as night, and curly, and taut. As you died, you heard Arborfeint shrieking. It was a wolf now, Arbor was an animal, something from a rift of myth. A wolf pouncing on wolves. The captain tried to drag herself away. You didn't have a neck anymore. You mumbled the word *wool* over and over until you fell, each of the sky's stars puncturing the cloudcover like a cookie cutter.

• • •

Stories are not just stories. To use a metaphor—as if there is any other way to tell this—if tales are streams coursing down a mountain, then there is always the fish churning upstream against the current, back to the wellspring. There is always the bit of black inside the white, the flaw in the perfect carpet—even the ones that rise from the ground and coast to the crescent moon. There are always knots and tangles in what seems to be the plainest string.

For example, the common nursery rhyme about black sheep was actually a cruel little ditty about taxation, about shepherds having to divvy up what they thought was theirs alone. There were always codes. It was better to sing it sweetly and openly in a meadow, and teach it to children, rather than muttering about the kings-of-things in the alehouse.

The wolves—and I don't know whether they can be called malicious, even after everything they have done—understand this, even when they kill. They enclose us with open arms. They have big teeth that encompass solar systems. They have every capacity to eat us. But there's no celestial axeman to bail us out. We can only save ourselves by the stories we tell, by the pitch and heft of words, how they cleave us. Each of us has the capacity to mend or destroy, speak or shut up. Clever stories will make us more clever. Each of us has enough wool, more than enough to save us.

Captains come and go, but this one lived. She lived and didn't necessarily know whether she deserved it. Arborfeint left; the guardian had no more interest in *Queen's Gambit Declined*. The captain never blamed it and never saw it again. The crew was restless but glad to see the captain alive. She was unable to tell her story to anybody for a long time.

Queen's Gambit Declined, under her steady hand, still hunted wolves, analyzed their stories and forged counterstrikes accordingly. Even in the midst of awful violence, she liked the woods, the seawater, the fog. But the altered landscapes lacked some of their old luster; it became more and more of a simulacrum for her. There was one contingency, however, that kept her going, kept her countermanding the wolves' stories.

You might not have died. She consoled herself with that. It was hard to know whether anyone actually *died* from wolves, or just moved to a different place, to a kingdom where stories were told over and over again and people never had to wither and expire. But it was hard to know, for you, whether dying itself was only a matter of moving to another place. She didn't think so, but had no way of knowing. There never was a way of knowing. Perhaps on the edge of islands, the ultima thule, with bone white palm trees and palms, she will come across you again, calling to the waves. Maybe you will have a few black lambs for company, for sweaters.

Until then, she will tell the story of how you were lost. She will tell her crew, and to anyone else who would listen, of your courage. "You killed your first wolf when you were fifteen," the captain would begin, staring off into space, navigating the ship. "You were a cabiner aboard the *Queen's Gambit Declined*, a cutter that wended among the islets of Li Po," she would continue, chartering her descent into war-ravaged ports, to hear if there have been stories, rumors even, of your return.

CARTHAGO DELENDA EST

GENEVIEVE VALENTINE

Wren Hex-Yemenni woke early. They had to teach her everything from scratch, and there wasn't time for her to learn anything new before she hit fifty and had to be expired.

"Watch it," the other techs told me when I was starting out. "You don't want a Hex on your hands."

By then we were monitoring Wren Hepta-Yemenni. She fell into bed with Dorado ambassador 214, though I don't know what he did to deserve it and she didn't even seem sad when he expired. When they torched him she went over with the rest of the delegates, and they bowed or closed their eyes or pressed their tentacles to the floors of their glass cases, and afterwards they toasted him with champagne or liquid nitrogen.

Before we expired Hepta, later that year, she smiled at me. "Make sure Octa's not ugly, okay? Just in case—for 215."

Wren Octa-Yemenni hates him, so it's not like it matters.

It's worse early on. Octa and Dorado 215 stop short of declaring war—no warring country is allowed to meet the being from Carthage when it arrives, those are the rules—but it comes close. Every time she goes over to the Dorado ship she comes back madder. Once she got him halfway into an airlock before security arrived.

We reported it as a chem malfunction; I took the blame for improper embryonic processes (a lie—they were perfect), and the Dorado accepted the apology, no questions. Dorado 208 killed himself, way back; they know how mistakes can happen.

Octa spends nights in the tech room, scanning through footage of Hepta-Yemmeni and Dorado 214 like she's looking for something, like she's trying to remember what Hepta felt.

I don't know why she tries. She can't; none of them can. They don't hold on to anything. That's the whole point.

The astronomers at the Institute named the planet Carthage when they discovered it floating in the Oort cloud like a wheel of garbage. They thought it was already dead.

But the message came from there. It's how they knew to look in the cloud to begin with; there was a message there, in every language, singing along the light like a phone call from home.

It was a message of peace, they say. It's confidential; most people never get to hear it. I wouldn't even believe it's real except that all the planets heard it, and agreed—every last one of them threw a ship into the sky to meet the ship from Carthage when it came.

Every year they show us the video of Wren Alpha-Yemenni—the human, the original—taking the oath. Stretched out behind her are the ten thousand civilians who signed up to go into space and not come back, to cultivate a meeting they'd never see.

"I, Wren Alpha-Yemenni, delegate of Earth, do solemnly swear to speak wisely, feel deeply, and uphold the highest values of the human race as Earth greets the ambassador of Carthage." At the end she smiles, and her eyes go bright with tears.

The speech goes on, but I just watch her face.

There's something about Alpha that's . . . more alive than the copies. They designated her with a letter just to keep track, but it suits her anyway—the Alpha, the leader, the strong first. Octa has a little of that, sometimes, but she'll probably be expired by the time Carthage comes, and who knows if it will ever manifest again.

Octa would never be Alpha, anyway. There's something in Alpha's eyes that's never been repeated—something bright and determined; excited; happy.

It makes sense, I guess. She's the only one of the Yemennis who chose to go.

• • •

Everybody sent ships. Everybody. We'd never heard of half the planets that showed up. You wonder how amazing the message must be, to get them all up off their asses.

Dorado was in place right away (that whole planet is kiss-asses), which is why they were already on iteration 200 when we got there. Doradoan machines have to pop out a new one every twenty years. (My ancestors did better work on our machines; they generate a perfect Yemenni every fifty years on the dot—except for poor Hex. There's always one dud.) Dorado spends their time trying to scrounge up faster tech or better blueprints, and we give our information away, because those were the rules in the message, but they just take—they haven't given us anything since their dictionary.

WX-16 from Sextans-A sent their royal house: an expendable younger son and his wife and a collection of nobles, to keep the bloodline active until the messenger arrived. We don't deal with them—they think it's coarse to clone.

NGC 2808 (we can't pronounce it, and sometimes it's better not to try) came out of Canis Major and surprised everyone, since we didn't even think there was life out there. They've only been around a few years; Hepta never met them. Their delegate is in stasis. Whenever that poor sucker wakes up he's going to have some unimpressed ambassadors waiting to meet him. They should never have come with only one.

Xpelhi, who booked it all the way from Cygnus, keep to themselves; their atmosphere is too heavy for people with spines. They look like jellyfish, no mouths, and it took us a hundred and ten years to figure out their language; the dictionary they sent us was just an anatomical sketch. Hepta cracked it because of something Tetra-Yemenni had recorded about the webs of their veins shifting when they were upset. The Xpelhi think we're a bunch of idiots for taking so long. Which is fine; I think they're a bunch of mouthless creeps. It evens out.

Neptune sent a think-tank themselves, like they were a real planet and not an Earth colony. They've never said how they keep things going on that tiny ship, if it's cloning or bio-reproduction or what; every generation they elect someone for the job, and I guess whenever

Carthage shows up they'll put forward the elected person and hope for the best. Brave bunch, Neptune. Better them than us.

Centauri was the smartest planet. They sent an AI. You know the AI isn't sitting up nights worrying itself into early expiration. It's not bothered by a damn thing.

Octa makes rounds to all the ships. She's the only one of them who does it, and it works. Canis Major sent us help once, when we had the ventilation problem on the storage levels. She didn't ask for help; they're not obligated to share anything but information. But when she came back, an engineer was with her.

"Trust me, I know everything about refrigeration," he said, and after the computer had translated the joke everybody laughed and shook his hand.

Octa stood beside him like a mother until they had taken him into the tunnels, and then she tucked her helmet under her arm like she was satisfied.

"They're good people," she said to the shuttle pilot, who was making a face. "With no ambassador to keep them going, they must feel so alone. Give them a chance to do good."

"I've got the scan ready," I said. (I scan her every time she comes back from somewhere else. It's a precaution. You never know what's going on outside your own ship.)

"Let's be quick, then," she said, already walking down the corridor. "I have to make some notes, and then I need to talk to Centauri."

(Centauri's AI is Octa's favorite ship; she's there far more often than she needs to be. "Easier to come to decisions when it's just a matter of facts," she said.)

Octa did a lot of planning, early on, like she had a special purpose beyond what Alpha had promised—like time was short.

Of all the copies, she was the only one who ever seemed to worry that her clock was ticking down.

All the Yemennis have been different, which is unavoidable. Even though each one has all the aggregated information of previous iterations without the emotional hangover, it can get messy, like

Hepta and Dorado 214. Human error in every copy. It's the reason her machines all have parameters instead of specs; some things you never can tell. (Poor Hex.)

It's hard on them, of course—after fifty years it all starts to fall apart no matter what you do, and you have to shut one down and start again—but it's the best way we have to give her a lifetime of knowledge in a few minutes, and we don't want Carthage to come when we're unprepared.

I don't know what's in the memories, what they show her each time she wakes. That's for government guys; techs mind their own business.

There's a documentary about how they picked Alpha for the job, four hundred years back. One man went on and on about "the human aesthetic," and put up a photo of what a woman would look like if every race had an influence in the facial features.

"Almost perfect. It's like they chose her for her looks!" he says, laughing.

Like Carthage is going to know if she's pretty. Carthage is probably full of big amoebas, and when they meet her they'll just think she's nasty and fragile and full of teeth.

They have a picture of Alpha up in the lab anyway, for reference. No one looks at it any more—nobody needs to. When I look in the mirror, I see a Yemenni first, and then my own face. I have my priorities straight.

Wren Yemenni is why we're here, and the reason none of us have complained in four hundred years is because she knows what she owes us. She's seen the video, too, with those ten thousand people who gave up everything because someone told them the message was beautiful.

No matter what her failings are, she tries to learn everything she can each time, to move diplomacy forward, to be kind (except to Dorado 215, but we all hate those ass-kissers so it doesn't matter). She knows what she's here to do. It's coded deeper than her IQ, than her memories, somewhere inside her we can't even reach; duty is built into their bones. Alpha passed down something wonderful, to all of them.

Octa doesn't look like Alpha. Not at all.

• • •

Just before Dorado 215 hits his twenty-year expiration, he messages a request that Octa accompany him on an official visit to the Xpelhi. There's something he wants to show them; he thinks they'll be interested.

Everyone asks her to go when they have to talk to Xpelhi. We gave everyone the code once we cracked it (we promised to exchange information, fair and square), but no one else is good at it and they need the help. The Yemmenis have a knack for language.

"I hate him," she says as I strap her into her suit. (It's new—our engineers made it to withstand the pressure in the Xpelhi ship. It's the most amazing human tech we've ever produced. Earth will be proud when they get the message.)

"If peace didn't require me to go . . . " she says, frowns. "I hope they see that what he's offering won't help anyone. It never does."

She sounds tired. I wonder if she's been up nights with the playback again.

"It's okay," I say. "You can hate him if you want. No one expected you to love him like the last one did. It's better not to carry the old feelings around. You live longer."

"He's different," she says. "It's terrible how it's changed him."

"All clones feel that way sometimes," I say. "Peril of the job. Here's your helmet."

She takes it and smiles at me, a thank-you, before she pops it over her head and activates the seal.

"I feel like a snowman," she says, which is what Hepta used to say. I wonder if anyone told Octa, of if she just remembered it from somewhere.

I stay near the bio-med readout while she's on the Xpelhi ship; if anything starts to fail, the suit tells us. If her lungs have collapsed from the pressure there's not much we can do, but at least we'll know, and we can wake up the next one.

Her heart rate speeds up, quick sharp spikes on the readout like she's having a panic attack, but that happens whenever Dorado 215 says something stupid. After a while it's just a little agitation, and soon she's safely back home.

She stands on the shuttle platform for a long time without moving, and only after I start toward her does she wake up enough to switch off the pressure in the suit and haul her helmet off.

I stop where I am. I don't want to touch her; I've worked too hard on them to handle them. "Everything all right?"

She's frowning into middle space, not really seeing me. "There's nothing on the ship we could use as a weapon?"

Strange question. "I guess we could crash the shuttle into someone," I say. "I can ask the engineers."

"No," she says. "No need."

It was part of the message, the first rule: no war before Carthage comes. We don't even have armed security— just guys who train with their hands, ready in case Octa tries to shove any more people in airlocks.

She hasn't done that in a while. She's getting worn down. It happens to them all, nearer the end.

"There's been no war for four hundred years," she says as we walk, shaking her head. "Have we ever gone that long before without fighting? Any of us?"

"Nope." I grin. "Carthage is the best thing that hasn't happened to us yet."

Her helmet is tucked under one arm, and she looks down at it like it will answer her.

The Delegate Meeting happens every decade. It wasn't mandated by Carthage; Wren Tetra-Yemenni began it as a way for delegates to have a base of reference, and to meet; no one has even seen the new Neptunian Elect since they picked her two years back, and they have to introduce Dorado 216.

We're not allowed to hear what they talk about—it's none of our business, it's government stuff—but we hang around in the hallways just to watch them filing in, the humanoids and the Xpelhis puttering past in their cases. The Centauri AI has a hologram that looks like a stick insect with wings, and it blinks in and out as the signal from his ship gets spotty. I cover my smile, though—that computer sees everything.

On the way in, Dorado 216 leans over to Octa. "You won't say anything, will you? It would be war."

"No," she says, "I won't say anything."

"It's just in case," he goes on, like she didn't already give him an answer. "There's no plan to use them. We're not like that—it's not like that. You never know what Carthage's plans are, is all." Then, more quietly, "I trusted you."

"215 trusted me," she says. "You want someone to trust you, try the next Yemenni."

"Watch it," he says. A warning.

After a second she frowns at him. "How can you want war, after all this effort?"

He makes a suspicious face before he turns and walks into the reception room with the rest of them.

Octa stands in the hall for a second before she follows him, shoulders back and head high. Yemmenis know their duties.

After the Delegate Meeting, Octa takes a trip to the Centauri AI. She's back in a few hours. She didn't tell anyone why she was going, just looks sad to have come back.

(Sometimes I think Octa's mind is more like a computer than any of them, even more than Alpha. I wonder if I made her that way by accident, wishing better for them, wishing for more.)

In the mess, the pilots grumble that it was a waste of shuttle fuel.

"That program shows up anywhere they need it to," one of them says. "Why did we have to drive her around like she's one of the queens on Sextan? They should expire these copies before they go crazy, man."

"Maybe she was trying to give us break from your ugly face," I say, and there's a little standoff at the table between the pilots and the techs until one of the language ops guys smoothes things over.

I stay angry for a long time. The pilots don't know what they're talking about.

Yemennis do nothing by mistake.

Alpha was the most skilled diplomat on the planet.

They don't say so in the documentary; they talk about how kind she is and how smart she is and how she looks like a mix of everyone, and if you just listened to what they were saying you'd think she hardly deserved to go. There were a lot of people in line; astronauts and prime ministers and bishops all clamoring for the privilege.

And she got herself picked—she got picked above every one of them; she was the most skilled diplomat who ever lived. She could work out anything, I bet.

There's an engineer down five levels who looks good to me, is smart enough, and we get married. We have two kids. (Someone will have to watch over the Yemennis when I'm gone, someone with my grandfathers' talents for calibrating a needle; we've been six generations at Wren Yemmeni's side.)

We celebrate four hundred years of peace. All the delegates put a message together, to be played in every ship, for the civilians. For some of them, it's the first they've heard of the other languages. Everyone on the ship, twelve thousand strong, watches raptly from the big hangar and the gymnasium level, from the tech room and the bridge.

They go one by one, and I recognize our reception room as the camera pans from one face to another. They talk about peace, about their home planets, about how much they look forward to all of us knowing the message, when Carthage comes.

Wren Octa-Yemenni goes last.

"I hope that, as we today are wiser today than we were, so tomorrow we will be wiser than we are," she says. Dorado 216 looks like he wants to slap her.

She says, "I hope that when our time comes to meet Carthage, we may say that we have fulfilled the letter and spirit of its great message, and we stand ready for a bright new age."

Everyone in the tech room roars applause (Yemennis know how to talk to a crowd). Just before the video shuts off, it shows all the delegates side by side; Octa is looking out the window, towards something none of us can see.

One night, a year before she's due to be expired, I find Octa in the development room. She's watching the tube where Ennea is gestating.

Ennea's almost grown, and it looks like Octa's staring at her own reflection.

"Four hundred years without a war," she says. "All of us at a truce, talking and learning. Waiting for Carthage."

"Carthage will come," I promise, glancing at Ennea's pH readout.

"I hope we don't see it," she says, frowns into the glass. "I hope, when it comes, all of us are long dead, and better ones have taken their places. Some people twist on themselves if you give them any time at all."

Deka and Hendeka are in tubes behind us, smaller and reserved, eyes closed; they're not ready. We won't even need them until I'm dead. Though it shouldn't matter, I care less for them than I do for Ennea, less than I do for Octa, who's watching me.

Octa, who seems to think none of them are worthy of Carthage at all. She's been losing faith for years.

None of these copies are like Alpha. They all do their duty, but she *believed*.

At the fifty-year mark, Octa comes in to be expired.

She hands over the recording device, and the government guys disappear to their level to put together the memory flux for Ennea, who will wake up tonight and need to know.

"You shouldn't keep doing this," she tells me as we help her onto the table and adjust the IV.

There are no restraints. The Yemennis don't balk at what they have to do; duty is in their bones. But Octa looks sad, even sadder than when she found out that the one before her had loved someone who was already dead.

"It's fine," I say. "It's the best way—one session of information, and she's ready to face Carthage."

"But she won't remember something if I don't record it? She won't know?"

Octa's always been a little edgy—I try to sound reassuring. "No, she won't feel a thing. Forget Dorado. There's nothing to worry about."

Octa looks like she's going to cry. "What if there's something she needs to know?"

"I'll get you a recorder," I say, and start to hold up my hand for the sound tech, but she shakes her head and grabs my sleeve.

I drop my arm, surprised. No one else has even noticed; they're already starting the machines to wake up the next one, and Octa and I might as well be alone in the room.

After a second she frowns, drops my hand, makes fists at her sides like she's holding back.

The IV drips steadily, and around us everyone is laughing and talking, excited. They seem miles away.

Octa hasn't stopped watching me; her eyes are bright, her mouth drawn.

"Have you seen the message?"

She must know I haven't. I shake my head; I hold my breath, wondering if she's going to tell me. I've dreamed about it my whole life, wondering what Alpha knew that made her cry with joy, four hundred years ago.

"It's beautiful," she says, and her eyes are mostly closed, and I can't tell if she's talking to me or just talking. The IV is working; sometimes they say things.

She says, "I don't know how anyone could take up a weapon again, after seeing the message."

Without thinking, I put my hand over her hand.

She sighs. Then, so quietly that no one else hears, Octa says, "I hope that ship never comes."

Her face gets tight and determined—she looks like Alpha, exactly like, and I almost call out for them to stop—it's so uncanny, something must be wrong.

But nothing is wrong. She closes her eyes, and the bio-feed flatlines; the tech across the room turns off the alarm on the main bank, and it's over.

We flip on the antigrav, and one of the techs takes her down to the incinerator. He comes back, says the other delegates have lined up in the little audience hall outside the incinerator, waiting to clap and drink champagne.

It's always a long night after an expiration, but it's what we're here to do, and it's good solid work, moving and monitoring and setting up the influx for Yemenni's first night. Nobody wants a delay between delegates. You never know when the Carthage is going to show up. We think another four hundred years, but it could be tomorrow. Stranger things have happened.

Wren Ennea-Yemenni needs to be awake, just in case; she'll have things to do, when Carthage comes.

RATS OF THE SYSTEM

PAUL McAULEY

Carter Cho was trying to camouflage the lifepod when the hunter-killer found him.

He had matched spin with the fragment of shattered comet nucleus, excavated a neat hole with a judicious burn of the lifepod's motor and eased the sturdy little ship inside; then he had sealed up his pressure suit and clambered out of the airlock, intending to hide the pod's infrared and radar signatures by covering the hole with fullerene superconducting cloth. He was trying to work methodically, clamping clips to the edge of the cloth and spiking the clips into the slumped rim of the hole, but the cloth, forty metres square and just sixty carbon atoms thick, massing a little less than a butterfly's wing, warped and billowed and twisted as gas and dust vented from fractured ice. Carter had managed to fix two sides and was working on the third when the scientist shouted, "Heads up! Incoming!"

That's when Carter discovered she'd locked him out of the pod's control systems.

He said, "What have you done?"

"Heads up! It's coming right at us!"

The woman was hysterical.

Carter looked up.

The sky was an apocalypse. Pieces of comet nucleus were tumbling away in every direction, casting long cones of shadow through veils and streamers of gas lit by the red dwarf's half-eclipsed disc. The nucleus had been a single body ten kilometres long before the Fanatic singleship had cut across its orbit and carved it open and used X-ray lasers and kietic bomblets to destroy the science platform hidden inside it. The singleship had also deployed a pod of hunter-killer drones, and after crash deceleration these were falling through the remains of the comet, targeting the flotsam of pods and cans and general wreckage. Carter saw a firefly flash and gutter in the sullen wash of gases, and then another, almost ninety degrees away. He had almost forgotten his fear while he'd been working, but now it flowed through him again, electric and strong and urgent.

He said, "Give me back my ship."

The scientist said, "I'm tracking it on radar! I think it's about to—"

The huge slab of sooty ice shuddered. A jet of dust and gas boiled up beyond a sharp-edged horizon and something shot out of the dust, heading straight for Carter. It looked a little like a silvery squid: a bullet-shaped head trailing a dozen tentacles tipped with claws and blades. It wrapped itself around an icy pinnacle on the other side of the hole and reared up, weaving this way and that as if studying him. Probably trying to decide where to begin unseaming him, Carter thought, and pointed the welding pistol at it, ready to die if only he could take one of the enemy with him. The thing surged forward—

 Dust and gas blasted out of the hole. The scientist had ignited the lifepod's motor. The big square of fullerene cloth billowed like a sail in a squall, and the hunter-killer smashed into it, tore it free from the clips Carter had so labouriously secured, and tumbled past him at the centre of a writhing knot.

Carter dived through the hatch in the pod's blunt nose. Gravity's ghost clutched him and he tumbled head over heels and slammed into the rear bulkhead as the pod shook free of its hiding place.

Humans had settled the extensive asteroid belt around Keid, the cool K1 component of the triple star system 40 Eridani, more than a century ago. The first generation, grown from templates stored in a seedship little bigger than a man's head, had settled on a planetoid and built a domed settlement and planted intercrater plains of water ice and primeval tars with vast fields of vacuum organisms. Succeeding generations had spread through Keid's asteroid belt, building domes and tenting crevasses and ravines, raising families, becoming expert in balancing the ecologies of small, closed biomes and creating new varieties of vacuum organisms, writing and performing heroic operettas, trading information and works of art on the interstellar net that linked Earth's far-flung colonies in the brief golden age before Earth's AIs achieved transcendence.

The Keidians were a practical, obdurate people. As far as they were concerned, the Hundred Minute War, which ended with the reduction of Earth and the flight of dozens of Transcendent AIs from the Solar System, was a distant and incomprehensible matter that had nothing to do with the ordinary business of their lives. Someone wrote an uninspired operetta about it; someone else revived the lost art of the symphony, and for a few years her mournful eight hour memoriam was considered by many in the stellar colonies to be a new pinnacle of human art. Very few Keidians took much notice when a Transcendent demolished Sirius B, and used trillions of tonnes of heavy elements mined from the white dwarf's core to build a vast ring in close orbit around Sirius A; no one worried overmuch when other Transcendents began to strip-mine gas giants in other uninhabited systems. Everyone agreed that the machine intelligences were pursuing some vast, obscure plan that might take millions of years to complete, that they were as indifferent to the low comedy of human life as gardeners were to the politics of ants.

But then self-styled transhuman Fanatics declared a jihad against anyone who refused to acknowledge the Transcendents as gods. They dropped a planet-killer on half-terraformed Mars. They scorched colonies on the moons of Jupiter and Saturn and Neptune. They dispatched warships starwards. The fragile web of chatter and knowledge-based commerce that linked the stellar colonies began to unravel. And then, a little over a thousand days ago, a Transcendent had barrelled into the Keidian system, swinging past Keid as it decelerated from close to light speed, arcing out towards the double system of white and red dwarf stars four hundred AU beyond. The red dwarf had always been prone to erratic flares, but a few days after the Transcendent went into orbit around it, the dim little star began to flare brightly and steadily from one of its poles. A narrowly focussed jet of matter and energy began to spew into space, and some of the carbon-rich star-stuff was spun into sails with the surface area of planets, hung hundreds of thousands of kilometres beyond the star yet somehow coupled to its centre of gravity. Pinwheeling of the jet and light pressure on the vast sails tipped the star through ninety degrees, and then the jet burned even brighter, and the star began to move out of its orbit.

Soon afterwards, the Fanatics had arrived, and the war of the 40 Eridani system had begun.

The scientist said, "The hunter-killers found us. We had to outrun them."

Carter said, "I was ready to make a stand."

The scientist glared at him with her one good eye and said, "I'm not prepared to sacrifice myself to take out a few drones, Mr Cho. My work is too important."

She was young and scared and badly injured, but Carter had to admit that she had stones. When the singleship struck, Carter had been climbing into a p-suit, getting ready to set up a detector array on the surface of the comet nucleus. She had been the first person he'd seen after he'd kicked out of the airlock. He'd caught her and dragged her across twenty metres of raw vacuum to a lifepod that had spun loose from the platform's broken spine, and installed her in one of the pod's hibernation coffins. She'd been half-cooked by reflected energy of the X-ray laser beam that had bisected the main section of the science platform; one side of her face was swollen red and black, the eye there a blind white stone, hair like shrivelled peppercorns. The coffin couldn't do much more than give her painblockers and drip glucose-enriched plasma into her blood. She'd die unless she went into hibernation, but she'd wouldn't allow Carter to put her to sleep because she had work to do.

Her coffin was one of twenty stacked in a neat five by four array around the inner wall of the lifepod's hull. Carter Cho hung in the space between her coffin and the shaft of the motor, a skinny man with prematurely white hair in short dreads that stuck out in spikes around his thin, sharp face as if he'd just been wired to some mains buss. He said, "This is my ship. I'm in charge here."

The scientist stared at him. Her good eye was red with an eightball haemorrhage, the pupil capped with a black data lens. She said, "I'm a second lieutenant, sailor. I believe I outrank you."

"Those commissions they handed out to volunteers like you don't mean anything."

"I volunteered for this mission, Mr Cho, because I want to find out everything I can about the Transcendent. Because I believe that what we can learn from it will help defeat the Fanatics. I still have work to do, sailor, and that's why I must decide our strategy."

"Just give me back control of my ship, okay?" She stared through him. He said, "Just tell me what you did. You might have damaged something."

"I wrote a patch that's sitting on top of the command stack. It won't cause any damage. Look, we tried hiding from the hunter-killers, and when that didn't work, we had to outrun them. I can appreciate why you wanted to make a stand. I can even admire it. But we were outnumbered, and we are more important than a few drones. War isn't a matter of individual heroics. It's a collective effort. And as part of a collective, every individual must subsume her finer instincts to the greater good. Do you understand?"

"With respect, ma'am, what I understand is that I'm a sailor with combat experience, and you're a science geek." She was looking through him again, or maybe focussing on stuff fed to her retina by the data lens. He said, "What kind of science geek are you, anyway?"

"Quantum vacuum theory." The scientist closed her eye and clenched her teeth and gasped, then said, her voice smaller and tighter, "I was hoping to find out how the Transcendent manipulates the magnetic fields that control the jet."

"Are you okay?"

"Just a little twinge."

Carter studied the diagnostic panel of the coffin, but he had no idea what it was trying to tell him. "You should let this box put you to sleep. When you wake up, we'll be back at Pasadena, and they'll fix you right up."

"I know how to run the lifepod, and as long as I have control of it, you can't put me under. We're still falling along the comet's trajectory. We're going to eyeball the Transcendent's engineering up close. If I can't learn something from that, I'll give you permission to boot my ass into vacuum, turn around, and go look for another scientist."

"Maybe you can steer this ship, ma'am, but you don't have combat training."

"There's nothing to fight. We outran the hunter-killers."

Carter said, "So we did. But maybe you should use the radar, check out the singleship. Just before you staged your little mutiny, I saw that it was turning back. I think it's going to try to hunt us down."

Carter stripped coffins and ripped out panels and padding from the walls. He disconnected canisters of the accelerant foam that flooded coffins to cradle hibernating sleepers. He pulled a dozen spare p-suits from their racks. He sealed the scientist's coffin and suited up and vented the lifepod and dumped everything out of the lock.

The idea was that the pilot of the singleship would spot the debris, think that the pod had imploded, and abandon the chase. Carter thought there was a fighting chance it would work, but when he had told her what he was going to do, the scientist had said, "It won't fool him for a moment."

Carter said, "Also, when he chases after us, there's a chance he'll run into some of the debris. If the relative velocity is high enough, even a grain of dust could do some serious damage."

"He can blow us out of the sky with his X-ray laser. So why would he want to chase us?"

"For the same reason the hunter-killer didn't explode when it found us. He wants to take a prisoner. He wants to extract information from a live body."

He watched her think about that.

She said, "If he does catch up with us, you'll get your wish to become a martyr. There's enough anti-beryllium left in the motor to make an explosion that'll light up the whole system. But that's a last resort. The singleship is still in turnaround, we have a good head start, and we're only twenty-eight million kilometres from perihelion. If we get there first, we can whip around the red dwarf, change our course at random. Unless the Fanatic guesses our exit trajectory, that'll buy us plenty of time."

"He'll have plenty of time to find us again. We're a long way from home, and there might be other—"

"All we have to do is live long enough to find out everything we can about the Transcendent's engineering project, and squirt it home on a tight beam." The scientist's smile was dreadful. Her teeth were filmed with blood. "Quit arguing, sailor. Don't you have work to do?"

A trail of debris tumbled away behind the pod, slowly spreading out, bright edges flashing here and there as they caught the light of the red dwarf. Carter pressurized p-suits and switched on their life-supports systems and transponders before he jettisoned them. Maybe the Fanatic would think that they contained warm bodies. He sprayed great arcs of foam into the hard vacuum and kicked away the empty canisters. The chance of any of the debris hitting Fanatic's singleship was infinitesimally small, but a small chance was better than none at all, and the work kept his mind from the awful prospect of being captured.

Sternward, the shattered comet nucleus was a fuzzy speck trailing foreshortened banners of light across the star-spangled sky. The expedition had nudged it from its orbit and buried the science platform inside its nucleus, sleeping for a whole year like an army in a fairytale as it fell towards the red dwarf. The mission had been a last desperate attempt to try and learn something of the Transcendent's secrets. But as the comet nucleus had neared the red dwarf, and the expedition had woke up and the scientists had started their work, one of the Fanatic drones that policed the vicinity of the star had somehow detected the science platform, and the Fanatics had sent a singleship to deal with it. Like all their warships, it had moved very fast, with brutal acceleration that would have mashed ordinary humans to a thin jelly. It had arrived less than thirty seconds behind a warning broadcast by a spotter observatory at the edge of Keid's heliopause. The crew of the science platform hadn't stood a chance.

The singleship lay directly between the comet and the lifepod now. It had turned around and was decelerating at eight gravities. At the maximum magnification his p-suit's visor could give him, Carter could just make out the faint scratch of its exhaust, but was unable to resolve the ship itself. In the other direction, the red dwarf star simmered at the bottom of a kind of well of luminous dark. Its nuclear fires were banked low, radiating mostly in infrared. Carter could stare steadily at it with only a minimum of filtering. The sharp-edged shadows of the vast deployment of solar sails were sinking beyond one edge as the jet dawned in the opposite direction, a brilliant white thread brighter than the fierce point of the white dwarf star rising just beyond it. Before the Transcendent had begun its work, the red dwarf had swung around the smaller but more massive white dwarf in a wide elliptical orbit, at its closest approaching within twenty AU, the distance of Uranus from the Sun. Now it was much closer, and still falling inward. Scientists speculated that the Transcendent planned to use the tidal effects of a close transit to tear apart the red dwarf, but they'd had less than forty hours to study the Transcendent's engineering before the Fanatic's singleship had struck.

Hung in his p-suit a little way from the lifepod, the huge target of the red dwarf in one direction, the vast starscape in the other, Carter Cho resolved to make the best of his fate. The Universe was vast and inhuman, and so was war. Out there, in battles around stars whose names—Alpha Centauri, Epsilon Eridani, Tau Ceti, Lalande 21185, Lacaille 8760, 61 Cygni, Epsilon Indi, Groombridge 1618, Groombridge 34, 82 Eridani, 70 Ophiuchi, Delta Pavonis, Eta Cassiopeiae—were like a proud role call of mythic heroes, the fate of the human race was being determined. While Carter and the rest of the expedition had slept in their coffins deep in the heart of the comet, the Fanatics had invested and destroyed a dozen settlements in Keid's asteroid belt, and the Keidians had fought back and destroyed one of the Fanatics' huge starships. Compared to this great struggle, Carter's fate was less than that of a drop of water in a stormy ocean, a thought both humbling and uplifting.

Well, his life might be insignificant, but he wasn't about to trust it to a dying girl with no combat experience. He fingertip-swam to the stern of the pod, and opened a panel and rigged a manual cutout before he climbed back inside. He had been working for six hours. He was exhausted and sweating hard inside the p-suit, but he couldn't take it off because the pod's atmosphere had been vented and most of its systems had been shut down, part of his plan to fool the Fanatic into thinking it was a dead hulk. The interior was dark and cold. The lights either side of his helmet cast sharp shadows. Frost glistened on struts exposed where he had stripped away panelling.

The scientist lay inside her sealed coffin, her half-ruined face visible through the little window. She looked asleep, but when Carter manoeuvred beside her she opened her good eye and looked at him. He plugged in a patch cord and heard some kind of music, a simple progressions of riffs for percussion and piano and trumpet and saxophone. The scientist said that it was her favourite piece. She said that she wanted to listen to it one more time.

Carter said, "You should let the coffin put you to sleep. Before—"

The scientist coughed wetly. Blood freckled the faceplate of her coffin. "Before I die."

"They gave me some science training before they put me on this mission, ma'am. Just tell me what to do."

"Quit calling me ma'am," the scientist said, and closed her good eye as a trumpet floated a long, lovely line of melody above a soft shuffle of percussion. "Doesn't he break your heart? That's Miles Davis, playing in New York hundreds of years ago. Making music for angels."

"It's interesting. It's in simple six/eight time, but the modal changes—" The scientist was staring at Carter; he felt himself blush, and wondered if she could see it. He said, "I inherited perfect pitch from my mother. She sang in an opera chorus before she married my father, and settled down to raise babies and farm vacuum organisms."

"Don't try and break it down," the scientist said. "You have to listen to the whole thing. The totality, it's sublime. I'd rather die listening to this than die in hibernation."

"You won't die if you do what I tell you."

"I've set down everything I remember about the work that was done before the attack. I'll add it to the observations I make as we whip around the star, and squirt all the data to Keid. Maybe they can make something useful of it, work out the Transcendent's tricks with the magnetic fields, the gravity tethers, the rest of it . . . " The scientist closed her eye, and breathed deeply. Fluid rattled in her lungs. She said softly, as if to herself, "So many dead. We have to make their deaths worthwhile."

Carter had barely got to know his shipmates, recruited from all over, before they'd gone into hibernation, but the scientist had lost good friends and colleagues.

He said, "The singleship is still accelerating."

"I know."

"It could catch us before we reach the star."

"Maybe your little trick will fool it."

"I might as well face up to it with a pillow."

The scientist smiled her ghastly smile. She said, "We have to try. We have to try everything. Let me explain what I plan to do at perhelion."

She told Carter that observations by drones and asteroid-based telescopes had shown that the Transcendent had regularized the red dwarf's magnetic field, funnelling plasma towards one point on photosphere, where it erupted outward in a permanent flare—the jet that was driving the star towards its fatal rendezvous at the bottom of the white dwarf's steep gravity well. The scientist believed that the Transcendent was manipulating the vast energies of the star's magnetic field by breaking the symmetry of the seething sea of virtual particular pairs that defined quantum vacuum, generating charged particles *ab ovo*, redirecting plasma currents and looped magnetic fields with strengths of thousands of gauss and areas of thousands of kilometres as a child might play with a toy magnet and a few iron filings. The probe she'd loaded with a dozen experiments had been lost with the science platform, but she thought that there was a way of testing at least one prediction of her theoretical work on symmetry breaking.

She opened a window in Carter's helmet display, showed him a schematic plot of the slingshot manoever around the red dwarf.

Carter said, "You have to get that close?"

"The half-life of the strange photons will be very short, a little less than a millisecond."

"I get it. They won't travel much more than a few hundred kilometres before they decay." Carter grinned when the scientist stared at him. He said, "Speed of light's one of those fundamental constants every sailor has to deal with."

"It means that we have to get close to the source, but it also means that the photon flux will increase anomalously just above the photosphere. There should be a sudden gradient, or a series of steps . . . It was one of the experiments my probe carried."

Carter said, "But it was destroyed, so we have to do the job instead. It's going to get pretty hot, that close to the star. What kind of temperatures are we talking about?"

"I don't know. The average surface temperature of the red dwarf is relatively cool, a little over 3000 degrees Kelvin, but it's somewhat hotter near the base of the flare, where we have to make our pass."

"Why don't we just skim past the edge of the flare itself? The flare might be hotter than the surface, but our transit time would be a whole lot less."

"The magnetic fields are very strong around the flare, and spiral around it. They could fling us in any direction. Outward if we're lucky, into the star if we're not. No, I'm going to aim for a spot where the field lines all run in the same direction. But the fields can change direction suddenly, and there's the risk of hitting a stray plume of plasma, so I can't fire up the motors until we're close."

Carter thought of his cutout. He said, "If you have to hit a narrow window, I'm your man. I can put this ship through the eye of a needle."

The scientist said, "As soon as I see the chance, I'll fire full thrust to minimise transit time."

"But without the thermal protection of the comet nucleus it'll still be a lot worse than waving your hand through a candle flame. I suppose I can set up a barbecue-mode rotation, run the cooling system at maximum. Your box will help keep you safe, and I'll climb into one too, but if the temperature doesn't kill us, the hard radiation flux probably will. You really think you can learn something useful?"

"This is a unique opportunity, sailor. It's usually very difficult to study Transcendent engineering because they keep away from star systems that have been settled. Some of us think that the Hundred Minute War was fought over the fate of the human race, that the Transcendents who won the war and quit the Solar System believe that we should be left alone to get on with our lives."

"But this one didn't leave us alone."

"Strictly speaking, it did. Forty Eridani B and C, the white dwarf and the red dwarf, are a close-coupled binary. Keid is only loosely associated with them. And they're a rare example of the kind of binary the Transcendents are very interested in, one in which the masses of the two components are very different. We have a unique opportunity to study stellar engineering. The Fanatics know this, which is why they're so keen to destroy anything which comes too close."

"They want to keep the Transcendents' secrets secret."

"They're not interested in understanding the Transcendents, only in worshipping them. They are as fixed and immutable as their belief system, but we're willing to learn, to take on new knowledge and change and evolve. That's why we're going to win this war."

Following the scientist's instructions, Carter dismantled three cameras and rejigged their imaging circuits into photon counters. While he worked, the scientist talked about her family home in Happy Valley on Neuvo California. It had been badly damaged in one of the first Fanatic attacks, and her parents and her three brothers had helped organise the evacuation. Her mother had been an ecosystem designer, and her father had been in charge of the government's program of interstellar commerce: they were both in the war cabinet now.

"And very proud and very unhappy that their only daughter volunteered for this mission."

Carter said that his family were just ordinary folks, part of a cooperative that ran a vacuum organism farm on the water- and methane-ice plains of San Joaquin. He'd piloted one of the cooperative's tugs, and had volunteered for service in the Keidian defence force as soon as the war against the Fanatics began, but he didn't want to talk about the two inconclusive skirmishes in which he'd been involved before being assigned to the mission. Instead, he told the scientist about his childhood and the tented crevasse that was his family home, and the herds of gengineered rats he'd helped raise.

"I loved those rats. I should have been smart enough to stay home, raise rats and make babies, but instead I thought that the bit of talent I have for math and spatial awareness was my big ticket out."

"Shit," the scientist said. "The singleship just passed through your debris field."

She opened a window, showed Carter the radar plot.

He felt a funny floating feeling that had nothing to do with free fall. He said, "Well, we tried."

"I'm sure it won't catch up with us before we reach the star."

"If we make that burn now—"

"We'll miss the chance to collect the photon data. We're going to die whatever we do, sailor. Let's make it worthwhile."

"Right."

"Why did you like them? The rats."

"Because they're survivors. Because they've managed to make a living from humans ever since we invented agriculture and cities. Back on Earth, they were a vermin species, small and tough and smart and fast-breeding, eating the same food that people ate, even sharing some of the same diseases and parasites. We took them with us into space because those same qualities made them ideal lab animals. Did you know that they were one of the first mammal species to have their genome sequenced? That's why there are so many gengineered varieties. We mostly bred them for meat and fur and biologicals, but we also raised a few strains that we sold as pets. When I was a little kid, I had a ruffed piebald rat that I loved as much as any of my sisters and brothers. Charlie. Charlie the rat. He lived for more than a thousand days, an awfully venerable age for a rat, and when he died I wouldn't allow him to be recycled. My father helped me make a coffin from offcuts of black oak, and I buried him in a glade in my favourite citrous forest . . . "

The scientist said, "It sounds like a nice spot to be buried."

Carter said, "It's a good place. There are orchards, lots of little fields. People grow flowers just for the hell of it. We have eighteen species of mammals roaming about. All chipped of course, but they give you a feeling of what nature must have been like. I couldn't wait to get out, and now I can't wait to get back. How dumb is that?"

The scientist said, "I'd like to see it. Maybe you could take me on a picnic, show me the sights. My family used to get together for a picnic every couple of hundred days. We'd rent part of one of the parklands, play games, cook way too much food, smoke and drink, play tig and futzball, and generally get outside of ourselves."

"My father, he's a pretty good cook. And my mother leads a pretty good choral group. We should all get together."

"Absolutely."

They smiled at each other. It was a solemn moment. Carter thought he should say something suitable, but what? He'd never been one for speeches, and he realised now that although the scientist knew his name—it was stitched to his suit—he still didn't know hers.

The scientist said, "The clock's ticking."

Carter said, "Yes ma'am. I'll get this junk fixed up, and then I'll be right back."

He welded the photon detectors to the blunt nose of the pod, cabled them up. He prepped the antenna array. After the pod grazed the base of the flare, its computer would compress the raw data and send it in an encrypted squawk aimed at Keid, repeating it as long as possible; repeating it until the Fanatic singleship caught up. It was less than ten thousand kilometres behind them now. Ahead, the red dwarf filled half the sky, the jet a slender white thread rooted in patch of orange and yellow fusion fire, foreshortening and rising above them as they drove towards it. Carter said that its base looked like a patch of fungal disease on an apple, and the scientist told him that the analogy wasn't far-fetched; before the science platform had been destroyed, one of the research groups had discovered that there were strange nuclear reactions taking place down there, forming tonnes of carbon per second. She showed him a picture one of the pod's cameras had captured: a rare glimpse of the Transcendent. It was hard to see against the burning background of the star's surface because it was a perfectly reflective sphere.

"Exactly a kilometre across," the scientist said, "orbiting the equator every eight minutes. It's thought they enclose themselves in bubbles of space where the fundamental constants have been altered to enhance their cognitive processes. This one's a keeper. I'll send it back—"

A glowing line of gas like a burning snake thousands of kilometres long whipped past. The pod shuddered, probably from stray magnetic flux.

Carter said, "I should climb inside before I start to cook."

The scientist said, "I have to fire up the motor pretty soon." Then she said, Wait."

Carter waited, hung at the edge of the hatch.

The scientist said, "You switched on the antenna array."

"Just long enough to check it out."

"Something got in. I think a virus. I'm trying to firewall, but it's spreading through the system. It already has the motor and nav systems—"

"I also have control of the com system," another voice said. It was light and lilting. It was as sinuous as a snake. It was right inside Carter's head. "Carter Cho. I see you, and I know you can hear me."

The scientist said, "I can't fire the motor, but I think you can do something about that, sailor."

So she'd known about the cutout all along. Carter started to haul himself towards the stern.

The voice said, "Carter Cho. I will have complete control of your ship momentarily. Give yourself to us."

Carter could see the singleship now, a flat triangle at the tip of a lance of white flame. It was only seconds away. He flipped up the panel, plugged in a patch cord. Sparce lines of data scrolled up in a window. He couldn't access the scientist's flight plan, had no nav except line-of-sight and seat-of-the pants. He had to aim blind for the base of the flare and hope he hit that narrow window by luck, came in at just the right angle, at just the right place where parallel lines of magnetic force ran in just the right direction . . .

"Carter Cho. I have taken control. Kill the woman and give yourself to us, and I promise that you will live with us in glory."

Or he could risk a throw of the dice. Carter ran a tether from his p-suit utility belt to a nearby bolt, braced himself against a rung. With his helmet visor almost blacked out, he could just about look at the surface of the star rushing towards him, could see the intricate tangles of orderly streams that fed plasma into the brilliant patch of fusion fire at the base of the jet.

"Kill her, or I will strip your living brain neuron by neuron."

"Drop dead," Carter said, and switched off his com. The jet seemed to rise up to infinity, a gigantic sword that cut space in two. The scientist had said that if the pod grazed the edge of the jet, spiralling magnetic fields would fling it into the sky at a random vector. And the star took up half the sky . . .

Fuck it, Carter thought. He'd been lucky so far. It was time to roll the dice one more time, hope his luck still held. He fired attitude controls, aimed the blunt nose of the pod. A menu window popped up into front of his face. He selected *burn* and *full thrust*.

Sudden weight tore at his two-handed grip on the rung as the motor flared. It was pushing a shade under a gee of acceleration, most humans who had ever lived had spent their entire lives in that kind of pull, but Carter's fingers were cramping inside the heavy gloves and it felt as if the utility belt was trying to amputate him at the waist. The vast dividing line of the jet rushed towards him. Heat beat through his p-suit. If its cooling system failed for a second he'd cook like a joint of meat in his father's stone oven. Or the Fanatic could burn him out of the sky with its X-ray laser, or magnetic flux could rip the pod apart . . .

Carter didn't care. He was riding his ship rodeo-style towards a flare of fusion light a thousand kilometres wide. He whooped with defiant glee—

—and then, just like that, the pod was somewhere else.

After a minute, Carter remembered to switch on his com. The scientist said, "What the fuck did you just do?"

It took them a while to find out.

Carter had aimed the pod at the edge of the jet, hoping that it would be flung away at a random tangent across the surface of the red dwarf, hoping that it would survive long enough to transmit all of the data collected by the scientist's experiment. But now the red dwarf was a rusty nailhead dwindling into the starscape behind them, the bright point of the white dwarf several seconds of arc beyond it. In the blink of an eye, the pod had gained escape velocity and had been translated across tens of millions of kilometres of space.

"It had to be the Transcendent," the scientist said.

Carter had repressurized the pod and the cooling system was working at a flat roar, but it was still as hot as a sauna. He had taken off his helmet and shaken out his sweat-soaked dreadlocks, but because the scientist's coffin was still sealed because her burns made her sensitive to heat. He hung in front of it, looking at her through the little window. He said, "I took the only chance we had left."

"No magnetic field could have flung us so far, or so fast. It had to be something to do with the Transcendent. Perhaps it cancelled our interia. For a few seconds we became as massless as a photon, we achieved light speed . . . "

"My luck held," Carter said. "I hit those magnetic fields just right."

"Check the deep radar, sailor. There's no sign of the Fanatic's singleship. It was right on our tail. If magnetic fields had anything to do with it, it would have been flung in the same direction as us."

Carter checked the deep radar. There was no sign of the singleship. He remembered the glimpse of the silver sphere sailing serenely around the star, and said, "I thought the Transcendents wanted to leave us alone. That's why they quit the Solar System. That's why they only reengineer uninhabited systems . . . "

"You kept rats, when you were a kid. If one got out, you'd put her back. If two started to fight, you'd do something about it. How did your rats feel, when you reached into their cage to separate them?"

Carter grinned. "If we're rats, what are the Fanatics?"

"Rats with delusions of grandeur. Crazy rats who think they're carrying out God's will, when really they're no better than the rest of us. I wonder what that Fanatic must be thinking. Just for a moment, he was touched by the hand of his God . . . "

"What is it?"

"I've finished processing the data stream from my experiment. When we encountered the edge of the flare, there was a massive, sudden increase in photon flux."

"Because of this is this symmetry breaking thing of yours. Have you sent the data?"

"I still have to figure the details."

"Send the data," Carter said, "and I'll button up the ship and put us to sleep"

"Perhaps there are some clues in the decay products . . . "

"You've completed your mission, ma'am. Let someone else worry about the details."

"Jesswyn Fiver," the scientist said. She was smiling at him through her little window. For a moment he saw how pretty she'd been. "You never did ask my name. It's Jesswyn Fiver. Now you can introduce me to your parents, when we go on that picnic."

THE POLITICAL OFFICER

CHARLES COLEMAN FINLAY

———◆———

Maxim Nikomedes saw the other man rushing towards him, but there was no room to dodge in the crate-packed corridor. He braced himself for the impact. The other man pulled up short, his face blanching in the pallid half-light of the "night" rotation. It was Kulakov, the Chief Petty Officer. He went rigid and snapped a salute.

"Sir! Sorry, sir!" His voice trembled.

"At ease, Kulakov," Max said. "Not your fault. It's a tight fit inside this metal sausage."

Standard ship joke. The small craft was stuffed with supplies, mostly food, for the eighteen month voyage ahead. Max waited for the standard response, but Kulakov stared through the hull into deep space. He was near sixty, old for the space service, old for his position, and the only man aboard who made Max, in his mid-forties, feel young.

Max smiled, an expression so faint it could be mistaken for a twitch. "But it's better than being stuck in a capped off sewer pipe, no?"

Which is what the ship would be on the voyage home. "You've got that right, sir!" said Kulakov.

"Carry on."

Kulakov shrunk aside like an old church deacon, afraid to touch a sinner less he catch the sin. Max was used to that reaction from the crew, and not just because his nickname was the Corpse for his cadaverous and dead expression. As the Political Officer, he held the threat of death over every career aboard: the death of some careers would entail a corporeal equivalent. For the first six weeks of their mission, after spongediving the new wormhole, Max cultivated invisibility and waited for the crew to fall into the false complacency of routine. Now it was time to shake them up again to see if he could find the traitor he suspected. He brushed against Kulakov on purpose as he passed by him.

He twisted his way through the last passage and paused outside the visiting officers' cabin. He lifted his knuckles to knock, then changed his mind, turned the latch and swung open the door. The three officers sitting inside jumped at the sight of him. Guilty consciences, Max hoped.

Captain Ernst Petoskey recovered first. "Looking for someone, Lieutenant?"

Max let the silence become uncomfortable while he studied Petoskey. The captain stood six and a half feet tall. His broad shoulders were permanently hunched from spending too much time in ships built for smaller men. The crew loved him so much they would eagerly die—or kill—for him. Called him Papa behind his back. He wouldn't shave again until they returned safely to spaceport; his beard was already quite full, and juice-stained at the corner with proscripted chewing tobacco. Max glanced past Lukinov, the balding "radio lieutenant" and stared at Ensign Pen Reedy, the only woman on the ship.

She was lean, with prominent cheekbones, but the thing Max always noticed first were her hands. She had large, red-knuckled hands. She remained impeccably dressed and groomed, even six weeks into the voyage. Every hair on her head appeared to be individually placed as if they were all soldiers under her command.

Petoskey and Lukinov sat on opposite ends of the bunk. Reedy sat on a crate across from them. Another crate between them held a bottle, tumblers, and some cards.

Petoskey, finally uncomfortable with the silence, opened his mouth again.

"Just looking," Max pre-empted him. "And what do I find but the Captain himself in bed with Drozhin's boys?"

Petoskey glanced at the bunk. "I see only one and he's hardly a boy."

Lukinov, a few years younger than Max, smirked and tugged at the lightning bolt patch on his shirt sleeve. "And what's with calling us *Drozhin's* boys? We're just simple radiomen. If I have to read otherwise, I'll have you up for falsifying reports when we get back to Jesusalem."

He pronounced their home *Hey-zoo-salaam*, like the popular video stars did, instead of the older way, *Jeez-us-ail-em*.

"Things are not always what they appear to be, are they?" said Max.

Lukinov, Reedy, and a third man, Burdick, were the Intelligence listening team assigned to intercept and decode Adarean messages—the newly opened wormhole passage would let the ship dive into the Adarean system undetected to spy. The three had been personally selected and prepped for this mission by Dmitri Drozhin, the legendary Director of Jesusalem's Department of Intelligence. Drozhin had been the Minister too, back when it had still been the Ministry of the Wisdom of Prophets Reborn. In fact, he was the only high government official to survive the Revolution *in situ*, but these days his constellation was challenged by younger men like Mallove, who'd created the Department of Political Education.

"Next time, knock first, Lieutenant," said Petoskey.

"Why should I, Captain?" returned Max, congenially. "A honest man has nothing to fear from his conscience, and what am I if not the conscience of every man aboard this ship?"

"We don't need a conscience when we have orders."

"Come off it, Max," snorted Lukinov. "I invited the Captain up here to celebrate. Reedy earned her comet today."

Indeed, she had. The young ensign wore a gold comet pinned to her left breast pocket, similar to the ones embroidered on the shirts of the other two officers. Comets were awarded only to crew members who demonstrated competence on every ship system—Engineering, Ops and Nav, Weapons, Vacuum and Radiation. Reedy must have qualified in record time. This was her first space assignment. "Congratulations," said Max.

Reedy suppressed a genuine smile. "Thank you, sir."

"That makes her the last one aboard," said Petoskey. "Except for you."

"What do I need to know about ship systems? If I understand the minds and motivations of the men who operate them, it is enough."

"It isn't. Not with this," his mouth twisted distastefully, "this *miscegenated*, patched-together, scrapyard ship. I need to be able to count on every man in an emergency."

"Is it that bad? What kind of emergency do you expect?"

Lukinov rapped the makeshift table. The bottles rattled. "You're becoming a bore, Max. You checked on us, now go make notes in your little spy log, and leave us alone."

"Either that or pull up a crate and close the damn hatch," said Petoskey. "We could use a fourth."

Lukinov waved his hand in clear negation, showing off a large gold signet ring. "You don't want to do that, Ernst. This is the man who won his true love in a card game."

Petoskey looked over at Max. "Is that so?"

"I won my wife in a card game, yes." Max didn't think that story was widely known outside his own department. "But that was many years ago."

"I heard you cheated to win her," said Lukinov. He was Max's counterpart in Intelligence—the Department of Political Education couldn't touch him. The two Departments hated each other and protected their own. "Heard that she divorced you too. I guess an ugly little weasel like you has to get it where he can."

"But unlike your wife, she always remained faithful."

Lukinov muttered a curse and pulled back his fist. Score one on the sore spot. Petoskey reached out and grabbed the Intelligence officer's elbow. "None of that aboard my ship. I don't care who you two are. Come on, Nikomedes. If you're such a hotshot card player, sit down. I could use a little challenge."

A contrary mood seized the Political Officer. He turned into the hallway, detached one of the crates, and shoved it into the tiny quarters.

"So what are we playing?" he asked, sitting down.

"Blind Man's Draw," said Petoskey, shuffling the cards. "Deuce beats an ace, ace beats everything else."

Max nodded. "What's the minimum?"

"A temple to bid, a temple to raise."

Jerusalem's founders stamped their money with an image of the

Temple to encourage the citizen-colonists to render their wealth unto God. The new bills carried pictures of the revolutionary patriots who'd overthrown the Patriarch, but everyone still called them temples. "Then I'm in for a few hands," Max said.

Petoskey dealt four cards face-down. Max kept the king of spades and tossed three cards back into the pile. The ones he got in exchange were just as bad.

"So," said Lukinov, glancing at his hand. "We have the troika of the Service all gathered in one room. Military, Intelligence, and—one card, please, ah, raise you one temple—and what should I call you, Max? Schoolmarm?"

Max saw the raise. "If you like. Just remember that Intelligence is useless without a good Education."

"Is that your sermon these days?"

"Nothing against either of you gentlemen," Petoskey interjected as he dealt. "But it's your mother screwed three ways at once, isn't it. There's three separate chains of command on a ship like this one. It's a recipe for mutiny. Has been on other ships, strictly off the record. And with this mission ahead if we don't all work together, God help us."

Max kept the ten of spades with his king and took two more cards. "Not that there is one," he said officially, "but let God help our enemies. A cord of three strands is not easily broken."

Petoskey nodded his agreement. "That's a good way to look at it. A cord of three strands, all intertwined." He stared each of them in the eyes. "So take care of the spying, and the politics, but leave the running of the ship to me."

"Of course," said Lukinov.

"That's why you're the captain and both of us are mere *lieutenants*," said Max. In reality, both he and Lukinov had the same service rank as Petoskey. On the ground, in Jesusalem's mixed-up service, they were all three colonels. Lukinov was technically senior of the three, though Max had final authority aboard ship within his sphere.

It was, indeed, a troubling conundrum.

Max's hand held nothing—king and ten of spades, two of hearts, and a seven of clubs. Petoskey tossed the fifth card down face-up. Another deuce.

CHARLES COLEMAN FINLAY

Max hated Blind Man's Draw. It was like playing the lottery. The card a man showed you was the one he'd just been dealt; you never really knew what he might be hiding. He looked at the other players' hands. Petoskey showed the eight of clubs and Lukinov the jack of diamonds. Max glimpsed a dark four as Ensign Reedy folded her hand and said "I'm out."

"Raise it a temple and call," Max said, on the off chance he might beat a pair of aces. They turned their cards over and it was money thrown away. Petoskey won with three eights.

Lukinov shook his head. "Holding onto the deuces, Max? That's almost always a loser's hand."

"Except when it isn't."

Petoskey won three of the next five hands, with Lukinov and Max splitting the other two. The poor ensign said little and folded often. Max decided to deal in his other game. While Lukinov shuffled the cards, Max tugged at his nose and said to the air. "You're awfully silent, Miss Reedy. Contemplating your betrayal of us to the Adareans?"

Lukinov mis-shuffled. A heartbeat later, Captain Petoskey picked up his spittoon and spat.

Reedy's voice was as steady as a motor churning in low gear. "What do you mean, sir?"

"You're becoming a bore, again, Max." Lukinov's voice had a sharp edge to it.

"What's this about?" asked Petoskey.

"Perhaps Miss Reedy should explain it herself," said Max. "Go on, Ensign. Describe the immigrant ghetto in your neighborhood, your childhood chums, Sabbathday afternoons at language academy."

"It was hardly that, sir," she said smoothly. "They were just kids who lived near our residence in the city. And there were never any formal classes."

"Oh, there was much more to it than that," pressed Max. "Must I spell it out for you? You lived in a neighborhood of expatriate Adareans. Some spymaster chose you to become a mole before you were out of diapers and started brainwashing you before you could talk. Now while you pretend to serve Jerusalem you really serve Adares. Yes?"

"No. Sir." Reedy's hands, resting fingertip to fingertip across her knees, trembled slightly. "How did they know women would ever be admitted to the military academies?"

Reedy hadn't been part of the first class to enter, but she graduated with the first class to serve active duty. "They saw it was common everywhere else, perhaps. Does it matter? Who can understand their motives? Their gene modifications make them impure. Half-animal, barely human."

She frowned, as if she couldn't believe that kind of prejudice still existed. "Nukes don't distinguish between one set of genes and another, sir. They suffered during the bombardments, just like we did. They fought beside us, they went to our church. Even the archbishop called them good citizens. They're as proud to be Jesusalemites as I am. And as loyal. Sir."

Max tugged at his nose. "A role model for treason. They betrayed one government to serve another. I know for a fact this crew contains at least one double agent, someone who serves two masters. I suspect there are more. Is it you, Miss Reedy?"

Lukinov and Petoskey had turned into fossils before his eyes. Petoskey stared at the young Intelligence officer across the table like a man contemplating murder.

Reedy pressed her fingertips together until her hands grew still. She refused to look to Petoskey or Lukinov for help. "Sir. There may be a traitor, but it's not me. Sir."

Max leaned back casually. "I've read your Academy records, Ensign, and find them interesting for the things they leave out. Such as your role in the unfortunate accident that befell Cadet Vance."

Reedy was well disciplined. Max's comments were neither an order nor a question, so she said nothing, gave nothing away.

"Vance's injuries necessitated his withdrawal from the Academy," Max continued. "What exactly did you have to do with that situation?"

"Come on, Max," said Lukinov, in his senior officer's cease-and-desist voice. "This is going too far. There are always accidents in the Academy and in the service. Usually it's the fault of the idiot who ends up slabbed. Some stupid mistake."

Max was about to say that Vance's mistake had been antagonizing Reedy, but Petoskey interrupted. "Lukinov, have you forgotten how to deal? Are you broke yet, Nikomedes? You can quit any time you want."

Max showed the roll of bills in his pocket and Lukinov started tossing down the cards. As he made the second circuit around their makeshift table, the lights flickered and went off. Max's stomach fluttered as the emergency lights flashed on, casting a weak red glare over the cramped room. The cards sailed past the table, and into the air. Petoskey slammed his glass down. It bounced off the table and twirled toward the ceiling, spilling little brown droplets of whiskey.

Petoskey slapped the ship's intercom. "Bridge!"

"Ensign!" barked Lukinov. "Find something to catch that mess before the grav comes back on and splatters it everywhere."

"Yes, sir," Reedy answered and scrambled to the bathroom for a towel.

"Bridge!" shouted Petoskey, then shook his head. "The com's down."

"It's just the ship encounter drill," said Lukinov.

"There's no drill scheduled for this rotation. And we haven't entered Adarean space yet, so we can't be encountering another ship . . . "

Another ship.

The thought must have hit all four of them simultaneously. As they propelled themselves frog-like toward the hatch, they crashed into one another, inevitable in the small space. During the jumble, Max took a kick to the back of his head. It hurt, even without any weight behind it. No accident, he was sure of that, but he didn't see who did it.

Petoskey flung the door open. "The pig-hearted, fornicating bastards."

Max echoed the sentiment when he followed a moment later. The corridor was blocked by drifting crates. They'd been improperly secured.

"Ensign!" snapped Petoskey.

"Yes, Captain."

"To the front! I'll pass you the crates, you attach them."

"Yes, sir."

"Can I *trust* you to do that?"

"Yessir!"

Max almost felt sorry for Reedy. Almost. In typical fashion for these older ships, someone had strung a steel cable along the corridor, twist-tied to the knobs of the security lights. Max held onto it and stayed out of the way as Petoskey grabbed one loose box after another and passed them back to Reedy. There was the steady sound of velcro as they made their way toward the bridge.

"What do you think it is?" Lukinov whispered to him. "If it's a ship, then the wormhole's been discovered . . . "

The implications were left hanging in the air like everything else. Max compared the size of Lukinov's boot with the sore spot on the back of his head. "Could be another wormhole. The sponge is like that. Once one hole opens up, you usually find several more. There's no reason why the Adarans couldn't find a route in the opposite direction."

Lukinov braced himself against the wall, trying to keep himself oriented as if the grav was still on. "If it's the Adareans, they'll be thinking invasion again."

"It could be someone neutral too," said Max. "Most of the sponge-divers from Earth are prospecting in toward the core these days, but it could be one of them. Put on your ears and find out who they are. I'll determine whether they're for us or against us."

"If they're against, then Ernst can eliminate them," laughed Lukinov. "That's a proper division of labor."

"Our system is imperfect, but it works." That was a stretch, Max told himself. Maybe he ought to just say that the system worked better than the one it replaced.

"Hey," shouted Petoskey. "Are you gentlemen going to sit there or join me on the bridge?"

"Coming," said Lukinov, echoed a second later by Max.

They descended two levels, and came to the control center. Max followed the others through the open hatch. Men sat strapped to their chairs, faces tinted the color of blood by the glow of the emergency lights. Conduits, ducts, and wires ran overhead, like the intestines of some man-made monster. One of the vents kicked on, drawing a loud mechanical breath. Truly, Max thought, they were in the belly of leviathan now.

"Report!" bellowed Petoskey.

"Lefty heard a ship," returned the Commander, a plug-shaped double-chinned fellow named Gordet. "It was nothing more than a fart in space, I swear. I folded the wings and initiated immediate shutdown per your instructions before our signature could be detected."

"Contact confirmed?"

"Yes, sir."

"Good work then." The ship chairs were too small for Petoskey's oversized frame. He preferred to stand anyway and had bolted a towel rack to the floor in the center of the deck. The crew tripped over it when the grav was on, but now Petoskey slipped his feet under it. With the low ceilings it was the only way he could keep from bumping his head. It was against all regulations, but, just as with his smuggled tobacco, Petoskey broke regulations whenever it suited him. It was a quality shared by many of the fleet's best deep space Captains. "Those orders were for when we entered Adarean space, Commander," Petoskey added a second later. "I commend your initiative. Put a commendation in Engineer Elefteriou's record also."

"Yes, sir." Gordet's voice snapped like elastic, pleased at the Captain's praise.

"Identity?"

"It's prime number pings up Outback. Corporate prospectors. Her signature looks like one of the new class."

Petoskey grabbed the passive scope above his head and pulled it down to his eyes. "Vector?"

"Intercept."

"*Intercept?*"

"It's headed in-system and we're headed out. At our current respective courses and velocities, we should come within spitting distance of it just past Big Brother."

Big Brother was the nickname for this system's larger gas giant. Little Brother, the smaller gas giant, was on the far side of the sun, out past the wormhole to home.

"Are they coming from the Adares jump?" Petoskey asked.

"That's what we thought at first," said Gordet. "But it appears now that they're entering from a third wormhole. About thirty degrees negative of the Adares jump, on the opposite side of the elliptic." He glanced over the navigator's shoulder at the monitor. "Call that one thirty-six degrees."

Petoskey continued to stare into the scope. "Shit. There's nothing out here."

Gordet cleared his throat. "It's million of kilometers out, sir. Still too far away for a clear visual."

"No! I mean there's *nothing* out here. This system won't hold their attention for long. It's only a matter of time before they find the opened holes to Adares and home." He paused. "Do that and they'll close our route back."

Indeed. Max had a strong urge to pace. If he started bouncing off the walls, he was certain Petoskey would order him off the bridge, so tried to float with purpose. Burdick, the third member of the Intelligence team, paused in the hatch, carrying a large box. He nodded to Lukinov and Reedy, who followed him forward toward the secure radio room. Max wondered briefly why Burdick had left his post.

"The intercept makes things easier for us," Petoskey concluded aloud. "Calculate the soonest opportunity to engage without warning. With any luck, the missing ship will be counted as a wormhole mishap." Absorbed by the sponge.

Elefteriou turned and spoke to Rucker, the First Lieutenant, who spoke to Gordet, who said, "Sir, radio transmissions from the ship appear to be directed at another ship in the vicinity of the jump. If we take out this one, then the other dives and lives to witness."

"Just one other ship?"

"No way of telling this far out without the active sensors." Which they couldn't use without showing up like a solar flare.

"The order stands," said Petoskey. "Also, Commander, loose cargo in the corridors impeded my progress to the bridge. This is a contraindication of ship readiness."

Gordet stiffened, as crushed by this criticism as he'd been puffed up by the praise. "It'll be taken care of, *sir!*"

"See to it. Where's Chevrier?" Arkady Chevrier was the Chief Engineer. He came from a family of industrialists that contributed heavily to the Revolution. His uncle headed the Department of Finance, and his father was a General. Mallove, Max's boss in Political Education, had warned him not to antagonize Chevrier.

"In the engine room, sir," answered Gordet. "He thought that the sudden unscheduled shutdown of main power resulted in a drain on the main battery arrays. I sent him to fix it."

"Raise Engineering on the com."

"Yes, sir," said Gordet. "Raise Engineering."

Lefty punched his console, listened to his earphones, shook his head.

Petoskey shifted the plug of tobacco in his mouth. "When I tried to contact the bridge from quarters, the com was down. If I have to choose between ship communications and life support, in the presence of a possible enemy vessel, I want communications first. Get a status report from Engineering, and give me a com link to all essential parts of the ship within the next fifteen minutes if you have to do it with tin cans and string. Is that clear?"

Sweat beaded on Gordet's forehead. His jowls quivered as he answered, "Yessir!"

Gordet did not divide his attention well, Max noted. The Commander had been so absorbed with the other ship, he had not yet noticed the ship communications problem. Several past errors in judgment featured prominently in his permanent file. He seemed unaware that this was the reason he'd been passed over for ship command of his own. But he was steady, and more or less politically sound.

He could also be a vindictive S.O.B. Max watched him turn on his subordinates. "Corporal Elefteriou," Gordet shouted. "I want a full report on com status. Five minutes ago is not soon enough! Lieutenant Rucker!"

"Sir!"

"Get your ass to Engineering. I want to receive Chevrier's verbal report on this com here!" He punched it with his fist for emphasis. "If it doesn't come in fifteen minutes, you can hold your breath while the rest of us put on space gear."

The First Lieutenant set off for Engineering. Petoskey cleared his throat. "Commander, one other thing."

"Yes?"

"We'll switch to two shifts now, six hours on, six off. All crew."

"Yes, sir."

Petoskey gestured for Max to come beside him.

"So now we wait around for three days to intercept," Petoskey said in a low voice. "You look like a damn monkey floating there, Nikomedes. We could surgi-tape your boots to the deck."

"That's not necessary." Petoskey wasn't the only captain in the fleet who'd tie his political officer down to one spot if he could. Max needed to be free to move around to catch his traitor.

"If you were qualified for any systems, I'd put you to work."

An excellent reason to remain unqualified. "And what would you have me do?"

"At this point?" Petoskey shrugged. Then he frowned, and jerked his head toward the Intelligence team's radio room. "Was that true? About . . . ?"

"This is *not* the place," Max said firmly. Illusion was not reality; the crew pretended not to hear Petoskey speak, but they'd repeat every word that came from his mouth.

"I hate the Adareans, I want you to know that," Petoskey said. "Anything to do with the Adareans, I hate, and I'll have none of it aboard my ship. So if there's any danger, even from one of the intelligence men—"

"There will be no danger," Max asserted firmly. "It is my job to make certain of that."

"See to it, Lieutenant."

"I will." Max was surprised. That was the most direct command any Captain had given him during his tenure as a political officer.

Petoskey returned an almost respectful nod. Max was about to suggest a later discussion when Lukinov shouted from the hatch.

"Captain. You might want to listen to this. We tried to raise you on the com, but it's not working."

Petoskey slipped his feet free and followed the Intelligence officer. Max invited himself and swam along.

Inside the listening room, Reedy sat at a long desk, wearing a pair of headphones, making notes on the translation in her palm-pad. Burdick had a truck battery surgi-taped to a table wedged in the tiny room's rounded corner. Wires ran from it to an open panel on the main concomsole, and Burdick connected others. He looked up from his work and grinned as they came into the hatch. "Gotta love the electrician's mates," he said. "They've got everything."

Lukinov laughed and handed a pair of headphones to Petoskey. "Wait until you hear this."

Petoskey slipped the earpieces into place. "I don't understand Chinese," he said after a minute. "Always sounds like an out-of-tune guitar to me."

Lukinov's smile widened. "But it's voices, not code, don't you see? The level of encryption was like cheap glue." He made a knife-opening-a-letter gesture with his hands.

"Good work. What have you learned so far?"

Lukinov leaned over Reedy's shoulder to look at the palm-pad. "Corporate security research ship. Spongedivers."

Petoskey nodded. "Bunch of scientists and part-time soldiers. Soft, but great tech. Way beyond ours. It's a safe bet their battery arrays don't go down when they fly mute. Lefty says there's another one parked out by the wormhole."

Lukinov confirmed this. "We know it because the radio tech is talking to his *girl*friend over on the other ship."

Burdick snickered, and Petoskey muttered "Mixed crews" with all the venom of a curse. He glared at Reedy so hard his eyes must have burned a hole in the ensign's head. The young woman looked up from her pad. "Yes, sir?" she asked.

"I didn't speak to you," Petoskey snapped.

Mixed crews were part of the Revolution, a way to double manpower—so to speak—in the military forces and give Jesusalem a chance to catch up. So far it was only in the officer corps, and even there it hadn't been received well. Some men, like Vance at the Academy, tried to openly discourage it despite the government's commitment.

Lukinov held the back of Reedy's seat to keep from drifting toward the ceiling. "The inbound ship's called the *Deng Xiaopeng*. Why does that name sound familiar?"

Petoskey shrugged. "Means nothing to me."

If they didn't know, then Max would give them an answer. He cleared his throat. "I believe that Deng Xiaopeng was one of Napoleon's generals."

Lukinov curled his mouth skeptically.

"That doesn't sound right," said Petoskey.

"I'm quite certain of it," said Max, bracing himself between the wall and floor at angle sideways to the others. "Confusion to the enemy."

"Always," replied Petoskey, apparently happy to find something he could agree with. "Always."

When Max's mind became restless, so did he. Two days after the spongedivers were sighted, his thoughts still careened weightlessly off the small walls. The presence of the ship from Outback complicated the ship's mission and his. Meanwhile, he was cut off from all his superiors, unable to guess which goal they wanted him to pursue right now. Or goals, as the case more likely was. So he was on his own again. Forced to decide for himself.

Nothing new about that, he thought ruefully.

He released the straps, and pushed off for the door to take a tour of the ship. He still had his traitor to catch.

When he opened the door, he saw another one cracked open down the corridor. Lieutenant Rucker peeked out and gestured for Max to come inside. Max checked to see that no one was in the hall and slipped into the room.

The blonde young man closed the door too fast and it slammed shut. "Didn't know if you were ever going to come out," Rucker said, producing an envelope. "This is from Gordet."

Max took the multi-tool from his pocket, and flicked the miniature vibra-knife on to slice open the seal. He studied the sheet inside. Commander Gordet had written down the codes for the safe that held the Captain's secret orders. Interesting. Max wondered if Rucker had made a copy for himself. "Did Gordet say anything specific?"

"He said to tell you that if we were to engage the Outback ship in combat and anything unfortunate were to happen to the Captain, you would have his full cooperation and support."

"So what did he tell the Captain?"

Rucker looked at the wall, opened his mouth, closed it again. He was not a quick liar.

Max gave him an avuncular clap on the shoulder. "You can tell me, Lieutenant. I'll find out anyway."

Rucker gulped, still refusing to meet Max's eyes. "He told the Captain that, um, if we were to engage the other ship in combat, and anything unfortunate were to happen to you, he'd make sure it was all clear in the records."

So Gordet was indecisive, trying to play both sides at once. That was a hard game. The Commander had no gift for it either. "What's your opinion of Gordet?" probed Max.

"He's a good officer. I'm proud to serve under him."

Rather standard response, deserving of Max's withering stare. This time Rucker's eyes did meet his.

"But, um, he's still mad about losing his cabin to you, sir. He doesn't like bunking with the junior officers."

"He'll get over it," said Max. "Just remind him that Lukinov is bunking with Burdick, eh?" He gestured at Rucker to open the door. Rucker looked both ways down the corridor, motioned that it was clear, and Max went on his way.

He headed topside, pulling himself hand over hand up the narrow shaft. When he exited the tube he found Kulakov conducting an emergency training drill in the forward compartments. Stick-its were hung up everywhere, indicating the type and extent of combat damage. Crews in full space gear performed "repairs" while the Chief Petty Officer graded their performance.

"You're dead," shouted Kulakov, grabbing a man by his collar and pulling him out of the exercise. "You forgot that you're a vacuum cleaner!"

"But sir, I'm suited up properly." His voice sounded injured, even distorted slightly by the microphone.

"But you're not plugged in," Kulakov said, tapping the stick-it on the wall. "That's open to the outside, and without your tether you're nothing more now than a very small meteor moving away from the ship! What are the rest of you looking at?"

He glanced over his shoulder, saw Max, and froze. The crews stopped their exercise.

"You just spaced another crewman," said Max, tilting his head toward a man who'd backed into the wall. "Carry on."

He turned away without waiting for Kulakov's salute. He didn't know why he had such an effect on that man, but now he was thinking he should look into it.

He proceeded through several twisting corridors, designed to slow and confuse boarding parties headed for the bridge, and passed the gym. He needed exercise. The weightlessness was already starting to get to him. But he decided to worry about that later.

He paused when he came to the missile room.

The Black Forest.

That was the crew's nickname for it. Four polished black columns rose four uninterrupted stories—tubes for nuclear missiles, back when this ship was intended to fight the same kind of dirty war waged by the Adareans. It was the largest open space in the entire ship. When the grav was on, the men exercised by running laps, up one set of stairs, across the catwalk, down the other, around the tubes, and up again.

Max went out onto the catwalk, climbed up on the railing, and jumped.

If one could truly jump in zero-gee, that was. He pushed himself towards the floor, and prayed that the grav didn't come on unexpectedly. On the way down he noticed someone who feared just that possibility making their way up the stairs.

Max did a somersault, extending his legs to change his momentum and direction, pushed off one of the tubes, and bounced over to see who it was. He immediately regretted doing so. It was Sergeant Simco, commander of the combat troops.

Every captain personally commanded a detachment of ground troops. It could be as big as a battalion in some cases, but for this voyage, with an entire crew of only 141, the number was limited to ten. Officially, they were along to repel boarders and provide combat assistance if needed. Unofficially, they were called troubleshooters. If crewmen gave the Captain any trouble, it was the troopers' job to shoot them.

Simco would enjoy doing it too. He had more muscles than brains. But then nobody had that many brains.

"Hello, Sergeant," Max called.

"Sir, that was nicely done."

"I didn't have you pegged for the cautious type."

Simco shook his head. "I don't like freefall unless I've got a parachute strapped to my back."

Typical groundhog response. "Are your men ready to board and take that Outback ship, Sergeant?"

"Sir, I could do it all by myself. They're *women*."

They both laughed, Simco snapped a perfect salute, and Max pushed off from the railing. When he landed on the bottom, he saw placards marked "Killshot" hanging on each of the four tubes. That meant that were loaded with live missiles, ready to launch. Something new, since the last time he'd passed through the Black Forest. He saw handwriting scrawled across the bottom of the placards, and went up close to read it. *A. G. W.*

Under the old government, the hastily thrown together Department of War had been called the Ministry of A Just God's Wrath. Considering the success of the Adareans, the joke had been that the name was a typo and should have been called Adjust God's Wrath. Some devout crewman still had the same goal.

On the lower level, Max continued to the aftmost portion of the ship, off-limits to all crew except for Engineering and Senior officers. Only one sealed hatch allowed direct entrance to this section. Max found an off-duty electrician's mate sitting there, watching a pocketvid. The faint sound of someone dying came from the tiny speaker.

Max stopped in front of the crewman. "What are you watching?"

The crewman looked up, startled. DePuy, that was his name. He jumped to his feet and went all the way to the ceiling. He saluted with one hand, while the thumb of the other flicked to the pause button. "It's *A Fire On The Land*, sir. It's about the Adarean nuking of New Nazareth."

"I'm familiar with it," Max replied. Political Education approved all videos, and practically ran the video business. "The bombing and the vid. Move aside and let me pass."

"Sorry, sir, the Chief Engineer said . . . "

Max turned as cold as deep space. He reached under DePuy to open the hatch. "Move aside, crewman."

"The Chief Engineer gave me a direct order, sir!"

"And I am giving you another direct order right now." Damn it, thought Max, the man still hesitated. "Rejecting an order from your Political Officer is mutiny, Mr. DePuy. A year is a very long time to spend in the ship's brig waiting for trial."

"Sir! A year is a very long time to serve under a chief officer who holds grudges, sir!"

"If I have to repeat my order a third time, you *will* go to the brig."

DePuy saluted and pushed off from the wall. Though he seemed to seriously consider, for a split second, whether he wouldn't rather be locked up than face Chevrier's temper.

Max went down the corridor and paused outside the starboard Battery Room. The hatch stood open on the two-story space. One of the battery arrays was completely disassembled and diagrammed on the wall, with the key processing chips circled in red. A small group of men, most of them stripped to their waists, crowded into the soft-walled clean room in the corner. A large duct ran up from it toward the ceiling, the motor struggling to draw air. A crewman looked up and tapped the Chief Engineer on the shoulder.

"You!" Chevrier shouted as soon as he saw Max. "This is a restricted area! I want you out of my section right now!"

"Nothing is off-limits to me," Max replied.

"Fuck your mother!" Chevrier thundered, shooting across the room and getting right in Max's face. Chevrier's eyes had dark circles around them like storm clouds, and red lines in the whites like tiny bolts of lightning. He probably hadn't slept since the spongediver was spotted; no doubt he was also pumped up on Nova or its more legal equivalent from the dispensary. That would explain his heavy sweating. It couldn't drip off him in the weightlessness, but had simply accumulated in a pool about a half inch deep that sloshed freely in the vicinity of his breastbone. Max noticed that the comet insignia was *branded* on Chevrier's bare chest. The Revolutionary government had banned that tradition, but the branding irons were still floating around some ships in the service. Chevrier was the type who had probably heated it up with a hand welder and branded himself. He jabbed a finger in the direction of the empty spot on Max's left breast pocket. "You haven't qualified for a single ship's system," he said, "and you sure as hell aren't reactor qualified. Now get out of my section!"

"You forgetting something, soldier?" Max asked, in as irritating a voice as he could manage.

Chevrier laughed in disbelief. "I wish I could forget! I've got a major problem on my hands, a ship with no fucking backup power."

Max took a deep breath. "Did somebody break your arm, *soldier*?"

Chevrier's eyes flickered. He made a sloppy motion with his right hand in the general direction of his head. Had Mallove sent word in the other direction too? Did Chevrier know that Max was supposed to leave him alone?

"Good. Give me a status report on the power situation."

The Chief Engineer inhaled deeply. "Screwed up and likely to stay that way. The crewman on duty panicked—he folded the wings and powered down the Casmir drive without disengaging the batteries first and fried half the chips. We are now trying to build new chips, atom by atom, but you need a grade A clean hood to do that. And our hood is about as tight and clean as an old whore."

Max had heard all this already, less vividly described, from the Captain's reports. "Go on."

"Normally, we could just switch over to the secondary array, but some blackhole of a genius gutted our portside Battery Room and replaced it with a salvaged groundside nuclear reactor so we can float through Adarean space disguised like background radiation in order to do God knows what."

"But you can switch communications, ship systems, propulsion, all that, over to the reactor, right?"

That was the plan: Dive into Adarean space, do one circuit around the sun running on the nukes while recording everything they could on the military and political communications channels, then head home again.

"We've already done all that," answered Chevrier, "but we can't power up the Casmir drive with it. It's strictly inner system, no diving."

He suddenly noticed the pool of sweat on his chest, went to flick it away, then stopped. "The Adareans won't scan us if we're running on nuclears, but they wouldn't scan canvas sails either, so we might as well have used them instead. We've got to fix the main battery at some point."

"Can you bring the grav back online?"

"Not safely, no, and not with the reactor. It's a power hog. Too many things to go wrong."

"Lasers?"

Chevrier ground his teeth. "You could talk to the Captain, you know. He sends down here every damned hour for another report, asking the same exact damn questions."

"Lasers?" repeated Max firmly.

"I recommended other options to the Captain, but if you want to turn some Outback ship into space slag, I'll give you enough power to do it. As long as you let me comb through the debris for spare parts once you're done. Might be the one way to get some decent equipment."

"Fair enough. How are your men holding up?"

"They're soldiers." He pronounced the word very differently than Max had. "They do exactly what they're told. Except for that worthless snot of a mate who apparently can't even guard a fucking sealed hatch properly."

Max didn't like the sound of that. Chevrier couldn't keep pushing his men as hard as he pushed himself, or they'd start to break. "Men are not machines," Max began . . .

"Hell they aren't! A ship's crew is one big machine and you're a piece of grit in the silicone, a short in the wire. With you issuing orders outside the chain of command, the command splits. You either need to fit in or get the hell out of the machine!"

Chevrier jabbed his finger at Max's chest again to punctuate his statement. This time, he made contact with enough force to send the two men in opposite directions.

It was clear that he didn't mean to touch Max, and just as clear that he didn't mean to back down. He glared at Max, daring him to make something of it. Aggressiveness was the main side effect of Nova. It built up until the men went supernova and burned out. On top of that,

Chevrier also had that look some men got when things went very wrong. He couldn't fix things so he wanted to smash them instead.

Max could bring him up on charges, but the ship needed its Chief Engineer right now. And if Mallove had promised his friends in government that he would protect Chevrier . . .

Max decided to ignore the incident. For the time being. "I'll be sure to make a record of your comments."

Chevrier snorted, as if he'd won a game of chicken. "If you have problems with any of the big words, come back and I'll spell them out for you." He flapped his hand near his head again, turned and went back to the clean hood.

The other men scowled at Max.

That was the problem with anger—it was an infectious disease. Frustration only made it spread faster. He continued his tour, looking into the main engine room and then at the nuclear reactors. Nobody was in the former because there was nothing to be done there, and nobody was in the latter because radiation spooked them. One man sat in the control room, reading the monitors. Max hovered near the ceiling a moment looking over the crewman's shoulder, comparing the pictures on the vids to the layout of the rooms. The crewman stared at the monitors intently, pretending not to see Max. Yes, thought Max, anger was very infectious. You never knew who might catch it next.

The hapless mate DePuy still guarded the hatch, whipping the vid behind his back as he snapped to attention. Max ignored him. Accidents happened. Some idiots would just slab themselves.

He went back through the Black Forest, acknowledging salutes from a pair of shooters, the Tactics Officer's mates. He swam through the air to the top level, and down the main corridor, past the open door of the exercise room. He turned back. If grav was going to be offline much longer, he needed to sign up for exercise time. Physically, he needed to stay sharp right now.

Max pushed the door open. The room was dark. It surprised him briefly that no one was there, but then, with the six-and-sixes, and all the drills, the men were probably too busy. He hit the light switch. Nothing came on. He moved farther into the room to hit the second switch. Something hard smashed him on the back of the head. He twisted, trying to get a hold of his assailant but there was no one behind him. He realized that the other man was above him, on the ceiling, too late, and as he twisted in the dark room, he suddenly became very dizzy, losing any sense of direction, any orientation to the walls and floors. A thick arm snaked around his throat, choking off his nausea along with his breath. Max got hold of a thumb and managed to pull it halfway loose, but he had no leverage at all.

He swung his elbows forcefully and futilely as black dots swam before his eyes like collapsing stars in the darkened room.

Then the darkness became absolute.

He experienced a floating, disconnected sensation, like being in the sensory deprivation tanks they'd used for some of his conditioning experiments. Max had hated the feeling then, of being lost, detached, and he hated it now. Then light knifed down into one of his eyes and all his pains awoke at once.

"Do you hear me, Lieutenant Nikomedes?"

"Yes," croaked Max. His throat felt raw. The light flicked off, then stabbed into the other eye. "That hurts."

"I should imagine that it's the least of your hurts. Has the painkiller worn off completely then?"

"I hope so, because if it hasn't . . . " His throat felt crushed and his kidneys ached like hell. The light went off and Max's eyes adjusted to the setting. He was in the sickbay, with the Doc hovering over him. His name was Noyes, and he was only a medtech but the crew still called him Doc. The service was short of surgeons. Command didn't want to spare one for this voyage.

"Your pupils look good," Noyes continued. "There's a ruptured blood vessel in the right eye. It's not pretty, but the damage is superficial. We had some concern about how long you'd been without oxygen when you came in."

Yeah, thought Max. He was concerned too. "So how long was it?"

"Not long. Seconds, maybe. A couple of the shooters found you unconscious in the gym."

"And so they brought the Corpse to sickbay?"

"You know that nickname?" Noyes administered an injection and

Max's pain lessened. "Whoever attacked you knew what he was doing. He cut off your air supply without crushing your windpipe or leaving any fingerprint type bruises on your throat. You're lucky—the shooters did chest compressions as soon as they found you and got you breathing again."

So this wasn't just a warning. Someone had tried to kill him, and failed. Unless the shooters were in on it. But who would do it and why? His hand shot up to his breast pocket. Gordet's note with the secret codes was still there.

"What's that?" asked Noyes, noticing the gesture.

"A list of suspects," replied Max. He wondered if someone had followed him from Engineering. "Did you hear the one about the political officer who was killed during wargame exercises?"

Suspicion flickered across the Doc's face. "No," he said slowly.

"They couldn't call it friendly fire because he had no friends."

Noyes didn't laugh. He was young, barely thirty, if that. But his face was worn, and he had a deep crease between his eyes. "Can I ask you a direct question?"

"If it's about who did this . . . "

"No. It's about the ship's mission."

"I may not be able to answer."

"It's just the crew, you know what they're saying, that this is a suicide mission. We're supposed to sneak into Adarean space, nuke their capital, and then blow ourselves up, vaporize the evidence."

"Ah," no, Max hadn't heard that one yet, though he supposed he should have thought of it himself. Sometimes there were disadvantages to knowing inside information; it limited one's ability to imagine other possibilities. "We could blow up their capital, but their military command is space-based, decentralized. That kind of strike wouldn't touch them at all. That doesn't make any sense, Doc."

"It doesn't have to make sense for the service to order it." Noyes laughed, a truncated little puff of air. "I was scheduled for leave, I was supposed to be getting married on my leave, and I got yanked off the transport and put on this ship without a word of explanation, and then found out I was going to be gone for a year and a half. So don't tell me the service only gives orders that make any sense."

Max had no answer for that. He knew how orders were.

"Is this a suicide mission?" asked Noyes. "Tell me straight. The shooters think that's why someone tried to kill you, because they don't have to worry about what would happen when they got back home."

And they could die knowing they'd offed an officer. There were definitely a few of that type on board. But Max didn't think it was that random. "And if it is a suicide mission?"

The medtech's face grew solemn. "Then I want to send some kind of message back to Suzan. I don't want her to think I simply disappeared on her. I don't want her to live the rest of her life with that."

Noyes couldn't be the only one having those thoughts. No wonder there was tension on the ship. "This isn't a suicide mission," Max said firmly.

"Your word on that?"

"Yes." This was a rumor he would have to try to kill. Even if it were true. Max touched his pocket again. What exactly were the secret orders? He thought he knew them, but maybe he didn't.

Noyes shook his head. "Too bad you're the Political Officer. Everyone knows your word can't be trusted." He handed Max a bottle of pills. "The Captain wants to see you on the bridge right away. Take one of these if you feel weak, or in pain, and then report back to sickbay next shift."

Max sat up, and noticed his pants pockets were inside out. So someone had been searching him after all, and the shooters had interrupted them. Unless that too was part of the ruse. For now, he'd stick to the simpler explanation.

Noyes helped him to his feet. "I ought to keep you for observation," he said.

"No," replied Max. "I'm fine." I'm as rotten a liar as Rucker is, he thought. He wondered if the First Lieutenant had changed his mind. Or changed his allegiances.

The door opened and Simco waited outside. His bulk seemed to fill up the small corridor. He snapped a crisp salute and whipped his hand down again. "Captain assigned me to be your guard, sir. He asks you not to speak about this incident while I'm investigating it. He also requires your immediate attention on the bridge."

"The assignment comes a little too late apparently, Sergeant," murmured Max. Simco smiled, and Max gestured for him to lead the way.

"You first, sir."

Trouble never came looking for him face to face, thought Max as he led the way through the corridors. It always came sneaking up behind.

The bridge was crowded because of shift change. Double the usual crew packed into the tight space, giving report to one another in low tones.

No one but the Captain bothered to look up when Max entered, and even he only glanced away from the scope for a second. Vents hissed above the muted beeps from the monitors. The two shooters Max had seen in the Black Forest were seated next to the Tactics' Officer. Max waited to make eye contact with them, to say thanks, but they were so absorbed in their work they didn't notice him. He gave up waiting, and slid over to stand by Petoskey.

"It's about damn time, Nikomedes," growled Petoskey.

"I had a slight accident."

"Well, I have a slight problem. The incoming ship boosted. They're in some kind of a hurry. So our window of opportunity is here, and it's closing fast."

He hadn't made up his mind yet, Max realized. "Have they detected us?"

"No. We're between them and the rings. They don't see us because we're floating dead, and because they don't expect to see anyone out here."

Max remained silent, running the calculations through his head. Outback's presence would not affect the Jesusalem's claim to the system, only the possible success of their mission through Adarean space.

" 'War is an extension of political policy with military force,' " prompted Petoskey, quoting regulations.

And it was the job of the political officer to be the final arbiter of policy. This was exactly the type of unforeseen situation that created the need for political officers on ships. "What are our options?"

Petoskey shifted his chewing tobacco into a spot below his lower lip.

"Chevrier says we could power up and hit them with the lasers, but we wouldn't get more than one or two shots. I don't like our chances at this distance. We could launch the nuclears at them. They'd see them coming, but we could bracket them so that they'll still take on a killer dose of radiation even if we don't score a direct hit. Or we could do nothing."

"What are your concerns?"

He sucked the tobacco juice through his teeth. "The last I heard officially, Outback was one of our trading partners."

"We have met the enemy," Max mused softly, "and they are us."

Petoskey scowled. "But Outback also trades with Adares. If they find our dive to their system, they'll let the Adareans know about it and that endangers our mission. So what's the politically correct thing for me to do?"

"I would suggest that we haven't been tasked with guarding the system or the other wormhole. I would point out that there are other ships in place specifically to do just that." He paused. "And as long as we dive undetected, our mission isn't really endangered."

Petoskey leaned back, and straightened, so that his head nearly scraped the pipes. He slammed the scope back into its slot and stared hard at Max. "So we let them pass?"

"They've got a second ship outside our range. We pop this one, and the other one sees us, then Jesusalem could face a war on two fronts." Although they weren't technically at war with Adares any longer, the capital was filled with rumors of war. "Politically, we're not ready to handle that."

"I'll tell you one thing," said Petoskey, with a slight shudder that mixed revulsion with unease. "I'm glad not to use the nukes. Those are dirty weapons to use. On people."

"I fail to see any difference," said Max. "Two kinds of fire. Lasers or nukes, they would be equally dead."

Petoskey had a lidded cup taped to the conduits on the wall. He pulled it off, spat into it, and taped it back up again. Pausing, so he could change the subject. "I understand that you were nearly dead a little while ago, Nikomedes. Simco has one of his men guarding Reedy."

"Why?" asked Max. Had the ensign been attacked also?

"Spy or not, it's obvious she's trying to get back at you for your comments in quarters the other day. I asked around and found out what she did to Vance. Shows what happens when you don't keep women in their place. Before I had her locked up, I wanted to make certain this wasn't something arranged between the two of you. Some kind of duel. Not that I thought it was, but . . . "

He thought it might be, finished Max to himself. Or hoped it might be. "It wasn't Reedy as far as I know. But let Simco's man watch her while Simco investigates. If Reedy's guilty, maybe she'll give herself away."

"Shouldn't have a woman on board anyway, even if she is language qualified. We can't afford dissension on a voyage like this one. I will personally execute anyone who endangers this mission. I don't care if it is a junior officer."

Or a woman, thought Max. "Understood," he answered. He looked up one last time, to see if he could catch the shooters' eyes. That's when he noticed Rucker and Gordet staring at him. They had been whispering to one another and stopped. "In fact, I think I'll head down to the radio room right now."

"You're dismissed from duty until Doc says you've recovered. And Simco or one of his men will stay with you at all times."

That was not what Max wanted, not at all. "Thanks. I appreciate that."

Petoskey nodded, dismissing him.

Max began to wish that whoever had attacked him had done a better job.

He went to the secure radio room and all three of the Intelligence officers stopped talking and turned towards the doorway. It's the Political Officer Effect, thought Max.

"What happened to your face?" Lukinov asked.

"I fought the law and the law won," Max answered impulsively.

Burdick burst out laughing. Even Lukinov smiled. "Why does that sound so damned familiar?" he asked.

"*Judas's Chariot*," answered Burdick. "The vid. It was one of Barabbas' lines."

"Yeah, yeah, I remember that one now. It had Oliver Whatshisname in it. I got to meet him once, at a party, when he did that public information vid. Good man." He twisted around. The smell of his cologne nearly choked Max. "Seriously, Max, what happened? And why has the Captain put a guard on one of my men?"

"Someone tried to kill me." Max was disappointed with the surprise in Lukinov's expression. In all of their expressions. Intelligence was supposed to know everything. "Captain suspects the ensign here."

"That's ridiculous!" Lukinov rolled his eyes. Anger flashed across Reedy's face.

"It wasn't my suggestion," Max replied. "But if you don't mind my asking, which one of you is just coming on shift?"

"I am, sir," Reedy answered immediately.

"And where were you?"

"In her quarters sleeping," interjected Lukinov. "Where else would she have been?"

"You were there with her?" No one wanted to answer that accusation, so Max slid past it. "You two usually work one shift together, and Burdick takes the other, right?"

The senior officer hesitated. "I doubled shifted with Burdick because of the information we were getting."

So. Reedy had been alone. Not that Max suspected her of the attack. But now he'd have to. Maybe he'd misestimated her in the first place. "What information is that?"

"The other Outback ship is doing some kind of military research defending the wormhole. Based on what we're overhearing from observers in the shuttles. We've got a name on the second ship. It's the *Jiang Qing*, same class as the other one." He paused. "You aren't going to try to tell me that Jiang Qing was one of Napoleon generals too, are you Max?"

"Why not?" asked Max flatly. "Historically, Earth has had women generals for centuries. Jesusalem was the only planet without a mixed service."

Lukinov's lip curled. "We finally tracked down Deng Xiaopeng. He and this Jiang Qing woman were both part of the Chinese revolution. Reedy found the information."

"The Chinese communist revolution," clarified the ensign. "They were minor figures, associated with Mao. Both were charged with crimes though they helped bring about important political changes that led to the second revolution."

"Ah," said Max. A wave of pain shot through him. If his legs had been supporting his weight, they would surely have buckled. "Please cooperate with Sergeant Simco until we can get this straightened out. Now if you will excuse me."

He didn't wait for their response, but turned back to the hall. Simco waited at parade rest, his hands behind his back. Another trooper stood beside him.

"I'm going to return to my cabin now," Max said.

"I've detailed Rambaud here to watch you while I begin my investigation," Simco replied. Rambaud was a smaller but equally muscled version of his superior officer. "I'll be rotating all my men through this duty until we find the culprit."

"Keeping them sharp?" Max said.

Simco nodded. "A knife can't cut if you don't keep it sharp."

"I couldn't agree more." Max barely noticed the other man shadowing him through the narrow maze of corridors. When he reached his room, he took a double dose of the doctor's pain killers, added one from his own stock, and washed them all down with a gulp of warm, flat water. He looked in the bathroom mirror at his damaged eye. That's when he started to shake. He had the ludicrous sensation that he was going to fall down, so he grabbed hold of the sink and tried to steady himself. Eventually it passed, but not before his breath was coming out in ragged gasps.

He'd come too close to dying this time. And why?

The rumor of the suicide mission still bothered him, and so did the problem of Reedy. When he drifted off to sleep, he dreamed that he was wandering an empty vessel searching for someone who was no longer aboard, through corridors that were kinked and slicked like the intestines of some animal. They started shrinking, squeezing the crates and boxes that filled them into a solid mass, as Max tried to find his way out. The last section dead-ended in a mirror, and when he paused to look into its silver surface an eye above a pyramid filled his damaged socket.

He woke up in a cold sweat. According to the clock, he'd slept nearly four and a half hours, but he didn't believe it. He wasn't inclined to believe anything right now.

He rose and dressed himself. He needed better luck. If it wouldn't come looking for him, he'd have to go looking for it.

Down in the very bottom of the ship rested an observation chamber that contained the only naked ports in the entire vessel. Max went down there to think, dutifully followed by Simco's watchdog.

Max paused outside the airlock. "You can wait here."

"I'm supposed to stay with you, sir."

"The lights are off, it's empty," said Max, realizing as soon as the words were out of his mouth what had happened the last time he went into a dark room alone. "If someone's waiting in there to kill me, then you've got them trapped. You'll get a commendation."

Rambaud relented. Max entered the room, closing the hatch behind him. It sealed automatically reminding Max of the sound of a prison cell door shutting.

Outside the round windows stretched the infinite expanse of space. The sun was a small, cold ember in a charcoal-colored sky dominated by the vast and ominous bulk of Big Brother. They were close enough that Max could see crimson storms raging on its surface, swirling hurricanes larger than Jerusalem itself. He counted three moons spinning around the planet, and great rings of dust, as if everything in space was drawn into satellite around the self-consuming fire of its mass.

A quiet cough came from the rear of the compartment.

Max pirouetted, and saw another man floating cross-legged in the air. As he unfolded and came to attention, light glinted off the jack that sat lodged in his forehead like a third eye. It was the spongediver, the ship's pilot, Patchett.

"At ease, Patchett," said Max.

Patchett nodded toward the port as he clasped his hands behind his back. "Beautiful, isn't it?"

"It's no place for a human being to live," Max said. "Give me a little blue marble of a planet any day instead."

The pilot smiled. "That figures."

"What do you mean?"

"You're a Political Officer, and politics is always about the place we live, how we live together." He gestured at the sweep of the illuminated rings. "But this is why I joined the service—to explore, to see space."

"Has it been worth it?"

"Too much waiting, too much doing nothing." He shifted in his seat. "The diving makes it worthwhile."

"Good," murmured Max, looking away.

"You and I are alike that way," Patchett said. "We both are the most useless men on the ship *except* for that one moment when we're the only one qualified to do the job." He stared out the port. "What happened to you, that was wrong, sir."

Max gazed out the window also, saying nothing.

"I'd guess I've been in the service as long as you have, nearly twenty years."

"Just past thirty years now." It wasn't all in the official records, but thirty years total. A very long time. Patchett clearly wanted to say something more. "What is it?" asked Max. "Speak freely."

"Things have been going downhill the past few years, sir. The wrong men in charge, undermining everything we hoped to accomplish in the Revolution. They all want war. They forget what the last one was like."

"Are you sure you should be telling this to your political officer?"

"You're the political officer. You have to know it already. You may be the only one I *can* say it to. Petoskey's an excellent Captain, don't get me wrong, sir. But he's too young to remember what the last war was like."

They hung there, in the dark, weightless, silence, watching the giant spin on its axis. If Patchett was right, there was one moment in the voyage only when Max's skills would make a difference. But what moment, and what kind of difference, there was no way to know in advance.

Simco was in the med bay when Max went to check in with Noyes. "I'd salute," said the Sergeant, "but Doc here's treating a sprain."

"Dislocation," corrected Noyes.

"What happened?" asked Max.

Simco grinned. "I scheduled extra combat training for my men.

Want to make sure they're ready in case they run into whoever attacked you. It doesn't really count as a good workout unless someone dislocates something."

Noyes snorted.

"Plus, Doc here says that we have to exercise at least an hour a day or we'll start losing bone and muscle mass."

"Nobody's had to deal with prolonged weightlessness in a couple of hundred years," added Noyes. "I'm only finding hints of the information I need in our database. The nausea, vertigo, lethargy, that I expected and was prepared for. But we're already seeing more infections, shortness of breath, odd stuff. And we've got orders to spend *months* like this? It's madness. Take it easy on this thumb for a few more days, Simco." He went to lay his stim-gun on the table and it floated off sideways across the room. "Damn. Not again."

Max snatched it out of the air and handed it back to the Doc. "Any word on who my attacker was?" he asked Simco.

"No." The Sergeant blew out his breath. "But I did hear that you picked a fight with Chevrier down in Engineering."

"Nothing even close to that."

"Good. He's a big man, completely out of your weight class."

"Right now, we're all in the same weight class."

That won Max a laugh from both Simco and Noyes. "Still, if you go see him again, about anything, please inform me first," the Sergeant said.

"You'll know about it before I do," promised Max.

After the Doc was done checking him, Max went back through the crate-packed corridors towards his quarters. On the way, he passed Reedy, whose mouth quirked in a brief smile as Max squeezed past her.

"What do you find so funny, Ensign?" Max growled.

Reedy's eyes flicked, indicating the trooper following her and the one behind Max. "For a second there, sir, I wondered which of us was the real prisoner."

Very perceptive. She had an edge to her voice that reminded him of Chevrier. He recalled that she had shown a strong aversion to confinement after the incident with Vance. "Remember who you're speaking to, Ensign!"

"Yes, sir. It won't happen again, sir."

"See that it doesn't."

He went into his room and swallowed another pain-killer. Even if the moment came when he could make a difference, would he be able to get away from his minders long enough to do it?

Eight more shifts, two more days, and nothing.

Max had no appetite, the food all tasted bland to him. He couldn't sleep for more than a few hours at a time. If he turned the lights off, he'd wake in a panic, disoriented, unsure of where he was. But if he slept with the lights on, they poked at the edge of his consciousness, prodding him awake. He tried to exercise one hour out of every two shifts, but everything seemed tedious. It just felt wrong, empty motions with nothing to push against.

On the bridge, he asked Petoskey if it was still necessary to have a guard.

"The attack's still unsolved," Petoskey said. "Until Simco brings me the man—or woman—who did it, I want you protected."

Max had the sinking feeling that might be for the rest of the voyage. "How are the repairs going?"

"Chevrier replaced all the chips in the dead array with new ones, but something failed when he tested it. He has an idea for rebuilding the chips with some kind of silicon alloy crystal. Says he can grow it as long as we stay weightless. Some other kind of old tech. Inorganic. He tried to explain it to me, but he's the only one that really understands it."

"Can we wait that long?"

"We can't power up to jump as long as those Outback ships are in the vicinity. They'd see us—and the wormhole—in a microsecond. So far they still haven't detected our buoy. Or if they have, they just took it for a pulsar signal." Which was the idea, after all. Petoskey tugged hard at his beard. There were dark stains of sleeplessness under his eyes. "Don't you have some work to do, some reports to write?"

He meant it as a dismissal. Max was willing to be dismissed. He was still no closer to catching his traitor, and his luck couldn't have been more execrable.

He went to the ship's library to read. Rambaud, his trooper again this the shift, had no interest in reading or studying vids of any kind. He writhed in almost open pain as Max made it clear that he intended to stay at a desk alone for several hours. Max decided that it wouldn't be murder if he bored Simco's men to death.

He sat there, scanning Fier's monograph on the Adarean war, skimming through the casualty lists in the appendixes, thinking about some of the worst battles, early on, and the consequences of war, when a voice intruded on his contemplations.

" . . . bored as hell down here. Uh-huh. Wargames. That sounds interesting. Can you understand that Outback lingo?"

Rambaud was whispering on the comlink to his compatriot in charge of Reedy. Max let the conversation turn to complaints about the exercise regimen and weightlessness before he flipped off his screen and rose to go.

The Intelligence radio room was on his regular circuit of destinations, so he made no excuse for heading there now. The door was propped open, and the scent of Lukinov's imported cologne hit Max's nose out in the corridor. He paused in the doorway. The trooper stood behind Lukinov and Reedy, with a pair of headsets on.

"So this is how well you keep secrets?" asked Max.

The trooper saw Max, yanked the earphones out of his ear, and handed them back to an ebullient Lukinov. "Wait until you hear this, Max!" Lukinov said.

The trooper who tried to squeeze by Max without touching him. Max stayed firmly in his way, making him as uncomfortable as possible. "Rambaud," he said to his own man, "I believe I left my palm-pad down in the library by accident. Retrieve it for me and bring it to this room immediately so I can record this conversation."

Rimbaud hesitated before answering. "Yes, sir."

The other trooper took up station outside the door. Max kicked the door shut and latched it.

"What's going on with the spongediver?" asked Max.

"They're testing a new laser deflector, using it for wormhole defense." Lukinov grinned. "Go ahead and listen."

Max picked up the headphones and fit the wires into his ears. Pilots chattered with tactics officers, describing the kind of run they were simulating. No wonder Outback outfitted their survey ships with the newest military equipment. The blind side of a wormhole dive was probably the only place in the galaxy they could test any new weapons without being observed. "Very standard stuff here," he said after a moment. "Is there just one channel of this?"

"Their scientists are on the other channel, the one Reedy's monitoring. But don't you see what an advantage this gives us if we can steal it? We can attack Adares with impunity and keep them from diving into our system."

Max switched the channel setting to the one Reedy listened to. "Do unto others before they do unto you?"

"Exactly!" replied Lukinov.

Reedy's eyes went wide open. She started tapping the desk to get their attention. "Sir," she said. "There's something you should . . . "

"Not right now," said Max.

Lukinov frowned at him. "Now see here—"

"No, you see here. Has the Captain been informed of this?"

"Not yet," replied Lukinov.

"You invite some grunt in here to listen to information that will certainly be classified top secret before you notify the Captain?" He sneered at Lukinov, pausing long enough to listen to the scientists talk. "You can be sure that my Department will file a record of protest on our return. In the meantime, I better go get the Captain."

Lukinov popped out of his seat. "No, I'll do that. I was just planning to do that anyway, if you hadn't interrupted."

"Sir," repeated Reedy. "*Sirs.*"

"Ensign," said Max, "Shut. Up."

The ensign nodded mutely, her eyes shaped like two satellite dishes trying to pick up a signal.

"I'm coming with you, Lukinov," Max said.

"No, you aren't, *Lieutenant,*" snapped the Intelligence officer. "I'm the one man on this ship you can't give direct orders to and don't you forget it."

Max saluted, a gesture sharp enough to have turned into a knife hand strike at the other man's throat. Lukinov stormed out of the room. Max turned back to the ensign, who simply stared at him.

"They just broadcast the complete specifications," said Reedy. "They were checking for field deformation—"

"I know that," said Max. And then he did something he never expected to do, not on this voyage. He said aloud the secret Intelligence code word for "render all assistance." Silently, to himself, he added a prayer that it was current, and that Reedy would recognize it.

"Wh-what did you say?" stammered the ensign.

Max repeated the code word for "render all assistance" while he pulled off his earphones and reached in his pocket for his multi-tool. His fingers found nothing, and he realized that it had been missing since his attack. "And give me a screwdriver," he added.

Reedy handed over the tool. "But . . . but . . . "

Max ignored her. In thirty seconds, he'd disconnected the power and disassembled the outer case of the radio. "Give me the laser," he said.

The ensign's hands shook as she complied.

"I need two new memory chips and the spare pod." Reedy just stared at him, uncomprehending. "Now!" spat Max, and the ensign dove for the equipment box.

Max shoved the loaded memory into his pockets and snapped the replacements pieces into their slots as Reedy handed them over. The radio was still a mess of pieces when someone rapped on the door.

"Stall them!" hissed Max.

The rap came again, and the door pushed open. Reedy flew toward it like a rocket. Rambaud pushed his head in partway. "Here's your palm-pad, sir."

"I'll take it," said Reedy, grabbing it and pushing the door shut again.

"Thanks!" called Max. He'd lost one of the screws, and when he looked up from the equipment to see if it was floating somewhere, he was temporarily disoriented. His stomach did a flip-flop and his head spun in a circle. "Shit!"

Rambaud pushed back on the door. "Are you safe in there, sir? I'm coming in."

Reedy wedged herself against the wall to block the door.

Max heard a plain thump as Rambaud bounced against it. He saw the screw floating near his ankles and scooped it up. He fixed the cover and powered the machine up again. Reedy grunted as the door pushed against her, cracking open. "I'm fine," Max said loudly.

Rambaud nodded, but he stood outside the cracked door peering in.

Reedy was breathing fast. A thousand questions formed and died on her lips when Max spun to face her. Max had taken the leap, and now he had to see how far that leap would take him.

"Ensign," he whispered.

"Yes, sir?"

"From this moment forth," his lips barely moved, "you will consider me your sole superior officer."

Her eyes jumped to the door. "Sir? But—"

"That is a direct order!"

"Yes, sir!"

"You will not tell anyone—"

But he did not get the chance to tell Reedy what she should and shouldn't say. The door swung open and Lukinov entered, followed by Captain Petoskey. Lukinov grinned like a party girl full of booze. "Wait until you hear this," he said. He put his headphones on, and handed one to Petoskey as Reedy slid quickly back into her place.

They listened for a moment. Petoskey squinted his eyes, and rounded his shoulders even more than usual. "Sounds like they're bringing the shuttles in, getting ready to leave. Radioing a safe voyage message to their other ship. What was I supposed to hear?"

"They're testing a new deflector for wormhole defense. If we attack their ship and kill them, we can take it. Their other ship will be stuck in-system and we can nuke them."

"Captain," said Max.

"Yes?"

"I didn't hear any evidence of this deflector. I can't recommend an attack."

Lukinov frantically punched commands into his keypad. "Let me back up to an hour ago." His face went as blank as the records he was trying to access. "I can't seem to find it. Reedy, what's going on here?"

"Sir," she muttered, with a pleading glance at Max, "uh, I don't know, sir."

"She's covering up," said Max.

Three faces stared at him with variations of disbelief.

"Look at the battery, it's not properly grounded." It was an awful explanation, but the best that Max could come up with on the spot. "Reedy was moving some equipment around, hit it with something. I didn't see what. Sparks flew and the screens all went dead. She got them back up right away, but she probably wiped the memories."

"Ensign!" screamed Lukinov. "Explain yourself!"

Reedy's mouth hung open. She didn't know what to say. Betrayal was written all over her face.

Petoskey took off his headset. "Lukinov, I trust you to take care of this. Nikomedes . . . "

"Yes, sir?"

Petoskey couldn't seem to think of any orders to give him. "I have to go talk to Chevrier. We have our mission. With the second ship out of the way, we have to prepare to dive."

Max followed Petoskey out into the corridor, but returned to his room to stash the stolen memory. Only two things mattered now: getting the information to his superior, and keeping Lukinov from getting it to his. It needed to be used as a defensive weapon, not as an excuse to start a war. Lukinov had access to the radio, and official channels. Max didn't. That stacked the cards in Lukinov's favor.

He had to do something with it soon, before they jumped to Adarean space. And he had to hope that a baby-faced ensign just out of the Academy didn't fold under pressure and give him away. It was like a game of Blind Man's Draw. Max had already put everything he had into the pot.

There was nothing else he could do at this point except play the card that he was dealt.

Meal time. Max sat by himself, as usual, at his own narrow table in the galley. Even the trooper guarding him sat with some of the other crewmen.

Lukinov entered, saw Max, and came straight over to him. "Reedy won't say that you were lying, but you were," the Intelligence officer said. "Not that it matters. The machines are buggered, the data's all gone. Even Burdick can't find it."

Max had a blank sheet in his pocket. He pulled it out, and a stylus, and passed it over to Lukinov. This was the way duels were proposed at the Academy. According to the Academy's cover story, it was the way Reedy had arranged to meet with Vance.

Lukinov looked at the sheet, then scratched 'observation room' and a time two hours distant on it. He pushed it back over to Max, who shook his head, and wrote 'reactor room.'

"Why there?" asked the Intelligence officer.

"They've got cameras there, but no mikes. It's off-limits to Simco's troopers, but not to us. We won't be there long."

"So this is just to be a private conversation? I should leave my weapons behind?"

"I wish you would."

"More's the pity," said Lukinov, and stormed out.

Max was putting his tray away, trying to resolve his other problem, when Simco came in. "Lukinov won't let us throw the ensign in the brig, not yet. But he thought it was best if I stuck with you personally in the meantime."

Perfect, thought Max, just perfect.

Two hours had never stretched out to such an eternity before, in all Max's life. Simco escorted him to his quarters and joined him inside.

"Do you want to follow me into the head and shake it dry for me?" asked Max on his way into the bathroom.

Simco laughed, but remained in the other room. Max retrieved a bottle of pills and an old pair of nail clippers from the medicine cabinet, putting them in his pocket. Then he led Simco on a long, roundabout trip through the corridors that ended up on the floor of the Black Forest. He stopped when he got there and snapped his fingers.

"I forgot something," Max said. "You don't mind if I borrow that multi-tool in your pocket, do you?"

Simco stuffed his hand automatically into his pants, wrapped it around the bulge there, and froze. "Sorry, sir, I don't have one with me," he said, grinning. "Got one in my locker. Or do you want to hit Engineering to borrow one?"

"No, it's nothing I need that badly." He jumped. "Meet you up top, in the exercise room." He grabbed hold of the service ladder outside one of the missile shafts, and pulled himself up. He used his momentum to spin, kicking off from the side of the shaft, and shot like a rocket towards the ceiling.

"Hold up there," called Simco, halfway up the stairs.

Max ducked into the upper corridor. He dove through the hall as fast as he could, past the exercise room, down the access shaft, and back out the corridor below, returning to the missile room. He watched Simco's feet disappear above him into the top corridor, and then he flew straight across the cavern to the section over Engineering, opened a portside hatch, and closed it again after himself.

A long time ago Max had modified his nail clippers to function as a makeshift tool. Bracing himself against the wall, he used it now to remove the grille from the ceiling vent—it was the supply duct for the HEPA filters in the clean hood corner of the battery room directly below. He squeezed inside, feet first, pulling the grille after him. There was no way to reattach it, but with no gravity he didn't need to. He simply pulled it into place and it stayed there.

It was an eighteen-inch duct and he was a small man. Even so, he felt like toothpaste being forced back into the tube. He had to twist sideways and flip over to get past the L-curve, but after that it was a straight trip down to the reactor room. With his arms pinned above his head, and no gravity to help him, he writhed downward like a rat caught in a drainpipe. He reached bottom, unable to go any further. His kicks had no effect at all and his heart began to race as he wondered if he'd be trapped inside the duct. Finally, by pressing his elbows out into the corners, and hooking one foot on the lip where the vent teed out horizontally, he was able to push the other foot downward until the duct tore open.

He eased downward into the plenum space above the hood ceiling, and kicked through the tiles. When he finally lowered himself into the battery room he was drenched in sweat, and his pants were ripped in the thigh. He hadn't even noticed. He undid his belt and looked at the scrape on his leg. It was mostly superficial. Not much blood.

He leaned in the corner, with the hood's softwalls pulled back, catching his breath. The cameras were all installed to monitor the reactor, so they faced the center of the two-story tall room. Most of them close-upped on specific pieces of equipment. He eased out, pushing himself up toward the ceiling.

He glanced at his chrono. Already seven minutes past his meeting time with Lukinov. He waited two more minutes before the hatch popped open. He had a split second to decide what he would do if it was one of the engineers.

But a familiar balding head thrust through the door. Max eased out of the hood area. "Hey, Lukinov."

"Max?" The other man twisted around to see him. He entered, closing the hatch behind him. "How the hell did you get in here? Chevrier's guard at the door gave me the runaround, swore he hadn't seen you! The mate watching the monitors said you never came in here either. What are you, some damn spook?"

Max ignored the questions. "You wanted to talk to me about the radio room. It was me. I stole the memory chips."

Lukinov came toward him, pale with fury. "You did what? By god, I'll see you hang."

"Intelligence won't touch me," said Max. "Not for this."

"I'll get Political Education to do it, you goddamn weasel," Lukinov vowed. He launched himself towards Max, keeping a hand against the wall to orient himself. "Your boss, Mallove, is a personal friend of mine. He won't like—"

Max jumped, tucking his knees and spinning as he sailed in the air. He wrapped his belt around Lukinov's throat, pivoted, twisting the belt as he pulled himself back to the floor. The motion jerked Lukinov upside down so that he floated in the air like a child's balloon.

"Your boss, Drozhin," whispered Max, "doesn't like the way you've been selling Intelligence's secrets out to Political Education and War."

Drozhin was Max's boss too. He'd moled Max in Political Education as soon as the new Department formed.

Lukinov panicked. He thrashed his arms and legs, disoriented, trying to make contact with any surface, clutching futilely at Max, who was behind his back and below him. Max twisted the belt, pinching the carotid arteries and cutting off blood flow to the brain. Lukinov was unconscious in about seven seconds. His body just went still. He was dead a few seconds later.

Drozhin had ordered Max to watch Lukinov, not kill him, but he couldn't see any other way around it. He shoved the body toward the corner, under the vent, and put his belt back on.

Still nobody at the hatch. Maybe they hadn't noticed. Maybe they were summoning Simco. There'd be no denying this one, not if he'd missed the location of any cameras.

But he had no time to think about failure. He didn't want anyone looking closely at Lukinov's body, and he didn't want the ship making the jump to Adares. Intelligence was publicly part of the war party, but Drozhin believed that war would destroy Jerusalem and wanted it sabotaged at all costs. Max took the medicine bottle from his pocket and removed the two pills that weren't pills. He popped them into his mouth to warm them—they tasted awful—while he removed the wire and blasting cap from the bottle's lid.

He couldn't blow any main part of the reactor, he understood that much. But the cooling circuit used water pipes, and a radioactive water spill could scuttle the jump. Max darted in, fixed the explosive to a blue-tagged pipe, plugged the wire in it, and hurried back to the hood. He pushed Lukinov's corpse in the direction of the explosive before he climbed through the hole into the vent.

There was a soft boom behind him.

Max cranked his neck to peer down between his feet and saw the water spray in a fine mist, filling the air like fog. All the radiation alarms blared at once.

They sounded far off at first while he wiggled upward. He thought he was sweating, but realized that the busted air flow was drawing some of the water up through the shaft. Droplets pelleted him with radiation, and that made him crawl faster. He got stuck in the bend for a moment, finally squeezing through, and thrusting the vent cover out of the way without checking first to see if anyone was in the corridor. But it was empty—so far his luck held! He retrieved the grille and screwed it back into place. One of the alarms was located directly beside him, and its wailing made his pulse skip.

He emerged into the shaft of the weapons compartment as men raced both ways, towards the accident and away from it. No one noticed him. He was headed across the void, toward his quarters when someone called his name.

"Nikomedes! Stop right there!"

He saw the medtech, Noyes, down by the corridor that led to Engineering. "What is it, Doc?"

"You don't have your comet, do you?"

Max touched the empty spot on his breast pocket. "No. Why?"

"Radiation emergency!" he screamed. "You're drafted as the surgeon's assistant! Come on!"

Max considered ignoring the command, but according to regulations, Doc was right. Anyone who wasn't Vacuum and Radiation qualified was designated an orderly to help treat those who were. Plus it gave him an alibi. He jumped toward the bottom of the Black Forest, and joined Noyes.

"Here, carry this kit," Noyes said, handing over a box of radiation gear, as he went back across the hall to grab another.

"Where is it?" asked Max. He held the gear close, covering the rip in his pants. "What's going on?"

"Don't know. The com's down again. But it has to be the reactor."

Nobody guarded the main hatch to Engineering so the two men went straight in. A crowd gathered in the monitor room, spilling out into the corridor. Noyes pushed straight through, and Max followed along behind him. Chevrier was shaking a crewman by the throat.

"—what the hell did you let him in there for?"

"He ordered me too!" the man complained. It was DePuy.

"There's water everywhere!" another one of the men yelled, coming back from the direction of the reactor room hatch. "The reactor's overheating fast!"

"It's already past four hundred cees," said one of the men at the monitors.

Chevrier tried to fling DePuy at the wall, but they just flopped a short distance apart. The Chief Engineer turned toward the rest of crew in disgust.

Rucker, the first lieutenant, showed up behind Max. "Captain wants a report! The com's down again!"

"That's because the reactor's overheating," Chevrier said. "The cooling system's busted."

"My God," said Rucker, invoking a deity he probably didn't believe in, thought Max.

Noyes slapped a yellow patch on the first lieutenant's shirt. "Radiation detectors, everyone! When they turn orange, you're in danger, means get out. Red means see me for immediate treatment!" He handed some to Max. "Make sure everyone wears one."

"We've got to go in there, fix the pipe, and cool the reactor," said Chevrier. Some of the men started to protest. "Shut the fuck up! I'm asking for volunteers. And I'll be going in with you."

Rucker wiped the blonde cowlick back off his forehead. "I'll go in," he said. Six other crewmen volunteered, most of them senior Engineers. Max slapped radiation badges on those men first.

"Here's the plan." Chevrier pointed to pictures on the monitors. "We're going to shut off these valves here and here, cut out and replace this section of pipe—"

Noyes, looking over his shoulder, said, "That man in there ought to come out at once. He looks unconscious."

"That man is dead," said Chevrier, "and it's a good thing too, or I'd kill him. Then we're going to run a pipe through here, from the drinking water supply—"

A moan of dismay.

"—shut up! We'll take it from the number three reserve tank. That ought to be enough, and it won't contaminate the rest of the water. Once we get the main engine back up, we can make more water."

Everyone had a badge now, and Max hung back with Noyes.

"I'd like someone to go in there and turn off these," Chevrier tapped spots on one of the monitors, "here, here, and here, while I get the repair set up."

"That'll be me," Rucker said. Like any junior officer, Max thought, trying to set a good example.

Chevrier gave him a nod. "This one here is tough. It'll take you a few minutes. It's right next to the reactor, and it's going to be hotter than hell." He gave Rucker the tools he needed and sent him off down the tube to the reactor room.

"I'll need a shower set up for decontamination," said Noyes.

Max found the air shower over by the other clean room, and showed him where it was. Noyes started setting up the lead-lined bags for clothing and equipment disposal.

By the time they went back to the monitor room, Chevrier had diagramed his repair. His volunteers double-checked the equipment lined up in the hall. He sent others, who hadn't volunteered, to run a connector line from the fresh water tank. They were just getting ready to go in, when Rucker staggered back out. He looked . . . cooked. Like the worst sunburn Max had ever seen. His clothes were soaked, and glowing drops of water followed through the air in his wake. Noyes was there, swiping the droplets out of the air with a lead blanket. He wrapped Rucker in it, and started leading him toward the shower.

The lieutenant's badge was bright red.

One crewman bolted, and another one threw up. Fears about radiation ran deep on the planet, fed by a generations worth of vids. No one said anything about the smell, but one of the men took off his shirt and tried to catch the vomit as it scattered through the air.

Chevrier ripped his badge off. "Won't need this. Just one more distraction. If we're going to go swimming, we might as well go skinny-dipping." He stripped off his clothes and the other volunteers followed his example. "Can't handle tools in those damn vacuum suits anyway."

Anger, fear, those things were contagious, Max reflected. But so were courage and foolhardy bravery. He hoped the price was worth it.

He supposed he ought to be at decontamination, with Noyes, but he couldn't tear himself away from the monitors. There were no cameras aimed directly at the spot where the men were working with the pipes, but they passed in and out of the vids. The radioactive water pooled in the air, drop meeting drop, coalescing into larger blobs like mercury spilled on a lab table and just as poisonous. The drops floated through the air like anti-bodies in a bloodstream. The men splashed into them as they moved and the water clung to their skin, searing wherever it touched.

Simco appeared at the door demanding a report for the Captain. Max ignored him. The reactor was so hot that the paint peeled off it, curling like bits of ash as it burned away. Water that hit its surface boiled away into steam, but the steam hit the other water, and became drops again instantly, a swirling rain that never fell. And, except for the dead tone of the radiation alarms, it all happened in silence, with no one in the monitor room speaking for long minutes, and no sound at all from the reactor room.

Noyes appeared beside Max. "That man needs to come out right now," he said, tapping at one of the monitors. There were glowing circles, spinning in slow lambent spirals on one man's buttocks.

Max laughed, a sound that came out of his mouth only as a breathless sigh. "Those are tattoos, Doc. Jets. Lightning bug juice impregnated in the subdermal cells."

"I've . . . never heard of that," said Noyes.

"It's supposed to bring a spacer safely home again."

"It's an abomination," blurted Noyes. The people of Jesusalem were against any mixing of the species. "Let's hope it does," he said.

"Indeed," replied Max.

DePuy stood beside them, shaking his head. "They're not getting it fixed."

Max was beginning to think he'd miscalculated badly. He hadn't wanted anyone to look too closely at Lukinov's corpse. He wanted the ship to turn around and head back home. But with the main engine down and the back-up scuttled, they were in big trouble.

The hatch flew open and two men came out.

"They've been in there almost an hour," said Noyes.

"Is it done?" the men in the monitor room demanded. Max heard his own voice blurt out, "Is it fixed?"

But their faces were mute. The blistered flesh bubbled off as Doc wrapped them in blankets. Noyes helped one towards the shower, and Max took the other. "This is hopeless," Noyes said, trying to clean the men. "You have to go back there now and get the other men out before they die."

"I think we all die with the ship if they fail," said Max.

Rambaud, one of the troopers, appeared in the door. "Message from the Captain, Doc. He wants you on the bridge."

"Tell him no."

The trooper's eyes kept flicking nervously to their badges. Max noticed his own was a sickly orange color. "Beg your pardon, Doc, but he's getting ready to abandon ship. If it's necessary."

"If he wants to give me an order, he can come down here and do it himself," said Noyes, pumping the burned man full of painkillers, and starting an IV.

Rambaud fled.

Noyes stared after him. "They were going to suicide all of us anyway, for nothing. If I'm going to die, it might as well be doing my job."

"Hell, yes." Max's job was getting the specifications on the deflectors to Drozhin. If the Captain took the escape shuttles and flew in system, then it was Max's duty to retrieve the chips from his quarters and get on a shuttle.

He followed Noyes back into the mouth of fire instead.

"They're coming out!" someone shouted.

Four more men this time, in worse shape than the others. Noyes had to hypospray them full of painkillers just to get them down to the shower, and it was the whole routine all over again. Max carried the man with the tattoos. They were coal black in his skin. Whatever lived in the cells and gave them their luminescence had been killed off by the radiation.

Before they finished the others, Chevrier was brought to them, covered with burn blisters, his hands raw meat, his eyes blind. He couldn't speak.

"Did he get it done?" shouted Max.

No one knew, so Max flew back towards the monitor room, where the handful of men that remained were arguing over the monitors. "The temperatures are still rising," shouted DePuy. His voice had risen an octave in pitch. "I tell you he didn't get it running."

"What's going on?" asked Max.

"The pipes aren't open," said one of the Electrician's mates.

"Somebody needs to go in there and turn this valve here," said DePuy. He pointed to one right in the middle of the steam put off by the overheating reactor. It was almost impossible to see in the fog.

No one volunteered.

They were boys mostly, eighteen or nineteen, junior crewmen. They'd all seen the others carried out, had smelled the burned flesh, had listened to their weeping. They were heirs to a hard-earned fear about radiation, and they couldn't get past that, couldn't overcome it.

The cut on Max's leg throbbed. His face and arms felt hot, burned. "I'll go in," he said.

Reactors were the only ship system he wasn't officially trained on, and all the reading he'd done before the voyage seemed inadequate to the task now. But it was his responsibility. He could go in there and turn a valve. He could do that much.

He went out to the corridor and found it blocked by a man in a vacuum suit, dragging a plasma cutter on a tether and reading the manual in his palm-pad. The man turned, his face gray behind the clear mask covering his face. It was Kulakov, the Chief Petty Officer.

For a second Max thought the man would freeze up.

Kulakov looked back down at his diagram. "Be sure to seal the locks tight behind me," he said. "Send someone right now to levels three and four, portside, directly above us, to clear the corridors and seal the locks there. You have to do that!"

"Will do," said Max. Then, "Carry on."

Kulakov passed through the hatch, but when Max went to seal it, the fresh water supply tubing blocked it. "Damn," he said, with a very bad feeling in the pit of his stomach. "Damn, damn, damn."

Then DePuy was there beside him with a clamp and some cutters. He severed the pipe, and tossed the loose end through the hatch after Kulakov. Max sealed the door. "Did someone go to three and four?"

DePuy nodded. "But I'll go double-check," he added, glancing at the bare spot where Max's comet should have been. No, he was looking at Max's radiation badge. It was orange-red, bleeding into a bright crimson.

"You better head over to see Doc," said the Electrician's mate at the monitors.

"Not yet," said Max.

On the video feed they watched Kulakov move methodically from point to point, comparing the hook-up and settings with the diagram on his palm-pad. It took him much longer than it had Chevrier when he was naked. A couple times it was clear that between the fog, and the loss of sensation caused by the suit, Kulakov became disoriented crossing an open space. He spun in circles until he found the right side up again. He reached the final valve but couldn't turn it. He peeled his gloves off, surrounded by the steam, and slowly cranked it over.

The Electrician's mate pounded the monitors. "It's running! Look at the temps drop!"

Max did, but he watched Kulakov too, as he struggled to put his gloves back on, picked up the plasma cutter, and then burned a hole through the hull.

The weeping sound of the radiation alarms was joined by the sudden keening of the hull breach alarms. There was a shudder through the whole ship, the bulkhead creaked beside him, and Max's ears popped.

But he kept his eyes fixed on the screen in the reactor room. The steam and all the radioactive water whooshed out of the ship. So did Lukinov's body. And so did Kulakov.

There was a dark, flat line straight across one of the screens, like a dead reading on a monitor.

Kulakov's tether.

"Hey look!" whispered one of the crewmen as Max entered the sick bay. "The Corpse is up and walking!"

They all laughed at that, the survivors, even Max. Chevrier was dead, and so was Rucker, and so were two other men. Of the six surviving men who'd received red badge levels of radiation exposure, only Max was strong enough to walk.

Kulakov sat in the middle of them. His hands were wrapped in bandages, two crooked, crippled hooks. Max nodded to him. "They still giving you a hard time?" he asked.

"You know it," grinned Kulakov.

"Well, it's not fair that he should be the only one who gets leave while we're on this voyage," said one of the men.

"How can it be shore leave without a shore, that's what I want to know," said Kulakov.

They all laughed again, even Max. That was going to be a ship joke for a long time, how Kulakov got liberty—hanging on a tether outside the ship.

"Papa sent me down here with a message," said Max. Captain Petoskey, Papa, had only been to the sick bay once since the accident, and quickly. Most of the other crewman stayed away as if radiation sickness were something contagious.

"What is it?" said Kulakov, the words thick in his throat.

"He wanted me to tell you that he's going to request that they rename the ship." The crewmen looked up at him seriously, all the humor gone from their eyes. "They're going to call it the *New Nazareth*."

New Nazareth had been nuked the worst by the Adareans. The land there still glowed in the dark.

Kulakov chuckled first, then the other men broke out laughing. Max saluted them, holding himself stiff for a full three seconds, then turned to go see Noyes. The medtech slumped in his chair, head sprawled across his arms on the desk, eyes closed. "I'm not sleeping," he muttered. "I'm just thinking."

"About your fiancée," asked Max, "waiting for you at home?"

"No, about the bone marrow cultures I've got growing in the vats, and the skin sheets, and the transplant surgery I have to do later this afternoon, that I've never done unassisted before, and the one I have to do tonight that I'm not trained to do at all." He twisted his head, peeking one eye out at Max. "And Suzan. Waiting for me. And the ship flying home. How are you feeling?"

"I'd be fine if you had any spare teeth," Max said, poking his tongue into the empty spots in his gums. That didn't feel as strange as having gravity under his feet again.

"They're in a drawer over by the sink," said Noyes. "Take two and call me in the morning."

Max walked through corridors considerably less crowded than they had been a few days before. Almost everything inside the ship had received some radiation. The crewmen went crate to crate with geiger counters deciding what could be saved and what should be jettisoned. With the grav back on, the men's appetites returned. They also had a year's worth of supplies and only a few weeks voyage ahead of them. So every meal became a feast. Some celebrated the fact that they were going home, and others the simple fact that they'd survived

Only Captain Petoskey failed to join the celebration. When Max entered the galley, Petoskey wore the expression of a man on the way to the lethal injection chamber. Max couldn't say for sure if was the condemned man's expression or the executioner's.

Ensign Reedy sat on one side of a long table, with two troopers standing guard behind her. Petoskey and Commander Gordet sat on the opposite side with Simco standing at attention. Petoskey looked naked without his beard, shorn before they recorded these official proceedings. Burdick, the other Intelligence officer, sat off to one end.

Petoskey invited Max to the empty seat beside him. "Are you sure you feel up to this, Nikomedes?"

"Doc says I'll be fine as long as it's brief."

"This'll be quick."

Petoskey turned on the recorder, and read the regulations calling a board of inquiry. "Ensign Reedy, do you wish to make a confession of your crimes at this time?"

Max looked at the youngster. He hadn't seen or spoken to her since he'd taken the chips in the radio room. If Reedy broke and told them what Max had done, then the entire gamble was for naught.

"I have nothing to confess," Reedy said.

"Corporal Burdick," continued Petoskey, "will you describe what you found in the radio room."

"The equipment had been disassembled, and the memory chips replaced with spares." He made eye contact with no one. "This happened sometime during the last shift when Lieutenant Lukinov and Ensign Reedy were on duty together."

"Sergeant Simco, please describe your actions."

"Sir, we made a complete search of Ensign Reedy's person and belongings looking for the items described by Corporal Burdick. We found nothing there, nor in any place he is known to have visited. We also searched Lieutenant Lukinov's belongings and found nothing."

"Lieutenant Nikomedes," continued Petoskey. "Would you describe what you saw in the radio room?" He added the exact date and shift.

Max repeated his story about the battery short circuit. "If Lukinov removed the chips that Ensign Burdick described, and he had them on him, then they were spaced."

Petoskey nodded. "Yes, I've thought of that. Ensign Reedy, can you explain what happened to the chips containing the communications from the neutral ship?"

"No sir, I can not."

"Were you and Lieutenant Lukinov working together as spies for the Adareans?"

"I was not," answered Reedy. "I can't speak for the Lieutenant, as I was not in his confidence."

Petoskey slammed his fist on the table. "I think you're a coward, Reedy. You're too weak to take responsibility for your actions. I'd tell you to act like a man, but you're not."

If Petoskey hoped to provoke Reedy, then his gambit failed. She sat there, placid as a lake on a still summer day.

"Can we conduct a medical interrogation?" interjected Max.

Petoskey went to tug at his beard, but his fingers clutched at emptiness. "I've discussed that already with the surgeon and Commander Gordet. Noyes is only a medtech, and not qualified to conduct an interrogation that will hold up in military court. Conceivably, we could even taint the later results of a test."

Max leaned forward. "Can we use more . . . traditional methods?"

"I won't command it," said Petoskey, looking directly into the recorder. He waited for Max to speak again.

Max ran his tongue over the loose replacement teeth, saying nothing, and leaned back. He might get out of this, after all.

"However, if you think . . . " said Petoskey.

Max looked at the camera. "Without an immediate danger, we should follow standard procedures."

Petoskey accepted this disappointment and concluded the proceedings with a provisional declaration of guilt. He ordered Reedy confined to the brig until they returned to Jesusalem.

As Max limped back towards his quarters afterwards he noticed that Gordet followed him.

"What can I do for you, Commander?" asked Max.

The bull-shaped second-in-command looked around nervously, then leaned in close. "There's something you should know, sir."

"What?" asked Max wearily. "That Petoskey ordered Simco to kill me, that he intended to blame it on Reedy, and then have her arrested and executed?"

Gordet jerked back, flabbergasted. "Did you check the secret orders too?"

"What does it matter now? Simco failed, Reedy's arrested anyway, and we're on our way home. A bit of advice for you, Mr. Gordet." He clapped him on the shoulder. "Next time you should pick your horse before the race is over."

He walked away. When he returned to his room, he recovered the sheet with the combination from its hiding spot, and destroyed it. He didn't know what the secret orders said. He didn't care.

There was only one thing he had left to do.

Third shift, night rotation, normal schedule. Max headed down to the brig carrying a black bag. One of Simco's troopers stood guard. "I'm here to interrogate the prisoner," Max said.

"Let me check with Sergeant Simco, sir."

Max had been thinking hard about this. Only two people knew that he had the plans for the deflector, and the only way two people could keep a secret was if one of them was dead.

"Sarge wants to know if you need help," said the trooper.

"Tell him that I take full responsibility for this, in the name of the Department of Political Education, and that no assistance will be necessary."

The trooper relayed this information, then gave Max a short, sneering nod. "He says he understands. Perfectly. But he wants me to make sure that you'll be safe in there."

Max patted a hand on his black bag. "If you hear screaming," he said, "don't interrupt us unless it's mine."

The trooper twitched uncomfortably under Max's glare. "Yes, sir." He opened the door for Max.

Reedy's wrists and ankles were cuffed, and she wore insignia-less fatigues. She sat up quickly on the edge of her bunk, and folded her hands on her knees, fingertip to fingertip. She couldn't salute, but Max doubted she would have.

He stepped inside. The room was barely eight feet by four, with a bed on one wall and a stainless steel toilet built into the corner opposite the door. "That'll be all, trooper," Max said. "I'll signal you when I'm done."

The hatch closed behind him and latched shut. He looked at Reedy. Her eyes were red and puffy but devoid of feeling, her cheeks hollow and drawn. A blue vein stood out vulnerably on her pale neck.

With his lips tight, Max gave her a small nod. "You look depressed," he said softly, holding the bag in front of him.

She shook her head, once. "No, I've been depressed before. This time it's not bad."

"Define *not bad.*"

"It's bad when you want to kill yourself. Right now, I just wish I was dead."

Max took that as his cue. He sat down with his back against the door placed and opened his bag. He removed two tumblers and a bottle of ouzo. The ensign remained perfectly still as Max pulled out a plate, and ripped open vacuum-wrapped packages of cheese, sausages, and anchovies to set on it.

"Not proper *mezedes* at all," he said, apologetically. "The fish should always be fresh."

He filled one cup and pushed it over towards Reedy, then poured and swallowed his own. It tasted like licorice, reminding him both of his childhood and his days as a young man, in completely different ways. Reedy remained immobile.

"I've been thinking." Max spoke very quietly, unbuttoning his collar. "When two men know a secret, it's only safe if one of them is dead." Good men had died already because of this. So would many more, along with the bad. "Therefore you don't know anything. Only I, and Lukinov, and Lukinov's dead. Do you understand this?"

"I don't know anything," said Reedy, with just a hint of irony. She reached over and lifted the glass of ouzo.

"My department will declare you the most politically sound of officers. Intelligence will know the truth, at least at the level that matters. Drozhin will get the Captain's official report, but he'll get another report unofficially. You'll be fine." He picked up an anchovy. "There will be a very difficult time, a very ugly court martial. But you can survive that."

"Again?"

"This one will not be removed from the record due to extenuating circumstances." Her attack on Vance had been one of self-defense. "But you'll be exonerated. You'll be fine. Things are changing. They'll be better." He believed that.

She leaned her head back and tossed down the ouzo. Max reached over and poured her another glass while her eyes were still watering. "When I got this assignment," she said, "I couldn't figure out if I was being rewarded for being at the top of the class in languages, despite being a woman. Or if I was being punished for being a woman."

"Sometimes it's both ways at once," Max said. He bit the anchovy and found he didn't care for the taste.

"Can I ask you one question?" asked Reedy.

Why did people always think he had all the answers? "Information is like ouzo. A little bit can clear your head, make you feel better. Too much will make you sick, maybe even kill you." He twirled his cup. "What's your question?"

"Did you really win your wife in a card game?"

"Yes." He drained his glass to cover his surprise. Though he'd won her with a bluff and not by cheating.

"Why did she leave you?"

Max thought about telling her that was two questions. Then he thought about telling her the truth, that his wife hadn't left him, that she waited at home for him, not knowing where he was or what he did, going to church in every day, caring for their two grandchildren. His daughter was about Reedy's age. But he'd kept his life sealed in separate compartments and wouldn't breech one of them now.

"Love, like loyalty," he said, "is a gift. You can only try to be worthy of it."

The silence lengthened out between them like all of the empty, uncharted universe. The food sat untouched while they drank. Max could feel himself getting drunk. It felt good.

AMID THE WORDS OF WAR

CAT RAMBO

Every few day-cycles, it receives hate-scented lace in anonymous packages. It opens the bland plastic envelope to pull one out, holding the delicate fragment between two forelimbs. Contemplating it before folding it again to put away in a drawer. Four drawers filled so far; the fifth is halfway there.

"Traitor," say some of the smells, rotting fruit and acid. "Betrayer. Turncoat. One who eats their own young." Others are simply soaked in emotion: hate and anger, and underneath the odor of fear. It lets the thoughts, the smells, the tastes fill it, set its own thoughts in motion. Then it goes downstairs and sits with the other whores, who make room uneasily for it.

It is an anomaly in this House. Most of the employees are humanoid and service others like themselves. It is here for those seeking the exotic, the ones who want to be caressed by twelve segmented limbs even though it is only the size of their two hands put together. They want to feel chitin against their soft skin, to look into the whirl of multicolored eyes and be afraid. For some, it only has to be there while they touch themselves to bring them to the flap and spasm of mammalian orgasm.

Others require its physical assistance, or its whispered obscenities telling them what they want to hear. It has learned what words to say.

It has never seen others of its race in this port. If it did, it would know that this place, far away from that distant front and its fighters, had been invaded by one side or the other, that soon the bombs, the fires, the killings would begin.

It was raised a soldier. It and its clutch-mates were tended until they were old enough to have minds, and then trained. It was one of six—a small clutch, but prized for its quickness and agility. They learned the art of killing with needle throwers, and once they had mastered that, they were given different needles: fragments that exploded, or shot out acid, or whistled until the ears of the soft-fleshed creatures who called themselves the Espen—their enemies—exploded.

They were provided with hundreds of Espen for them to train on. They were allowed to select their favorites. Some of them played unauthorized games. They told the prey they would be freed if they killed a hunter or if they killed each other, because it made them fight harder. When they were dead the clutch mates were allowed to take fluid from their bodies.

It liked the taste of their spinal liquid: salty plasma tinged with panic, complicated enzymes that identified where they came from. It became a connoisseur; it could name each of their three continents and tell you on which its victim had been spawned. None of its siblings could do the same.

The names such creatures call their clutch-mates differs according to many factors: the social position both hold, the spatial relationship, the degree of affection in which they are held that day.

For the sake of simplicity, think of it as Six of Six, and think of the clutch as One through Five of Six. One was simple-minded but direct, and never lied, in contrast to Two, who loved to talk and tell stories. Three was jealous of everyone; anytime the others were talking, it would intervene. Four was kind-hearted, and had to be prodded before it killed for the first time. (And even after that it would hesitate, and often one of the others would perform the final stroke.) Five and Six were often indistinguishable, the others said, but they thought themselves quite separate.

In those early days they lived together. They groomed the soft sensory hairs clustered around each other's thoraxes, and stroked the burnished chitin of carapaces. It did not matter if what each of them touched was itself or another. They sang to each other in symphonies of caress, passing thoughts back and forth to see how they unfolded in each other's heads.

They were not a true hive mind. They depended on each other, and one alone would die within the year lacking the stimulation of the others' scent, the taste of their thoughts, to stir their own. But they possessed their own minds. Six of Six acted by itself always, and no other mind prompted its actions; when it was questioned by the Interrogator, it insisted that until the end.

They were like any clutch; they quarreled when opinions differed, but when others intruded, they held themselves like a single organism, prepared to defend the clutch against outsiders. At sleep time, they spun a common web and crawled within its silky, tent-like confines to jostle against each other, interlocking forelimbs and feeling the twitches of each others' dreams.

Five and Six had the most in common, and so they quarreled most often. Everything Six disliked about itself, the fact that it was not always the quickest to act and sometimes thought too long, it saw in Five, and the same was true for the other. But there was no fighting for position of the sort that happens with a clutch that may produce a queen or priest. They knew they were ordinary soldiers, raised to defend the gray stone corridors in which they had been born. And beyond that—raised to go to war.

There is a garden in the center of this house, which is called The Little Teacup of the Soul. Small, but green and wet. Everything is enjoyment and pleasure here—to keep the staff happy, to keep them well. This spaceport is large, and there are many Houses of this kind, but this one, the manager says, is the best. The most varied. We'll fulfill any need, the manager says—baring its teeth in a smile—or die trying.

The whores's rooms are larger than any spacer's and are furnished as each desire.

Six of Six's cell is plain, but it has covered the walls with scent marks. It has filled them with this story, the story of how it came here, which no one else in this house can read. It sits in its room and dreams of the taste of hot fluid, of the way the Espen training creatures struggled like rodents caught in a snare.

One of its visitors pretends that it is something else.

Tell me that you are laying eggs in my flesh, he says, and Six crawls over him and says the words. But it is not a queen, and its race does not lay eggs in the living. It holds his skin between two pincers and tears it, just a little, so he will feel the pain and think it is an egg. He lies back without moving, his eyes closed.

My children will hatch out of you, it says, and makes its voice threatening.

Yes, he says, yes.

The pleasure shakes him like a blossom in the garden, burdened by the flying insects that pollinate it.

Everything was war, every minute of every day. The corridors were painted with the scent of territoriality—the priests prayed anger and defense, and the sound of their voices shook the clutch-mates to the core. They were told of the interlopers, despoilers, clutch-robbers, who would destroy their race with no thought, who hated them simply because of what they were. They massed in the caverns, the great vast caverns that lie like lungs beneath the bodies of their cities, and touched each other to pass on the madness.

They were smaller than the Enemy, the soft fleshed. With limbs tucked in, they were the size of an Enemy's head at most, and every day the Espen people carried packages, bags, that size. So they sent ships laden with those willing to give their lives for the Race, willing to crawl through their stinking sewer tunnels or fold themselves beneath the seats of their transports, blood changed to chemicals that would consume them—and the Enemy—in undying flame, flames that could not be quenched but burned until they met other flames. They watched broadcasts of their cities, their homes, their young, burning, and rejoiced.

They put One, Three, and Six in armor of silver globules, each one a bomb, triggered by a thought when they were ready. They flew at night, one of the biological planes with no trace of metal or fuel, so it could elude their detection, and entered their city. Dropped at a central point, they clung to the darkness and separated, spreading outward like a flower.

Six found a café, full of the Enemy, drinking bitter brews that frothed like poison. They had no idea it was so close. The little ones ran around the tables and the adults patted them indulgently. They did not resemble the hatchlings Six knew, and each one was different in its colors. On the walls were pictures that did not show war: they showed clouds, and sun, and birds flying. It could smell the liquid in their bodies and knew it was on the third continent. It had tasted them before.

A child saw Six where it lurked, up near the eaves, and screamed. Some force took over its limbs and it could no longer move. The area emptied, and it watched the death numbers tick downward as the blast radius cleared, trying to figure out what to do. Their soldiers shot it with a ray like crystal, a ray that made the world go away.

When it awoke, its armor was gone, and it could destroy no one, not even itself. Even the little bomb that would have shattered its body and freed it was gone, an aching, oozing cavity where it had rested so long inside its body the only trace left behind.

The Espen talked to Six. They said they were its friends, they said they were its enemies. They said it would be spared, that it would be killed. They cut away two of its limbs but ceased when they saw it did not hurt. They burned it with fire and acid, and laughed when it made sounds of pain. They mocked it. They said it would be alone forever, that its race had been killed. They said they would kill it too, if it did not communicate, if it did not tell them what they wanted to know, even though it had no knowledge and did not know what the priests at home would do next.

When it could make sounds no longer, they made it into a trade. They gained three of their own in exchange. And when it was back among its own kind, the questioning began again, although this time it was by the priests. The Interrogator was a large, dark-chitined creature; from what the assistants said, Six gathered that the Interrogator's clutch-mates had all died in the war.

The first day the Interrogator came and asked questions: What had it said to the Espen? What had it revealed about their own armies and weapons? Why had they kept it alive?

Why indeed? It did not know and said as much. The Interrogator looked at its mutilated body, at the stumps of limbs, at the raw places where they had pried away the carapace and burned the soft exposed patches, and went away without another question that night, trailed by its two assistants.

The next day the Interrogator appeared and ran through the list again. What had Six said? What had it revealed? Why was it alive? Six said it did not know and the Interrogator came closer to where it crouched, favoring its injuries. It reached out a forelimb and rested it lightly on a pain point. The touch was like fire all over again.

I don't know, it said. Torture me if you like, as they did, and I will tell you everything I told them, which was nothing.

The Interrogator leaned still further in, pressing harder with its forelimb, smelling the scents it gave off while sunk deep in pain. Finally the Interrogator pulled back, and left the room.

The Interrogator repeated this act every few hours. In the dim light of the cell, as the cycles passed, as it came again and again, Six began to regrow its severed limbs, and the places where they had pried away pieces of carapace healed and thickened, except for the spot the Interrogator had chosen for his torment, which was ulcerated and sore, not healing.

Long after Six of Six's regenerated limbs could flex as their predecessors once had, Five was allowed to see it. It stood well away, flanked by guards, so Six could not touch it from where it lay bound, no matter how it yearned toward its clutch-mate.

It asked the same question the Interrogator had. Why was Six still alive? One and Three had accomplished their mission, it said, and Four had died in a similar operation. Only Two and Five were left. But now they were suspect, clutch-mates of a renegade and no longer trusted soldiers.

They had found work as cleaners, and subsisted on the gruel fed to drones, barely enough to keep their specialized frames alive. Five's eyes were dull, its delicate claws blunted from rough work. It did not think Two could survive much longer.

What can I do, Six asked. It felt itself dying inside, untouched. The Interrogator stood to one side, watching the interaction, sniffing the chemicals released into the air as they talked.

We are suspect, because no one knows what you have done, Five said. Tell them what you have done, and that we are not involved.

I do not understand, Six said. It was slower in those days. Its mind talked to itself but no one else, and it had grown lonely and unaccustomed to thinking. I have done nothing, Six said.

Then Two and I will work until we die, Five said.

Six could feel the thoughts pressing against its own, trying to shape it. I understand, it said finally. And Five went away without another word.

And so Six confessed to the Interrogators an hour later that it had told the Espen of their tactics, of the caverns full of training captives, of the plans it knew. It said its clutch-mates knew nothing. The Interrogator stood watching it talk. Six could not tell what it thought of the lie, but after that it came no longer.

A few days later, they placed Six in a cage, hung high in the air, and the armies marched past to look at it. It saw Two and Five, reinstated, but they would not look at it with their faceted, gleaming eyes. It looked at them, touching them with its sight, hoping that they would be well, that they would remember it.

Six thought the priests would kill it then, but they sent it back to the Espen, with the message, *Here is your spy.* And they sent Six to another planet and then another, until finally someone opened the door of the cage and said, we will provide for you no longer, you're on your own.

It lived as it could for a while, hiring itself out for high-altitude or delicate work that clumsy fingers could not perform. But there are many drifters on a space station like TwiceFar, and people hire their own kind. It was not until it met the manager here that it realized uniqueness could be an asset.

The Universe is large, and the war of its people and that race of soft-fleshed is very far away now. But Six's race remembers its missing member, the one who they believe sold them all for life. Its image hangs on their corridors amid the words of war, and tangles of foul scent adorn it.

Without the touch of its clutch-mates, it feels its intelligence fading, but each time the webs rouse it for a moment, and remind it who it is, who it was. And then it goes downstairs and finds a patron who wishes it to bring him pleasure, to torture him, or be tortured, or who will pay it to say what he wishes, and earn enough to keep it alive another day.

It has six drawers in its room holding the emotions that keep it alive—the thoughts of those who would see it dead.

It has six drawers. Soon all six will be full.

A SOLDIER OF THE CITY

DAVID MOLES

ISIN 12:709 13" N:10 18" / 34821.1.9 10:24:5:19.21

Color still image, recorded by landscape maintenance camera, Gulanabishtiïdinam Park West.

At the top of the hill is a football court, the net nearly new but the bricks of the ground uneven, clumps of grass growing up from between the cracks. On the same side of the net are a man and a young girl. The hollow rattan ball is above the girl's head, nearing the apex of its trajectory; the girl, balanced on the toes of her bare right foot, her left knee raised, is looking toward the man.

The man is looking away.

Cross-reference with temple records identifies the man as Ishmenininsina Ninnadiïnshumi, age twenty-eight, temple soldier of the 219th Surface Tactical Company, an under-officer of the third degree, and the girl as his daughter Mâratirşitim, age nine.

Magnification of the reflection from the man's left cornea indicates his focus to be the sixty-cubit-high image of Gula, the Lady of Isin, projected over the Kârumishbiïrra Canal.

Comparison of the reflection with the record of the Corn Parade ceremonies suggests a transmission delay of approximately three grains.

1. Corn Parade

In the moment of the blast, Ish was looking down the slope, toward the canal, the live feed from the temple steps and the climax of the parade. As he watched, the goddess suddenly froze; her ageless face lost its benevolent smile, and her dark eyes widened in surprise and perhaps in fear, as they looked—Ish later would always remember—directly at him. Her lips parted as if she was about to tell Ish something.

And then the whole eastern rise went brighter than the Lady's House at noonday. There was a sound, a rolling, bone-deep rumble like thunder, and afterwards Ish would think there was something wrong with this, that something so momentous should sound so prosaic, but at the time all he could think was how loud it was, how it went on and on, louder than thunder, than artillery, than rockets, louder and longer than anything Ish had ever heard. The ground shook. The projection faded, flickered and went out, and a hot wind whipped over the hilltop, tearing the net from its posts, knocking Mâra to the ground and sending her football flying, lost forever, out over the rooftops to the west.

From the temple district, ten leagues away, a bright point was rising, arcing up toward the dazzling eye of the Lady's House, and some trained part of Ish's mind saw the straight line, the curvature an artifact of the city's rotating reference frame; but as Mâra started to cry, and Ish's wife Tara and all his in-laws boiled up from around the grill and the picnic couches, yelling, and a pillar of brown smoke, red-lit from below, its top swelling obscenely, began to grow over the temple over the temple, the temple of the goddess Ish was sworn as a soldier of the city to protect, Ish was not thinking of geometry or the physics of coriolis force. What Ish was thinking—what Ish knew, with a sick certainty—was that the most important moment of his life had just come and gone, and he had missed it.

34821.1.14 10:9:2:5.67

Annotated image of the city of Isin, composed by COS Independence, on Gaugamela station, Babylon, transmitted via QT to Community Outreach archives, Urizen. Timestamp adjusted for lightspeed delay of thirteen hours, fifty-one minutes.

Five days after the strike the point of impact has died from angry red-orange to sullen infrared, a hot spot that looks like it will be a long time in cooling. A streamer of debris trails behind the wounded city like blood in water, its spectrum a tale of vaporized ice and iron. Isin's planet-sized city-sphere itself appears structurally intact, the nitrogen and oxygen that would follow a loss of primary atmosphere absent from the recorded data.

Away from the impact, the myriad microwave receivers that cover the city's surface like scales still ripple, turning to follow the beams of power from Ninagal's superconducting ring, energy drawn from the great black hole called Tiamat, fat with the mass of three thousand suns, around which all the cities of Babylon revolve. The space around Isin is alive with ships: local orbiters, electromagnetically accelerated corn cans in slow transfer orbits carrying grain and meat from Isin to more urbanized cities, beam-riding passenger carriers moving between Isin and Lagash, Isin and Nippur, Isin and Babylon-Borsippa and the rest—but there is no mass exodus, no evacuation.

The Outreach planners at Urizen and Ahania, the missionaries aboard *Liberation* and *Independence* and those living in secret among the people of the cities, breathe sighs of relief, and reassure themselves that whatever they have done to the people of the cities of Babylon, they have at least not committed genocide.

Aboard COS *Insurrection*, outbound from Babylon, headed for the Community planet of Zoa at four-tenths the speed of light and still accelerating, the conscientious objectors who chose not to stay and move forward with the next phase of the Babylonian intervention hear this good news and say, not without cynicism: I hope that's some comfort to them.

2. Men giving orders

Ish was leading a team along a nameless street in what had been a neighborhood called Imtagaärbeëlti and was now a nameless swamp, the entire district northwest of the temple complex knee-deep in brackish water flowing in over the fallen seawall and out of the broken aqueducts, so that Ish looked through gates into flooded gardens where children's toys and broken furniture floated as if put there just to mar and pucker the reflection of the heavens, or through windows whose shutters had been torn loose and glass shattered by the nomad blast into now-roofless rooms that were snapshots of ordinary lives in their moments of ending.

In the five days since the Corn Parade Ish had slept no more than ten or twelve hours. Most of the rest of the 219th had died at the temple, among the massed cohorts of Isin lining the parade route in their blue dress uniforms and golden vacuum armor—they hadn't had wives, or hadn't let the wives they did have talk them into extending their leaves to attend picnics with their in-laws, or hadn't been able to abuse their under-officers' warrants to extend their leaves when others couldn't. Most of the temple soldiery had died along with them, and for the first three days Ish had been just a volunteer with a shovel, fighting fires, filling sandwalls, clearing debris. On the fourth day the surviving priests and temple military apparatus had pulled themselves together into something resembling a command structure, and now Ish had this scratch squad, himself and three soldiers from different units, and this mission, mapping the flood zone, to what purpose Ish didn't know or much care. They'd been issued weapons but Ish had put a stop to that, confiscating the squad's ammunition and retaining just one clip for himself.

"Is that a body?" said one of the men suddenly. Ish couldn't remember his name. A clerk, from an engineering company, his shoulder patch a stylized basket. Ish looked to where he was pointing. In the shadows behind a broken window was a couch, and on it a bundle of sticks that might have been a man.

"Wait here," Ish said.

"We're not supposed to go inside," said one of the other men, a scout carrying a bulky map book and sketchpad, as Ish hoisted himself over the gate. "We're just supposed to mark the house for the civilians."

"Who says?" asked the clerk.

"Command," said the scout.

"There's no *command*," said the fourth man suddenly. He was an artillerist, twice Ish's age, heavy and morose. These were the first words he'd spoken all day. "The Lady's dead. There's no command. There's no officers. There's just men giving orders."

The clerk and the scout looked at Ish, who said nothing.

He pulled himself over the gate.

The Lady's dead. The artillerist's words, or ones like them, had been rattling around Ish's head for days, circling, leaping out to catch him whenever he let his guard down. *Gula, the Lady of Isin, is dead.* Every time Ish allowed himself to remember that it was as if he was understanding it for the first time, the shock of it like a sudden and unbroken fall, the grief and shame of it a monumental weight toppling down on him. Each time Ish forced the knowledge back the push he gave it was a little weaker, the space he created for himself to breathe and think and feel in a little smaller. He was keeping himself too busy to sleep because every time he closed his eyes he saw the Lady's pleading face.

He climbed over the windowsill and into the house.

The body of a very old man was curled up there, dressed in nothing but a dirty white loincloth that matched the color of the man's hair and beard and the curls on his narrow chest. In the man's bony hands an icon of Lady Gula was clutched, a cheap relief with machine-printed colors that didn't quite line up with the ceramic curves, the Lady's robes more blue than purple and the heraldic dog at her feet more green than yellow; the sort of thing that might be sold in any back-alley liquor store. One corner had been broken off, so that the Lady's right shoulder and half her face were gone, and only one eye peered out from between the man's knuckles. When Ish moved to take the icon, the fingers clutched more tightly, and the old man's eyelids fluttered as a rasp of breath escaped his lips.

Ish released the icon. Its one-eyed stare now seemed accusatory.

"Okay," he said heavily. "Okay, Granddad."

BABYLON CITY 1:1 5" N:1 16" / 34821.1.14 7:15

"Lord Ninurta vows justice for Lady of Isin"

"Police to protect law-abiding nomads"

"Lawlessness in Sippar"

—*Headlines, temple newspaper* Marduknaşir, *Babylon City*

BABYLON CITY 4:142 113" S:4 12" / 34821.1.15 1:3

"Pointless revenge mission"

"Lynchings in Babylon: immigrants targeted"

"Sippar rises up"

—*Headlines, radical newspaper* Iïnshushaqiï, *Babylon City*

• • •

GISH, NIPPUR, SIPPAR (various locations) / 34821.1.15
"THEY CAN DIE"
—Graffiti common in working-class and slave districts,
after the nomad attack on Isin

3. Kinetic penetrator

When Tara came home she found Ish on a bench in the courtyard, bent over the broken icon, with a glue pot and an assortment of scroll clips and elastic bands from Tara's desk. They'd talked, when they first moved into this house not long after Mâra was born, of turning one of the ground-floor rooms into a workshop for Ish, but he was home so rarely and for such short periods that with one thing and another it had never happened. She kept gardening supplies there now.

The projector in the courtyard was showing some temple news feed, an elaborately animated diagram of the nomads' weapon—a 'kinetic penetrator,' the researcher called it, a phrase that Tara thought should describe something found in a sex shop or perhaps a lumberyard—striking the city's outer shell, piercing iron and ice and rock before erupting in a molten plume from the steps directly beneath the Lady's feet.

Tara turned it off.

Ish looked up. "You're back," he said.

"You stole my line," said Tara. She sat on the bench next to Ish and looked down at the icon in his lap. "What's that?"

"An old man gave it to me," Ish said. "There." He wrapped a final elastic band around the icon and set it down next to the glue pot. "That should hold it."

He'd found the broken corner of the icon on the floor not far from the old man's couch. On Ish's orders they'd abandoned the pointless mapping expedition and taken the man to an aid station, bullied the doctors until someone took responsibility.

There, in the aid tent, the man pressed the icon into Ish's hands, both pieces, releasing them with shaking fingers.

"Lady bless you," he croaked.

The artillerist, at Ish's elbow, gave a bitter chuckle, but didn't say anything. Ish was glad of that. The man might be right, there might be no command, there might be no soldiery, Ish might not be an under-officer any more, just a man giving orders. But Ish was, would continue to be, a soldier of the Lady, a soldier of the city of Isin, and if he had no lawful orders that only put the burden on him to order himself.

He was glad the artillerist hadn't spoken, because if the man had at that moment said again *the Lady's dead*, Ish was reasonably sure he would have shot him.

He'd unzipped the flap on the left breast pocket of his jumpsuit and tucked both pieces of the icon inside. Then he'd zipped the pocket closed again, and for the first time in five days, he'd gone home.

Tara said: "Now that you're back, I wish you'd talk to Mâra. She's been having nightmares. About the Corn Parade. She's afraid the nomads might blow up her school."

"They might," Ish said.

"You're not helping." Tara sat up straight. She took his chin in her hand and turned his head to face her. "When did you last sleep?"

Ish pulled away from her. "I took pills."

Tara sighed. "When did you last take a pill?"

"Yesterday," Ish said. "No. Day before."

"Come to bed," said Tara. She stood up. Ish didn't move. He glanced down at the icon.

An ugly expression passed briefly over Tara's face, but Ish didn't see it.

"Come to bed," she said again. She took Ish's arm, and this time he allowed himself to be led up the stairs.

At some point in the night they made love. It wasn't very good for either of them; it hadn't been for a long while, but this night was worse. Afterwards Tara slept.

She woke to find Ish already dressed. He was putting things into his soldiery duffle.

"Where are you going?" she asked.

"Lagash."

"What?"

Tara sat up. Ish didn't look at her.

"Lord Ninurta's fitting out an expedition," Ish said.

"An expedition," said Tara flatly.

"To find the nomads who killed the Lady."

"And do what?" asked Tara.

Ish didn't answer. From his dresser he picked up his identification seal, the cylinder with the Lady's heraldic dog and Ish's name and Temple registry number, and fastened it around his neck.

Tara turned away.

"I don't think I ever knew you," she said, "But I always knew I couldn't compete with a goddess. When I married you, I said to my friends: 'At least he won't be running around after other women.' " She laughed without humor. "And now she's dead—and you're still running after her."

She looked up. Ish was gone.

Outside it was hot and windless under a lowering sky. Nothing was moving. A fine gray dust was settling over the sector: *the Lady's ashes*, Ish had heard people call it. His jump boots left prints in it as he carried his duffle to the train station.

An express took Ish to the base of the nearest spoke, and from there his soldiery ID and a series of elevators carried him to the southern polar dock. As the equatorial blue and white of the city's habitable zone gave way to the polished black metal of the southern hemisphere, Ish looked down at the apparently untroubled clouds and seas ringing the city's equator and it struck him how normal this all was, how like any return to duty after leave.

It would have been easy and perhaps comforting to pretend it was just that, comforting to pretend that the Corn Parade had ended like every other, with the Lady's blessing on the crops, the return of the images to the shrines, drinking and dancing and music from the dimming of the Lady's House at dusk to its brightening at dawn.

Ish didn't want that sort of comfort.

• • •

34821.6.29 5:23:5:12.102

Abstract of report prepared by priest-astronomers of Ur under the direction of Shamash of Sippar, at the request of Ninurta of Lagash.

Isotopic analysis of recovered penetrator fragments indicates the nomad weapon to have been constructed within and presumably fired from the Apsu near debris belt. Astronomical records are surveyed for suspicious occlusions, both of nearby stars in the Babylon globular cluster and of more distant stars in the Old Galaxy, and cross-referenced against traffic records to eliminate registered nomad vessels. Fifteen anomalous occlusions, eleven associated with mapped point mass Sinkalamaïdi-541, are identified over a period of one hundred thirty-two years. An orbit for the Corn Parade criminals is proposed.

4. Dog soldier

There was a thump as Ish's platform was loaded onto the track. Then *Sharur's* catapult engaged and two, three, five, eight, thirteen, twenty times the force of Isin's equatorial rotation pushed Ish into his thrust bag; and then Ish was flying free.

In his ear, the voice of the ship said:

—First company, dispersion complete.

On the control console, affixed there, sealed into a block of clear resin: Gula's icon. Ish wondered if this was what she wanted.

And Ninurta added, for Ish's ears alone:

—Good hunting, dog soldier.

At Lagash they'd wanted Ish to join the soldiery of Lagash; had offered him the chance to compete for a place with the Lion-Eagles, Ninurta's elites. Ish had refused, taking the compassion of these warlike men of a warlike city for contempt. Isin was sparsely populated for a city of Babylon, with barely fifty billion spread among its parks and fields and orchards, but its soldiery was small even for that. When the hard men in Ashur and the actuaries in Babylon-Borsippa counted up the cities' defenders, they might forget Lady Gula's soldiers, and be forgiven for forgetting. What Ninurta's men meant as generosity to a grieving worshipper of their lord's consort Ish took for mockery of a parade soldier from a rustic backwater. It needed the intervention of the god himself to make a compromise; this after Ish had lost his temper, broken the recruiter's tablet over his knee and knocked over his writing-table.

"You loved her—dog soldier."

Ish turned to see who had spoken, and saw a god in the flesh for the first time.

The Lord of Lagash was tall, five cubits at least, taller than any man, but the shape and set of his body in its coppery-red armor made it seem that it was the god who was to scale and everything around him—the recruiting office, the Lion-Eagles who had been ready to lay hands on Ish and who were now prostrate on the carpet, the wreckage of the recruiter's table, Ish himself—that was small. The same agelessness was in Ninurta's dark-eyed face that had been in Lady Gula's, but what in the Lady had seemed to Ish a childlike simplicity retained into adulthood was turned, in her consort, to a precocious maturity, a wisdom beyond the unlined face's years.

Ish snapped to attention. "Lord," he said. He saluted—as he would have saluted a superior officer. A murmur of outrage came from the Lion-Eagles on the floor.

The god ignored them. "You loved her," he said again, and he reached out and lifted Ish's seal-cylinder where it hung around his neck, turned it in his fingers to examine the dog figure, to read Ish's name and number.

"No, Lord Ninurta," Ish said.

The god looked from the seal to Ish's face.

"No?" he said, and there was something dangerous in his voice. His fist closed around the seal.

Ish held the god's gaze.

"I still love her," he said.

Ish had been prepared to hate the Lord of Lagash, consort of the Lady of Isin. When Ish thought of god and goddess together his mind slipped and twisted and turned away from the idea; when he'd read the god's proclamation of intent to hunt down the nomads that had murdered 'his' lady, Ish's mouth had curled in an involuntary sneer. If the Lord of Lagash had tried to take the seal then, Ish would have fought him, and died.

But the god's fist opened. He glanced at the seal again and let it drop.

The god's eyes met Ish's eyes, and in them Ish saw a pain that was at least no less real and no less rightful than Ish's own.

"So do I," Ninurta said.

Then he turned to his soldiers.

"As you were," he told them. And, when they had scrambled to their feet, he pointed to Ish. "Ishmenininsina Ninnadiïnshumi is a solder of the city of Isin," he told them. "He remains a soldier of the city of Isin. He is your brother. All Lady Gula's soldiers are your brothers. Treat them like brothers."

To Ish he said, "We'll hunt nomads together, dog soldier."

"I'd like that," Ish said. "Lord."

Ninurta's mouth crooked into a half-smile, and Ish saw what the Lady of Isin might have loved in the Lord of Lagash.

For the better part of a year the hunters built, they trained, they changed and were changed—modified, by the priest-engineers who served Ninagal of Akkad and the priest-doctors who had served Lady Gula, their hearts and bones strengthened to withstand accelerations that would kill any ordinary mortal, their nerves and chemistries changed to let them fight faster and harder and longer than anything living, short of a god.

The point mass where the priest-astronomers of Ur thought the hunters would find the nomad camp was far out into Apsu, the diffuse torus of ice and rock and wandering planetary masses that separated Babylon from the nearest stars. The detritus of Apsu was known, mapped long ago down to the smallest fragment by Sin and Shamash, and the nomads' work had left a trail that the knowledgeable could read.

The object the nomads' weapon orbited was one of the largest in the near reaches of Apsu, the superdense core of some giant star that had shed most of its mass long before the Flood, leaving only this degenerate, slowly cooling sphere, barely a league across. The gods had long since oriented it so the jets of radiation from its rapidly spinning magnetic poles pointed nowhere near the cities, moved it into an orbit where it would threaten the cities neither directly with its own gravity, nor by flinging comets and planetesimals down into Babylon.

It took the hunters two hundred days to reach it.

The great ship *Sharur*, the Mace of Ninurta, a god in its own right, was hauled along the surface of Lagash to the city's equator, fueled, armed, loaded with the hunters and all their weapons and gear, and set loose.

It dropped away slowly at first, but when the ship was far enough from the city its sails opened, and in every city of Babylon it was as if a cloud moved between the land and the shining houses of the gods, as the power of Ninagal's ring was bent to stopping *Sharur* in its orbit. Then the Mace of Ninurta folded its sails like the wings of a diving eagle and fell, gathering speed. The black circle that was Tiamat's event horizon grew until it swallowed half the sky, until the soldiers packed tight around the ship's core passed out in their thrust bags and even *Sharur*'s prodigiously strong bones creaked under the stress, until the hunters were so close that the space-time around them whirled around Tiamat like water. Ninagal's ring flashed by in an instant, and only Lord Ninurta and *Sharur* itself were conscious to see it. *Sharur* shot forward, taking with it some tiny fraction of the black hole's unimaginable angular momentum.

And then Tiamat was behind them, and they were headed outward.

BABYLON CITY 1:1 5" N:1 16" / 34822.7.18 7:15
    "All cities' prayers with Lord of Lagash"
    "Police seek nomad agents in Babylon"
    "Lord Shamash asks Lord Anshar to restore order"
        —*Headlines, temple newspaper* Marduknaṣir, *Babylon City*

BABYLON CITY 4:142 113" S:4 12" / 34822.7.16 1:3
    "An eye for an eye"
    "Nativist witch-hunt"
    "Ashur to invade Sippar"
        —*Headlines, radical newspaper* Iïnshushaqiï, *Babylon City*

5. Machines

At Lagash they had drilled a double dozen scenarios: city-sized habitats, ramship fleets, dwarf planets threaded with ice tunnels like termite tracks in old wood. When the cities fought among themselves the territory was known and the weapons were familiar. The vacuum armor Ish had worn as a Surface Tactical was not very different from what a soldier of Lagash or Ashur or Akkad would wear although the gear of those warlike cities was usually newer and there was more of it. The weapons the Surface Tacticals carried were deadly enough to ships or to other vacuum troops, and the soldiers of the interior had aircraft and artillery and even fusion bombs although no one had used fusion bombs within a city in millennia. But there had been nothing like the nomads' weapon, nothing that could threaten the fabric of a city. No one could say with certainty what they might meet when they found the nomad encampment.

Ish had seen nomad ships in dock at Isin. There were ramships no larger than canal barges that could out-accelerate a troopship and push the speed of light, and ion-drive ships so dwarfed by their fuel supplies that they were like inhabited comets, and fragile light-sailers whose mirrors were next to useless at Babylon, and every one was unique. Ish supposed you had to be crazy to take it into your head to spend a lifetime in a pressurized can ten trillion leagues from whatever you called home. There wouldn't be many people as crazy as that and also able enough to keep a ship in working order for all that time, even taking into account that you had to be crazy in the first place to live in the rubble around a star when you could be living in a city.

But that wasn't right either. Because most of the people that in Babylon they called nomads had been born out there on their planets or wherever, where there were no cities and no gods, with as much choice about where they lived as a limpet on a rock. It was only the crazy ones that had a choice and only the crazy ones that made it all the way to Babylon.

The nomads Ish was hunting now, the assassins somewhere out there in the dark, he thought were almost simple by comparison. They had no gods and could build no cities and they knew it and it made them angry and so whatever they couldn't have, they smashed. That was a feeling Ish could understand.

Gods and cities fought for primacy, they fought for influence or the settlement of debts. They didn't fight wars of extermination. But extermination was what the nomads had raised the stakes to when they attacked the Corn Parade and extermination was what Ish was armed for now.

—There, said *Sharur's* voice in his ear.—There is their weapon.

In the X-ray spectrum Sinkalamaïdi-541 was one of the brightest objects in the sky, but to human eyes, even augmented as Ish's had been at Lagash, even here, less than half a million leagues from the target, what visible light it gave off as it cooled made it only an unusually bright star, flickering as it spun. Even under the magnification of *Sharur's* sharp eyes it was barely a disc; but Ish could see that something marred it, a dark line across the sickly glowing face.

A display square opened, the dead star's light masked by the black disc of a coronagraph, reflected light—from the dead star itself, from the living stars of the surrounding cluster, from the Old Galaxy—amplified and enhanced. Girdling Sinkalamaïdi-541 was a narrow, spinning band of dull carbon, no more than a thousand leagues across, oriented to draw energy from the dead star's magnetic field; like a mockery of Ninagal's ring.

—A loop accelerator, the ship said.—Crude but effective.

—They must be very sophisticated to aspire to such crudeness, said Ninurta.—We have found the sling, but where is the slinger?

When straight out of the temple orphanage he'd first enlisted they'd trained Ish as a rifleman, and when he'd qualified for Surface Tactical School they'd trained him as a vacuum armor operator. What he was doing now, controlling this platform that had been shot down an electromagnetic rail like a corn can, was not very much like either of those jobs, although the platform's calculus of fuel and velocity and power and heat was much the same as for the vacuum armor. But he was not a Surface Tactical any more and there was no surface here, no city with its weak gravity and strong spin to complicate the equations, only speed and darkness and somewhere in the darkness the target.

There was no knowing what instruments the nomads had but Ish hoped to evade all of them. The platform's outer shell was black in short wavelengths and would scatter or let pass long ones; the cold face it turned toward the nomad weapon was chilled to within a degree of the cosmic microwave background, and its drives were photonic, the exhaust a laser-tight collimated beam. Eventually some platform would occlude a star or its drive beam would touch some bit of ice or cross some nomad sensor's mirror and they would be discovered, but not quickly and not all at once.

They would be on the nomads long before that.

—Third company, Ninurta said.—Fire on the ring. Flush them out.

The platforms had been fired from *Sharur's* catapults in an angled pattern so that part of the energy of the launch went to slowing *Sharur* itself and part to dispersing the platforms in an irregular spreading cone that by this time was the better part of a thousand leagues across. Now the platforms' own engines fired, still at angles oblique to the line joining *Sharur's* course to the dead star.

Below Ish—subjectively—and to his left, a series of blinking icons indicated that the platforms of the third company were separating themselves still further, placing themselves more squarely in the track of the dead star's orbit. When they were another thousand leagues distant from *Sharur* they cast their weapons loose and the weapons' own engines fired, bright points Ish could see with his own eyes, pushing the weapons onward with a force beyond what even the hunters' augmented and supported bodies could withstand.

Time passed. The flares marking the weapons of the third company went out one by one as their fuel was exhausted. When they were three hundred thousand leagues from the ring, the longest-ranged of the weapons—antiproton beams, muon accelerators, fission-pumped gamma-ray lasers—began to fire.

Before the bombardment could possibly have reached the ring—long before there had passed the thirty or forty grains required for the bombardment to reach the ring and the light of the bombardment's success or failure to return to *Sharur* and the platforms—the space between the ring and the third company filled with fire. Explosions flared all across Ish's field of view, pinpoints of brilliant white, shading to ultraviolet. Something hit the side of the platform with a terrific thump, and Ish's hand squeezed convulsively on the weapon release as his diagnostic screens became a wash of red. There was a series of smaller thumps as the weapons came loose, and then a horrible grinding noise as at least one encountered some projecting tangle of bent metal and broken ceramic. The platform was tumbling. About half Ish's reaction control thrusters claimed to be working; he fired them in pairs and worked the gyroscopes till the tumble was reduced to a slow roll, while the trapped weapon scraped and bumped its way across the hull and finally came free.

—Machines, machines! he heard Ninurta say.—Cowards! Where are the *men?*

Then the weapon, whichever it was, blew up.

34822.7.16 4:24:6:20—5:23:10:13

Moving image, recorded at 24 frames per second over a period of 117 minutes 15 seconds by spin-stabilized camera, installation "Cyrus", transmitted via QT to COS Liberation, on Gaugamela station, and onward to Community Outreach archives, Urizen:

From the leading edge of the accelerator ring, it is as though the ring and the mass that powers it are rising through a tunnel of light.

For ten million kilometers along the track of the neutron star's orbit, the darkness ahead sparkles with the light of antimatter bombs, fusion explosions, the kinetic flash of chaff thrown out by the accelerator ring impacting ships, missiles, remotely operated guns; impacting men. Through the minefield debris of the ring's static defenses, robotic fighters dart and weave, looking to kill anything that accelerates. Outreach has millennia of experience to draw on, and back in the Community a population of hundreds of billions to produce its volunteer missionaries, its dedicated programmers, its hobbyist generals. Many of the Babylonian weapons are stopped; many of the Babylonian ships are destroyed. Others, already close to Babylon's escape velocity and by the neutron star's orbital motion close to escaping from it as well, are shunted aside, forced into hyperbolic orbits that banish them from the battlefield as surely as death.

But the ring's defenders are fighting from the bottom of a deep gravity well, with limited resources, nearly all the mass they've assembled here incorporated into the ring itself; and the Babylonians have their own store of ancient cunning to draw on, their aggregate population a hundred times larger than the Community's, more closely knit and more warlike. And they have Ninurta.

Ninurta, the hunter of the Annunaki, the god who slew the seven-headed serpent, who slew the bull-man in the sea and the six-headed wild ram in the mountain, who defeated the demon Ansu and retrieved the Tablet of Destinies.

Sharur, the Mace of Ninurta, plunges through the battle like a shark through minnows, shining like a sun, accelerating, adding the thrust of its mighty engines to the neutron star's inexorable pull. Slender needles of laser prick out through the debris, and *Sharur's* sun brightens still further, painful to look at, the ship's active hull heated to tens of thousands of degrees. Something like a swarm of fireflies swirls out toward it, and the camera's filters cut in, darkening the sky as the warheads explode around the ship, a constellation of new stars that flare, burn and die in perfect silence: and *Sharur* keeps coming.

It fills the view.

Overhead, a blur, it flashes past the camera, and is gone.

The image goes white.

The transmission ends.

6. Surviving weapons

It was cold in the control capsule. The heat sink was still deployed and the motors that should have folded it in would not respond. Ish found he didn't much care. There was a slow leak somewhere in the atmosphere cycler and Ish found he didn't much care about that either.

The battle, such as it was, was well off to one side. Ish knew even before doing the math that he did not have enough fuel to bring himself back into it. The dead star was bending his course but not enough. He was headed into the dark.

Ish's surviving weapons were still burning mindlessly toward the ring and had cut by half the velocity with which they were speeding away from it, but they too were nearly out of fuel and Ish saw that they would follow him into darkness.

He watched *Sharur*'s plunge through the battle. The dead star was between him and the impact when it happened, but he saw the effect it had: a flash across the entire spectrum from long-wave radio to hard X-ray, bright enough to illuminate the entire battlefield; bright enough, probably, to be seen from the cities.

Another god died.

There was a sparkle of secondary explosions scattered through the debris field, weapons and platforms and nomad fighters alike flashing to plasma in the light of Ninurta's death. Then there was nothing. The ring began, slowly, to break up.

Ish wondered how many other platforms were still out here, set aside like his, falling into Apsu. Anyone who had been on the impact side was dead.

The weapons' drive flares went out.

The mended icon was still where he had fixed it. Ish shut down the displays one by one until his helmet beam was the only light and adjusted the thrust bag around the helmet so that the beam shone full on the icon. The look in the Lady's eyes no longer seemed accusatory, but appraising, as if she were waiting to see what Ish would do.

The beam wavered and went dark.

BABYLON CITY 2:78 233" S:2 54" / 34822.10.6 5:18:4

Record of police interrogation, Suspect 34822.10.6.502155, alias Ajabeli Huzalatum Taraämapsu, alias Liburnadisha Iliawilimrabi Apsuümasha, alias 'Black'. Charges: subversion, terrorism, falsification of temple records, failure to register as a foreign agent. Interrogator is Detective (Second Degree) Nabûnaïd Babilisheïr Rabişila.

Rabişila: Your people are gone. Your weapon's been destroyed. You might as well tell us everything.

Suspect: It accomplished its purpose.

Rabişila: Which was?

Suspect: To give you hope.

Rabişila: What do you mean, "hope"?

Suspect: Men are fighting gods now, in Gish and Sippar.

Rabişila: A few criminal lunatics. Lord Anshar will destroy them.

Suspect:	Do you think they'll be the last? Two of your gods are dead. Dead at the hands of mortals. Nothing Anshar's soldiers do to Sippar will change that. Nothing you do to me.
Rabişila:	You're insane.
Suspect:	I mean it. One day—not in my lifetime, certainly not in yours, but one day—one day you'll all be free.

7. A soldier of the city

A ship found Ish a few months later: a ship called *Upekkhâ*, from a single-system nomad civilization based some seventeen light-years from Babylon and known to itself as the Congregation. The ship, the name of which meant 'equanimity', was an antimatter-fueled ion rocket, a quarter of a league long and twice that in diameter; it could reach two-tenths the speed of light, but only very, very slowly. It had spent fifteen years docked at Babylon-Borsippa, and, having been launched some four months before the attack on the Corn Parade, was now on its way back to the star the Congregation called *Mettâ*. The star's name, in the ancient liturgical language of the monks and nuns of the Congregation, meant 'kindness'.

Ish was very nearly dead when *Upekkhâ's* monks brought him aboard. His heart had been stopped for some weeks, and it was the acceleration support system rather than Ish's bloodstream that was supplying the last of the platform's oxygen reserves to his brain, which itself had been pumped full of cryoprotectants and cooled to just above the boiling point of nitrogen. The rescue team had to move very quickly to extricate Ish from that system and get him onto their own life support. This task was not made any easier by the militarized physiology given to Ish at Lagash, but they managed it. He was some time in recovering.

Ish never quite understood what had brought *Upekkhâ* to Babylon. Most of the monks and nuns spoke good Babylonian—several of them had been born in the cities—but the concepts were too alien for Ish to make much sense of them, and Ish admitted to himself he didn't really care to try. They had no gods, and prayed—as far as Ish could tell—to their ancestors, or their teachers' teachers. They had been looking, they said, for someone they called *Tathâgata*, which the nun explaining this to Ish translated into Babylonian as 'the one who has found the truth'. This Tathâgata had died, many years ago on a planet circling the star called Mettâ, and why the monks and nuns were looking for him at Babylon was only one of the things Ish didn't understand.

"But we didn't find him," the nun said. "We found you."

They were in *Upekkhâ*'s central core, where Ish, who had grown up on a farm, was trying to learn how to garden in free fall. The monks and nuns had given him to understand that he was not required to work, but he found it embarrassing to lie idle—and it was better than being alone with his thoughts.

"And what are you going to do with me?" Ish asked.

The nun—whose own name, *Arrakhasampada*, she translated as 'the one who has attained watchfulness'—gave him an odd look and said:

"Nothing."

"Aren't you afraid I'll—do something? Damage something? Hurt someone?" Ish asked.

"Will you?" Arrakhasampada asked.

Ish had thought about it. Encountering the men and women of *Upekkhâ* on the battlefield he could have shot them without hesitation. In Apsu, he had not hesitated. He had looked forward to killing the nomads responsible for the Corn Parade with an anticipation that was two parts vengefulness and one part technical satisfaction. But these nomads were not those nomads, and it was hard now to see the point.

It must have been obvious, from where the monks and nuns found Ish, and in what condition, what he was, and what he had done. But they seemed not to care. They treated Ish kindly, but Ish suspected they would have done as much for a wounded dog.

The thought was humbling, but Ish also found it oddly liberating. The crew of *Upekkhâ* didn't know who Ish was or what he had been trying to do, or why. His failure was not evident to them.

The doctor, an elderly monk who Ish called Dr. Sam—his name, which Ish couldn't pronounce, meant something like 'the one who leads a balanced life'—prounounced Ish fit to move out of the infirmary. Arrakhasampada and Dr. Sam helped Ish decorate his cabin, picking out plants from the garden and furnishings from *Upekkhâ*'s sparse catalog with a delicate attention to Ish's taste and reactions that surprised him, so that the end result, while hardly Babylonian, was less foreign, more Ish's own, than it might have been.

Arrakhasampada asked about the mended icon in its block of resin, and Ish tried to explain.

She and Dr. Sam grew very quiet and thoughtful.

Ish didn't see either of them for eight or ten days. Then one afternoon as he was coming back from the garden, dusty and tired, he found the two of them waiting by his cabin. Arrakhasampada was carrying a bag of oranges, and Dr. Sam had with him a large box made to look like lacquered wood.

Ish let them in, and went into the back of the cabin to wash and change clothes. When he came out they had unpacked the box, and Ish saw that it was an iconostasis or shrine, of the sort the monks and nuns used to remember their predecessors. But where the name-scroll would go there was a niche just the size of Ish's icon.

He didn't know who he was. He was still—would always be—a soldier of the city, but what did that mean? He had wanted revenge, still did in some abstract way. There would be others, now, Lion-Eagles out to avenge the Lord of Lagash, children who had grown up with images of the Corn Parade. Maybe Mâra would be among them, though Ish hoped not. But Ish himself had had his measure of vengeance in Apsu and knew well enough that it had never been likely that he would have more.

He looked at the icon where it was propped against the wall. Who was he? Tara: "I don't think I ever knew you." But she had, hadn't she? Ish was a man in love with a dead woman. He always would be. The Lady's death hadn't changed that, any more than Ish's own death would have. The fact that the dead woman was a goddess hadn't changed it.

Ish picked up the icon and placed it in the niche. He let Dr. Sam show him where to place the orange, how to set the sticks of incense in the cup and start the little induction heater. Then he sat back on his heels and they contemplated the face of the Lady of Isin together.

"Will you tell us about her?" Arrakhasampada asked.

ABOUT THE
CONTRIBUTORS

Ken MacLeod was born in Stornoway, Isle of Lewis, Scotland, on August 2, 1954. He is married with two grown-up children and lives in West Lothian. He has an Honours and Masters degree in biological subjects and worked for some years in the IT industry. Since 1997 he has been a full-time writer, and in 2009 was Writer in Residence at the ESRC Genomics Policy and Research Forum at Edinburgh University. He is the author of thirteen novels, from *The Star Fraction* to *Intrusion*, and many articles and short stories. His novels and stories have received three BSFA awards and three Prometheus Awards, and several have been short-listed for the Clarke and Hugo Awards. Ken MacLeod's blog is The Early Days of a Better Nation: kenmacleod.blogspot.com. His twitter feed is: @amendlocke

Suzanne Palmer is a writer and artist who lives in western Massachusetts. In keeping up with current SF author trends, she has chosen "twins" as the most efficient means of distraction from writing, but sometimes they fall asleep and words happen anyway. Her stories have appeared in *Asimov's, Interzone*, and *Black Static*.

Charles Oberndorf is a graduate of Clarion East. He's the author of three novels and five stories, all science fiction. He teaches English at University School in Cleveland, Ohio where he lives with his wife and son. He's written book reviews for the *Cleveland Plain Dealer* and the *New York Review of Science Fiction*. He's currently working on a thematic sequel to "Another Life" as well as a biographical novel about an American veteran of the Spanish Civil War.

Yoon Ha Lee lives in Louisiana with her family, but has not yet been eaten by alligators. Her fiction has appeared in *Clarkesworld, Lightspeed,* and *The Magazine of Fantasy and Science Fiction*. This story was inspired by Admiral Yi Sun-Shin's victories in the Imjin War, although it is probably not possible to improve on.

Alastair Reynolds was born in Barry in 1966. He spent his early years in Cornwall, then returned to Wales for his primary and secondary school education. He completed a degree in astronomy at Newcastle, then a PhD in the same subject at St Andrews in Scotland. He left the UK in 1991 and spent the next sixteen years working in the Netherlands, mostly for the European Space Agency, although he also did a stint as a postdoctoral worker in Utrecht. He had been writing and selling science fiction since 1989, and published his first novel, *Revelation Space*, in 2000. He has recently completed his tenth novel and has continued to publish short fiction. His novel *Chasm City* won the British Science Fiction Award, and he has been shortlisted for the Arthur C Clarke award three times. In 2004 he left scientific research to write full time. He married in 2005 and returned to Wales in 2008, where he lives in Rhondda Cynon Taff.

Catherynne M. Valente is the *New York Times* bestselling author of over a dozen works of fiction and poetry, including *Palimpsest*, the Orphan's Tales series, *Deathless*, and the crowdfunded phenomenon *The Girl Who Circumnavigated Fairyland in a Ship of Own Making*. She is the winner of the Andre Norton Award, the Tiptree Award, the Mythopoeic Award, the Rhysling Award, and the Million Writers Award. She has been nominated for the Hugo, Locus, and Spectrum Awards, the Pushcart Prize, and was a finalist for the World Fantasy Award in 2007 and 2009. She lives on an island off the coast of Maine with her partner, two dogs, and an enormous cat.

Robert Reed is the author of several novels and a small empire of short fiction. His novella, "A Billion Eves" won the Hugo. Reed lives in Lincoln, NE with his wife and daughter, and his new best friend, a NOOK Tablet.

Sandra McDonald is the author of the recent gender-bending collection *Diana Comet and Other Improbable Stories* and the novels *The Outback Stars, The Stars Down Under,* and *The Stars Blue Yonder.* Her short fiction has appeared in more than thirty national, small press and online magazines. She holds an MFA in Creative Writing and teaches college in Jacksonville, Florida. Visit her at www. sandramcdonald. com

Adam-Troy Castro's seventeen books include *Emissaries from the Dead* (winner of the Philip K. Dick award), and *The Third Claw of God,* both of which feature his profoundly damaged far-future murder investigator, Andrea Cort. His next books will be a series of middle-school novels about the adventures of a strange young boy called Gustav Gloom, the first of which will be *Gustav Gloom and the People Taker,* due out from Grossett and Dunlap in August 2012. His short fiction has been nominated for five Nebulas, two Hugos, and two Stokers. Adam-Troy, who describes the odd hyphen between his first and middle names as a typo from his college newspaper that was just annoying enough to embrace with gusto, lives in Miami with his wife Judi and a population of insane cats that includes Uma Furman and Meow Farrow.

Beth Bernobich is a writer, reader, mother, and geek. Her short stories have appeared in *Asimov's, Interzone,* and *Strange Horizons,* among other places. Her first fantasy novel, *Passion Play,* appeared from Tor Books in 2010, with three more to follow in the series. She currently lives in Connecticut with her husband and two idiosyncratic cats.

Tom Purdom's contributions to the science fiction field include novels, short fiction, magazine articles, book reviews, and an anthology of science writing by leading science fiction writers. He started reading science fiction in 1950, when it was just emerging from the pulp ghetto, and sold his first story in 1957, just before he turned twenty-one. In the last two decades, he has produced a string of novelettes and short stories that has appeared in *Asimov's* and anthologies such as the best of the year books edited by David Hartwell and Gardner Dozois. Outside of science fiction, his literary output includes magazine articles, essays, science writing, brochures on home decorating, an educational comic book on vocational safety, and twenty-five years of classical music criticism. He lives in downtown Philadelphia where he devotes himself to a continuous round of pleasures and entertainments.

Kristine Kathryn Rusch is a bestselling writer in the United States and Europe. She has won the Hugo award twice, the World Fantasy Award, and several readers choice awards in both mystery and science fiction. She also writes under half a dozen pen names in a variety of genres. To find out more about her work, go to www. kristinekathrynrusch.com

Geoffrey A. Landis is a physicist who works at the NASA John Glenn Research Center on developing advanced technologies for human and robotic space exploration. He is also a Hugo- and Nebula- award winning science fiction writer; the author of the novel *Mars Crossing,* the short-story collection *Impact Parameter and Other Quantum Realities,* and more than eighty short stories, which have appeared in places including *Analog, Asimov's, The Magazine of Fantasy & Science Fiction,* and numerous best-of-the-year volumes. Most recently, his poem "Search" won the 2009 Rhysling award for best science-fiction poem, and his poetry collection *Iron Angels* appeared from Van Zeno in 2009. His most recent story, "Sultan of the Clouds," appears in the September 2010 issue of *Asimov's.*

Nancy Kress is the author of thirty books, including fantasy and SF novels, four collections of short stories, and three books on writing. She is perhaps best known for the "Sleepless" trilogy that began with *Beggars in Spain.* Her work has won four Nebulas, two Hugos, a Sturgeon, and the John W. Campbell Award. Most recent books are a collection, *Fountain of Age and Other Stories,* a YA fantasy written under the name Anna Kendall, *Crossing Over*; and a short novel of eco-terror, *Before the Fall, During the Fall, After the Fall*. Kress lives in Seattle with her husband, SF writer Jack Skillingstead, and Cosette, the world's most spoiled toy poodle.

Alan DeNiro is the author of *Skinny Dipping in the Lake of the Dead*, a story collection from Small Beer Press; and *Total Oblivion, More or Less*, a novel from Spectra. Stories set in the same world as "Have You Any Wool" have appeared or are forthcoming in *Asimov's, Strange Horizons*, and *Talebones*.

Genevieve Valentine's fiction has appeared or is forthcoming in *Clarkesworld, Strange Horizons, Lightspeed*, and *Apex*, and in the anthologies *The Living Dead 2, Running with the Pack, Teeth*, and more. Her nonfiction has appeared in *Lightspeed, Tor.com*, and *Fantasy Magazine*, and she is the co-author of *Geek Wisdom*. Her first novel, *Mechanique: A Tale of the Circus Tresaulti*, has won the 2012 Crawford Award. Her appetite for bad movies is insatiable, a tragedy she tracks on her blog, genevievevalentine.com.

Paul McAuley is the author of more than twenty books, including science-fiction, thriller, and crime novels, three collections of short stories, a Doctor Who novella, and an anthology of stories about popular music, which he co-edited with Kim Newman. His fiction has won the Philip K Dick Memorial Award, the Arthur C. Clarke Award, the John W Campbell Award, and the Sidewise and British Fantasy Awards. After working as a research biologist and university lecturer, he is now a full-time writer. He lives in North London.

Charles Coleman Finlay is the author of four novels and more than forty stories, some of which have been finalists for the Hugo, Nebula, Sidewise, and Sturgeon Awards. He is married to novelist Rae Carson; they live in Ohio with their two sons and an endless supply of story ideas. His website is www.ccfinlay.com.

Cat Rambo lives and writes in the Pacific Northwest. Her one hundred plus published stories include appearances in *Asimov's, Weird Tales,* and *Tor.com*. Links to her fiction and more information can be found at www.kittywumpus.net

David Moles has been writing and editing science fiction and fantasy since 2002, and is a past finalist for the Hugo Award, the World Fantasy Award, and the John W. Campbell Award for Best New Writer, as well as the winner of the 2008 Theodore Sturgeon Memorial Award, for his novelette "Finisterra." David's most recent book is the novella *Seven Cities of Gold*. He currently lives in San Francisco.

PUBLICATION HISTORY

"Her Husband's Hands" by Adam-Troy Castro. © 2011 by Adam-Troy Castro. Originally published in *Lightspeed*.

"Remembrance" by Beth Bernobich. © 2006 by Beth Bernobich. Originally published in *Sex in the System*.

"Palace Resolution" by Tom Purdom. © 2004 by Tom Purdom. Originally published in *Microcosms*.

"The Observer" by Kristine Kathryn Rusch. © 2008 by Kristine Kathryn Rusch. Originally published in *Front Lines*.

"The Long Chase" by Geoffrey A. Landis. © 2002 by Geoffrey A. Landis. Originally published in *Asimov's*.

"Art of War" by Nancy Kress. © 2007 by Nancy Kress. Originally published in *The New Space Opera*.

"Have You Any Wool" by Alan DeNiro. © 2006 by Alan DeNiro. Originally published in *Twenty Epics*.

"Carthago Delenda Est" by Genevieve Valentine. © 2009 by Genevieve Valentine. Originally published in *Federations*.

"Rats of the System" by Paul McAuley. © 2005 by Paul McAuley. Originally published in *Constellations*.

"The Political Officer" by Charles Coleman Finlay. © 2002 by Charles Coleman Finlay. Originally published in *F&SF*.

"Amid the Words of War" by Cat Rambo. © 2010 by Cat Rambo. Originally published in *Clarkesworld*.

"A Soldier of the City" by David Moles. © 2010 by David Moles. Originally published in *Engineering Infinity*.

ABOUT THE EDITORS

Rich Horton is a software engineer in St. Louis. He is a contributing editor to *Locus*, for which he does short fiction reviews and occasional book reviews; and to *Black Gate*, for which he does a continuing series of essays about science fiction history.

Sean Wallace is the founder and editor for Prime Books, which won a World Fantasy Award in 2006. In the past he was co-editor of *Fantasy* and two-time Hugo Award winning and two-time World Fantasy nominee *Clarkesworld*; the editor of the following anthologies: *Best New Fantasy, Fantasy, Horror: The Best of the Year, Japanese Dreams*, and *The Mammoth Book of Steampunk*; and co-editor of *Bandersnatch, Fantasy Annual, Phantom* and *Weird Tales: The 21st Century*. He lives in Rockville MD with his wife, Jennifer, and their twin daughters, Cordelia and Natalie.